MAGGIE GEE

THE FLOOD

SAQI

The author thanks Christine Casley, the most skilful of editors, everyone at Saqi, and the Hawthornden Foundation for its generous hospitality in Scotland.

British Library Cataloguing-in-Publication Data
A catalogue for this book is available from the
British Library

ISBN 0 86356 315 5

Saqi Books
26 Westbourne Grove
London W2 5RH
www.saqibooks.com

*For Musa and Nina, with love
and, always, for Rosa*

Before

I am going to tell you how it happened. How I came to be here, with so many others, in this strange place I often dreamed of, or glimpsed in the distance, across the river – the lit meadows, the warm roof-tops, caught in those narrow shafts of sunlight, in this moment that lasts for ever. A city hovering over the darkness. Above the waters that have covered the earth, stained waters, rusty waters, pulling down papers, pictures, peoples; a patch of red satin, a starving crow, the last flash of a fox's brush. A place which holds all times and places. And we are here. We are all still here.

I lived my life in the earthly city. The earthly city, down on the plain. Designed for humans. And pets, their playthings.

What else was there? Billions of microbes. Snails and worms. And birds, of course; visiting the gardens: nesting, foraging. Quivering, flashing on the flowering quinces. Calling sharp warnings against the cats. Jackdaws, thrushes, pigeons, starlings with dark silk rainbows on the wing. On Daffodil Hill, near the City Zoo, you saw how many, how beautiful: sky-wide, skimming trapezia of starlings, smoking at the edges as they turn on the blue.

And urban foxes. Twisting and fossicking, yipping and screaming mobs of red musk. Narrow-faced, amber-eyed, rufous, fearless. And swarming rats, and mice, and pigeons.

Outside the city there was always war. The earthly city was built for war: armies were raised, weapons stockpiled; people could be immured and defended. When things went wrong, there were massacres.

But most of the time, we kept war outside, and sent our soldiers against other cities, and tried to eliminate the fleas and the vermin, the seething enemy within.

Mr Bliss set hawks to reduce the pigeons, but rebellious old people turned up with sacks of birdseed and pop-corn to woo them back. The arrests were partial and inefficient. The city-dwellers liked their pigeons.

That year in the city it was always raining. When the sun broke through, we were ready to worship.

And there in the distance was the other city, the city of dreams, the place we half-know we have seen at night, when we wake happy from somewhere forgotten.

Perhaps the dead can move through time. If time is an endless unspooling ribbon, the living see only the short bright section to which they cling, panting, struggling, peering out, blinded, from the spot-lit moment. Perhaps the dead see the whole of the road, stretching out for ever, before, behind, three thousand human generations. Under the city, the dead travel onwards. Searching for something. Homing, homing.

That year in the city it was always raining.

One

After months of rain, the sun broke through.

The earth turned towards it, in absolute beauty.

Light poured along dull black streets which were briefly steep runnels of gold and red. Old brick semis blushed like roses. Early spring hedges glowed sharp in the light.

A white-haired widow, May, looked out and was suddenly glad it was her who survived, not him. May, not Alfred, dearly though she'd loved him. And briefly remembered how to be happy –

For here was the sun.

Alfred loved the sun.

Spring was coming. The world was gilded.

May stood at the window, smiling at the street, the narrow impoverished street she loved, and thought, thank God for small mercies. The rains have ended. I've got the children; life goes on, and I'm still here. She put on a kettle, and made some tea.

May had two new grandsons, Winston and Franklin, who came to see her once a week. Shirley, their mother, was a good daughter.

Yet the choices Shirley made had set the cat among the pigeons. She liked black men. Elroy was black.

Sometimes May felt Shirley had wrecked their lives, because Dirk, May's son, was still in prison for killing Winston, Elroy's brother. His own sister's brother-in-law. It wasn't Winston's fault he was black, but Alfred and Dirk had feelings about it. People said the dead boy was homosexual, but the colour business had made it all worse, though May liked black people as much as anyone.

Fortunately, since her grandchildren were mixed. One of them was named after the dead boy, Winston. May was used to colour; she no longer saw it, and she still felt sad about what Dirk had done. The kids looked like Alfred, and May, and Shirley, although their skin was so like Elroy's.

Her whole life had been about her children, except for the little pockets of time when she was alone, with her books and her poems, a tiny woman in a world of light, blown like a leaf towards the wall, and the beautiful words are whirling round her, *Oedipus, Charon, Persephone* – then all of life seemed to come to a point, the trees, the white clouds, the cat on the pavement pouncing on a skipping string of dry grass. In those moments, the world felt enormous, with everything bright and sharp as glass, and May wanted to weep just to be alive, this little quivering leaf of a woman. And soon, she thinks, she will blow off the edge, a speck of dust spinning out across the void, towards nothingness, maybe –

Or perhaps towards Alfred, for somewhere, surely, deep underneath the city of pain and music and crisp packets, there is a vault leading into blue air, and they are all walking, crowds of strangers, the dead, pressing onward with small mute faces, and if she searched for ever she would find the ones who mattered; her mother and father, and Alfred – marching – Alfred would always be on the move – and the dead boy, Winston – should she feel ashamed? – but maybe she could tell him about her grandchild, little Winston, who carried his name on into the future.

May wasn't religious, but she knew there was something. There had to be; there was so much beauty. Tennyson, her favourite poet, was religious. And May was reading a book of Greek myths, a present from Shirley, who was very thoughtful. It took May back to childhood happiness, reading about the gods in her Newnes' Encyclopedia.

She hoped her grandchildren would read.

Winston and Franklin. May doted on them. She had three more grandchildren who lived abroad, and they were white as paper, but she never saw them. She'd rather have mixed ones who came round for tea. For she herself was not prejudiced, had never been part of the menfolk's silliness. Indeed, she had a soft spot for Elroy, who was handsome (as Dirk, her son, had never been handsome) and had a good job in the Public Health Service, the poor old struggling Public Service.

Which she hoped would last long enough to see her out: a nice clean bed; the soft hands of the nurses. Sunlight through a window. The blue beyond.

Away in the prosperous north of the city, nobody uses the Public Service. There is higher ground, better services: trichologists, reflexologists, manicurists, chiropodists, naturopaths, osteopaths, homeopaths, and chic small shops with tiny pots and parcels of exquisitely expensive animal parts, lungs, roes, embryos, fractions of hoof and horn and tail, which people offer each other as gifts; and silvered or gilded brocade clutch-bags, minuscule cards with jokes and mirror-lets, frail silk peonies, porcelain teddy bears, toys too delicate and dangerous for children. Because there is money, objects can be useless.

A rich woman, Lottie, turns over in bed in her sprawling house in the north of the city. Each of these houses holds soft sleeping bodies, sparsely distributed among the big rooms, sleeping well because they have eaten well, and drunk good wine, and been lucky in life. Though Lottie herself hasn't slept so well, lately, as if she were secretly growing older, but Lottie refuses to grow older.

Harold was asleep beside her. She loved him, of course, his saturnine profile, the fine line of his Roman nose, though he was losing his hair – there was some on the pillow – and in many ways not quite up to the mark. Men of his age so often weren't; men in general, when she thought about it. Still she had decided to love him; she loved him. And really, Harold was lovable. (And in certain respects, certain private respects, where Lottie had always had high standards, Harold was very – satisfactory. He satisfied her, every time.)

Lottie loved light, and the day was alight. The morning poured in, glorious, between the curtains she never closed. Lottie heard birds, though she didn't know which ones – if only Harold were awake, she could ask him – and she lifted her head and glimpsed blossom outside, bobbing blossom in February, Japanese something, Harold had said, scarlet flowers with golden centres, Japanese Quince, for the whole world was connected, red cups blazing on black leafless branches, glorious against the blue.

Lottie let her head fall back again. She never stirred till her tea was brought up. But she gazed, with a smile of cat-like content, at the only picture she totally loved (although, she was still quite fond of her Bonnard), a picture with which she identified, a painting which spoke to her inmost being, for she certainly had an inmost being, though Harold teased her that her life was just shopping.

The woman in the picture was Lottie's *alter ego*, but noticeably less pretty than her. It must be worth eight or nine million, now, though her father had bought it when Hoppers were cheap. *Morning Sun: Soleil du Matin*. A middle-aged woman sat on a bed, feet and knees drawn up on the mattress, her tight dress raised to show sturdy thighs, blonde hair pulled back from a strong jaw-line, staring at the light pouring in through the window, a flood of bright gold from

the wide open window, sensual, worshipping, passive,
intent. Lottie knew Hopper had painted her spirit. She
stretched luxuriously against the sheet.

Her linen is changed twice a week. Soon she'll poke Harold
gently to wake him up, and he will bring up Lottie's
breakfast. Not too much later, Faith will arrive, basically to
nag Lottie's teenage daughter, so Lottie herself can remain
sunny. But life *is* sunny; life is easy.

Eastward, southward, there are no more gardens. Every
scrap of land has a building on it. Light shears between
blackened towers in the east, scraping against the rain-
washed sky. The towers are packed with rushing bodies,
checking their pockets for pens, keys, looking for umbrellas,
overalls, tool-kits. Parents scream and children wail; a young
mother smiles as she hugs her baby, trying to get him to take
the breast, but her milk hasn't come, and he's yellow with
jaundice. It doesn't matter; she has her baby, the single
glorious irreplaceable thing, and the sun is shining, the sun
is shining.
    The first day for weeks without constant rain. A cold
wind bangs at an open window, though most of the
windows never open. Postmen drudge on with their heavy
bags, blessing the sun that is drying the walk-ways, cursing
the freebies that weigh their bags down, damning the e-mails
that lessen the letters. 'No one writes letters any more,' they
complain. But they like the rare postcards, because they can

read them, poking a line of kisses through someone's door, bending a Caribbean sunset through another.

Their arms ache, and their knees are arthritic. Life is chilly; life is hard.

Bruno knows that the end is coming. 'The last days,' Bruno Janes intones. 'The last days. In these last days ...' He has the gents to himself, this morning. It is kept very clean, with a dark steel mirror which makes him look stronger, more certain than ever.

He is practising his riffs, in front of the mirror, telling himself, convincing himself. He sways to the mirror, to his own dark shape, his bony head with its faint gleam of fur. The old black attendant is watching him, from her scented cupboard where the radio tinkles, but Bruno rises above her gaze. 'There will be signs and wonders, in these last days ...'

The rich and the decadent would suffer: old women, who he hated the most; painted women; weak women; adulterers, actors, celebrities, the smug pink faces in the papers, the falsely happy, the vilely lucky, drug-takers, stockbrokers, exercise addicts, youth-perverters, lazy foreigners, lying prophets, all those whose sins had brought destruction on the city. They were sores upon the face of the earth, but God would wash it clean again.

He yearns towards himself, two wire-thin forms that charm each other, snake on snake. Bruno has always lived alone, even before he went into prison for trying to murder a dirty old woman, but now he's found God, and forgiveness, and a following. Now he is washed in the blood of the Lamb. Bruno likes blood, and Bruno likes washing, scrubbing his skin with a worn-down nail-brush, wrapping the wounds neatly every day. The mad old woman is shaking her head, shaking her head as she watches him.

'Cha! Are you takin' dem rubbish ting wid you?' she calls after him, picking up the dressings he has discarded, but he doesn't understand foreign languages, foreign people, old women, he keeps on walking into the future.

Back in the car, the Book lies open, the only book Bruno needs to read, the only pages of the only book, though that's not what he says to Jews and Muslims.

St John is writing to the seven churches. The hour of fulfilment is coming nearer. These are the words of the One who holds the seven spirits of God, the seven stars … The scroll is still fastened with seven seals, but soon all secrets will be revealed, soon his justice will come upon them. 'How long, sovereign Lord, holy and true, must it be before thou wilt vindicate us and avenge our blood on the inhabitants of the earth?'

The great day of vengeance was at hand, and who would be able to stand before God?

Bruno knows that the end will come.

'Then the seven angels that held the seven trumpets prepared to blow them.'

Two

Winston and Franklin, May's grandchildren, sons of Shirley and Elroy Edwards, can't go to nursery school today, because it is closed for teacher training. Usually Shirley, who is doing a degree with a view to becoming a teacher herself, would leave the boys with their grandmother, but May has just had her house treated for woodworm, and Shirley fears it's toxic.

And so the boys fight each other, soundless, possessed, within the box of steel that drives them to the Towers.

They love each other as twins do; adore each other with wordless belonging. They hate each other like a blade and a cut. They somehow need to be one, not two, and they maul each other to make it happen. The boys need exercise, air and sunlight, but days of rain have hemmed them in.

As Shirley drove towards the east of the city, the streets outside grew smaller, dingier, jammed with battered vehicles because there were no garages. Franklin had his finger up Winston's nose: Winston was biting hard on something pink and chunky; yes, the thumb-pad of Franklin's hand. 'You hurt Bendy Rabbit,' he shouts at Franklin. Bendy Rabbit is sacrosanct. Oddly, Franklin doesn't have a favourite animal. Winston is his favourite animal.

Shirley frowned forward into the traffic. She was late. Doubly late, for the sitter, Kilda, aged fifteen, and her Accessing Culture class back in the centre. And she worried. Kilda was too flighty to mind two four-year-olds alone all day, but Shirley couldn't miss another class. Kilda was a sniffing, nasal redhead at the sullen epicentre of her teens, who had come to Shirley through her mother Faith, Shirley's former cleaner.

(Shirley was fond of Faith in a way. Fat little Faith, bucketing onwards, who helped her out before her first husband died. But Faith's daughter Kilda was an unknown quantity; Kilda was an accident, Faith had once confided. Kilda was beautiful, sweaty, and silent, statuesque where her mother was short. She had huge grey eyes that to Shirley seemed blank, though Elroy said they were beautiful.)

Now she frowned and drove, drove on the brakes and the accelerator, not swearing through recourse to her religious faith. 'Sugar. Sugar, sugar. Shoot, shoot ...' The streets were slippery and parts of them were flooded; her tyres were soft; the car handled badly. She wanted to be somewhere else, another person, in another life, a slimmer, younger, childless person. She blinked with shock at her disloyalty, she who had longed all her life for children –

In the split second when Shirley's eyes were closed, a dented yellow rust-bucket, blinded by the sun blazing down the road, suddenly pulled out from the kerb, straight across her, making her swerve.

'Shoot ... oh *shoot* ...'

Franklin's finger slipped out of Winston's nose and jabbed, quite by accident, into his eye, a good result for Franklin, till Winston, roaring with surprise and pain, crushed his elbow into Franklin's genitals. Both of them bellowed like startled bulls. Shirley span the wheel hard and the crucifix hanging in the front of the car swung wildly and hit the roof.

'Oh shoot ... *Shit* ... oh FUCK.'

She had hit something, something not very hard, low to the ground, something living. The boys stopped yelling to turn round in their seats and pick out in the dazzle a dark awful shape outlined in gold dragging itself across the road between the cars. It was a mangled tabby cat. Something dying.

'You hit a pussy!'

'Stop, stop!'

'It's all bleeding.'

'It's fell over! *Mum*! Mum!'

The two boys put their arms round each other and hugged tightly, with big grave eyes. Their tiny digits played light rapid grace-notes in their opposite's skin, till the fluttering calmed them. On two different notes, they began to hum. Being two was easier when they were one.

Gripping the wheel with big white knuckles, Shirley roared on towards the Towers.

They loomed towards her out of the haze, standing up like guns, identical, as if the architect had only one idea, which had replicated, blindly, where people were poor. They rose above the earth like a forest of dead trees, their tips in sunlight, their root-balls dark.

Dirk has been out of prison three months. He still doesn't quite believe he is free when he wakes from sleep, shaking and terrified.

Dirk was in prison long enough for the bolts and bars to grow inside him. His original sentence was considered light, insultingly so by the victim's family. The barrister got the charge reduced to manslaughter, claiming the victim had made a sexual suggestion, which had naturally horrified his client in his state of distress over his dying father.

Dirk felt quite hard done by, hearing this speech. That Winston geezer was a fucking pervert!

Though he got full remission for good behaviour, and some extra wangled by the prison chaplain, who was always happy when the men found God, prison seemed to Dirk like the unending hell he has teetered on the edge of all his life.

Why has no one helped him to make a life? It can't be too late. He is only in his twenties.

Other white prisoners liked him at first, since the man he killed was black, and also a poofter. 'One less of them does no harm,' someone hissed. He came in with a rep for having bottle.

But quite soon the others turned against him. They said he smelled bad. They called him Banana-Face; he looked in the mirror and saw it was true, prison had made him look yellow and crooked. And his hair was thinning, which made him wretched. Like he had to grow old before he'd had any chances.

And the cell had been small. Small and stinking. There was trouble with the drains, with all the rain. Some days the sun never seemed to shine. Life had got smaller, uglier. Smaller and darker. If possible. Life with May and Alfred had been small enough. Dirk got the crap bedroom, because he was the youngest. He had the crap job, in a newsagent.

There'd been poofters in prison, wherever you looked. Nowhere you could go to escape them. There were things that had happened at night, sometimes, which made him twitch with disgust the next day. In there it had been a jungle, or a pigsty. In there he had had to let standards slip. For a few minutes life flashed red and alive, but afterwards shame made it worse. There was no ... no ... Whatever it was that his cow of a mother hadn't given him wasn't here either. People did it to each other out of hatred, and they hated Dirk, of course, and he hated them, but still he had to do it. And live with it, half-closing his eyes. Swearing never again – never again. Knowing it would always happen again.

But now he's found something he thinks is his own. Dirk has his own vision of heaven, a mount of blood and gold and glory, a place where his enemies will burn like straw, all the people who picked on him.

One day some priests had come to visit. All the lads volunteered to go, to wind them up. Dirk had looked at the slip of paper. He didn't read as fast as some. *'The Brothers and Sisters of the Last Days'*. (Sisters and brothers. What good were they? Dirk's sister Shirley had married a darkie, and his big brother Darren had fucked off abroad.)

Dirk read it, very slowly and effortfully, because he was bored, because he wanted something, he wanted anything, he needed, he needed – it was like hunger, pressing him on.

'We believe in saving souls,' he made out. 'Anyone can be saved. Come home to the One Who is All.' (At first he read it as 'the One Who is Ali,' and thought, disgusted, they must be Muslims.) 'One Way, One Truth, One Path. Open your hearts, and come home.'

Something like a pain, like indigestion, had risen up towards his throat, and an odd hot feeling scratched at his eyes. When he'd read it again, for the meaning, the pain got clearer, catching him out, sneaking up on him. He had crumpled the paper into a ball, flung it into his chamber-pot, watched it go yellow, then dark, then sink into the foul depths ...

Mum had come to see him a few times in prison, and told him some lies, but quite soon, she stopped. Even when she came, she had never stayed long. Then she started writing letters, but they made him depressed, going on about Shirley having babies and Darren getting divorced again, all the normal achievements that seemed beyond him.

In fact, his mother hated him.

She always had done. (There was nothing, no one.)

So did Shirley, his sister, who had once seemed to love him. That was over for ever, since Dirk had killed Winston. The pansy fucking brother of Shirley's black boyfriend.

(It was the one moment in Dirk's life to date when he had felt like himself, or at least like *someone*. They were in the park, where his father was God, but Dad was in hospital, on his last legs, and the coloureds took advantage, they were everywhere, laughing, and this one had lured Dirk into the toilets, and Dirk went in after him to do Dad's work, to protect the park, to stand up for justice, but then the man played with himself, in the dark, and Dirk had to kill him to save himself from the raw red hunger that came upon him. For once he had power over another body. But the blood was soon everywhere, the mess, the terror, and he had been left as before, alone, creeping back like a rat before his mother could see him.)

But Mum must have noticed. Must have gone to the police. She tried to blame Dad, when she first came to visit, but Dirk knew Dad would never have told of him. They all said it, though, even the police, and Shirley, the one time his sister came to see him, they all pretended Dad had grassed him up. But Dad had been fond of him. Hadn't he? Dad had tried to teach him football, in the park, for weeks, and only gave up because Dirk was hopeless.

Now Dad was dead, the only one who'd loved him.

They had sent Dirk to Gallwood, the city prison, which was only a bus ride from where Mum lived, but she didn't bother. She'd forgotten him.

So he hadn't told her he was out of prison. She wouldn't be glad. She wouldn't want to know. He didn't need Mum, or Darren, or Shirley.

It didn't matter now, because he had a new family. Now Dirk had Brothers and Sisters again, the Brothers and Sisters of the Last Days. He was accepted at last. He was one of them.

He was, wasn't he? He went to the meetings. No one had actually turned him away.

'Open your hearts, and come home.'

'Oh *here* you are dear,' said Faith (insincerely, for when the women she worked for weren't around she sometimes called them 'that cow' or 'that bitch') as she finally opened the door to Shirley. 'I hope you haven't had to wait.'

It had seemed an age to Shirley, who was horribly late, who had climbed the stairs, because the lift was broken, who felt she'd stood for ever on the bleak, echoing landing above the narrow, precipitous stairwell, clutching the hands of the twins, afraid; they were trying to wrest away from her. It felt dizzily far above the dank basement. She clutched the boys tighter, though they yelled louder, and tried not to hear what Faith was saying, what she had somehow known she would say – 'I did say eight thirty and I don't want to, you know, make a big thing of it but we are trying to, you know, help you out, I should have been in the centre by nine because Mrs Segall's kid can't really be trusted to go to school even though Lola is sixteen now –'

She broke off briefly and at last let Shirley and the twins in through the door to the welcome fug of warmth with its undernote of damp, but as Shirley let go the little hands at last Faith's small eyes glittered and she pounced again. '– But then, the mother's got more money than sense. You car-drivers,' she said, with a meaningful look, 'whizzing round polluting everything, no offence, but do a good turn when you can, is what I say, it's very central, it's on your way –'

'But Faith, you don't know where I'm going –'

'– I don't suppose you know Mrs Segall, Lottie? Used to be a looker, now she's getting on a bit, just drop me off there and then we'll all be happy.'

'I thought you were going to be here with Kilda?' Shirley asked blankly. But the large determined bottom had barrelled away. 'Where *is* Kilda?' Shirley asked the wall.

'Mummy kills cats!' shouted Franklin triumphantly, hugging Winston, who hugged him back. The two boys began kissing each other's faces like cats licking each other, making little breathy noises of happiness. Franklin broke off first. 'Mummy drives on top of cats! The cat got dead!'

'That cat got dead. Poor cat,' said Winston, and suddenly began to cry, big tender tears in which, as Shirley stooped to wipe them, she briefly saw a perfect miniature ribbon-crossed parcel of light, the reflection of the four-paned kitchen window; a black cross on a white background. There had been a large cross just inside the front door. Perhaps Faith or Kilda had become religious. Shirley felt glad; it would keep her sons safe. But the tears kept welling from Winston's eyes.

Faith reappeared in a blue velvet coat with frogging, which Shirley guessed had once belonged to an employer. It gaped over Faith's big reddened chest. 'I can't hang about,' she said. 'Don't worry about the kiddies, Shirley.'

'Where is Kilda exactly?' Shirley inquired, finding herself hustled out of the door, as the boys began to understand she was leaving and set up a desolate caterwaul.

'Well she has to wash her hair, obviously,' Faith said.

'But the boys —' said Shirley, more insistently.

With a martyred air, Faith screamed like a banshee: 'KILDA! GET YOUR ARSE IN HERE AT ONCE OR I'LL KILL YOU!' To Shirley she said calmly, 'She loves her bed. Sleep is very good for them, at that age.'

Kilda came stomping through from the bathroom. Red eyes, pale face, Medusa rats' tails of dark red hair, a strong jaw in a jut of temper. She said loudly right in her mother's face: 'Do you mind, Mum? I was washing my hair.' But she winced swiftly away when her mother yelled back at full volume: 'WELL YOU'VE DONE IT NOW HAVEN'T YOU YOU LAZY COW?' And then continued in a normal voice, quite as if nothing had gone amiss, 'Mrs Edwards wants to see you having a nice play with the boys.'

A frown creased Kilda's forehead over wet-pearled eyebrows. Then her face relaxed, and you saw her gleaming beauty: her waxen skin, cream-pale, unmarked; her cheek like the curve of an altar-candle: the serene, full symmetry of her lips.

Youth, thought Shirley, was beauty. In that second Kilda was as lovely as a saint glowing in a window, looking down from the glory of her height, for Shirley wasn't small, but the girl was much taller. 'Shall I put a video on?' the vision inquired. Her voice was low and musical. 'No, don't worry,' Shirley said hastily. 'But you can't really leave them on their own, you know, Kilda, they're, you know, always on the move —'

'Well they are a bit difficult,' said Kilda with a queenly condescension she had learned from her mother. 'But they're all right with me. I don't mind kids. I think we've got *Ram Raiders Three* somewhere.'

'Good,' said Shirley uncertainly, scouring her memory. 'Oh yes, *Raiders of the Lost Ark*. Lovely.'

'Later on I might take them out.'

Shirley decided not to ask more. 'I'll pick them up at two and take them to the zoo.'

'Kilda's lazy,' said Faith loudly, to Shirley, but speaking entirely for Kilda's benefit. 'She never gets off her arse, you know —' She suddenly seemed to remember that this person was the one she was recommending to Shirley.

Was this the best Shirley could manage? Yes, she told herself silently as she trotted after Faith down the endless steps back to the drenched car park.

'If the rains keep on, we'll be in boats,' said Faith, with a kind of perverse satisfaction. 'They say they are diverting the floods from the centre. No one cares about people round here.'

'That can't be true,' said Shirley, desperately, partly because her boys were there. 'In any case, it'll soon dry out. If the sun holds up. Which I expect it will.'

By the time she reached the Institute it was gone eleven. The sun had disappeared. It was raining again. She was red in the face with shame and frustration.

As Shirley parked, badly, and ran towards the door, a large blonde woman in a sleek grey fake fur was just flinging some money at a taxi driver. 'If you'd listened to me,' she was shouting, loudly, 'we'd have got here much sooner, and I wouldn't be late.'

Shirley recognized her suddenly: someone from her
Accessing Culture class which all first year students had to
go to, a chic woman, fortyish, who came irregularly. Close-
up, she saw the fur was probably real. What was her name?
Lottie Something. That was a coincidence. 'You're for Paul
Bennett's class, aren't you?' Shirley panted in passing, and at
once Lottie turned away from her fight with the driver and
her face lit up in a beatific smile. She had blonde springy
curls, seeded with rain-drops. In fact, she might well be older
than forty, but she had a perfect, polished look, as if every
curve of her skin was buffed and burnished.

Shirley wished her own hair looked like that. Lottie's
lipstick was glossy, she smelled exquisite, her shoes and bag
looked impossibly groomed. Before Shirley had children, she
too looked like that. This woman probably didn't have
children.

'Oh how wonderful. Someone else is late. Come along,'
said Lottie, pushing Shirley forward, a surprisingly strong
hand in the small of her back. 'I'm Lottie by the way. Lottie
Segall-Lucas. You're Sheilah, aren't you? Haven't you got
two little boys? I saw you with them, gorgeous, I could have
eaten them. I always think half-castes are so attractive! My
son Davey's got a lovely black girlfriend, frightfully brainy,
not that I'm a judge ...'

'God said to Noah, "The loathsomeness of all mankind has
become plain to me, for through them the earth is full of
violence. I intend to destroy them, and the earth with them."
The Lord said, "Make yourself an ark with ribs of

cypress ..."' In Victory Square, there was a wide raft of people round a placard like a mast, painted in red. The letters dripped and ran down like blood. 'LAST DAYS', it proclaimed. 'ONE WAY OUT.' 'Awake,' roared the man, addressing the crowd. 'Awake and look around you! What do you see? Filth! Corruption! In God's sight the world has become corrupted, for all men are living corrupt lives on earth.' The rest was inaudible, but every so often, 'Awake' surged up again, like an island in the flood.

Around the preacher stood a little knot of the faithful, facing outward, like soldiers, towards the crowd, clutching hundreds of pamphlets of cheap thin paper. The face of a young black man gleamed with faith: Samuel believed that the good would be saved. Next to him, his white wife Milly pulled back her shoulders and threw up a 'Praise him'. She felt happy; she began a new job tomorrow, cleaning at the City Swimming Pool. Next again, a middle-aged white woman with a thin pinched face sighed and yearned, eyes turned ecstatically up to heaven. 'Amen,' Moira called, 'Amen, Brother.' As she spoke, one bony hand ruffled, then smoothed the coat of an enormous red-brown mongrel with the longing eyes of a labrador. She dropped a few pamphlets and began to panic, hissing explanations as she crouched to pick them up. 'They're wet,' she lamented. 'Everywhere's wet.' As she spoke, it started to rain again. 'Be still now, Moira,' said Samuel, kindly. 'We've thousands of copies of the thing.'

In a twenty-storey tower two blocks away, people who made books were arguing.

'Thing is,' said Delorice Edwards firmly, 'it isn't original.' She was talking about Emma Dale's new book, provisionally titled *A Breast in Winter*, an 'upbeat rural cancer saga', as the marketing department's notes informed them. Delorice hadn't meant to say this – wrong time, wrong place – but the constant rain made her feel depressed. There was a nagging sense that her years of study, the way she had turned her life around, her amazing coup with Farhad Ahmad, had not finally brought her the thing she wanted; just a room of polished surfaces and blank whiteness.

Ten faces swung towards her round the oval table. In the centre, a glinting hi-tech tin of waxen lilies, rather larger than life, stuck up boldly, redolent of incense, interrupting their eye-lines. The expressions she could see ranged from annoyed to amused. Mohammed, who was newer than her, looked interested.

Briefly Delorice flunked the challenge. She gazed out of the window: two pigeons swooped past, dive-bombing downwards through the sunlit rain. Somewhere desolate, sirens wailed. A plane engine gnawed like a distant headache.

She had had a major breakdown when her brother was murdered. Brilliant Winston, who had always been their pride. Delorice's mother had to care for little Leah; now her daughter was five and still living with her grandmother. They had all come back from the edge of despair (and she herself from the edge of madness) through Delorice becoming what Winston had been, the straight-A student, the hope of the family.

Now she pulled herself back into the lily-drugged room,

and made herself smile sweetly as she said, 'This book is naff and sentimental and dated.'

Helena Harp, Headstone's editorial director, felt a sudden twinge of hatred for the girl she had hired, who sat before them, smiling, all glossy with newness. Delorice must have thought she had it all: that lacquered black hair, pulled back from a face with high cheek-bones and dark clever eyes; a reputation as the brightest new kid on the block; the glozing trade profiles, which never failed to mention the tragedy of the murdered brother; that whiff of grief and integrity.

Ignorant, she thought. And arrogant.

'You don't think it's original?' she said, and smiled. Then the smile snapped to nothing, like a rubber band. 'It is a mistake,' she enunciated, slowly, 'to think our job's about looking for genius.'

'Course, I didn't mean −' Delorice flushed with embarrassment.

Then, just as swiftly, she was furious. At college she had proved to be brilliant at English, since she'd always been a reader, in every spare moment: in bed; in the bath; when she breast-fed Leah. Her shyness, too, had quickly vanished as she learned to use the language of her lecturers. Delorice was afraid of nobody, now.

Patricia forged onwards. 'The bottom line is, Emma Dale makes a lot of money for us.'

Sid, the sales manager, was frowning slightly. 'Well, the figures for *Lover in Clover* weren't brilliant −'

Patricia interrupted. 'Thirty thousand hardbacks of *Farmyard Matters* plus three hundred thousand paperback!'

Delorice tried again, more determinedly. 'Look, it's hard to make sex and cancer boring, but this book does. Have you read it, Patricia?'

'Of course.' The older woman glared back. Delorice knew at once that she hadn't.

'Point is,' Brian said, rushing in to mollify, anxious at the turn the conversation was taking, for if people started asking if publishers read books, the game would be up for all of them – 'I reckon we could shift half a mill of this one, if it's as raunchy as *Farmyard Matters*.'

'But,' Delorice tried, one last time, 'the public is going to see it's rubbish.'

'Writers can't all be Farhad Ahmad,' hissed Patricia, rearing up like a snake, the white cords in her long neck standing out sharply. (She never could pronounce his name; Farhad Ahmad had been discovered by Delorice, and gone on to win the Iceland Prize, the most prestigious of the book prizes.) 'Emma Dale is not trying to be Angela Lamb.' (Another winner of the Iceland Prize.) 'And we aren't Third Dimension, Delorice.'

Now everyone sniggered except Delorice, and Mohammed, who didn't get the reference. Everyone at Headstone hated Third Dimension. This was why they'd been so glad to woo Delorice away from their younger, hipper, rivals. Delorice's protégé Farhad Ahmad was beautiful, young, foreign, sexy, and mega-selling, after winning the prize. Headstone had assumed he would come with Delorice, but instead he'd done a massive deal with Dingleberry.

'It's nothing to do with Farhad or Angela,' Delorice protested, feeling hot again. 'I just think, it's like, a real pity if we print all these copies of something that's bullshit.'

A barrage of voices broke out around the table.

'We'd get coverage on the sex-and-cancer angle.'

'I can see it in the *Post*'s "Good Health" pages.'

'The book clubs are bound to come on board.'

'Patsy Rowan will give a good quote. They're mates.'

'And Bea Browning will give a quote for anything.'

'Rocco could do the cover. Sort of "Tasteful Tits" –'

'Would the tits be a reference to the breast cancer?' Delorice interrupted, brutally. Everyone looked politely away. Of course, she had a chip on her shoulder.

Their target sales were half a million copies.

Delorice decided to go home early.

Afterwards she wandered through Victory Square. A crowd straggled over the Monument steps. It was raining, lightly, in little gusts. The centre of the square was submerged in water, but the sun was burning through the clouds. Somewhere, she thought, there would be a rainbow.

The crowd was carrying banners and placards; there were crackling speeches; someone shouted 'Amen'. It was that strange new religious cult, she realized, the One Way Brothers, the 'People of the Book', who claimed to unite Jews and Christians and Muslims because they all shared the same sacred texts. (She'd heard that the Christians and Muslims in One Way were already worshipping in different places, however. And that not a single Jew had joined. They were doing very well, though, where people were poor.) It was queer that 'the Book' should be so honoured – not what she was used to, in publishing.

She wondered, grimly, what they'd think of Emma Dale. If all those copies of *A Breast in Winter* were spread out across the square, they would cover it completely. Half a million copies would spill over the side-streets, infect the libraries, infest the bookshops. The city published thousands of books every year, spewing them out then pulping them.

And yet, she was somewhere on top of this heap, and part of Delorice was still pleased to be there. Another part wondered how on earth she'd done it. It was dream-like, uneasy. It all seemed random.

The defining moment was her brother's death. She would never escape it: it had turned her life around. While Winston was alive, he had been the clever one. Delorice could hide and dream in his shadow, read novels during lessons, drift into motherhood. Her gain had been built on that terrible loss.

Sometimes she saw Winston, walking down the street, slim and rangy, reading a book. Once she had even called out his name; it was another young man, with another book. Chance made those spectres cross her path. And yet she believed her brother was somewhere. His long, dancing limbs, his golden eyes. He would be walking along, talking to himself, quoting Baldwin, discussing, laughing. Winston had always talked to himself. It was part of what made him special, different. And he had high standards; he believed in things. She wished she could embrace his long, wiry body, press her cheek against his rougher one.

They had never thought they could lose Winston. That he could be murdered by a stupid racist. Chance, blind chance, for despite the rumours she knew that her brother had been no battyman.

Perhaps everything in life was nothing but chance. At her feet, two pigeon-feathers skimmed across a puddle; wind shook the banners of the crowd across the way.

It was chance, too, meeting Farhad Ahmad at college, when he hadn't long arrived in the city. He was two-thirds of the way through writing a novel, but it was already eight hundred pages long. Reading it, she knew at once what to do. The delicious certainty of the editor's itch. After they became lovers, she cut and rewrote, and the three-hundred page result was snapped up by Third Dimension, who asked her to start a list of young black writers. Then she broke up with Farhad, who was eager to forget her once he got the big prize and the ecstatic reviews.

And now she was here, and still wondering why. Sometimes she felt dizzy at her lack of experience, the terrifying speed of her ascent. Every morning Delorice felt that fear again in Headstone's superfast lift with its see-through floor, which made her hover and swoop over nothing. Would she ever believe in anything they published? Sometimes her job seemed like a kind of germ warfare.

But then there was love, small and real. What she felt for Leah, Davey, her sister – Viola had always been there for her.

As Delorice dipped down into Victory Metro Station, she looked back for a second across the square. The rain had stopped. The black water glittered. The sun lit up faces, blank and identical, all turned submissively in one direction.

'Look, we have to be prepared for germ warfare,' Mr Bliss said eagerly, raising his eyebrows, to a roomful of grumpy ministers. They stared at the president, dully, and said nothing. Perhaps he was on speed. He seemed horribly young. Yet his floss of pale curls had begun to recede.

'Is there any evidence they've got biologicals?' someone grunted, at length, from beyond Bliss's eye-line. Far down the table, he would soon go further.

'Intelligence is preparing a dossier.' Mr Bliss tried to ignore a deep suppressed titter that broke from the bottom of the room. He was a sensitive man; disbelief stung him. 'But that's not the point. We have to be pro-active. We think they've got nuclear as well.' His candid eyes sought those of his colleagues. Why were they looking away from him?

'I'll brief the press,' said Anwar Topping, his closest friend, the government's spokesman. 'But the public is going to demand protection.'

'Attack,' said Bliss, 'is the best form of defence.' He hoped his voice didn't sound excited. He sat more erect and straightened his jacket. 'It's unpalatable, guys, but we have to face it.'

There was silence, for a second, in the rich, dark room. Everyone wondered, briefly, how they'd come to this moment.

'But we *have* attacked them,' said the same dissenting voice. (Bliss knew who it was; it was Darius Blow. He'd been

given a job, which they'd hoped would enlighten him. It
hadn't worked, so he would soon lose it.) 'We've been
bombing them for years,' Darius went on, coarsely. 'It hasn't
made them any nicer.'

'But now you're talking something of a different order,'
said Anwar to Bliss, drawing him out, crossing and re-
crossing small plump knees. His little eyes were bright,
pleased. Something enormous was going to happen.

'We have to be realistic, guys,' said Bliss, spreading out
soft pink hands and smiling. He knew he was right, but he
wanted them with him. He frowned, for a change, to be
statesman-like. 'I sense a new mood among our people.
There is a historic opportunity here. We have to be big
enough to seize it.'

The dissenters sulked, and slouched in their chairs.

Jenner Footle, one of the inner circle, came in on a
pragmatic note. 'If the rains continue, we have to do
something. The people are restless around the Towers. A
common enemy will unite us –'

'Not that that's the point, of course,' said Bliss.

'What time-scale are we thinking of?' prompted Anwar
Topping.

'We have to get men and weapons in place. And then
there will be national security issues.'

'Mass vaccinations?' probed Hogben, from Health.
'There's nothing very plausible around for anthrax. Or most
of the nasties they could throw at us. Do we have any
detailed information –'

'Look, guys, what they have is academic,' said President
Bliss, with an engaging grin. 'We're not going to give them
the chance to use it.'

'March?' suggested Anwar Topping. 'What is the thinking in Hesperica?'

'Mr Bare's very much onside,' said Mr Bliss. 'We're thinking May. Provisionally. But if things worsen, we could go in April.'

There was a small, collective, exhalation. The thing was spoken; a date had been named. Fear, still tiny, but sharp and cold, skated into the room. The president shivered.

In Victory Square, the crowd had trebled. The sun was steadying, almost hot. A beautiful girl, very tall and pale, hove gracelessly through the ranks of gawkers. She tugged two little boys by the hand, pulling them through by main force, ignoring their wails and squawks of protest. 'Come on, Winston. Get a move on, Franklin. Have they prophesied yet?' she called to Moira. As the crowd yelled and the microphone howled, volleys of banned pigeons took fright and wheeled skywards, their dark wings flaring into fans of bright silk when they hit the buffeting wind and white sunlight.

The man who was watching from his car across the square anxiously reached for his sunglasses, rubbing a damp finger across dry lips. He made a gun with his fingers, pow-pow-pow, but there were too many of them, too dirty, too free, and the light on their wings was a pain in his forehead, and there wasn't enough air, with the windows closed, but he was afraid to open them.

Sanctity, for Bruno, remained indoors; outdoors, life was multiple, uncontrollable; he kept himself pure, while the others went out and did God's work in the market place. But he found, to his horror, he was sweating in here. He tried to remove from his mind the suspicion that a piece of old food was mouldering somewhere.

The crowd was doing well. Gathering, breeding. From this distance, they all looked alike, turned towards the placards with their letters of blood. It would do for a start. Bruno nodded, gratified, but somewhere a buzzing scratched at his brain.

Something disgusting was in his car. Something had hatched, or squeezed through the crack that he always left open in case of suffocation. The bluebottle hung there, low and sleepy, as if the sun had just poked it awake. A fat black body trailing fat black legs that might have dragged through unspeakable fluids, women's nastiness, excrement, wings that had circled the stinking city, tainted with blood and sour money. Now it was here, corrupting his air.

Bruno carefully took aim with his newspaper, then trapped the fatness against the window, feeling its juiciness under his thumb. He held it there, trembling, feeling his power, though the moment of joy was lost as he squashed it. He flicked the thing, horrified, out of the car.

They were all the same, but now there was one less.

And out in the square, goodness was growing. Calm spread through him as he watched the crowd, more stick figures drawn in to join the others, moving slowly together, unstoppable. It reminded him of something they had once done at school, an experiment with magnets and iron filings. Twenty years later he had understood. Though the other boys elbowed him out of the way, he had glimpsed over their shoulders a great ... Becoming. The tiny ants shuddered and shot into line. The will of the One: the One who was All. When the One was with Bruno, he was not alone. He was quiet, and good, and contained great multitudes, swollen with infinite power and love. Bruno picked up the Book, on the seat beside him, and read the future of the world: 'The first angel blew his trumpet. And there came hail and fire mixed with blood, and this was hurled upon the earth. A third of the earth was burnt, a third of the trees were burnt, and all the green grass withered.'

Three

When Shirley picked up the boys from the Towers, she was
surprised to find them in their overcoats. 'We just got back,'
Kilda said, brightly. 'I thought they needed a bit of air.'

'Brilliant,' said Shirley. 'I hope they aren't tired, though. I
thought I would take them to the zoo.' It was what mothers
should do, take children to zoos, mothers who were proper
mothers, that is, mothers who were younger than Shirley
was, mothers who weren't struggling to do a degree and
dumping their kids with fifteen-year-olds. 'You like animals,
don't you, boys?'

'I liked the pussy,' said Winston, thoughtfully.

'Sorry,' said Shirley. 'Oh by the way, Kilda, your mother
said I should give the money to her. She's going to pass it
straight on, she said.'

Kilda's grey beautiful eyes widened, then narrowed, and
she whispered something under her breath.

'Have you got their books?' Shirley was distracted, trying to get all their belongings together.

'Mrs Edwards, Mum won't give it me.'

'What do you mean? I'm sure she will.'

'She's always, like, I owe her money. Like, just by breathing I owe her money. She never gives me pocket money, because she never got pocket money, but that was back in the, you know, Ark.'

'Sorry, Kilda. I didn't know ...'

'Kilda lost it,' Franklin said.

'Lost what, Franklin?'

'She lost my book.'

'I'm sure she didn't.'

'And my book, too,' Winston competed.

'I'm sure you didn't, did you, Kilda?'

'It wasn't my fault,' Kilda began.

'Sorry, Kilda, we have to go. I know you'll get them back again. They are library books, you see. The boys like them.'

'I, you know, left them on the underground,' said Kilda. 'Because there was a bomb scare. It wasn't my fault. You could get them back from the Lost Property, maybe.'

So it wasn't Kilda's job to get them back.

Sighing, Shirley drove towards the zoo, which was on the hill in the centre of the city. Elroy was cynical about the bomb scares; he thought they came from the government. She liked the zoo, although it was expensive, and closed quite early in February. The boys snored and farted in the back of the car. They had obviously been eating horrible things. Perhaps she should just have taken them home.

But once she reached the zoo, and had woken the boys,

and stopped them crying, and wooed them through the gates, and made them go carefully, for the paths were a mudslide, the three of them walked into happiness: the top of the hill was alive with late sunlight, the mountain goats leaped on their artificial mountain, the water-birds thronged above the lake, their wings washed with gold as they prepared for sunset, the tigers, usually sleepy, were awake, and the silverback gorilla strolled up to inspect them, a burly, aristocratic grey figure with muscular buttocks and a shiny black naked weight-lifter's chest, staring opaquely out at the boys from under his massive, stony brow-ridge, playing with something whitish in its wrinkled, delicate fingers.

'Look at the lovely gorilla,' Shirley said.

'Lovely grilla,' Winston nodded, staring. 'It's eating its poo. Can I eat poo?'

'You did eat poo, Mum told me,' said Franklin. 'You are a baby. You eat poo!'

They started fighting. Shirley looked away. An elderly couple with a little red-haired girl perhaps a year or two older than the twins were standing not far away by the rails, and they looked at Shirley as if she should stop the violence, but Shirley knew it would only last a moment. She gave them a smile. They were grandparents looking after a child, and she thought of her mother, patient May, who often struggled to the zoo with the boys, though she got fed-up if they hit one another.

Why did males fight? she wondered. Mr Bliss seemed very keen on war. The older male apes could not be kept together. Her father used to lose his temper at home. But then there was Faith, always shouting at her daughter. And

Shirley hadn't always got on with her mother. At the back of
the cage, two female gorillas, smaller, lighter versions of the
male, sat companionably picking fleas off one another,
gazing at the products on their long ridged nails.

The little girl watched the twins fight, transfixed. She had
wide blue eyes clouded with grey and chestnut hair that
suddenly burned red when something caught her attention
and she climbed up the fence and into the sunlight. For a
moment Shirley thought she looked familiar. Her face was
memorable, a broad pale heart, full lips, smiling, a small
fierce chin. Yes, she had surely seen her before. 'There's a
butterfly,' the girl said, frowning, peering. 'It thinks it's
summer.'

'Get down, Gerda, please,' the old woman said. 'That's
dangerous, you know. Your mummy will worry.'

The red and brown butterfly had marks like eyes, big sad
eyes, on its scalloped wings, either side of its furry body. It
crawled on the glass, just above the fence. 'She won't,' said
Gerda, not getting down.

'She has a point,' the man muttered, with a smile to his
wife, but to the child he said firmly 'Now get down for
Grandpa. See, there's a notice: "Stay away from the fence."'

'But Winston and Franklin are climbing the fence.'

In the split second in which Shirley was registering that
the red-haired child knew the twins' names, the boys were
actually over the outer fence and making a bee-line for the
male gorilla. It pivoted massively upon his haunches, and
looked at them thoughtfully, then sidled towards them.
Shirley screamed and with no conscious decision was
suddenly hurting her back and arms as she yanked them

both, violently, up over the barrier, with both boys kicking furiously. 'Naughty boys,' she shouted, frightened, and they stared at her with big surprised eyes, but her anger dissolved once she saw they were safe.

'The butterfly will freeze, won't it?' asked Gerda. 'Or drown. Unless summer comes tomorrow. Can I take it home, Grandma, please? If it gets to summer it will be all right.'

'Excuse me,' said Shirley. 'How do you know the twins?'

'They're always naughty,' Gerda said.

'That's not nice, Gerda,' her grandpa rebuked her.

Gerda thought about it for a second. 'Winston isn't,' she added, untruthfully. Gerda had a soft spot for Winston.

'Gerda's not my friend,' said Franklin.

'I think they're friends from school,' contradicted the grandma. 'Don't worry about the butterfly, Gerda. There will be lots of new ones in summer.'

'Bendy Rabbit is eating its poo,' said Winston.

'The twins are just nursery,' Gerda said. 'I'm at big school. I do swimming. I like this butterfly. This one is special.'

'Gerda? That's an unusual name,' Shirley commented. 'Is it German?'

'See, her mother's a writer,' the grandpa said, a gleam of pride behind his round wire glasses. 'Angela Lamb. She's quite well known. And she gave the child this fairy-tale name.'

'From *The Snow Queen*, Henry,' the grandma said.

'Angela Lamb? She's famous,' said Shirley. 'I'm not a reader, but I've heard of her. There are lots of copies of her books in the library. I bet my mum's read her. She lives and breathes books ... You must be very proud of your daughter.'

'She took her mother's name,' said the grandpa. 'She's a Ship, really, but she chose to be Lamb.'

'We are proud of her,' the woman asserted.

'Bendy Rabbit is a rabbit-gorilla,' Winston shouted. Everyone ignored him.

'What happens to the butterfly?' Gerda asked. 'If it dies, where does it go?'

Her grandparents exchanged a strange, veiled look. 'Very proud of this one and all,' said the grandpa. 'You're our pride and joy, aren't you Gerda?'

Gerda was bored with the butterfly now. 'Come *on*,' she said, darting off towards the lake. 'I want to see the painting man.' Winston and Franklin set off in pursuit.

The adults followed, chatting amiably, introducing themselves as they dodged the puddles. They reminded Shirley faintly of her own parents, trying to catch up with the new generation, proud of their daughter but puzzled by her. They said they had moved back from the coast to live with Angela and look after Gerda.

'There isn't a dad around, you see,' the woman, whose name was Lorna, confided. 'That's the way of it, with this generation. My daughter's busy with her career. Your little boys are lucky to have you.'

'I'm not a perfect mother,' said Shirley, hastily. 'I'm trying to get a degree, you see.'

'My daughter hardly leaves her study,' the other woman said, sadly.

'Hold on, Lorna,' the grandfather said. 'She does her best. It's the pressures of fame.'

'I worked,' said Lorna. 'As you know, Henry. Shop, factory, whatever I could get. But I tried to put the children first. Still, I wasn't gifted like Angela. It's what you have to do, if you're gifted.'

The children were running headlong towards the lake, sending up sprays of water as they went. A lonely male figure in a long black overcoat stood by his easel near the willows. The sun had already set on the water, the shadows were deepening around the rushes, but higher up, the treetops were golden, the birds were roosting thick as leaves, and away in the lemon- and rose-rinsed sky others were circling, calling for sunset, herons trailing long reed-like legs, wood-pigeons whir-clapping their wings, a volley of white doves, palely gilded. The drenched grass round the lake was strewn with bird-shit and feathers, both of which Winston and Franklin were collecting, splashing about and shrieking with pleasure. Wherever they went, the birds flurried upwards.

'Don't frighten the birdies,' Gerda instructed them. 'Ian is painting them, aren't you, Ian?'

'It's OK,' the man said, in a strong Scottish accent. 'It's all in my head. It doesn't bother me.'

'Boys,' said Shirley, but without conviction, 'Your shoes will be soaked. Your hands will be filthy.'

'They're grand little boys,' the painter said. 'You have to eat a peck of dirt once in your life. That's what my father said, any reet.' He had a weather-beaten, world-worn face, a sensuous mouth, reddened cheeks, sharp grey-white eyes with something scary about them: the face, Shirley thought, of an ex-alcoholic, till he smiled, and she decided, 'He's handsome.' But shortish, thickset, more builder than painter.

'Do you come here a lot?' she asked. 'Aren't you cold? You should wear a scarf. Gloves. A hat.'

'He's always here,' Lorna told her. 'I think he doesn't feel the cold.'

'I feel the cold,' Ian corrected her. 'But I like the animals to see I've got skin. I want them to know I'm an animal, see.'

Lorna looked puzzled, but Shirley smiled.

'I'm an animal, aren't I, Ian?' Gerda asked, pulling at his coat-sleeve.

Ian nodded. 'Correct, young lady.'

'You aren't really,' Lorna insisted, but quietly, not to contradict the painter. 'You're a little human, aren't you, dear?'

'Animals shouldn't be locked up. That's what Ian says. Isn't it, Ian?' Gerda asked him.

'Good girl. Now run and see the swans.' He patted her arm, and she was gone. He had moved his body, while they were there, so his easel was invisible. The adults stood in a companionable group, talking about what everyone talked about, whether the endless rains would stop, but because today had brought some hours of sunlight and sun felt normal, once it returned, they ignored the predictions, they felt optimistic; perhaps it was over; they wanted to be happy. Ian said nothing, but he listened, nodding.

The children had run to the top of the bank and crouched there, bathed in the rich late light, the flame-haired girl, the golden-skinned boys. Now Gerda had hauled Winston on to her lap. The boy was nearly as big as she was, but she was trying to rock him like a baby, while Franklin was pulling him away by his feet.

Ian found his cigarettes, and offered them around. Shirley, who never smoked, took one.

'Mummy's smoking,' Franklin suddenly shouted. 'Mummy will get dead tomorrow.' Both the boys came slithering down the bank, indignant. 'Silly Mummy. You mustn't smoke.'

'I'm not really going to,' Shirley yielded. 'See, I'm giving it back to Ian. Sorry, Ian,' she said, embarrassed.

'You're a nice woman,' he said, smiling.

Painters, she decided, could say things like that. He tucked the cigarette in his jacket pocket, and Shirley found her cheeks felt hot. Above the lake, above the hill, the pinks in the sky were deepening, the smallest scraps and tatters of cloud suddenly burning an ardent red. Just for a few minutes the whole sky caught fire, the pinks and scarlets intensified to crimson, and then the sun slipped behind the bank; both clouds and circling birds turned black. Somewhere, a whistle blew for closing. 'Make your way to the nearest gates …'

'Do you like being outside?' Shirley asked Ian. 'My father always liked to be outside. He was a park keeper, you see.'

'I don't like cities,' Ian told her. 'I came here when I was a lad of seventeen. My life went wrong. There were a lot of lost years. Too young to be a barman, I suppose. I went crazy. Tried to smash up a hotel. Then I kicked the bottle and went to art school.'

'So why do you stay here, if you don't like cities?' Shirley asked him, half over her shoulder, turning to call the boys and go. Lorna and Henry and Gerda were leaving.

'Dunno. Painting. I've done quite well at it. Complicated.' He shrugged. 'I should get out. We should all get out.' His eyes were hard to read.

Shirley sighed, 'In any case, we've got to go. Winston! Franklin! Time to go home!' It was nice to meet an artist. She felt on the threshold of something important, one of those windows that opened in life and showed her things she had never imagined. Elroy and she didn't talk much now, with the boys always there, and Elroy's promotion. 'So what are you painting, can I just ask you?'

'The end and the beginning of the world,' Ian said.

Four

Lola and Gracie – just back from school, giggling with delight at the boys on the bus who had stared at their legs and asked for e-mail addresses; yelping with glee at the boys' total hopelessness, hopping from one coltish leg to another as they dragged huge school-bags up the path, shrieking with panic as they splashed into the puddles – were ecstatic to discover that no one was home, in the cavernous house Lola's mother had inherited. Faith, though too late to harry Lola in the morning, had come in later and filled up the fridge. That meant they could eat mountains of ice-cold cheesecake, sample the juices, the smoothies, the thickies, plunder the chocolates, catch up with their e-mails, and watch TV at deafening volume.

(Elsewhere, south and east of the city, children come home to cold houses, rattle the tin for cheap biscuits, care for other, younger children, put the washing on to please their mothers, then watch TV at the same volume. TVs blink and blare all over the city.)

Lola had been raised with lots of money; Lottie's wealth had come from fur, her father having made millions in the trade long before people disapproved of it. Money was the air the Segall-Lucases breathed; fur was something soft and scented that Lola's pretty mother wore in winter, something Lola liked to put her face against.

Then adolescence hit, with its souring knowledge. Some of her friends at private school had got in on scholarships, through brains, not money. She began to understand the whole world wasn't rich.

Her best friend changed every month or so, but for several months now it had been Gracie, though they quarrelled vividly every other fortnight, and made up with fleets of passionate notes, secretly launched across the class-room.

This friendship, like Lola's other friendships, seemed to be about shopping and music. In fact it worked at the deepest level – they liked the selves they had found with each other. Gracie, less rich and indulged than Lola, could take a brief dip in consumer paradise, spray herself with musk-rose and lily-of-the-valley and other, sharper, more elegant smells from the continental masters of perfume; riffle through Lottie's delicious handbags – the strawberry suede, gold-embossed Verso, the ultra-slender cream clutch by Parade – and be, for an evening, teenchild in paradise, glossy, an It-girl, Gracie the Ditsy.

In fact she had dimensions Lola lacked. Gracie's mother

Paula was a radical journalist who'd made her name investigating the security services. A single parent, a nag, a bore. Mysteriously, though when Gracie was home she couldn't bear her mother's carping, her predictable, puritanical opinions, her arguments with the television news – though Paula as a mother was faintly ridiculous, a potential source of public shame in tracksuit bottoms and turquoise anorak – mysteriously, when Gracie was away from her, at times when she felt she was on the line, her mother's opinions leaped to her lips, her mother's world-view became her own.

Now Gracie and Lola sat in Lola's bedroom, listening to hundreds of decibels of hip-hop, picking out, biting into, and discarding the expensive chocolates they'd filched from Lottie's dressing room. 'This one's disgusting … Banana praline.'

'This one's good. It's sort of brown.'

'A bit of brown never lets you down.' Both of them instantly fell about laughing, till Gracie remembered she didn't understand it.

'It's something my dad used to say, you know … I haven't seen my dad for two years. Mum had a row with him. I miss him. He was much nicer than that *byaatch* my mother.' Gracie was still giggling, but her eyes, which were large and black, were sad. Her dark curviness came from her father, who most people thought of as big and fat, but to Gracie he was the missing hero. And her lucky big sister lived with him, whereas Gracie had got stuck with her mother.

'I like your mum,' said Lola, cautiously. It never did to criticize mothers. Friends had to like them, though you did not. But Lola didn't really like Gracie's mother. Her clothes were shameful. Her hair sagged down like a couple of sand-bags. Unlike her own mother, she was always depressed.

'You're lucky,' Gracie said, throwing over a praline, which Lola liked and Gracie hated. It missed, and fell on the cream wool rug, and when Lola went to pick it up, she trod on it. She scraped up half of it, and left the rest. 'Yuck! These chocolates are so disgusting!'

'Shall we put back the rest of the box?'

'No, my mother will never notice.' That was nice about Lottie, her not noticing. The worst kind of parent noticed too much.

They began to dance, frantic, to the music, their hips gyrating, fluid, slick, their faces parodying ecstasy, their big feet beating time on the carpet, long hair whirling out like mermaids, stamping the chocolate into the mat, singing along with the Hesperican voices that took them over when they sang, and when they bought, and when they ate, for the city was part of the satellite lands of the Hesperican empire, in its final decades.

'Do we feel like a smoke?' Lola asked.

'Weed or tobacco?' Gracie said.

'You know I don't do weed, disgusting, though my stupid dad has always got some ... Shall I go and get some from his dressing-room?' Lola asked.

'Are you serious? Your *dad* smokes weed? That's really cool,' said Gracie, uncertain.

'No it's not, it's pathetic,' said Lola. 'My mum says it's pathetic, too. Not that my dad is pathetic,' she rushed to say, just in case there was doubt. 'My dad's really clever. He knows everything.'

'What does he do, exactly?' asked Gracie. 'He goes to an office somewhere, doesn't he?'

'It's kind of a study, actually. He's writing a book,' said Lola, defensive. 'It's about philosophy. Time. Things happening,' she said, to prove it, and then regretted having said so much. She had only recently grown defensive. Until she was thirteen or so, she was convinced that her father, Harold Segall, was the cleverest man in the universe, and one of the handsomest, as well, though it was a pity he had gone bald. Then something her mother had said sank in. 'Why don't you *do* something, Harold?' she had shouted, in the middle of a row they had one evening. 'You've been writing this book for nearly twenty years. Don't you think perhaps you should get a job?'

'You don't believe in me,' Dad had said. 'But I'll finish it in the next few years. My book might actually be important.' 'Oh poppycock, Harold, you'll never finish it.' His face became ashen, awful with hurt, and Lola ran in and put her arms round him, but she heard her mother, from the edge of what was bearable, say, 'Really Harold, don't be so pathetic. And you, Lola, stop making a fuss.'

'I hate you, Mum,' Lola had shouted. The first time she'd said it; it felt horrible. But now she said it every week. Though the one time her mother had said it back, furious, desperate, ugly with tears after Lola called her a hideous old cow (which she should have been cool enough to ignore), Lola remembered it for weeks, and swore to her mother that she'd never forgive her.

But actually, Lola adored her mother. She was very cuddly, and wore nice clothes, and smelled exquisite, and

laughed a lot. She handed out money on request. She told
Lola she was beautiful, which Lola needed to hear daily.
'You look exactly like I did at your age. Everyone was in love
with me.' She didn't complain when Lola borrowed her
tights, her pants, bras, shirts, makeup, partly because she
had so much of everything, though she once got cross when
Lola tipped a bottle of her favourite perfume in the bath, the
one Babe Grimaldi wore at her wedding, which cost three
hundred dollars an ounce. She wasn't virtuous, like Gracie's
mother. Her good points far outweighed the bad, or so Lola
thought on the happy evenings when she and her mother
curled up in bed with pizza and chips and ice-cream and
videos.

But now Lottie was doing something quite out of
character, a City Institute course in the History of Art. Lola
was convinced this wouldn't last. In some ways Mum was
very stupid, not half so bright as Lola's dad. Lottie didn't
understand about school work, and said the wrong things at
parents' evenings. 'I don't think children should work too
hard. There's plenty of time for her to learn things. I am just
starting, and I'm middle-aged,' was her robust reply to a
form teacher who thought that Lola should work harder.
'Don't turn her into a boffin, please,' when the head of
science suggested A-levels. 'Lola is artistic, like me,' she
asserted. 'I hardly think she wants to do science.' 'No, *you*
like art, Mum,' Lola had hissed. 'Ignore my mother,' she
told Ms Tansy. 'We're not the same person,' she screamed at
Lottie later.

They did look alike, though. Everyone said so. This
wasn't too bad, since Lottie was pretty. Though Lola was

taller and slimmer, thank God. She must have got that from
Harold, her father. Together with her brains, hopefully.

'So what did you say your dad's book is about?' asked
Gracie. Gracie was a reader.

'Time' sounded rather a weedy subject, so Lola decided
to avoid it. 'Non-fiction, I think.'

'Is it political?' In Gracie's house, most things were
political.

'He's quite political. Yes, he is. He definitely says he's a
socialist.' Lola lost confidence in that. He didn't actually do
anything socialist. 'Let's look at the web-site again,' she
said.

For Gracie and she had got a new interest. They had both
become anti-capitalists. This had lasted a long time; at least
two weeks.

They sat together over Lola's lap-top. Nothing much
happening this weekend. All the exciting stuff was in other
cities. Protests in Varna where a massive new dam was said
to be threatening the whole coastline. A chunk of the island
as big as a city could apparently fall into the sea. Eco-
protesters envisaged tidal waves, global disaster, millions
drowned.

'They go over the top a bit, don't they?' said Lola. Things
like that made her feel very nervous, as if it could suddenly
all be dissolved, the comfortable, perfumed, glittering city,
the only thing that she had known. She wanted to attack it,
but not actually destroy it.

'It could be true though,' Gracie insisted.

'Not much we can do about it any case. Varna's a long
way away, isn't it?'

'Not far enough, Lolo, Lollikins. It says tidal waves would sweep around the world.'

The two girls stared riveted, for a moment, at a computer simulation of a tidal wave. Tiny people struggled like ants. Something big and important at last. Something marvellous that would sweep them away and spare them the slow bits of growing up. Something massive, sexual, final.

Yet they loved their playthings, their friends, their homes.

'I could ask Davey. Davey would know. Davey knows everything about science.'

Davey was Lola's half-brother, her favourite person in the whole world. He had done a degree in science, she thought; after that he'd been a salesman of scientific health-food, then written for a magazine called *SpaceTime* which was a monthly guide to the galaxy, actually ending up as editor; then presented science on kids' TV, and had now become CTV's Mr Star-Lite, fronting a weekly programme on astronomy. Its ratings were very high.

'I think your brother's so cool,' said Gracie. 'You know, I watch his show on TV. He's really handsome, for, like, an older guy.'

'He's not really old. His thirtieth birthday was, like, just a few years ago, I can't remember,' his sister said, defending him. 'Our mother says he knows everything. Not that she knows anything.'

It was tea-time in the City Institute, where Lola's mother was working in the library (as Shirley Edwards would have liked to be). Lottie's tongue was caught between big white teeth as she wrote an essay on 'Conservation'. It could have been about pictures or buildings, but Lottie, with a newly discovered enthusiasm, wanted to write about books and manuscripts. Lottie was searching the internet. She had previously used it to buy flights and flowers, but the world of information was a marvellous surprise, gleaming with brainy-ness and cleanliness. She stretched like a cat and smiled to herself.

Paul Bennett, her lecturer, was watching her, amused, from a carrel twenty metres away. He loved his wife Alma, but all the same, his female mature students sometimes tickled his fancy. It was one of the good things about making his move from schools to universities; some of your students were not off-limits. Lottie Whatwashername – ah yes, Segall-Lucas – was sexy, absurd, good-looking, fun.

Quarter of an hour later, Lottie's sense of fun was deflated. She was reading about the 'Memory of the World' programme. The title really appealed to her, but the content was incredibly lowering. Most of it was about loss and forgetting. Except for Hesperica, which only fought wars in other countries, the biggest cause of loss to libraries was 'armed conflict'. Way down the scale came accidental fire, flood, mould, damp, dust, insects. Even fire and flood quite often came about as a result of contractors 'improving' the libraries. Lottie knew this was an irony: her third Art History lecture was all about irony. Irony had a bitter taste, not the kind of humour Lottie enjoyed. She kept on reading. The metal taste got worse. Some of the libraries destroyed by fighting in the last ten years were full of books salvaged from the second world war. The last fifty years had been the worst in the history of the world for losses to libraries. And there was another, nightmare problem: more and more writing was being produced, more and more copies of more and more documents, until no library system could cope, and Lottie found her eyes glazing over … She shook herself awake from an enjoyable dream about fire-fighting librarians with long, thick hoses. Human beings were impossible, she decided: they wrote the words, a great flood of words that was meant to explain and record the whole world, then they fought the wars that destroyed the lot.

Mind you, war was important. She wasn't against it.

Elsewhere on the campus, Angela Lamb, Iceland winner and minor celebrity, mother of the red-haired girl called Gerda who was watching a Painted Lady butterfly at the zoo, had a tea-time date with an academic. It wasn't something she looked forward to. Fifteen years ago, before she was successful, before she had won the Iceland Prize, she had been grateful to receive a letter from a Dr M. Penny, senior lecturer in English at City Institute, enclosing a paper she had written on Angela. The signature was illegible; for some reason Angela assumed she was male. Being between boyfriends, at the time, and liking men who admired her work, Angela sent back a sheet of sharp comments with a charming letter asking Dr Penny to lunch. Thus she had got landed with what she described in unbuttoned moments as 'that daft old biddy'.

At first Moira was quite pleasant. Both of them were fairly young at the time; Moira was in her late thirties, still

hopeful of fame and love and a baby or two, Angela half a
decade younger. Moira was sure she had the upper hand. She
could give this girl the patronage she needed – a sympathetic
(and brilliant) reading, her work discussed at feminist
conferences. Angela was virgin territory. The novelist's flat
was poor and small, allowing Moira to feel kindly towards
her.

Angela, for her part, quickly recovered from the
disappointment of Moira being female, and turned her
attention to correcting her errors. But Moira, when
challenged, swiftly changed the subject, and later, when
Angela tried to insist that some of the 'influences' couldn't
be right, because she simply hadn't read those authors,
Moira said, smiling, chin held high, 'Influences aren't quite
that simple. I'm adducing a pattern of intertextuality, setting
your work in its cultural context. You tell me you haven't
read *Jude the Obscure*, but how do I know you aren't
unconsciously suppressing it? In any case, some texts are
just in the air – to put a lay-person's gloss on it.' As she said
that, her large long-sighted eyes stared suddenly very hard at
Angela.

'*Jude the Obscure*? In the air?' queried Angela.

But that first time they agreed to differ. Both of them
thought there was something to gain. Angela gave Moira
some first editions, which she signed, sweetly, 'To Moira;
thank you from my heart for your interest in my work.'
Moira, for her part, invited Angela to a well-endowed
conference in Barcelona.

They kissed each other's cheeks on parting, and just for a
moment their eyes met appraisingly. Moira's slightly bulging

brown ones stared into Angela's blue-grey gaze. Moira was older and more established. Angela was younger and prettier. Moira was a critic, with a PhD; Angela, though, was the artist. When the chips were down, she was the source. The chicken came before the egg collector.

Then Angela won the Iceland Prize. The Iceland meant the global big-time; even Hesperica took notice of it. Angela jetted to New Work a few times, but decided to stay in the satellite cities. A certain loyalty impelled her to assent when Moira wrote to say she had been offered a contract to write the first critical biography.

Soon strains entered their relationship. Things had been going less well for Moira. The menopause found her still childless, loveless. Despite a good record of publications, she was only a reader, not a professor, because of prejudice, she insisted, against the female authors she wrote about.

Angela thought it was more likely to be because Moira was impossible to work with. Moira never actually agreed with anything, specializing in amused dissent, even to remarks about the weather, with a certain expression like a sneering camel that Angela began to anticipate, wincing. Moira never seemed to change her mind. To her, the author was a kind of appendage, useful to know, but not a source of knowledge.

Then Angela committed the unspeakable crime. Two years after winning the big prize, she conceived a child, by a Danian writer of fairy-tales she met at a conference.

'Are you going to have an abortion?' asked Moira, when Angela confided she was six weeks pregnant. Moira happened to know the Danian writer's wife, a suicidal sculptor. 'You never said you wanted to be a mother.' (She meant, *It's unfair: I have longed for a child.*)

'I didn't,' said Angela, 'but soon I shall be. I think it's a girl. My baby girl.' That was the way she imagined it; a tiny beauty who lay at her feet.

Moira could never forgive Angela that naked statement that she would be a mother. *My baby girl.* The words were white knives, in a city full of childless women.

Now, six years later, they hated each other. Moira's biography was long overdue, though she always insisted it was near completion. They hadn't met in the flesh for three years.

Today's rendezvous in the City Institute's café had been arranged by Angela, following a letter from Moira asking her to read a draft of the biography, 'to check the spelling of personal names'. She had also written, vaguely but alarmingly, of 'certain new spiritual commitments'. Angela realized, reading this letter, that Moira had never asked her any questions about her childhood, her love-life, her daughter. What kind of biography, she wondered, would leave all these areas a blank?

Moira turned out to be reluctant to meet. Angela had learned over the years that it was vital to Moira to have more commitments than anyone else, even as it became increasingly apparent that she didn't have a boyfriend, and wouldn't have children. Meetings involved a long and tortuous process of negotiation. Umbrage was taken if Angela didn't pay tribute to Moira's crowded schedules. The 'spiritual commitments', though, were new.

They finally met in the 1930s café overlooking the drenched campus as the sun went down. Angela was shocked by the change in her appearance. Moira looked gaunt, pale and mad. Her hair lay long and grey on her shoulders, with a greasy lankness suggestive of dirt. She had aged ten years in the three since they'd met. She sat in the window in the cruel late daylight, her hand clamped round a mug of water.

Was it the menopause? Angela wondered. 'Hello,' she hailed her, nervously. 'Lovely to see you. I'll get us some tea.'

'But I don't drink tea,' said Moira, frowning. 'Why do you assume that I drink tea?'

'Coffee? Juice?' Angela asked.

Moira ignored her. 'You're late,' she said.

'Only five minutes, surely. I couldn't find the café, you see. Some of the paths were blocked off, with the flooding.'

'Oh, it's all right,' said Moira, with a thin smile that meant the opposite. 'I rushed back from an important meeting in the centre of the city to be here, that's all, and now I'm stuck here waiting.'

Angela retreated to buy herself some coffee. There were anti-war posters everywhere. A sturdy, youngish woman with dark curling hair was standing on a chair, sticking up the last few: the man behind the hatch called across to her, 'I think we've got enough now, Zoe.' The most popular poster had a flock of vultures, each with a replica of Mr Bliss's face, brooding over a field of corpses. Angela looked at them dispassionately. Once she had believed in all that. It was harder, when you got rich and soft. (She wondered, briefly, if she still existed, somewhere, the sullen schoolgirl she had been? Awkward, pious, Angela Ship, the girl who refused, with her father's name; her friends called her Ange; she wrote ardent, embarrassing poems against starvation and nuclear war: 'Children of Dust', 'The Bone-shadows'. Thank God that most of them had never been published. And her brother George, whom she'd loved so much, who had been her friend when they were both children, was dead; and so was her younger brother, Guy. And she had survived as a different person.)

Thank God she was a different person.

While she was queuing, two students came up to her, all shy smiles, to say they liked her work. She got rid of them as soon as she decently could, but was aware of Moira craning round in her seat, frowning at them, looking at her watch.

(Lottie, taking a break from her essay and drinking a cup of dreary herb tea, spotted Paul Bennett at a nearby table. She was about to join him when the silly young woman who'd been sticking her anti-war posters everywhere went over and started harassing him. Lottie hoped the lecturer would tell her off, but to her surprise Paul started laughing, and when she left, she kissed his cheek.)

Angela brought two slices of cream-spliced carrot cake back to the table where Moira sat.

'Would you like one?' Angela asked. 'They look frightfully healthy.'

'Why do you assume that I need health food?' Moira asked, on a rising note.

'That's OK, I'll eat them both.'

But Moira watched her eat the cake resentfully, hungrily. Angela saw she was much too thin. That white bent wrist, with the knobbed bones showing, those skeletal fingers, plucking at crumbs.

'Are you sure you don't want some?'

'Do you think I want your food? Do you think I eat leftovers?'

'Of course not, Moira. But it's, you know, delicious. Don't worry, I'm really enjoying it.'

Though by now there was only a morsel or so left, Moira suddenly plunged on it like a heron, stabbing the cube off Angela's plate and snapping it down, her throat briefly bulging.

This was something new in the scale of hostility.

Angela began to feel annoyed, but she tried again. 'Those students,' she said. 'I'm so grateful to you, really. You actually seem to have made them like me. You must be a terrific teacher.' Somewhere Angela had read this advice: to win over any human being in the world, try a smile, money, or flattery.

But something had gone extremely wrong. Moira suddenly flushed red, from pale.

'Why do you assume,' she was nearly shouting, 'that I am the person teaching your work?'

'Well, I'm sorry, it did seem likely – Aren't you?'

That expression appeared, the contemptuous camel, the mouth curling, the eyes half-closed, and Angela remembered that camels could spit. And kick, surely. Her chair inched backwards.

'The department in its wisdom has given other, junior staff my graduate teaching.'

Angela looked at her narrowly. Moira's face was working

wildly. There was something furious yet absent in her mouth, her eyes, her twitching fingers.

'Is something wrong?' Angela asked.

'I have been ill,' Moira announced. 'You never asked if I was ill. It never seems to have occurred to you.'

This was so unfair that Angela fell silent. Moira always put her on the defensive. Around them the café was emptying. In the latticed window the sky burned scarlet, then crimson, magenta, preparing for dark. The red reflected on Moira's face, flared in her iris: mayhem, fury. There was another world outside the window. Angela longed sharply for escape. Somehow she had to calm Moira down.

'I was busy,' said Angela. 'I had my daughter –'

'Why do you think I want to know about *her*?'

This time the words were ejected with such venom that Angela actually flinched, and moved back. She looked at her hands, and tried again. 'Well if you're doing a biography, I think that Gerda might have to come in. They change your view of the world, you know.'

'*My* view of the world? *My* view of the world? What do you know about my view of the world? What do you know about my book? Why do you think I wanted children?' Moira had stood up, and was shouting loudly. People in the café were turning to look.

(Lottie stared from her adjacent table. One of those women looked vaguely famous, and the other one absolutely barking. If you were too clever, you clearly went mad. Still, cleverness was not Lottie's problem.)

Angela Lamb was far from unselfish, but she saw a

person in awful distress, a person who was surely damaging herself, losing her temper here in the café in front of students, in front of colleagues. She got up too, put her hand on Moira's shoulder, and said, quite gently, 'I don't mean to upset you, Moira. I think you're very unhappy about something. Why don't we go outside for a walk. We don't have to talk about the book today.'

'The book is rubbish,' Moira said, quieter, but still with terrible intensity. 'The book doesn't matter any more. I have been given a sign, today. Father Bruno has spoken. All the books will drown. Even your books, Angela. Your books which follow me and contradict me. Except the One Book, the One True Book. "God said to Noah, 'I intend to bring the waters of the flood over the earth to destroy every human being under heaven that has the spirit of life; everything on earth shall perish ...' The second angel blew his trumpet, and what looked like a great blazing mountain was hurled into the sea. A third of the sea was turned to blood, A THIRD OF THE LIVING CREATURES IN IT DIED, AND A THIRD OF THE SHIPS ON IT FOUNDERED ..."'

By the time she finished Moira was shrieking, a long metal ribbon of screaming sound, one arm lifted to the fluorescent ceiling, the other gesturing towards the red window, and all the faces, the eager, the indolent, city-worn faces, tired clever faces, innocent, ardent faces of the young, were fixed, startled, on the old woman prophesying.

Lottie decided it was time to leave the café. As she did so, somebody touched her shoulder. 'Well that was quite something,' said Paul Bennett. 'I need a stiff drink, after that. Coming?'

At half-past six, Lottie still wasn't home. Lola began to feel cross with her. She ought to come home every day at five so she could make Lola and her friends some tea. Lola was sixteen, but that wasn't the point. She had homework to do, and so did Gracie. They might do it and they might not, but they shouldn't have to waste time on housework. Her mother had been less reliable lately, since she'd started doing this Art History.

(They had found a cold chicken in the fridge, true, but it wasn't Lola's normal favourite kind. Faith didn't understand how to shop. It was wrapped in bacon, with chestnut stuffing. They had flipped off the bacon, desultorily – 'I'm a vegetarian, I don't eat bacon' – eaten some breast, got bored and abandoned it, on the kitchen floor where they happened to be sitting. 'Is it free range?' Gracie had asked, sternly, her mouth full of meat, eyes suddenly horrified. Lola had checked on the label. It wasn't. 'We usually only buy organic,' she said, but both of them at once stopped eating.)

Mum at the City Institute! It didn't make sense. She would never stick it.

Lola had spoken to her seriously. 'Mum, you don't have to do this, you know. We love you as you are. You don't have to be clever.'

'Thank you, darling. I'm not trying to be clever. I just thought I'd like to learn something new. I mean I do have quite a good eye for pictures. And I did, you know, get quite a few from Grandpa.'

'But honestly, Mum. You will be home most nights?'

'I can't promise,' Lottie said. 'I'll try of course. But I might make new friends. Even mothers do that. I might use the library. I might have classes. Faith will put food in the fridge, darling. I could even get her to come back in the evenings. I'm not quite sure about her cooking, though. And you two haven't been getting on well.' (Faith had been with the family ever since she came to the city, young and desperate, with a tiny baby. Yet Lola and she had never bonded. Faith, who was passionately partisan, tended to quote Kilda against her – 'My Kilda always cleans her room' – 'My Kilda hems her trousers' – though Kilda was nearly a year younger than Lola. The recent row, awesome, total, was because Faith had disposed of two of Lola's toy animals, a huge golden lion and a metre-high bear, which Lola happened to have left on the floor.

For a year or so, admittedly.

'She stole them,' Lola had sobbed, broken-hearted. 'She always does it. She takes my things.' 'Don't be silly, Lola. She threw them away.' 'They were like my most favourite possessions, Mum.' 'Funny I never saw you with them.' 'I loved Leo Lion with my *whole heart*.' 'You still should not have called her a thief.' This was the only insult that Lola had confessed to, but Faith insisted, 'she used language, Mrs Segall. Awful. Terrible. Effing and blinding. The worst I've heard.' In any case, Faith had demanded a large bonus before she continued working for them. Now she and Lola had a state of armed truce.)

'No please, Mum, don't, I'll manage,' Lola had said, hastily. Anything would be better than evenings with Faith.

Still, Lola felt aggrieved. Her mum had always been there. What always had been, always should be.

Besides, Lola felt protective of her. Mum knew practically nothing of any use, except about paintings, and clothes, and money. She would surely fail, and be disappointed, and then she'd take it out on Dad. In the meanwhile, who would look after Lola?

'I'm starving,' Gracie said at seven o'clock.

'Let's go and get chips,' Lola said. It didn't seem much fun, on a February day. She cast about for something to cheer them both up. 'And let's do, you know, an action somewhere. A protest thing. Our first protest.' (That would show her mother for not feeding her, and punish her weedy father, too, for skulking uselessly in his study.)

'Oh cool, cool, that's a great idea.' Gracie thought for a moment. 'What, though?'

'We ought to, like, hit at commerce,' said Lola, parroting the phrases she had read on the net.

'What's commerce exactly?' Gracie asked.

'Banks. Shops.'

'But Lol, we like shops.'

'Advertising, I suppose,' said Lola. 'It's "The Great Evil", like the web-site says. It sells powdered milk to Africa.'

'Does it?' This didn't seem quite right to Gracie. Surely the powdered milk was something different. 'So have they all got TVs in Africa?'

'Yes.' Lola didn't believe in backing down. 'If we were there, we could smash their TVs.' Actions would be easier, if they were in Africa. Here things seemed more complicated. After all, she got her allowance from a bank. If they hit banks too hard, she might lose her money, just when she was planning on going to the sales.

But Gracie had an idea at last. 'Well didn't you say that woman was in advertising, that one who yelled at you for having the party, who came in here and snatched the plug from the wall? And your mum called her a silly old fool?'

'Oh, Gloria. Yes. Our next-door neighbour. They made friends after that. Mum said we had to. She sent her about a thousand dollars' worth of flowers. But Gloria still moans if I play loud music.'

'So why don't we go and like do her over?'

'Cool,' said Lola. 'Yeah, cool.' But she didn't move. She knew Gloria. Gloria had sponsored her on charity walks. Knowing her made her seem somehow less capitalist. Most anti-capitalist actions seemed to involve paint, or posters, or flour. She imagined flour all over Gloria's sofa. And the indigo stair carpet, crusted with paint. Poor Gloria had only decorated last year. Couldn't they find some capitalists who weren't their friends?

'You're scared,' said Gracie. 'Anyway, I'm starving. Let's go for the chips and like see how we feel.'

'Let's take off our uniforms and put dark clothes on.'

Giggling, looking at themselves in the mirror, jumping on each other to make themselves scream, they both dressed up in head-to-toe black, tights, roll-necks, gloves and hoodies. The gloves were cashmere, lined in silk; Lottie had two dozen pairs like that, in shades from black to ice-cream pink.

'We look like cats.'

'We look like burglars.'

'We could be anyone, dressed like this.'

Suddenly they felt they could do it. If they weren't themselves, they could do anything. Two panthers prowled into the darkening city. They left the lights on, and both doors open.

Ten minutes later, Dirk strolled through, after a cursory ring on the front doorbell. He had found something he was good at, at last. It no longer mattered if Dirk was wanted; he got in anywhere, and took what he liked, remembering tips he had picked up in prison and learning quickly as he went along, for his brain had always been good at some things, though life had never given him the chances. Small, wiry people were good at burgling. It wasn't really burgling, since it was for God. Father Bruno had explained all that. They needed funds for their posters and leaflets, their fares and food, and the leaders' salaries. In any case, Dirk only burgled rich ponces who didn't deserve nice things in the first place. Now he had a profession, and a cause to believe in, the One Way, which made all things right, and a couple of knapsacks, which were filling up nicely.

Half an hour later, a fox arrived. He shouldered his way through the fuchsia hedge and splashed through the garden, angled, eager. He had woken up hungry, earlier than usual after mating vigorously last night. His eyes were a good deal sharper than Dirk's, with an extra layer of light-reflecting cells which made his amber irises glow green in car headlights. He had eaten, to date: three worms, two of which he pounced on from more than two metres away, a thin mouse, and a schoolchild's discarded packet of raisins. The raisins were his favourite, delicious, but it wasn't sufficient for a rutting dog-fox. Nearer the house it smelled horribly of humans, but the door to the kitchen swung wide open, the electric human light glared out. On the floor, within view, a plump gold-pink chicken blushed beside broken rashers of bacon. Spittle dripped on to the polished tiles as his jaws snapped shut and crushed the carcass.

Lottie Segall-Lucas was not in her element: a golden Koi carp in ditch-water. On their way into the bar, which was more bar than wine-bar, slopping out cloudy pints of beer to scruffy students shouting at each other, Paul was hailed by a large, softish-looking man who introduced himself to Lottie as Thomas. For a micro-second he looked interesting – curly dark hair, olive skin – but he turned out to be a special sort of librarian who worked out theories of librarianship. Lottie thought, I bet you make them up, and this government gives you money for it. Besides, he was poor; he was drinking shandy. The two men discussed a forthcoming conference whose finer details escaped Lottie. She perked up a bit when the talk became personal. Thomas had evidently been let down by some pretty young woman who found him dull. Lottie chipped in with some words of comfort – 'But that's what today's young women are like! My daughter and her friends are shockingly shallow. If you've got no money or looks, you're a zero. I'm afraid you'll have to get used to it.' Oddly, the man didn't seem cheered up. In fact, he had looked distinctly sulky. 'Don't worry,' she added, 'you'll be over her in weeks.' 'But Melissa left me a year ago.' And Paul didn't flirt with her at all (of course she would have discouraged it, if he had been man enough to do it, but still Lottie felt a bit disappointed). The young woman sticking up the silly posters in the café turned out to have been Paul's daughter Zoe. 'My daughter isn't at all shallow. Rather too earnest, if you ask me.' So was Lola's shallowness Lottie's fault?

Perhaps in future she'd go straight home.

Some time after sunset, the rain began. It beat against the window as Shirley cooked tea. We had the best of the day, she thought.

She got the boys into their bath. They were nearly too big to take it together, but they loved bath-times; with their clothes shucked off in a heap on the floor, they turned into one bucking and dipping body, giggling, slippery, deeply intertwined, spouting and gargling for happiness when they weren't fighting for space or soap. She left them to it, usually, after standing and watching for a bit.

Sometimes a question came into her head unbidden as she watched her two naked babes at play.

They were very alike, but they weren't identical.

Franklin was heavier and lighter-skinned, in company the shyer of the two: Winston was slighter, more imaginative, with light brown eyes like his murdered uncle; he made up stories; he was sociable.

Shirley had slept with another man around the time the

twins were conceived. She had confessed to Elroy, but in general terms, not making a point of the dates or times, and he had been too upset to ask. They had never mentioned her confession again. But in her head, the questions whispered. The man had been white, but Mediterranean-looking, with olive skin and dark curly hair. Sometimes when she looked at Franklin, his powerful body reminded her of Thomas ... but these were thoughts that she had to suppress before they leaked through and infected Elroy.

Today she was too tired to watch the bath. As she was washing up the tea-things, Elroy came home. He took off his jacket, called 'Hello', and stood in the doorway to the kitchen. 'Kiss,' he said. 'I need a kiss.'

She pecked his cheek and asked, 'How was your day?'

'Oh, usual problems. There's water in the basement. It might affect the electrical systems. I'm dealing with it.' He was faintly dismissive. These days he didn't bring his problems home. 'Where are the boys?' he asked, more warmly.

'They're in the bath.'

'They're early, then.'

'Yes, there wasn't any school today. I took them to the zoo.' She didn't add, 'I went to college, and left the boys with Kilda in the Towers, and she may have taken them God knows where.'

He nodded, approving of her as a mother, which made Shirley feel fraudulent. 'What's for dinner?' he asked, commandeering the paper she'd meant to read after washing up.

'I didn't know you were coming home. I ate with the

boys. But I'll fix you something.' Shirley was tired, and her voice was reluctant, though she loved Elroy, and the wifely part of her thought her husband deserved a hot supper after working all day in the hospital. Why couldn't he ring, though, and give her some warning?

'It's OK,' said Elroy, picking up her tone, turning away abruptly and making for the hall. 'I might ring Colin. We'll pick up some food.'

Which meant they would stay out till midnight.

He didn't sound annoyed, just resigned; she was often tired when he came home.

Too tired to talk, or make him supper, but not too tired to study, she thought. She heard him talking on the phone. Then he dipped back into the kitchen, and smiled. 'I'm going to go say hello to the boys. I'll get them into their pyjamas.'

'Take Winston Bendy Rabbit, will you?' Winston adored his Bendy Rabbit. Much of life consisted in re-uniting them. Elroy took it through, waggling its ears at her.

She was left by the draining-board feeling guilty. Her mum had always cooked tea for her dad; it would be waiting when he came in from the park, and they ate together, at the little table; the children were fed earlier and shooed out of the way, for it was understood that Dad came home exhausted. And afterwards he always said 'Thank you, May,' and sank into his armchair for a read of the paper. And then she would wash up, and come and join him. They sat there, silent, in a circle of light. Somewhere, surely, they must still be sitting there, lit by the table lamp, stooped companionably ...

Where? She would never go home again.

And it wasn't perfect – Dad could be a bastard, and look at Mum now, so slight, so tiny, as if she only half exists, without him.

Shirley wasn't May, and Elroy wasn't Alfred, and twins were tiring, and so was study.

Mum never managed to do a degree. I do my best, Shirley thought, as so often. She wiped the surfaces, washed the cloth, and went into the sitting-room to read her text-book, thinking, if I keep quiet, Elroy might do the boys' bed-time.

Slowly the domestic fog slipped away and her mind began to tune into pleasure. Culture, to Shirley, still meant the far continent, the world away from this flooded city. Elegant voices, silver architecture, long straight roads, a world of luxury –

Though Shirley and Elroy were far from poor. She was a wealthy widow when she married him; Elroy, who had then been younger, less established, had a new job now, more money, more status, high up in hospital management. Both of them had grown busier, older. The relationship had changed, but then, Mum said that children always changed a relationship. 'One day they'll be gone, and then you'll miss them.'

Briefly, Shirley thanked God for the boys.

Then she sighed, and lost herself in her assignment.

About half an hour later, Elroy came through. He looked harassed; his voice was accusing. 'Winston's crying. He wants his mother.'

'I'm a little bit busy ... Could you do it, Elroy?'

'Thing is, I don't know what's up with him. He's talking about you killing a cat, and a man shouting, and lots of people, and everyone will die, and I told him it must be something he's seen on TV, it isn't real, nothing's going to happen, but it seems this Kilda girl has told him it's true. Why she been looking after my boys? You tell me you take them to the zoo, Shirley.'

They were always *his* boys when he disapproved, though Shirley knew that the truth was more complex, he'd never be sure if the boys were his, because she, Shirley, was a wicked woman. She could never tell him. Her sin lay between them. One day, surely, he would pay her back. Or had he already? How could she blame him? Yet he was a doting, passionate father.

Later she was thoughtful as she lay in bed. Winston and Franklin had been hard to comfort. Perhaps the boys had seen some frightening news; most TV news was frightening, at the moment. Mr Bliss was banging the war drum again. We must have war, or there would never be peace. There was a lot of footage of troops moving, and reports of 'liberated' cities far away. Dark-eyed, frightened, liberated people stared back as reporters waved microphones under their noses and asked if they would like to thank Mr Bliss. Ragged, uncomprehending clapping.

Or maybe they'd heard something about the rains. The rising tide of water was scary for everyone. Or Kilda might have been talking wildly. To Shirley she seemed shy, but people were mysterious. Kilda hadn't told her where she had taken the boys.

Guilt pushed up again, black, powerful. She should never have dumped the boys on Kilda. If she hadn't done that, the boys would be sleeping. And that poor cat would still be alive. She had driven straight on; that really *was* wicked. She winced at the memory of its small squashed body. Somewhere an owner might be weeping.

One of the boys started crying again, and the rain hammered hard against the window.

Shirley prayed for the everlasting arms to bear her up, but it was one of those times when Jesus seemed distant, and all that came back was her own small voice, and the empty wind, and the night was black, wet, endless.

May sat in her kitchen trying to read, with darkness pressing against the pane. She loved poetry, and myths, and novels, but she didn't really have an education. (Shirley was getting an education.) May didn't understand about wood-boring insects, she didn't know history, or geography. Maybe she had married Alfred too young, and too many things had been left to him. How old had she been when they took up together?

A kid, really. A chit of a girl ...

She'd been driven to the kitchen by the throat-searing smell of the chemicals the woodworm men had used. Her kitchen still kept its old tiled floor; having no wood, it had not been treated. But there wasn't any heating, and the air was chill.

Feeling slightly wicked, she had switched on the oven, and sat by its warmth, clutching her book, unable to rid herself of the worry that Alfred would tell her off for extravagance.

And yet, she thought, if he did, oh if he did, if I heard his feet coming down from upstairs and his voice, slightly gruff, calling my name, if his dear red face should appear at the door ...

Unpredictable, familiar, the tears welled up, and the grief came back, the old hopeless stone, to press on her chest, crushing, stupid. How could anyone so real and particular – angular, awkward, his look, his smell, the little phrases only Alfred used, Alfred, love, my dear, my duck – how could *Alfred* disappear for ever?

Where had he gone? Alfred, Alfred.

'Stay with me, dear,' she whispered to him. 'You'll never be dead while I am alive.'

Why had she never understood? She hadn't realized that anyone died.

'This won't do,' she heard Alfred say. 'Pull yourself together, May. Make an effort.'

She put down the book, went to the cupboard and took out some flour to make a cake. When you lived alone, you could do what you liked; it didn't matter what time it was. Since she had the oven on, she might as well use it, though Shirley was funny about her cooking. None of May's children would eat her cakes, but as Shirley said, 'The twins will eat anything.'

Alfred actually liked my cakes.

She suddenly knew he was sitting next door, in his old chair, waiting for his bedtime cocoa. She could open the door and slip through to join him, in another world, where they would sit together, where everything that had been, still was, just a little way off, slightly blurred, faded.

The hairs on her arms stood on end. The light on the dresser made them burn pale gold, as if she were still that sunlit girl ...

He was waiting for her, and she should go, but the doorway to the next room looked dark.

She turned her back on it, and sifted the flour, and the beauty of its slow white fall softened the moment, fell across the slope where she struggled alone through the watches of the night with the endless question, where do we go?

Five

Lights had come on all over the city. Signs flashed, gorgeous, over Victory Square, indigo, purple, silver, gold, striped and eyed, zigzagged, pulsing; selling Hesperican sugars, fats, drugs, shows, sex, hopes, holidays. Headlights queued in rows on the motorways, workers trying to escape the city, their exits slowed by the many detours put into place where roads were flooded. Water on roads, walls, bridges, washed the lights into long slurs of colour, peacock-eyed where the traffic lights stared. Trapped motorists listened to their radios; more rains predicted; demonstrations in the south and east, where the populace claimed they were being neglected, their basements left flooded, their drains left blocked. Business as usual. They sighed and switched off.

Davey, Lottie Segall-Lucas's elder child, woke up

ridiculously late, as usual, the day after doing his *Star-Lite Show*. Creeping back to bed with a cappuccino, he skip-read an extraordinary brief for a programme in the pipe-line for April, a two-hour special being billed as *The End of the World Spectacular*. Target audience: treble their usual. Lots of publicity was promised. The planets were due to line up in the heavens: great excitement at CTV House. They were working on computer simulations: the repercussions could be cataclysmic. The footage, his producer promised, would be stunning. 'Hope you're as excited about this as we are.'

Davey did feel excited, briefly, about the possible jump in viewing figures, but there was something flakey, flakier than usual, about the concept of the show, a worm of doubt that gnawed at him, briefly. Would the planets really line up in the skies, or was it as unreal as an eclipse? Was it just an earth's eye optical illusion?

No point asking, he told himself. Davey had never forgotten the shaming moment when, early in his days in children's TV, he had questioned the validity of a bit of science, and the producer took him aside and said, his face briefly contorted with malice, 'Look Lucas, we know you're a clever little cunt but that's not why we're employing you, right?'

He tried to forget the end of the world as he ate his breakfast in the evening.

It was a strange life Davey had ended up living; not quite the life he had meant to have. A cartoon version of the life he once wanted. He had only ever managed to explain this to Delorice. Although she was young, or because she was young, she understood dreams, and the pain of surrendering them, here in the city that gorged on dreams.

No one on the show seemed to care what was true. Whereas Davey, in some humble, deeply buried part of him, believed in truth, and accuracy. But he lived in a world that preferred entertainment, and he did embarrassingly well in it. 'Davey you are my success story,' his mother would shriek when he went to visit. 'Lola is ditsy and Harold is feeble, but *you*, darling ... – Oh, hello there, Harold.'

When Davey was a boy he had loved the night skies, watching them almost every night from his room with its skylight on to the roof. He had a gift for maths, might have done astrophysics and fulfilled his dream of becoming an astronomer, but chance had deflected his path from the stars. His progressive school, St Herod's, was weak on science; his mother assumed that he would choose arts, and Davey did love books, and plays; then Lola was born when he was doing his A-levels, so his mother was too busy to stop him spliffing up; his results were a crushing disappointment, and the better universities were closed to him. He'd done a degree in Theatre Studies, followed, after a few dismal years of finding he was never going to be an actor, by a one-year diploma in Earth Sciences with a half-baked, one-term astronomy option (for how could Davey be a perpetual student when his mother already had one on her hands? His step-father, Harold, spent all his time reading for the great book he had been writing for decades. Harold was clever, and Davey loved him, but he wasn't practical, he wasn't worldly, and why should poor Mum have two hopeless men?)

And Davey had done a lot better than Harold, in the hard currency of the city. Davey worked frenetically; his sleep was erratic; Davey was famous; Davey earned money. Maybe Davey sometimes took a few too many tranx to soften the edges, when he got stressed; maybe he used a little crank or coke to keep himself ahead of the game; but that was all part of the life he lived, the tricksy, glitzy, life of the city, which perhaps he'd never wanted to keep up with, but how did you jump off a speeding train?

At nine o'clock Davey sat talking to his lap-top, TV's 'Mr Astronomy', finishing his 'Star-Lite' column for *The Biz* and listening with a tenth of his mind to the news. (He didn't have to listen, it was more of the same; another distant city was resisting liberation; nearer home, more riots had erupted in the Towers, in a block which had had no power for seven days.)

His doorbell rang loudly, a triumphant tattoo.

Davey opened his door on two wildly excited, shrieking, laughing, black-encased figures. 'Lola,' he said. 'What are you up to?'

'Let us in quick, quick, quick, and shut the door, they're chasing us,' Lola managed to pant out between hoots of laughter. They fell into the hallway, doubled up.

His sister's springy gold curls were concealed by a black beret splashed with big sequins of rain, but she still looked beautiful under the light, her eyes, half-closed with laughter, green and narrow like their mother's, her wide cheeks pink and shining with excitement. Davey was proud of his little sister. Just lately, though, she had been getting into scrapes, and having arguments with their mother. Davey sympathized; he'd been there, a decade or so ago. Mum had left him alone since he'd become successful.

'Are you Davey?' the other black figure inquired. She had pert features, a big smile, white teeth, red lips, wide dark eyes that took him in. A strand of dark hair escaped from her hoody.

'Are you really being chased?' Davey asked, frowning, and made to push past them to open the door, but the chorus of squawks that greeted this move – 'No, no please, they'll *get* us, Davey,' – made him give up, and let himself be clutched, hugged, kissed, trampled on, smothered.

He sat them down in his yellow-painted sitting-room, which was suddenly chaotic with limbs and laughter, and made them hot chocolate, and demanded explanations, but they both became so incoherent with excitement and please for him not to tell anything to anyone that he decided to let it be.

'Davey, you know everything about weather, don't you?' Lola suddenly asked him, eagerly.

'Not everything, Lola, actually.' Davey felt the usual twinge of discomfort that came when anyone questioned him: a nervous sifting of finite resources, the fear that gimcrack foundations were shifting. As a TV astronomer, he mostly relied on other, lesser-paid, people's research.

'He does,' said Lola, turning to her friend. 'Astronomy includes the earth. Davey, is it true this stuff about Varna, this, like, most of an island that's going to fall into the sea because of the dam the government's building, and there's going to be tidal waves and stuff, and, like, half of the world's population's going to drown?'

'Probably not,' Davey said firmly.

'Do you know about it, though?' asked Gracie, suspicious.

'I do know what you're talking about, and this dam project does sound pretty unsound, but I think the danger's been overhyped. There are real things to worry about, you know, girls. The war, for example. The floods, for another.'

But they didn't want to worry about real things, the things they lived with every day.

'You see,' said Lola, triumphant, her mouth made clown-like by a chocolatey stain. 'I told you Davey would know about it.'

'I'm not an expert,' Davey said. 'But most of these things never happen, remember. The odds are usually on our side. You girls needn't lose sleep over it.' Then a spurt of self-importance drew him on. 'I mean, every year there are meteors which could hit the earth if their course veered slightly, and if that happened we'd really be in trouble, you know, flash floods, dust covering the sun, the kind of thing that killed the dinosaurs ... Point is, in fact, they generally miss us. Matter of fact, we're just planning a programme about something more dramatic than collapsing islands.'

He broke off, realizing this wasn't helpful, but Gracie was gazing at him, bright-eyed, enthralled. 'For example? Go on, tell us. We're young. Young people have a right to know. We could fly to Australia, if we had warning.'

It was hard to resist such rapt attention. 'It wouldn't help you much, in this case. It really isn't something you should worry about, but – it seems all the planets are going to line up. In a month or two, not long away. I'm just getting my head round the researcher's notes. It might affect gravity, and tides, and so forth. They claim there could be massive floods. Something that would, you know, make Varna look tiny. I'm not at all sure I believe it, though.'

'Still dams are dangerous, aren't they?' asked Gracie, who hadn't entirely been listening to his answer because she was winding herself up to say something worthy of this interesting man. 'It's capitalism, isn't it? Exploiting nature. You're really lucky to deal with the stars,' she said. 'I mean there isn't any capitalism, up there. There's nothing Hesperican up there. Just beauty, I guess.' And then she blushed, in case he saw that she partly meant, *you* are beautiful. And he was very handsome; dark brows, kind eyes, thick ruffled hair, and the strong jaw-line of his mother and sister, though there was something uncertain about his mouth. Gracie, like her mother, was rarely uncertain.

'No advertising up there,' shouted Lola, slapping Gracie exuberantly on the shoulder, and they instantly both exploded again, giggling and kicking each other on the sofa, before they subsided, looking suddenly sober.

'I'd better go home,' said Gracie. 'My mother will be worrying.'

Paula Timms was a heavy kind of mother, a worrier, and since she had broken up with Gracie's father, rather too focused on her daughter; Lola and Davey's mother was mostly quite light, but Lola didn't want her to float away completely.

'Well our mother has abandoned us,' Lola announced, enlisting Davey's support. 'She's gone mental and gone off to college, hasn't she?'

'I'm rather pro it, as a matter of fact. Why shouldn't our mother do a degree?' Davey hadn't done the degree he wanted; if Lottie, did, he would be happy.

'Because it's my turn,' Lola said, real indignation widening her eyes. 'She ought to be home, encouraging me.'

It was gone eleven when Lottie phoned Davey at the City Observatory, sixty kilometres outside the city, where CTV paid for access to the instruments. It was the best thing about his job, one of the times when Davey felt completely happy, when he got a turn at the giant Caroline Herschel telescope – though for months there had been only fleeting visibility.

'Davey! This is your mother talking' (as if it could possibly be anyone else). 'THANK GOD you had Lola to supper! I am so grateful, darling. The most dreadful thing's happened. Everyone, but everyone has been burgled. By a dangerous maniac of a burglar. Our house. Gloria's house next door. Paula's house, that's Gracie's mother, I've never liked her but it's still a shame. And the girls would have been in, he might have stabbed them or raped them, but luckily they had come round to you!'

'I don't deserve any credit,' said Davey, trying to digest this information. 'I was just sitting there, and they turned up.'

'No you're wonderful, Davey, you always were, a wonderful son, a wonderful brother. Of course I feel guilty. Should I give up college? It wouldn't have happened if I'd been home. I mean, poor little Lola just sitting on her own and this creepy burglar comes barging in … I would have flattened him, Davey, as you well know. I would have beaten him to a pulp.'

This was the other side of their mother.

'Lola's not entirely helpless,' said Davey, remembering the girls in their black cat-suits. 'What have you lost?'

'Oh, just the fucking jewellery. It's always the jewellery. Luckily a lot of it was locked in the bank. But the burglar must have been completely weird, you know, some kind of *crazed starving were-wolf*, he went in the kitchen and found a cold chicken and absolutely *ripped it apart with his jaws*, there was meat and bones all over the floor, all over my beautiful ceramic tiles ... Lola is wild because the TV's gone, the tiny one you could take into the bath, and her new lap-top, and of course her phones. Gloria next door is going demented because, she says, he got into her computer and erased all this stuff she needed for work and left rude messages everywhere, raving on as if advertising was the devil ... Now even the burglars have got fucking political! I blame the floods. And the government. None of this would happen if I were in power. Still I never shall be, now I'm giving up my degree. Lola is being, you know, a bit blaming. Teenagers are hot on blame.'

'Don't be hasty, Mum. It's not your fault. Why can't Harold do something? He could work from home. And do more with Lola.'

'Oh *Harold*, darling. He's just a man. As you are, Davey, of course, but – better. One day I think you'll be a wonderful father.'

His mother had never said that before.

After she was gone, Davey sat and thought, staring out

across the flood-plains towards the distant city, the flush of
pink electric on the clouds above it, the warm coral stain of
the human animal. The long grids of light stretched out
towards the sea. All over the world there were grids like this,
spreading nerve-centres of streaming electrons, and people
moving in overlapping circles who suddenly found that their
fingers touched.

The richer city-dwellers all lived in separate houses. They
thought they were safe behind walls and windows, in nice
green neighbourhoods, far from the Towers. But actually
nothing was separate any more. The walls had become as
thin as paper. Thieves moved though doors and windows
like smoke. The rage round the Towers spread out in slow
ripples. The Towers weren't as distant as he had once
thought; he'd been shocked, and told himself not to be
shocked, when he learned that Delorice sometimes stayed
there with her sister ...

Davey's love for astronomy attracted him to patterns. It
didn't always give him a sense of perspective – his mother,
for example, could sometimes seem enormous, a kind of
tsunami or waterspout (though she was behaving quite well
at the moment), and Delorice often made him so happy he
couldn't work, or breathe, or think – but the truth was
humans were brief, ant-like. The earth itself was a flash of
dust, briefly flaring in the light of the sun, fading, as the
Herschel telescope moved out in space and the net of light
extended for ever, into the faintest snowfall of planets, lost
in the edgeless fields of stars.

Yet there Davey sat, at the centre of his moment. Mr Star-
Lite, the TV astronomer. He was in work, in the pink, in

love. Davey was over thirty years old; he'd made more than thirty circles around the sun.

His step-father said nothing could ever be lost. Harold's great book would explain it all. The two men had talked about it many times: Davey still half-believed Harold would write it, though Lottie had always been dismissive. Harold's answer lay in the physics of time (unsurprisingly, perhaps – his own father was a physicist). All that had ever been, still was. OK, the book might never be published, but the ideas had made a deep impression on Davey.

Harold's physics allowed for no past or future, only a single infinite structure. A hall of time from which the moments opened, a mansion of many sunlit rooms. Davey imagined an unending honeycomb (his nanny, Amanda, had taken him to church: *in my father's house are many mansions*).

Under the flat pink electric city there were other cities, flickering with firelight, a labyrinth of rooms lit by pin-pricks of flame. Over the city other cities would rise, long after everyone he knew had been forgotten. With a sudden sharp pang Davey thought of his sister, his beautiful sister – then his sister's children – fading, carried away from him on the great plain of time flattening out into the distance, and Delorice – Delorice, who he loved completely – and theory dimmed before Delorice's face, her full, humorous mouth, the high curve of her cheek. Davey stopped his train of thought, switched off his computer, began collecting his things to go home.

I must have children, he thought in his car. I wonder if

Delorice wants children? I'm in my thirties, after all. Have I
already left it too late?

It was one o'clock as he drove through the city. At a junction,
a Mercedes drew up beside him, a newish model with its
windows open and Jamiroquai blasting out into the night.
The driver, who was black, looked across at him; beside him
a beautiful young black woman sat singing and miming to
the music; the light showed the beauty of her cheeks, her
breasts; the man's glance seemed to say, 'And you're on your
own'. Davey felt briefly piqued, then annoyed, and tried to
beat the man on the lights, but the other car drew away
effortlessly, a lit cigarette flew out of the window and
splashed into a puddle on the road, and Davey forgot about
it, hungry for home.

　　Elroy got in about half an hour later, having dropped off
his passenger near the Towers. She had asked him in: he had
almost accepted.

May woke, in unease that turned rapidly to terror, for no
reason, as she lay there alone. Somewhere, loud music was
fading away. Whatever had alarmed her was already over,
but fear, for May, was so real, so visceral.

　　When she was a girl, fear was always there. Her father
had terrorized her mother. Then Alfred, for all his good
qualities, would get into rages with her and the kids. She had
always told herself it didn't matter, he was a good man and
she knew he loved her. His job was stressful, he meant no
harm … But sometimes they'd been afraid for their lives.

Her conscious mind had forgotten it all, but now, in the night, as she lay there sweating (since Alfred was gone, she used too many blankets), her body remembered it, alive with adrenalin, her breath speeding up, her heart racing. Lying in the dark, she raged at him. *It's cowardly to hit a woman ...*

She thought of Shirley. He'd been bad to Shirley. She supposed in some funny way he'd been jealous, of both Shirley's husbands, both of them black men.

But May really liked them. She thought they were handsome. And neither of them had ever hit Shirley. They were tall, and smiling, and kept their hair. In fact, she thought they were *fanciable*. She put out her tongue, in the dark, at Alfred.

The fear ebbed away. May fell asleep.

Elroy opened his front door as quietly as he could, slipped off his soaked shoes on the doormat, went and brushed his teeth and showered away the smoke on his hair. Tiptoeing past the boys' bedroom, he glimpsed Franklin asleep, bedclothes thrown off in the familiar tangle, kneeling up, head down, pyjama bottoms off, mumbling something passionate his father couldn't hear. Bendy Rabbit lay on Winston's head like a hat. 'I love you, boys,' Elroy whispered.

Shirley was sleeping flat on her back, her creamy skin lightly pearled with sweat, one heavy arm outside the bedclothes, her blonde hair darkened, sticking to her forehead. She was snoring lightly, like a swarm of bees. She was utterly open to him, like this, looking like the woman he had fallen in love with so completely ten years ago, in the innocent past, before anything happened, his brother's death, Shirley's unfaithfulness, her brother Dirk's conviction for murder, all the broken things that had piled up between them. He knelt beside her on the floor in the dark, and he wanted to make some reparation, he was going to say something, say it all, whatever it took to dissolve the hurt, he was going to pray, as he once used to, before life stamped upon his prayers; but then she moaned, and her eyes opened, and looked at him as if she saw what he was, saw where he'd been, saw him as guilty, and the smile she gave him was lost and blank. 'What time is it?' she asked, not expecting an answer, and then, turning over, turning away, her face blind now, her eyes closing, 'It's too late, Elroy. Go to sleep.'

Davey expected the house to be empty. His top-floor tenants, Chloe and Olivia, biologists from the Institute, were at a conference on cloning, and Delorice only stayed over at weekends, because her job, in publishing, was right in the centre. The street-light outside had been broken for weeks; the council had its work cut out dealing with the water. Davey felt in his coat pocket for his torch, to help him get his key in the lock. He jumped like a nervous horse when there was a sudden violent clatter by the dustbins. Burglars, he thought, so now it's my turn, and swung round ready to defend himself or die. It was the moment every city-dweller waited for, and Davey, who had never hit anyone, Davey, who was the mildest of people, even when he was a boy at school, began breathing fast, electric with adrenalin, but all he could hear was the smallest of movements, someone shuffling, panting, lurking somewhere, waiting for him, crouching in the dark, terrifying, just out of sight.

Then he dropped his keys, his torch swung wildly, his foot crunched over some broken biscuits – no, not so soft, a pile of small bones –

Suddenly the master was there before him, magnificent, original, every hair clear in the arcing beam, a red fox, quivering, poised to confront him, black shining eyes, sharp highwayman's nose. He could smell it too, he realized, suddenly, feeling a visceral excitement. *Near enough for us to smell each other.*

He held his torch steady. In that instant, they were linked.

The man and the animal crouched in the moment.

Six

It was a Tuesday in March; rather early for the Gardens. But Lottie was having a stressful morning. Lottie had had a very stressful month. The whole city, of course, was in disarray, but the populace, surely, could adjust to all that. The Tower-dwellers did keep making a fuss, but life had definitely been worse for her.

Her house had five floors, some rarely used. After the burglary, she'd checked most places – the burglar seemed to have taken little things, jewellery, money, *objets d'art*, and the randomness suggested he was thick as two planks, as well as psycho, and dangerous – but she hadn't gone into the mezzanine, the blue rooms which had once been Davey's. It was Faith who had discovered something missing, weeks later. There was a square of darker blue on the mezzanine wall.

'Didn't there use to be a picture there, Mrs Segall? Quite old, a bit messy, not a very big one, I don't suppose you like it or you wouldn't have put it there. But something's definitely gone.'

There was a stunned silence, and then: 'What do you mean?' Lottie screamed at full volume, looking suddenly larger, her green eyes bulging. There was only one painting in the mezzanine. 'Why didn't you mention this before?'

'It's probably nothing,' Faith said nervously. In fifteen years with Lottie, she had lost her temper twice, and Faith didn't like to remember it.

'It's only my fucking Bonnard,' Lottie said, quite quietly, but immensely threatening. 'Just a fucking major master-piece, that's all. Oh just my Bonnard. Well thanks for telling me.'

'*I* didn't steal it,' Faith grunted, cowed. She occasionally removed things she felt they didn't value – Lola obviously had far too much, more than was good for a child of that age, beautiful objects she crumpled or messed or left to get dusty on the floor, and Kilda could obviously sometimes use them, then everyone was happy, and no harm done – but she certainly wouldn't steal a painting. That was real stealing. That meant the police. She would like to, yes, but she wouldn't dare. In any case, screwing up her brains, she remembered the painting as queer and blurry, with a naked couple who looked all the wrong shape. She couldn't understand why Lottie chose it.

(In fact, the painting had a history. A former flame of Lottie's, an art dealer called Hugo, had given her the Bonnard when she was in her twenties. After she dropped him, Hugo tended to regretful visits, staring at the Bonnard with heavy, pensive meaning. In the end Lottie put it in the mezzanine. She did still love it, it wasn't that, there was something miraculous about the light, jewelling the squared floor of the bedroom, and the flat, cat-like planes of the woman's body, the liquid blues, yellows, violets – and it was unusual in Bonnard's *œuvre* to find two naked figures, not one. Still, the painting always made her think of sex with Hugo, and now she was with Harold, it didn't seem right. In any case, sex with Harold was better.)

Now the painting was gone, Lottie longed for it. Hers, hers; how dare they take it away? The prospect of an insurance pay-out of several millions was swiftly removed when the police found the door had been left unlocked, though Lola and Gracie fiercely denied it, so of course the policy wouldn't pay a cent.

Then this week the whole thing shifted into farce when the police investigation managed to establish that Bonnard's 'Bedroom: Sunny Afternoon' was in a continental museum, and had been there for twenty-seven years, so Lottie's Bonnard was a high-class fake.

'Why aren't you pleased?' asked Harold. 'At least this way the burglar is shafted.'

'But I was shafted for twenty-five years! That slimewad Hugo shafted me!' As she said it, Lottie noticed the double meaning, but didn't point it out to Harold, who could be sensitive about her past.

'I don't see why, if you really liked it.'

'Because I loved something – not real,' Lottie said. 'A copy of something can't be real. I like real things. You know, special things. Done by just one person, just for me. It's like the difference between theatre and cinema. I'd always choose theatre. Wouldn't everybody?'

'You're, you know, over-privileged, Mum,' her daughter informed her, dipping through the kitchen, scooping up a kiwi smoothie from the fridge, spilling chocolate brownie on the floor. 'Some people in the world haven't got the choice. In Africa I'm sure it's just DVDs.'

Lottie was not yet resigned to this newly thoughtful, political daughter. 'Try locking doors when you go out, and don't be smart, Lola.'

Today Lola had decided not to go to school.

'It's just another capitalist institution,' she said. 'I've seen through it, Mum. You can't make me.'

Her mother was next door, in the kitchen with Faith, and Lola could hear Faith hissing instructions. 'She's done this before, you know, Mrs Segall. When you've been at college, she sometimes bunks off, and gets under my feet, and begs me not to tell you. I mean, you have given me authority, haven't you?' (Lottie had encouraged Faith to be her enforcer, but recently Lola had gone a bit bonkers. Given a free hand, Faith could have sorted it: Kilda could still be slapped into submission.) 'Lola tried to bribe me, would you believe?' (Faith didn't mention that she sometimes succeeded.) 'You don't want to let her get like my Kilda. She's bunked off non-stop ever since she started her periods. And look at Kilda. Does she get off her arse? No, she thinks she's a fortune-teller. It's not exactly a career, is it? Though she claims people say that she's good at it –'

Lola interrupted, forgetting about school, forgetting what a cheek Faith had, yelling cheerfully through into the kitchen, 'Did you say Kilda was a fortune-teller? That's so cool, being a fortune-teller. Does she, like, you know, do it for money? Would she, like, do it free for me and Gracie?'

Lottie came through and stared hard at her daughter. When the chips were down, she was still the mother. Heavier, older, richer, stronger. 'Lola, dear, you get an allowance. But you're going to lose it if you don't go to school. Education is a commitment, you know, that's what they're always saying at college.'

Lola stared back at her, pebble-eyed, mocking. 'I don't have to go. You can't drag me there. I'm sixteen now. I can do what I like. You told Ms Johnson I shouldn't work too hard.'

One of the awful things about children was that they expected you to be consistent. Lottie considered the options, briefly. Would she win if she physically pushed her out of the door? Everything subtly changed once kids grew taller than you, though Lottie had an extra stone of muscle. Still if she failed, all was lost. Instead, Lottie tried an adoring smile. It came quite naturally; she did adore Lola. 'If you leave right now I'll get Daddy to drive you and I'll put some chocolate cake in your lunch-box.'

'Oh cool,' said Lola, forgetting her politics. 'And will you give me money for being good?'

Faith watched the bribe being given in silence. The sum was more than her morning's wages.

Harold did as he was asked, as usual, but came back home

in an awkward mood. Faith had gone off to the
supermarket. Lottie was just getting ready to go out; she had
an Art History class at eleven. She'd vowed she would not be
late again.

She was tempted to tell the class all about the Bonnard.
So far she'd kept quiet about that kind of thing. For some
reason she'd felt it might make the wrong impression if she
mentioned her Ingres, when they were studying him. Some
of the students were really quite scruffy. One of them was
black, so probably poor. But all of them would surely
sympathize about the Bonnard.

Harold interrupted her train of thought. 'I'm just a
chauffeur to you, Lottie.' His high, handsome forehead was
furrowed. She always enjoyed looking at his face, but he
really wasn't looking his best this morning, having pulled on
a jumper over his pyjamas in order to get Lola to school on
time.

'Did you mind taking her, darling? Sorry.' Lottie
continued doing her mascara.

'You never ask me about my work. I always ask you about
your classes.'

Lottie stopped in her tracks, and stared at him. Harold
almost never talked like that.

'Are you feeling sad, Harold? Sorry. How is the book? Did
you have a bad day yesterday?'

'You don't believe in my book, do you?'

'You did have a bad day. You're not all right.' Lottie came
over and stroked his back, and pressed her cheek against his
neck.

'Well something happened yesterday. Something I didn't
tell you.'

'Did the computer go wrong again? Oh dear. I keep offering to buy you a new one.'

'No –'

'The printer, then. Darling, let's go shopping. We'll get some more paper at the same time.' She knew how Harold liked his paper. Whatever it took to keep him happy.

There was a pause. He seemed to have a sore throat. 'The thing is, Lottie, I finished it.'

'Of course, Harold, that's why we need some more.'

'No, Lottie, please, *I finished my book!*'

Lottie sat there, winded. This was earth-shattering. No wonder Harold seemed so upset. Almost as long as they'd been married, he'd been writing it. She simply didn't know what to say.

'Never mind, darling, you can start another one,' she tried, tentatively.

It wasn't the right answer.

'You don't believe I will publish it. I'm a joke to you. I'm a joke to Lola. You'd be better off without me, wouldn't you, Lottie?'

They made love vigorously on the carpet. Afterwards both of them felt a lot better, and they fled upstairs, clutching their clothes and giggling, hearing Faith come back, one floor below.

'I think I might take some days off, for once,' Harold said, experimentally. 'I suppose you're very busy, Lottie. Of course you are, with your degree.'

Lottie realized at once that he'd been feeling jealous. Perhaps she had neglected him recently. 'Darling, I'm never too busy for you. Well sometimes I am, admittedly. Shall we go to a gallery? The zoo? The Gardens?'

Forgetting her commitment to education, Lola's mother bunked off for the day.

Shirley woke up feeling leaden. March was her least favourite month; the year was already less young and hopeful. One or other twin always seemed to be ill, so she rarely got them both to nursery. And the world felt frightening, at the moment. The war was unpredictable. Not that war ever ended, of course, but sometimes it blazed up, horribly alive. Great movements of men and weapons had started. Pop-eyed Mr Bliss was always on telly, telling the people that peace meant war. When you had children, war meant fear.

Shirley had been praying and reading the Bible, but these days she did it on her own. After his brother Winston had been murdered, Elroy had suffered a crisis of faith. Once it had linked them; they had gone to church together, often twice in one day, on Sundays. Now Elroy only went one week in four as a way of pacifying his mother, Sophie. Mostly Shirley went alone with Sophie and the boys, feeling wistful, just one more single-parent family.

And she was worried that Elroy was having an affair. What did he do when he was out so late?

And her little garden, which she loved and cared for, had been impossible to walk in for weeks.

She lay in bed, thinking about her snowdrops. They must have rotted. She would have to start again. All through February, she had kept hoping. She saw them vanishing, her hopes for this year, the small bells of white, so exquisite in close-up with their little clapper and frill of pale green and tiny gold stamens like matches burning, drowned stars now in the sludge of darkness.

The year rolled onwards, bringing only chaos. Dirty bombs might be dropped on the city. Elroy would leave her; he would take the boys. She would fail her studies and never become a teacher.

She lay there listening for the sound of the rain, only slowly registering that she heard nothing. (Yet part of her that was deeply tired longed for the kindness of a black wall of water, so she could go under and sleep for ever.)

Just at that moment, Elroy came in. 'Brought you a cup of tea,' he said, sitting on the bed, rubbing her shoulder. 'Guess what, it's a beautiful morning.'

The morning stopped, and became beautiful.

He opened the curtains, and let the light in, and they lay there together on the big new bed which had long ago replaced the one from her first marriage, looking out at the sun on the cherry trees. Pink petals broke from the black elbows of the branches. Her cherries, up to their knees in water, were still exhaling great clouds of pale blossom.

'You'd think their roots would have rotted,' Shirley said to him, laying her head against his shoulder. She suddenly thought about her dead father; he was a park keeper; how he loved spring. She wished he could somehow see her blossom. Perhaps he could, perhaps he was there.

'It's all right, Shirley. Everything's all right,' Elroy kept repeating, and kissing her hands, pressing her warm palm against his full lips.

The boys were in the sitting-room, watching television. Cautiously, tenderly, with infinite excitement, looking deep into each other's eyes, Elroy and Shirley made love.

Seven

Harold and Lottie walked to the subway station hand in hand, chattering like birds. At first Harold tried to talk about his book, but Lottie said, 'It's a beautiful day, don't feel you *have* to talk about it darling. I absolutely know your book's wonderful. You don't have to prove a thing to me ... And if not, your next one certainly will be.'

After that, Harold shut up about the book. He was used to Lottie. He didn't much mind. He had put six copies of the finished book into the post to publishers yesterday: he'd wanted to impress her with his drive and ambition, but after twenty years, it was too much to hope for. Instead, as so often, they talked about Lola. The Giant Baby, as they called her.

'I try to remember if Davey was like that,' Lottie said. 'It was years ago, of course. But I think he wasn't. He always seemed quite grown up. I think he used to tell me off about things.'

'Boys are different,' said Harold, absently. 'I don't really know any, but I was one once. There weren't any teenagers then, of course. Now they're a tribe, especially the girls.'

'Oh God,' said Lottie, 'there aren't any trains.'

The track was flooded between Central and Gardens.

They decided to drive. The route was circuitous, bringing them round to the Bridge of Flowers through parts of the city they didn't know. The water did not come above their axles, and Lottie drove as fast as she could; there wasn't much traffic, considering. She had never been a patient driver, and she wanted to get there while the sun lasted. More rain was forecast for later that day.

The diversion led through a council estate. In the distance, though, they caught a glimpse of the river; it was one of the parts of the city where rich and poor lived packed together. Lottie came slightly too fast round a corner and found herself braking furiously, surrounded by a mob of yelling people, frightened faces, placards, banners, waving hands, black open mouths, all of them spattered with the spray of muddy water that Lottie's speeding tyres had thrown up. Their shouts were loud enough to pierce the car windows.

'Stop,' said Harold.

'Are you kidding?' asked Lottie, thrusting the bonnet of the car forwards in a series of furious, powerful jerks. Now there was someone on the bonnet. A large pale face briefly stared through the window, tipped sideways, clutching at the glass with big hands, but Lottie, dauntless, accelerated. The figure clung on briefly, then slid to the ground; the voices grew louder and then died away as Lottie roared, aquaplaning, down to the bridge.

'For God's sake, Lottie, you can't do that.'

'Shut up, Harold. If I'd stopped, they'd have killed me. They were just a rabble. A mob of thieves.' Lottie was still driving much too fast, but a glance at her white face told him she'd been frightened.

'But it was a girl. Maybe younger than Lola.'

'Fuck off, Harold, or I'll drive into the river.'

Outside the window, the water extended, gleaming metal, over half the landscape. The bridge just skimmed the top of the flood. Near the edges of the new, powerful river were shallow-looking houses, a row of roofs, only their top storeys clearing the water, the windows like eyes above a shining scarf that had suddenly engulfed their past. Most of them must have been abandoned, Harold thought. And this wasn't the Towers, where things always went wrong, where people expected things to break down. The Bridge of Flowers was a showpiece area. Rich people lived here, especially politicians, because fast river launches could whip them down to Government Palace, bypassing the subway and the morning traffic.

So now even politicians couldn't protect themselves.

'It was some kind of religious group, in point of fact,' Harold resumed, still disapproving. Lottie was a force of nature, but sometimes you had to stand up to nature. 'What if you've hurt her, Lottie, honestly?'

'Why aren't you on my side, Harold? It wasn't my fault. They were all over the road. I wasn't to know they were religious. I don't expect they were. I expect they were rioters. They would have taken everything we had.'

'You splashed them,' he said. 'They got angry. They were carrying placards about the Last Days. I think they must have been that One Way lot who have been all over the papers recently. All over the walls as well. Copies of their posters seem to be everywhere.'

Lottie saw a parking space on slightly higher ground. She screeched to a halt and sat there for a moment clutching the wheel before she relaxed. There was a film of sweat on her small, neat features. That girl on the bonnet had reminded her of someone.

'Harold. Cuddle me. I'm upset. I should have gone to college. This is meant to be fun. It was you who suggested we came here in the first place.'

Harold had a choice; yield, or suffer. Were there any choices, really, in life? He put his arm around her. After all, he loved her. There was only one Lottie. Yielding, he suffered.

The Gardens, thought Harold, would cheer them up. They had hills, and temples, and landscaped walks which at this time of year should be lighting up with colour. But at the gates, where they showed their card, the uniformed man said, 'You'll be needing a boat.' Both of them laughed, automatically. For months all the jokes had been about flooding.

'We do have boats,' the man repeated, unsmiling. 'Just wait where it's dry. They'll be along in a minute. Here are some headphones. We're asking our visitors to listen to the commentary.'

He gave them leaflets headed 'PLEASE GIVE GENEROUSLY'. Harold read it; Lottie ignored it (it was dreadful the way people picked on the rich, always expecting her to give money, even if she'd been burgled, or had a bad day. They couldn't have a clue what Lola cost her. Or Harold. He was the costliest of all, if you added on what he wasn't earning, what she might once have reasonably expected him to earn. Or Faith, who cost thousands of dollars per year).

Lottie suddenly remembered the big white face of the girl who had fallen off the bonnet of her car. Kilda, Faith's daughter. That was who she looked like. But of course it couldn't possibly be her.

A group of people were waiting for the boat, standing in a row whose straightness was explained when Harold and Lottie waded across and found they were all standing on a low brick wall. The two newcomers inspected them, subdued and nervous. Things seemed to have gone further than they'd realized.

Later, as they were rowed through the drowned kingdom, they saw the beauty and the havoc. The river stretched out like a golden flood-plain. Only a scattering of birds traced lines on its surface. Where a great throng of specimen oaks once stood, every one of them different, from all over the world – Turko, Malai, Anaturia – the water now shone, inscrutable. Not a twig, not an acorn, waved above. A magpie flared across the bronze. 'One for sorrow,' said a small man with glasses, winking at Lottie in a way she disliked. The water was dazzling, but desolate.

While they stared at nothingness, two magnificent swans came powering across and led them on. It was like following a cloud, Lottie thought; a full-blown, snow-white, cumulus of feathers. Above the water, above the boat, some wisps of real cloud were thickening, greying, but rain shouldn't come till the afternoon.

She looked to her left, and life came back. A hill of daffodils rose out of the dark waters, brilliant, saturated with sun, joyfully yellow, glorious. On top was the white shape of the small temple of remembrance where Lottie and Harold once had lunch, over a year ago when the Gardens were green. Names of the gardeners who had died in the wars were engraved in gilt inside the portico; she remembered Harold reading some aloud.

'Timeless, isn't it?' asked the man with glasses who, like Lottie, wasn't listening to the audio commentary. Lottie didn't want to study on her day out, and in any case, she would look awful in earphones. The little man kept staring at her. He was thin, quite old, not a suitable admirer, and didn't seem to realize that she was with Harold. 'Sort of keeping all the memories safe,' he continued. 'My son's name's written there, you know. He died in Germania. My son George. Did a year here as a trainee gardener, and I'm happy to say they honoured his memory. If only he'd stayed, but he had to join the army … My name's Henry. How do you do?'

He's trying to make me unhappy, thought Lottie,

nodding repressively, and pointedly not extending her hand
to shake his thin veined one. As if I hadn't got enough on my
plate. (She couldn't bear to think of Davey dying in a war,
but the government were talking about conscription. Just
after he had met this nice girl, when she'd started to think
about grandchildren ...) Besides, the old creep was being
smug about the temple. 'I'm afraid it was full of graffiti last
year,' she said, rudely, turning up her coat collar. 'And if the
floods get worse, it could be swept away. Nothing's safe. Not
me, *not you*.'

That 'you' sounded distinctly personal. Henry looked
down at his boots, offended.

For some reason, Lottie's thoughts turned to college and
her essay on conservation. The Institute was on high
ground, like the zoo. But what if the waters kept coming?
What if they overwhelmed the flood defences, so that instead
of being diverted to outlying regions, as at present, the
waters swept into the centre? What if the flood breached the
library?

Lottie had the neophyte's reverence for books (it didn't
extend to her husband's, of course, because it wasn't an
object with a jacket, just a sprouting, burgeoning forest of
paper). She had actually taken some home, and read them.
She was careful not to spill her wine on the pages, or else
wiped it off almost straightaway. Harold teased her, of
course, because he'd always been a reader. She looked at his
face now, grave and absorbed, listening to his headphones as
they swept along, with some black and white coots bobbing
beside them, their feet a frantic blur of orange on the dark
as they tried to keep up with the big wooden boat.

The bespectacled man chucked a white bread sandwich. 'No feeding, sir,' said the oarsman sharply. 'Your commentary will help you with the regulations.'

But what if the whole Institute were flooded? There would surely have to be a plan to save things. Rare things, precious things, her tutor would know. Paul had once been a head teacher, so he must be practical. If he could deal with kids like Lola, he'd certainly know about disaster management. Lottie had just handed in her first two assignments. It would be a real tragedy if those got wet.

Harold had taken off his headphones. 'Look,' he said, smiling, touching her knee. 'Look over there. Isn't that fantastic?'

Though clouds had covered half of the sky already, creeping back, thickening, towards the sun, it still blazed down on a stand of black monkey-puzzle trees which stuck up proudly, cartoon-like, surreal, their broad up-curved fingers as simplified as cactus, and then she saw what Harold was pointing at, for the half-drowned trees seemed to bend and shift, every sturdy black branch was swelling and shrinking, and then she realized they were covered with crows, a crawling black congregation of crows, hopping over each other, jostling, cawing, a deafening chorus of harsh raw sound. Some of them flew up like a storm of black ash and hovered, squawking, above the boat. They looked large, and old. They had heads like hammers.

'Scary,' she said, shivering. 'I think I need a coffee, Harold.'

But the cafés were closed, submerged, gone. A white painted sign was afloat on its back; 'Open For Lunch', it told the sky. 'Lunch' had been crossed out and replaced by 'Tea'. As Lottie read it out, and the passengers laughed, a gun-shot sounded, and the sun went in.

'Er, was that a shot?' Harold asked their oarsman.

'Sounded like it.' His face was expressionless.

'Are they shooting at us?' A big red-faced woman panicked. 'Is it rioters?'

'I doubt it, madam.' He decided to explain, as the muttering spread the length of the boat. 'It's the birds, you see. Sitting ducks, so to speak. There are more of them than usual because of all the water. So a small minority of troublemakers come and shoot stuff for their dinners. We simply haven't got the manpower to catch them.'

There was another long volley, then the silence returned, broken by the oars and a crescendo of bird-calls as startled water-birds fled up into the sky. Lottie realized how diminished the hum of traffic was, its volume a fraction of the usual low roar, as if the Gardens had sailed out into the country, as if the present, and the city, was dissolving, and then it hit her what else was gone. The Bridge of Flowers was on the flight path of the City Airport, and when she and Harold used to come here regularly, when Lola was little, and they brought picnics, every ten minutes or so a plane would roar over like a huge stiff bird coming in to land, and the visiting families would point and crane upwards. Today, however, the planes had vanished. She remembered, then, reading in the papers, a week or so ago, in disbelief, that soon civilian planes might be grounded, if the staff could no longer clear water from the runways.

It had happened, then, the unbelievable thing. No more

planes coming into the city. The skies had gone back to clouds and birds. It didn't feel good, though; it didn't feel comfortable.

Then Lottie thought something even more disquieting. Perhaps no planes were leaving the city. Perhaps they were trapped, but that was impossible. Lottie would never let herself be trapped.

And then she thought: there'd be helicopters. She imagined her little family, jammed in.

Her foot sneaked across the bottom of the boat and found Harold's Wellington boot, and pressed against it, and she wished it were leather, not cold rubber, she wanted the friendly warmth of his body. The wood underneath them felt thin and fragile, the ground swayed horribly from side to side, and below the boat there might be fathoms of black water.

Harold was nudging her, frowning slightly. 'Have you got a headache, darling?' he asked. 'Would you like a mint, my sweet?'

She took it, gratefully, and smiled at him, and the world came back, in that moment of love. Of course the planes would soon be flying again. The army would certainly be working on the runways. The government was hopeless, but this was so basic. Lottie wished, as so often, that she was in charge; she had a brief flash of thousands of buckets, satisfyingly shiny, capacious buckets, with workers she could knock into shape. There was no excuse, at present, for any unemployment. These bracing thoughts made her happy again.

A little further on, an island of green was salted with pale wood anemones. The boat paused while they rested their eyes on the kindness of detail after so much blankness. Moles had survived, they had left black earth-works; primroses starred their wrinkled leaves. There were cream narcissi with ruched red centres, satiny tulips, gold and blue irises curled like delicate tips of tongues. The long grass whispered, *hope, beauty*.

They had swept around in a great wide arc and were returning, now, down the opposite wall of the Gardens, the side that was highest and furthest from the river, where the museum was, and the laboratories, the botanical gallery, the glass-houses. The buildings still stood square and grey though the water was lapping at their feet. Some of them were over two hundred years old, facing up stoically to the future.

'Have you got room there to store threatened species?' a studious-looking young woman asked, rolling up one brown plait as she spoke.

'Should have,' the grey-haired oarsman answered. 'Though the politicians want to get their hands on it,' he added, in a grumpy undertone that only Harold, who was squashed up against him, managed to make out, bending closer. Harold was about to question him when the sun made one last dying effort, sending long rays across the water.

Suddenly something spun into view like a red-gold Catherine wheel of fur, weaving, unweaving, three metres wide, hurling itself down the lawns near the buildings, flaring scarlet into the shallows which sent up a fountain of whirling spray, then spiralling on towards the boat, entirely puzzling, fluid, gorgeous, drawing the sun into itself, a careening planet of liquid copper, a flowing, plaited ring of red silk – and then suddenly broke into a family of foxes, who barked frantically for a second at the boat and then swam singly back towards the banks, where they ran dark and drenched up the green towards the buildings.

As they disappeared, the bright world turned brown, and in another second it began to rain. The little old man started talking again. 'I've got a daughter, you know,' he said. 'A daughter, *and* a granddaughter.'

'Miss,' said Gerda, although she had been told many times not to call the teacher Miss. All the girls called their teacher Miss. 'Why does it have to be wet play again? This morning it was fine, and we played outside.'

'I can't stop the rain,' said Rhuksana Habib. She was only listening with half an ear. She was thinking about her sister-in-law, her husband Mohammed's beloved Jamila, whose city Mr Bliss was attacking. Last week her water had been cut off. It was back on now, but her tree had suffered, which Jamila usually watered every day, the desert rose that grew in her courtyard: the first pink flowers had fallen off, leaving it 'grey as an elephant'. 'I hope it's alive,' she had written. 'If only we could have some of your rain.' Jamila wrote to them every week, and they looked forward passionately to her letters, though recent ones had been harrowing.

'Can't anyone in the world stop the rain?' asked Gerda.

'Don't worry about the rain,' said Rhuksana.

It wasn't good enough, she knew. All the children were worried; so were their parents; everyone in the city was worried. Some schools were shut because buildings were flooded. All over the city, houses felt smaller, mothers were more desperate, more children got slapped, because the rain was closing schools.

Her husband, Mohammed, was worried too, because the floods threatened Headstone House, the publishing conglomerate where he worked. It was touching that he should care so much, when the country where both of them had been born, the country where many of their family still lived, was being reduced to rubble by bombing. But then, Mohammed had always loved learning.

'God can stop the rain,' Rhuksana tried, tentative. She could never remember which children were Christians.

'Well can he do it now then?' asked Gerda. 'I don't want to be the leader again.'

Wet play was a problem for the teachers, because the children stayed in the class-room. The teachers missed the break they usually got while the children roared around the playground outside. Most of them delegated power, for wet play. This resulted in various levels of mayhem. Gerda, being a precocious reader, and considered old for her age, was often left in charge of the reading corner.

'The thick ones ask me to read to them,' she said, frowning. 'It isn't fair. I want to read my book, but they won't let me, so I have to read to them, but I don't want to, and then Adil gets cross and hits me because he says I'm reading too fast.'

'Sorry,' said Rhuksana, but she wasn't really listening.

Gerda was not a child with problems. She was white, she was healthy, she was super-bright. Gerda Lamb would have to look after herself. Though the father was missing, and the mother was a pain, the grandparents were always around, and besotted.

'I know,' said Gerda, suddenly beaming. (She really was an enchanting child, and Rhuksana, who had come into this profession because she loved children, was caught by the sweetness of her gap-toothed smile, her wide blue eyes, her high clever forehead beneath its cap of burnished copper, the trust which Gerda placed in her, and she laid aside her marking and her prejudice, and listened.) 'Can I read them my Hans Andersen, Miss?'

'Do you think it might be a bit hard for them?'

Gerda's shining face fell, and she looked at her feet, and shook her head, mute, stubborn. 'It isn't hard. It's a fairy-tale. The boys should listen. Because they don't like it.'

'I see,' said Rhuksana, and sighed. The boys needed football, and air, and fighting. (Once again she thought about Jamila in Loya. Loyan boys liked to play football on the streets; her husband, Mohammed, had once been a star goalie, captain of the Loyan Youth Eleven. At night the boys all spilled out on to the beaches and the car parks, wherever there was space, and electric light; but because of the war, now, they had to stay home. Cooped up inside, they were mutinous; Jamila's nephews were driving her mad …)

A story could never be as good as football. But the rain rained, and the light was going, and the afternoon break began in one minute. 'Oh well, try it,' she said to Gerda, and gave the child a little hug, though a city protocol forbade hugging. 'Try it, Gerda, my sweet. Why not?'

May was picking up the twins from nursery. She was near the gates, valiantly standing her ground in a surging scum of mothers, all of them fighting for their place in the shallows. In some parts the water was up to their ankles. No one would deliberately thrust her aside, but she had got so much smaller of late. It was that osteo-whatever the doctor talked about, her own bones shrinking, silently receding, as if her whole body was slowly being drawn through a tiny invisible gap in the world, through which she would slip, one day, entirely, and emerge whole on the other side.

But I have to stay here, I'm a grandmother.

The twins need me, Shirley needs me, she told herself, frustrated, squaring thin shoulders, trying to push like the others did.

The first line of children burst out into the daylight from the tall Victorian doors of the school. They had to go carefully, single file, negotiating a temporary walk-way. How tall they looked, the older ones. How quickly they grew, how bold, how loud, but still, one day they would shrink again.

There were Winston and Franklin, grappling, as usual, but then she saw they were helping each other, arms wound tenderly around each other, stopping each other from falling in the water. She thought, they will always have each other. Two was always so much better than one.

But I shall be just one for ever.

She shook off the thought, and shouted, joyful, 'Winston! Franklin! I'm over here!'

'Granny!' called Winston, beaming to see her, since Granny brought sweets, and Mum did not, and throwing Franklin off him, so they almost fell over, raced his brother to get to her, his light golden eyes shining, shining. At that age happiness was total, like sorrow.

They walked down the road, each clinging to one arm, surprisingly strong, robust, demanding. I'm three, she thought. I'm not one at all. As long as they need me, I'm part of them.

And yet, she knew they would grow too heavy, or she would grow too light for them. Inside her body, she was still retreating.

One day soon she would know where she was going.

One day I shall see Alfred again.

Eight

It had not been a good day for the One Way Brotherhood. They had nearly been killed by the devil woman who drove them down near the Bridge of Flowers, leaving most of them piebald with mud; they had been told they needed a bath by jeering teenagers, later, underneath the Towers; the police moved them on in Victory Square.

Now the 'home prayer' session was not going well, in the disused church they had taken a lease on, its interior gutted, its windows boarded up except for the rose window at the top of the nave, where they were trying to restore the sanctuary, which had a central lozenge of the Holy Spirit, a halo of white around the head of the dove. This afternoon, it felt dark, and dead, though fluorescent lights blinked and nagged above them.

'I think it's when the sun shines,' Kilda said. 'People don't take us seriously when the sun shines. When it's, like, raining, the public gets down. And when they're down, they listen to us.'

Moira glared at her, dismissive. 'Why do you think,' she snorted, 'that the success of our mission depends on the sun? Don't you believe we are in God's hands, and that he will reward us according to our deserving? Perhaps some among our number have sinned.'

'Well if you mean me, I haven't,' said Kilda, reddening. She couldn't stand Moira; she was old and batty, with a frightening white face and pointy nose and a tail of grey hair like a pantomime horse. Besides, Kilda got too much hassle from her own mother to put up with any more snash from a stranger. And she hated Moira's whining voice, thin, posh, ugly, screeching. Kilda knew she herself had a beautiful voice.

'Hush, Sister Kilda,' said Bruno Janes. Unusually, today, he had come among his people, partly because of his expertise with guns, which had come in useful when they were at the Gardens. Now his presence held them, magnetized. Without his pale-lidded, pale-eyed stare, without the white gleam of the fluorescent tubes making something inhuman of his polished scalp, Moira might have physically flown at the girl. (Kilda was young, and stupid, and bursting with hormones, and the Brothers loved Kilda more than her.)

Today had been particularly tormenting for Moira, because Kilda, quite by chance, had been hit by the car (probably, Moira thought, because she was slow-witted, while Moira, who was not, had got out of the way). The girl had been carried along on the bonnet, with all the Brothers and Sisters screaming, until the car swerved and threw her off. And then they were all round her, making a fuss of her, saying it was a miracle that her fall had been cushioned by a privet hedge, thanking God for her delivery. Throughout the whole process, Kilda was quite silent, after a vague moo-ing sound when it hit her, which the Brothers and Sisters thought showed her faith, but Moira knew just meant she was dim. Yet all day the wretched girl had kept this special lustre, the enviable glow of the delivered martyr.

Father Bruno was moving in Kilda's direction with the curiously stiff, mechanical gait that reassured them he was more than human, and the room fell silent, in awe and dread, for there was something unearthly about their leader, something that chilled and tranquillized, something that said all things were possible; he must have the power to raise the dead. Now Bruno took Kilda's head in his hands, her dark chestnut hair in his long white hands, with their big blue knuckles and perfect nails, and kneaded her scalp, with an odd expression that looked like a mixture of ecstasy and horror, and ran his white bony fingers through her hair, which after a few passes, stood out, electrified, an arm-wide halo of crackling current, a living force-field around her head. The room went quiet; everyone stared.

It was a metre across, a burning bush, a wheel of glory where the soul could be wracked. 'A sign, a sign,' voices whispered. Bruno, in a convulsive gesture, suddenly wrenched his hands away and wiped them, frantic as crabs, on his vestments, clawing the fabric up towards him, but Kilda's halo still burned dark red.

'Testify,' Milly and Samuel were urging. 'Now you must testify, Sister Kilda.'

Moira sat furious, gnawed by envy, tearing fragments off a piece of lined paper.

Kilda looked surprised, and faintly embarrassed, but everyone was staring, which she quite liked. She'd felt like dropping it all today, with the mud, and the rain, and those fit boys jeering – boys never usually jeered at Kilda – and no lunch to speak of, and the sick-making dead birds they were supposed to hump back to the Towers with them, and that silly old woman on her case, though the Brothers and Sisters had been especially nice to her.

'I could, like, tell you what's going to happen,' she said. 'To each of you, I mean. I can do that. I can see the future. My mother was the seventh of a seventh of a seventh –'

'Come with me, Sister Kilda,' Bruno Janes said, his pale eyes fixing her into silence, his pale claw lighting on her shoulder, and she got up, hypnotized, and followed him through to the sanctuary under the stained-glass dove.

Milly and Samuel led praises for the others while Bruno and Kilda stood apart, in the shadows. *Special, chosen*, the words flayed Moira, who was agonized with jealousy; they pretended to be holy, but really they were sexual. She was sitting with her back to the sanctuary, but she kept craning over her shoulder to watch them, pulling at her hair, which was tied into a rope, a dusty rope of dying matter. Once she had had shining red hair like Kilda. All she could hear was the young woman muttering – almost chattering, her tone matter of fact – in a virtually constant stream of sound. Then it stopped, and Bruno turned towards them.

Silence fell. 'Praise the Lord,' he said.

'Praise him,' they chorused, in ragged passion.

'He has seen fit to grant Sister Kilda a vision. In his goodness he has comforted us; he has given a sign to his people. As it says in the One Book, Brothers and Sisters: God blessed Noah and his sons and said to them, "Be fruitful and increase, and fill the earth. The fear and dread of you shall fall upon all wild animals on earth, on all birds of heaven, on everything that moves upon the ground and all fish in the sea; they are given into your hands. Every creature that lives and moves shall be food for you; I give you them all, as once I gave you all green plants …" And so you see, my Brothers, that on a day when some of you doubted the fitness of my teaching, that we should go to the Gardens and kill and eat, for some of our number were hungry, God has reminded us, through Sister Kilda, that every creature that lives shall be food for us. Even as I said, even as I taught you.'

'Amen,' Milly called, and 'Yea, Father,' Samuel roared.

'And this is for a purpose, God's great purpose,' Bruno continued. 'For when cities fall, and dominions and palaces come to nothing, our day will come, we shall fill God's earth. You must be fruitful and increase, swarm throughout the earth and rule over it.'

Now Samuel and Milly's alleluias crescendo-ed, and even Moira found herself shouting 'Glory, glory, praise his name,' and the hot tears ran down her dry cheeks.

It was Moira who had questioned Father Bruno's instructions about killing the creatures of God in the Gardens. But now she bowed and yielded to him, for she was no longer lost and lonely, she was no longer demeaned, ignored, she was flying with them, God's chosen people, and all things good would be granted her: greenness and fruitfulness; the kind light of heaven in which her wasted life would be washed, in which all her hurts could be known and forgiven; the birds in the air and the beasts of the field; she would have dominion over warm living things, they would come to shelter against her wracked body, she would feel their soft coats and their small hearts pulsing. Now her barren womb is become a garden; she will be fruitful and increase; it is not too late, for the Great Day is coming; 'Amen,' she calls, stroking her belly and weeping, 'amen, Brothers, amen, amen.'

Kilda sat down looking pleased at first, and joining eagerly in the acclaim, but then, as she realized Bruno had finished, as he started his parting benediction, she briefly looked aggrieved, or puzzled. She almost looked as if she might get up and say something, but there was no room for her to say anything; when Bruno was there, his spiritual power lay over them like a net of white ice, leaving his disciples locked, synchronized, lost in the steely perfection of grace.

As they shut the big wooden door behind them, and moved away in ones and twos into the drenching rain and the fading daylight, Kilda caught up with Brother Dirk. Some of the Brothers and Sisters were afraid of Dirk, with his twisted mouth and shadowy past, though Father Bruno told them God had brought Brother Dirk to the fold. Still, their fear judged; he had been in prison. But Kilda, who had grown up in the Towers and gone to school with the sons of thieves and killers, just saw a white bloke, poor, like her, not black, not posh, not foreign, not educated – more like her, in fact, than most of the rest.

'Dirk,' she said, 'That was weird. It wasn't, you know, what I told Bruno.'

'What wasn't?' said Dirk, only half-listening because he was trying to gauge the depth of the puddles.

'That stuff he said about us increasing, and filling the earth, and like ruling all the animals. He got all that from the Bible. It wasn't what I actually said to him.'

'What did you say to him, then?'

Kilda was trailing her long velvet scarf in the water. A long time ago, in another life, it had belonged to Mrs Segall's posh bitch daughter. Sometimes Mum got nice stuff from there. 'I just said all the things I knew about people. I'm, like, a fortune-teller. I've got the sight.'

'You're winding me up,' said Dirk, flatly.

'I'm not.' Kilda felt happy, suddenly. This was something that she could really do, unlike the subjects they had taught at school, though her mother thought she just made things up. Things she was good at made her feel better. 'Have a polo,' she said, on a generous impulse.

Dirk stared at her transfixed. Was she having a laugh? But the mints still hung from her hand in front of him.

'All right,' he said, feeling suddenly shy. The peppermint was making his eyes go prickly. He stuffed three polos into his mouth and choked them down before she changed her mind.

'Go on then,' she said, grinning at him. 'Ask me something. I'm good at this.'

'Go on then, tell me something about – I dunno. Can you do the past, as well? Cos if you do the past, I'll know if you're right. You could say complete bollocks about the future. Not being funny,' he added, to be nice, with something he hoped was a friendly smile, because he had noticed they did it a lot: the Brothers and Sisters always smiled at people.

'Are you all right?' Kilda asked him, alarmed. 'Your face went really weird, for a moment.' But she wanted to get on with her fortune-telling. 'Say who you want me to tell you about. Past, future, I can do both.'

Dirk thought of himself, naturally. But his past was something to avoid with people. The Brothers and Sisters had a policy: 'Total Truth and Total Forgiveness'. It couldn't actually apply to him, though. Some of them knew what he had done, in outline – that he had been forced to defend himself – but they didn't seem to want him to go into detail, and that, of course, was fine by him. They all held hands and confessed their sins, all except Father Bruno, naturally, but Dirk's sins seemed to be off the scale – there wasn't a single murderer among the lot of them, which was disappointing, given the numbers.

The future was a problem, too. He'd never been able to imagine his future, which was why the Last Days provided the answer. This was the way it was going to end, for him and God and everyone else. That was where all his enemies were headed, the immigrants, the coloureds, the filth-bags in prison who had made him do things he could never forget, his sister's husband, his brother, his sister. His fucking awful mother, who never really loved him. When they got to God's

Kingdom, so Bruno said, it would all be made up to them, everything bad, all the unfairnesses, the hurts, the insults. And the wicked would be scourged, which meant whipped till they bled, then tipped into the burning lake. (Dirk loved the idea of a lake, burning, black with his enemies, trying to get out. What a laugh he'd have, looking down from heaven!) Though Bruno wouldn't promise how soon it would be. The important thing was to be ready, and Dirk was ready, now he was a Brother, and had, at long last, a proper family. Kilda wasn't bad: he didn't mind her. She didn't seem to hate him, like his real sister.

But now Dirk began to feel a bit unhappy that Kilda had her own ideas about the future. Which made you think it was a long way off, the things he was looking forward to, the flaying and scourging, the milk and honey, though he personally meant to stay off the milk, which had made him throw up ever since he was a baby, when Mum didn't breast-feed him, so she said, because all her milk had gone to the two others, and so he just got silver top, which nearly killed him. That was May for you; she was a crap mother.

He thought of someone at random to ask about. 'Thingy,' he said. 'You know. That white woman who goes around with the big ugly coloured bloke. African, I think he is.'

'Milly?' Kilda said. 'She's with Samuel right? Samuel's quite fit, as a matter of fact. Well she's going to marry him, isn't she? I can see that.' She thought for a while; she appeared to be listening, and every so often nodding and smiling, or having a little chat to herself. (Dirk thought, she's got to be a bit mental. But Father Bruno seemed to think she was holy.)

Kilda continued, full of confidence. 'They're going to have a little boy, called Saul. And a grandson called Luke, I can only see one, but then he has, like, a whole tribe of children.' She was off, then, chattering, smiling away, going on and on like she had in church, '… and it all, like, happens, a long way away,' she finished triumphantly. Her cheeks were all pink, like she'd been really clever.

'Well done,' said Dirk, after a short pause. He had learned people liked it when you praised them. He couldn't give a monkey's about Milly and Samuel. 'So how about you?' he said. 'If you're so clever – I mean, being so clever – can't you tell what's going to happen to yourself?'

'No,' said Kilda. 'I don't want to. Perhaps it's unlucky, I don't know –' She paused, and seemed to be thinking, for a moment, then frowned, and rubbed her forehead. 'Can't see anything for you, either. I can just see, you know, night, and, like, floods. And you're in the Towers, I think, with Father Bruno. There's someone else there who's been very wicked but – I've got a headache, I can't see her face. Then someone turns up who really upsets you. Then –' She clutched at her chest as if in pain.

The bus came along at that moment. Listing heavily, packed to the gills, wallowing and splashing through the water, its headlights briefly illuminated them, the tall beautiful girl with her clumsy, heavy body, the grim little man with his twisted face, the two of them trapped in a circle of light where the lines of rain were like golden wire, a moment's cage they might never escape, with the cold and dark of the flood all round them.

'I expect I'll be famous though,' she said, as they fought their way through to a space at the back.

She's really up herself, Dirk thought. But then she said something he would never forget. Just as he was starting to hate her, she stopped him. 'You will be too. We'll both be saints.'

Kilda included him, she let him in.

When Rhuksana came back at the end of break, the level of noise in the class-room was normal, and two of the boys were climbing up the window-bars, with others watching and urging them on, so at first she didn't notice the little vortex of quiet around the reading corner. Half a dozen children sat on the felt mat, and a dozen more stood near, leaning inwards, and the centre of the stillness was Gerda's voice.

'That child is amazing,' she told Mohammed later, as they sat eating the Chinese takeaway he had picked up to save her cooking. They had married for love, with their parents' blessing, though Mohammed's mother would have liked him to pick a wife from Loya: foreign Muslim women could be very independent. 'She was reading them *The Snow Queen*, it's a Hans Andersen story which has her name in, and you wouldn't believe some of the ones who were listening, Darren, for example, who can never sit still.'

'The power of imagination,' said Mohammed. He had been brought up for the first sixteen years of his life in Loya, so he had missed a lot of books, though his nurse had told him, every night, magical stories about the village. He didn't know Hans Andersen, or Grimm, or Laing. When he was sent abroad, to go to school in the city, he started to read:

Dickens, Melville, Austen, Flaubert, Tolstoy. Mohammed had three degrees in literature. 'They don't value imagination, at Headstone.'

Headstone had wanted a Muslim on their staff. They hoped to start an Islamic list, which would surely save them from terrorist attacks, though Mohammed laughed and said no one would attack them. (A few of them were clearly afraid of him, particularly after the bomb on the subway supposed to have been planted by Loyan activists. The morning after, no one would look at him. He wanted to say, 'I detest violence'; he wanted to say, 'This is un-Islamic'; he wanted to say, 'Perhaps it was planted by someone wanting to make everyone hate us'; he wanted to say, 'Sometimes they come to the Mosque, people like this, and everyone avoids them, because it's like a virus, and we don't want to catch it'; he wanted to shout at their averted faces, 'Of course it's appalling to anyone intelligent, but my country is being bombed every night. Why doesn't everyone think *that*'s appalling?' He said none of these things, it was too embarrassing. Saying nothing, he suffered acutely.)

He didn't much want to do an Islamic list, since so many of his favourite authors were western. He asked if he could try to revitalize the backlist, which had some classic writers from the days when the publisher was Head & Stone, Limited. With marketing, he thought they could sell well again. But no one listened, he was just Mohammed, a new acquisition they were rather proud of whose presence took care of 'the Islamic issue'. They didn't know how much they shocked him with their trivial banter, their callowness, the way they thought of authors as disposable cash-cows.

He tried to explain some of this to Rhuksana, who thought he must be exaggerating. 'Some of them must love books,' she said. 'If they saw the way my children love books … They're hungry for books, but the school can't afford them.'

Now there were fresh problems at Headstone. The archives were kept in the basement. The files went back for a hundred and fifty years, to the days when they'd been a great publisher, with some of the best writers in the world on their list. One night last week for the first time the waters had risen above the doorstep. Letters and papers had got wet; boxes of documents were actually afloat, bobbing round the staff, who went in barefoot, trousers rolled up, fretful, ignorant, snatching things up and dropping them.

'They haven't a clue what's there,' he explained. 'It's just a great muddle of loss and forgetting. Now they're talking about what ought to be done, but half of them are already bored with the problem. They've lost so many sales because of these rains that some people say we can't afford to do anything, not even get in an archivist. "It's just the past," is what Patricia said. "It's all very well, but we can't live on it. If the rains continue, we won't have a future."'

'Don't they believe in memory?' asked Rhuksana.

'No, just money,' Mohammed said. 'But one good thing happened. Or might happen. I got given an amazing manuscript to read, by someone I've never heard of. H. I. – or H. J.? H. Something Segall. It's about – well, everything, really. This fellow has spent twenty years writing it. It's about time, and simultaneity. The way everyone's moment happens at once, wherever they are, however different, and every atom is interconnected. It's full of the most amazing stuff. For example: did you know that Napoleon lost the battle of Waterloo because of a volcano erupting that spring? There were massive floods, and he couldn't move his armaments. A lot of huge changes come to pass because two or three unconnected things coincide ... Are you listening, Rhuksana?'

'Yes ... sorry. I agree. I was thinking about one of the parents at school. He lost his job, his mother died, then his leg was crushed by a runaway lorry ... It all happened in a matter of weeks ... That must be what it's like in Loya. Darling, have you read the letter from Jamila?'

Mohammed's young sister had been trying for a year to get an exit visa from Loya. Rhuksana knew how much Mohammed loved her. They had both been hoping she would come and live with them and study at the City Institute; and maybe, with Jamila around to help them, Rhuksana would be able to have a baby. She wanted one badly, she ached for one. But Jamila was trapped, as the troops marched nearer the outskirts of the distant city where both their families had lived for centuries. The night sky was red with explosions, there were constant power cuts, the mosque had been hit. Sometimes the letters were unbearable. Too much was happening; too many things at once.

'I'll wait till I've recovered from my journey.'

Coming home was a nightmare every day, as he waited for non-existent transport, taking a more and more roundabout route as the network of viable streets shrank further. The corpse of a rat had washed up, gleaming, on to the platform of the bus that evening. The conductor kicked it off, cursing. Rhuksana had found a drowned fox in the garden that ran from the flats down to the canal. Its eyes were open. She was very upset.

There was a pause while they ate their Chinese Chicken, listening to the whisper of the rain on the window. Lots of the takeaway menu had been crossed out; 'suppry plobrems', the man explained. No sweetcorn, no Chinese Leaves, no carrots; everything came with water chestnuts. Mohammed wondered if the chicken was fresh.

'In any case,' said Rhuksana, brightening, 'there was little Gerda, reading her story, and some of the naughtiest kids in the class just sat at her feet, enthralled. A story like *The Snow Queen* never dates. Poor Mohammed, I suppose you didn't read it. It's about a young girl who has to cross the world to find a little boy, her playmate. He's been lured away by the wicked Snow Queen, who put a sliver of ice in his heart. When the girl finally finds him in the Snow Queen's palace, he seems to have forgotten her, but she kisses him, the chip of ice melts, and they run away, hand in hand, and there, outside the palace, it's summer, "full glorious summer", and they have grown up. So the story has everything kids like – courage, love, a happy ending. Hans Andersen will never die.'

'Unless all the readers do,' said Mohammed.

'Art will never die,' declared Lottie, lofty, in the taxi, to Harold, on the way to the opera. She was Accessing Culture; her course tutor would be pleased.

The Gardens had left her unusually thoughtful. She needed something to cheer her up; spending money nearly always helped. She needed crowds of well-dressed people, flamboyant music, heat, light; she needed red plush and heroic emotion, perfume, alcohol, her flame-red dress. She needed to make love; they had done it again (in that respect, happily, Harold was unbeatable). Christian had designed her a one-off evening number, something she had never worn till today, a full-length column of liquid scarlet with a built-in corset and a plunging neckline, engineered to flatter her every curve, making her breasts rise creamy and delectable out of the tightly-whorled rosebud of a bodice.

She had smoothed the shiny cups up over her nipples, examining herself in the bedroom mirror, starting to feel better, starting to feel good. This morning in the Gardens, life had felt empty, the ground she walked on was suddenly thin, as if they were floating on a sheet of paper – nothing happier or safer than a sheet of paper – with the flood-water already darkening the corner, preparing to pull them all down into nothingness, her luck, her marriage, her house, her money, the people of the city, their hopes, their stories (she had warmed at the last to the little old man with glasses, when he started telling her about his granddaughter, a child called Gerda, who loved the zoo, and came to feed the birds in the Gardens. His wife had made Gerda a red satin dress; the detail instantly made Lottie like him; she had seen the girl in her mind's eye – a patch of red satin, a sun-blanked face – on her grandfather's lap in the cruising boat, in that fragile company, so small, on the waters, all of them together, chattering, nervous, linked by a sudden fear of the future).

Which was ridiculous, of course. As if it could just vanish, the whole glittering city. When she, Lottie, was afraid of nothing.

But money had always been her shield. And she liked to think she was creative with it. First she had rung the Opera House: yes, they had four premium tickets. In fact, they had dozens of premium tickets. 'People just aren't going out, madam.' 'How feeble of them,' said Lottie. Then she rang Davey, in invincible mode. He was to get himself to the Opera House, by any means possible, with a 'nice date' – 'Mum, I have a girlfriend, as you know, I don't do dates' – 'Exactly, Davey. I remember her. And her name was – ?' 'Delorice.' 'Delorice, quite. A very nice girl, frightfully brainy, I approve, darling. Do you think she has got a decent frock?' 'Several, Mother. But she may be busy.' 'Davey, this is the *Opera House*.' She needed her family around her – not Lola, of course, who only liked hip-hop.

Now Lottie paused, as she dressed for the opera, and stared at the woman in her wonderful Hopper, *Morning Sun: Soleil du Matin*. So solidly grounded on that gleaming bed, bending forward, eagerly, into the morning, the living, rinsed-gold light of morning which poured full-tilt through the open window. In that perfect world it would never rain.

Perhaps the woman had the wrong lover, for the other half of the bed was vacant, perhaps she was even a prostitute, for she'd woken wearing a scanty pink dress; maybe her face had a clownish look, daubed, it appeared, with last night's makeup, a slash of red on her lips and cheeks, the head-on light making her skin a mask (here Lottie broke off to complete her makeup). But however

Lottie read it, however long she looked – and this picture had survived a lifetime of looking; the family had owned it since she was six – the painted woman was part of her, a woman four-square in the blaze of morning, leaning towards the empty, beautiful, sun-kissed city outside her window, the warm red brick of the eternal street.

Touching palms with twenty years of affection, Lottie and Harold let themselves out.

'Art will never die,' Lottie repeated, more urgently, plucking at Harold's cashmere coat, for her husband was staring out at people wading with bags and brief-cases on their heads, lit up wherever the lights were still working, oddly medieval, lurching, struggling, as the grumpy taxi-driver wove through the streets, swearing to himself at every diversion; the journey was taking three times longer than usual.

'I hope you're right,' said Harold, laughing, surprised by her intensity. That kind of statement was not like Lottie, but hearing the hunger in her voice, the way she needed to believe it, he tried again: 'Of course you're right.'

'And we're all happy, except for the floods. You managed to get to the end of the book. Lola has got that nice little friend, who I hope is a good influence. And Davey's doing so well at the moment.'

'Yes, Lottie darling. I'm proud of him.'

'He says he's made a programme about the end of the world. I mean, he does take on the big subjects.'

'Yes, Lottie. Marvellous.'

'But Harold, it isn't really so marvellous. I think it's scheduled for the day after the Gala.'

'The end of the world, you mean?' said Harold, and laughed uproariously.

'Yes, actually, Harold. Don't laugh, dear. That, and the programme. Both of them. It's very scientific. To do with the planets. But Davey doesn't seem to take it seriously.'

'Then we shan't either – all right, darling? Let's just enjoy the opera.'

Forty minutes later, Lola rushed in from drama rehearsals at her school, which had had to be stopped when part of the drama studio's roof collapsed under the weight of water. They had all had a fright; no one had been hurt, but there were several minutes of tears, and screams, and the Ramada twins fainted and were taken to hospital. Lola was still shaking with excitement, and ate: two packets of prawn cocktail crisps; a bowl of sweet cereal with two spoons of honey; a bar and a half of organic chocolate flavoured with organic coffee-beans; three meringues, which she filled with jam; then three different vitamin pills for her health. She longed for her parents; she'd almost died, and they ought to be here, to sympathize. She found their note, and felt cross with them; they were far too old to need to go out; nicked one of Harold's cigarettes, to spite them; coughed horribly; painted her nails; hated the colour, and cleaned it off again; changed into a wonderbra and micro-mini; remembered she had lots of homework to do; phoned a friend, Rosa, to talk about it; Rosa hadn't done it, but was sure it would be easy; arranged to meet Rosa at Sweaty Feet; jammed on her earphones to listen to Coldplay; pulled the front door to, as she rushed out, swearing as she plunged her new shoes into a puddle; failed to hear that the lock hadn't caught.

Two hours later, Dirk arrived. He wasn't imaginative, he knew this area; he had done very nicely here before. But even Dirk was pleasantly surprised to find Lottie's front door wide open again. The One God was really providing for them. This time Dirk had brought a van.

Davey and Delorice were both on edge as they journeyed towards the Opera House. Delorice and Lottie had met twice before, but Lottie had been vague about her on the phone. And it was Delorice's first time at the opera. The Opera House seemed ordinary to Davey; he'd been going to the opera since he was a kid, 'and people don't dress up as much as they did', he told Delorice, trying to help; he only dressed up to please his mother. But what he said emphasized the differences between them; he was a decade older than Delorice; paler, richer, more blasé. Some things he did still shocked her; the church had made her strongly opposed to drugs, so he rarely used when he was with her … Maybe this relationship was never going to work.

They had allowed three hours to get there, but the journey deteriorated into farce as they traipsed, dressed in evening gear and giant galoshes, through a makeshift patchwork of buses and water-buses. Waiting was muddy and nerve-wracking.

But the trip ended with a brilliant flourish. For the last

stretch, across the flooded square, the Opera House had acquired gilded gondolas, lit at prow and stern by blazing flambeaux, ferrying latecomers in silk and velvet over the black waters around the white mansion, light flickering across pale arms and blonde hair, and flaring and guttering on Delorice's skin, which glinted in the dark like rare black satin. By then she was terrified, chattering wildly, but the boat glided on, full of beauty and money, bearing them up over the surface of the night.

Lottie spotted them across the foyer, debouched, with ten others, from the gondola, tugging off their boots, tussling with their evening shoes. She sailed across, a golden figurehead breasting the tide in ruby red, all delighted laughter, big arms out-stretched, and embraced them both to her creamy bosom, Delorice just as warmly as Davey. Harold hovered, smiling benignly.

'How do you do, Mr Lucas, Mrs Lucas,' said Delorice, sounding like a virtuous schoolgirl.

'Harold and Lottie, please,' said Lottie. 'Don't fuss about your boots, my darling children. Just leave them there.'

'Mum, we can't. We're going to need them afterwards.'

'Lottie –' Harold tried to restrain her, but Lottie waved him impatiently away.

'Of course you won't. I'll get you a taxi. The gondolas take you to the taxi rank. And I'll buy you both some more boots tomorrow. You don't want to lump those things about with you.'

'Sorry to be late, Mum, darling. I wasn't expecting to need so many boats.'

'But didn't you adore those gorgeous gondolas!'

Lottie pulled them by the hands across the crimson foyer. Dark stains on the carpet where the flood had leaked in. 'It's *Madama Butterfly* of course, which I love, though Butterfly's hardly a role model, is she? I'm quite a feminist, Delorice, in my way. Did Davey *force* you to come tonight? He always says I'm frightfully bossy ...'

Davey knew at once it would be all right. Delorice was smiling at his mother, charmed. At least Lottie didn't let anyone be shy. He was surprised, all the same to hear Delorice say 'Thing is, Mrs Lucas –' 'Please, call me Lottie' – 'The thing is, Lottie, it's my very first time. I've never been to the opera before.' In the gondola Delorice had sworn him to secrecy!

'How wonderful! You're going to adore it. You must sit by me so I can see you enjoying it.' And then Lottie linked arms with her, and swooped her ahead of Harold and Davey, and the two men watched proudly as the two pretty women, one blonde and voluptuous, rain-drenched with diamonds ('Did you have to put the *whole lot* on, Mum?' 'I've got them out of the bank, I'm going to bloody well enjoy them'), the other dark and athletic and sinewy, walked in front of them up the red staircase, chattering and laughing loudly together. Every head turned to look at them, though Davey, trotting along in their wake, noticed, as he did from time to time, that Lottie's feet under the satin were a little large.

'She likes her,' said Harold, his eyebrows in overdrive, doing a thumbs up sign at Davey. The 'she' in that equation was definitely Lottie.

'She'll have to, I'm going to marry her,' said Davey, and having said it, felt completely astonished, but also certain he'd got it right, and Harold punched his arm with great emotion, and said, apparently inconsequentially, 'Your mother and I have been so happy; happier than anyone could ever imagine.'

'Although Mum can be –'

'Yes, she can be.'

The opera, though, gave him pause for thought. It began, as they had begun, all blossom, clouds of lit pink in a garden of cherries. Captain Pinkerton told the American ambassador about his plan to take a temporary bride from the imaginary country of Japan.

Davey, on Delorice's other side, told her in a whisper, 'America is really Hesperica, of course.'

'That's obvious,' she hissed back. 'But is it going to be sad? Will Butterfly love Pinkerton too much?'

His heart sank a little. 'You'll have to see.'

The familiar arias poured out, glorious. Pinkerton left Butterfly: the child was born, a touching little elf, a blond Japanese, and Lottie managed, with terrific tactfulness, not to say, as Davey feared she would, 'Isn't he gorgeous? I just love half-castes,' but the way she was smiling, when the child was on stage, suggested she was having just those thoughts. Butterfly sat waiting through that heart-stopping day and night and morning for her love to return. The inevitable tragedy closed upon them; for Davey, the stage was blurred with tears. A quick glance to his right showed both women were weeping, and Lottie was offering a handkerchief – 'I always bring two to *Butterfly*.'

'So good on imperialism,' Harold enthused, afterwards, as they sat in the three-quarters empty restaurant awaiting an implausibly costly meal; Delorice widened her eyes at the prices.

'But it was romantic,' protested Delorice. 'I thought it was romantic, not political.'

'Of course it is,' Lottie put in, eating the last bit of bread in the bowl. 'Harold is ridiculous.' Their party made up, in life and noise, for the missing people in the room.

'But Lottie –' said Harold.

'But *nothing*, Harold. Get me some more bread, will you, darling?'

'The way they used the American flag,' he continued, unruffled, drinking deep of his wine. 'It was just like the way Mr Bliss and Mr Bare make use of the flag of the Hesperican empire. The director was very strong on satire.'

'But the music –' said Delorice, and then looked embarrassed. 'I'm not an expert, right. But to me the music was all about love. Having it, then losing it. I mean she loses her husband, then her child ...' She fell silent; Davey guessed she was thinking about Leah.

He rushed in to help out. 'But she's true to herself. She's true to her love.' He was thinking, that's why Butterfly is wonderful. We all make shabby, temporary compromises. We are all Pinkertons, wracked with guilt. And Puccini's music is all the things we long for: love, artistry, loyalty, eternity.

'I wish she didn't die,' said Delorice. 'Why do they always have to die?'

The food had arrived, not exactly what they ordered, because of difficulties with supplies, but there was plenty of wine, and nobody minded.

'No one ever dies,' said Harold, suddenly, emptying another glass, and smiling, transformed from the usual shy, ironic Harold who let his wife take centre stage. 'In my book, I say that no one ever dies. Good moments, like this one, go on for ever. It's just that our bodies leave them behind. Our minds don't have to. We can choose to be happy.'

Lottie beamed upon him, proud but baffled. 'That's awfully clever, Harold. But is it true?'

'In my book it is,' he smiled back at her. 'The eternal return, the eternal moment –'

'Did you make that up?' Lottie asked him, tenderly.

'Not exactly. I wish I had.'

'It's true in art,' said Delorice, suddenly. 'Butterfly always lives again. Every night, she comes alive again. In a garden full of cherry-blossom.'

'You mean, every time they perform the opera,' Lottie said, thrilled to understand. 'But I said the very same thing to Harold, just this evening, didn't I, Harold? Tell them, will you?' (He nodded, patient.) 'I'd been looking at my wonderful Hopper, the one with the woman gazing out of her window, and I said to Harold, just like that, "Art will never die!" It's astonishing.' She beamed approval at Davey's girlfriend: Lottie was a fan of positive thinking.

'It's the same in books, isn't it?' Delorice went on. 'The characters in books don't have to die. At least, not for ever. They're always there.'

'You ought to be a writer, like Harold,' said Lottie. 'I've rather forgotten what you do.'

'I'm a publisher,' said Delorice. 'At Headstone Books.'

'HAROLD!' shrieked Lottie, leaning over the table and seizing his hand in hers. The fish on his fork fell off on the table, his favourite mouthful, saved till last. 'That's simply perfect. Did you hear that, darling? You could actually think about publishing your book. Delorice is *a publisher!*'

'Lottie,' said Harold, sterner than Davey could ever remember him being to Lottie, 'leave the poor girl alone. I have already sent off my book to publishers.' He had chosen six, at random, and tried to remember if Headstone was one of them.

'*Really*, Harold?' Lottie was astonished. 'You sent it off, on your own? Without telling me? Harold you're wonderful … did you, *really?*'

'A toast to Harold's book,' said Davey, and the four of them, glowing with wine and laughter, their bloodstreams lavished with nourishment from fish and flesh and vine and vanilla, raised crystal glasses to the chandelier; the bubbles burst, softly, and kept on bursting; they wished for success, they wished for the future.

At home, the front door banged on the night.

Nine

Moira knelt, by her dog, who twitched, and licked her, under the window of her attic room at the top of the student building she had moved to since she had been expelled by the City Institute. The hypocrites had told her they were not sacking her; they pretended they wanted her to get better, though Moira had never felt better or clearer. The pain of rejection had nearly killed her, but she knew it was all part of what was written; she must be cast out for her Master's sake. She corrected herself – she was going astray; Father Bruno was not her Master, but he was so strong, so masterful.

Moira had resigned from the wicked Institute, to show her colleagues they could not hurt her, or weaken her spirit, but they were cunning, and refused to accept it, saying they felt she needed time to consider. Now Moira had outwitted them; they kept paying money into her account, their dirty payments sneaking in like lizards, flickering up under her skirts like snakes, but she took the reptiles by their throats, turned them away from her, cast them out, gave all the money to the One Way Mission.

Now she was here. Now she was safe; she had humbled herself, she had left her house with its sinful weight of books and papers, its television, its tormenting music, Debussy and Ravel who seduced and sorcered, tempting her to think that life should be beautiful, tempting her to be broken-hearted. Now she was alone, unaccommodated, kneeling on the boards beside Fool, her dog, in the cold, in the dark, preparing for light, though part of her hoped day would never break, for the time drew nearer when God would dissolve the painful borders between day and night, when God would ease those exhausting crossings; the time drew near, and Moira was ready.

This morning, for once, the house was quiet. The glass of the window, which whispered and chattered, had become silent now the rain had stopped. It was the third morning of perfect silence. She prayed, humbly, that now she might hear him, Jesus, the still small voice of calm, gentling the terror of her racing heart. Stroking the dog's silk neck, she listened; then she pressed herself further down on the floor-boards, rasping her face against the hurtful grain; the Labrador cross watched her, trembling; Moira waited, trustful, but no voice came. She found she was shouting: 'Master, come! Come, Master! Your servant is ready!'; she prayed for herself in the singular, for the others were surely not humble enough, they preened themselves, they boasted, like Kilda, they drew attention to their petty triumphs.

'Come, Master! Master, come!' Moira screamed, and beat her hands upon the floor-boards. Dark, so dark, and no sign of dawn. Hungry, helpless, she began to moan and thrust her body against the harsh planks, licking up dust, gnawing at splinters, catching the edge of her tooth on a nail, pressing her tongue on the sour stub of metal, knowing this suffering came from God, lifting it up to him with sore, scraped hands ...

Whining, crying, Fool ran to the door, and then Moira's ears were blessed with thunder, a great roaring, a great shouting, and 'Yes, Lord, yes,' Moira called once more before the red dog's whimpers destroyed her epiphany, keening and quivering as he pawed at the handle, and she realized someone human was out there.

'Will you shut the fuck up?' a male voice demanded.

She was still lying there, twitching and whispering, her fingers bloodied, as the sun came up, prostrate, torn between hell and heaven.

The sun came up; beauty, beauty.

'The Gala,' Davey heard, as he tuned his car radio, catching it, missing it, 'the Gala ... expectations ... critics ...'

Davey was cruising back into the watery city as the sun's first rays hit the tops of the Towers, having spent the night at the Observatory. He registered another cloudless sky. That he was driving into light, without the faint fretting of windscreen wipers in his vision. That the surface of the motorway was almost dry. And last night the dark had been teeming with stars.

Perhaps it was over. Could it be over? Could they get on with their lives again?

His mind was racing, though his body was chilled: sometimes he thought they were no longer connected. He needed to be in bed with Delorice. She put him back together again.

And now his mother had fallen for her. The visit to the opera had been a success, as much of a success as it could possibly have been – except for the burglary, of course. Davey didn't find out about it till next day.

But his mother seemed curiously unfazed, this time. 'Fortunately, darling, I had *all* my jewels on.' Once again lots of Lola's gadgets had gone, 'but I can't say I mind a bit about that, she'll just have to learn to manage without them. She's losing her allowance for the next ten years. Of course I'll have to replace her television, and she can't do homework without a mobile phone –' The worst loss was Lottie's favourite picture, the beautiful Hopper he had known since childhood. Even here she almost managed to be philosophical. 'It's not the value, Davey, as you know. I wasn't ever going to sell it. The worst thing is, it might disappear completely. What if no one ever sees it again? What if whoever's got it doesn't even like it? It would be nice to think someone's looking at it … Hmm. With luck God will strike them blind.'

For Lottie, amazingly, the burglary was almost overshadowed by her revived enthusiasm for Delorice. 'Did you notice, darling, she was just like me? We kept on having the same opinions. I suppose it's natural, since you love your mother. Davey, Harold and I both think she's a catch. Not all pallid and snooty like your last one, not anorexic, not a sneerer' (Lottie had suspected Davey's last girlfriend of laughing at her, not without reason). 'You mustn't let this one get away.'

He smiled to himself. And Delorice liked Lottie. His life felt good, in the early morning sunshine. He cruised along thinking about his girlfriend: her finely cut, laughing, cushiony lips which opened, with love, like a sea-anemone, the way her fingers smoothed his back, the way she laughed at him, her truthfulness, the way she kept his feet on the ground. And Delorice did something in the world (although she always deprecated it). Unlike him, she had a proper job. It was one of the things that most impressed him.

And now she wanted to edit Davey! The woman who'd edited Farhad Ahmad, the youngest-ever winner of the Iceland Prize! Davey's agent was setting up a deal with Headstone for him to write a series of guided trips around the universe. The first idea Headstone came up with had made him shudder – *Star-Lite Trips*, 'journeys round the universe done in the style of a "sixties acid trip"' – but Delorice explained it had come from Marketing. 'You do see, Delorice, this must be educational,' he'd told her, 'if you're doing it for teenagers like my sister Lola. They know *nothing* – less than nothing.' 'Of course,' said Delorice, though she looked a little anxious. 'Don't worry, Davey.' He trusted her. They had settled on *Star Trips,* a more neutral name.

On the radio now, a government spokesman was saying the worst of the floods was over. A full inquiry had been launched into apparent failures of emergency planning, with particular reference to the 'alleged' lack of pumps and boats around the Towers in the east. The government was 'unable to substantiate' rumours that sabotage had been involved. 'Links to a foreign power' should be 'treated with caution'. (The government habitually denied its own rumours, so the item must be a government leak. The 'foreign power' would obviously be the one they were at war with.) But 'the rioters' voices would be fully heard'; the government was meeting their leaders today. 'Full and constructive' discussions were expected.

There had been no rain now for forty-eight hours, the longest intermission for over two months. Government meteorological experts 'confidently expected' drier weather to continue. 'The message is, we are on top of things.' Long-term restoration works would soon be underway, and the clean-up campaign had already started. 'It's very good news,' said a government spokesman. 'Especially today, with the City Gala.'

This Gala had been planned for a decade. It marked the twenty-fifth year since the city's docks had been turned into a pleasure zone for international tourists (and the twenty-fifth anniversary of the dockers' riots, in which ten people had been killed, though no one was keen to remember that). In the drubbing rain, rumours had redoubled that the government meant to call the Gala off: the rioters had demanded it, celebrities swore they would not attend, firemen and ambulancemen threatened a boycott, media pundits said it was tasteless with war boiling up in the lands around Loya, safety experts said it was pointless, the city was sinking into the flood.

But underneath it all, the city had been hoping that the giant party would go on. They had been oppressed, by the rains, by the shortages, the winter that seemed to have eaten the spring. Almost no one had been going out, as the buses and subways grew erratic and lawless; a bus had been swept away down river, fifty-three passengers had been drowned, the taxi drivers were demanding double money ... Now suddenly the worst was over, and at once, the city needed its Gala. The government would take charge of things. They were drafting an edict capping taxi rates, they were clearing debris from roads in the centre, they promised to lay on 'special river-buses', 'whatever it takes to get our people to their Gala' – though most of 'their people' weren't invited, of course.

The Gala was of pressing concern to Davey, since he was one of its star presenters. The biggest event of a quarter century, televised all over the world. Lottie and Lola were fizzing with pride, and even Delorice got quite excited, Delorice whose head wasn't easily turned and who was so rude about television. Delorice would be there, looking beautiful. Once his stint was over, they could dance all night, and then stay in bed and make love all morning, since the day after the Gala was a public holiday.

Suddenly now he heard his own name, and flushed with pleasure – 'Davey Lucas' – instantly followed by a shiver of shame as the voice continued 'the well-known astrologer'. He would be derided throughout the profession! But part of him knew he deserved to be. Part of him knew he was over-promoted, and some of the hype was his own fault. When TV had dubbed him 'Mr Astronomy', he'd asked them not to, but half-heartedly, and unsurprisingly, the name had stuck.

He suspected that the savagery of the response from within the academic establishment on his 'planetary line-up' spectacular partly derived from spleen at his title. Professor Sharp, for example, had called him 'a childishly unsophisticated thinker', though most of the thinking hadn't been Davey's. Sharp was almost certainly jealous.

And how could Davey help being flattered when Kylie Spheare, of Extreme Events, who was at every party, with her tiger-striped hair, called him and purred, into his surprised silence, 'Davey Lucas, you're the man we need. Frankly, at the moment, only you could do it. The kids love you, but you're, like, an intellectual, so you'll be able to remember all those foreign names. Bliss will be delighted to go on with you, it will help him, like, get cred with the youth –'

'*Bliss* go on with me?' Davey interrupted, trying not to sound too excited.

'Yeah, well I know he's a bore,' Kylie said, 'but we have to have the politicians on. But you, Davey, you're gorgeous, and you're, like, *serious*. The city is willing to pay for the best. Tell me you're not going to turn me down.' Her voice had become very low and sexy. Naturally Davey had to say 'Yes', though part of him was panicking. Why was all this happening to him? Had he ever asked for any of it?

Still, Davey had never been a purist. Lottie had taught him to enjoy what came.

Listening to the good news about the floods, Davey started to feel positively cheerful. Even the radio presenter, a sceptical countryman who usually savaged politicians from the city, sounded more optimistic today.

(However, CTV had really blown it, since the *Star-Lite End of the World Spectacular* was scheduled for the evening after the Gala. They'd had lots of tabloid coverage at the weekend, with everyone in apocalyptic mood, but now the sun was shining, people had lost interest. The floods were going down; of course the world couldn't end!)

Besides, for the first time in what seemed like months, there had been a completely clear night sky. Davey had OD-ed on the telescope, playing with some of his ideas for *Star Trips*. He wanted to explore, for teenagers, some of the wider questions in astronomy: one expanding universe, or many? Plural universes linked by worm-holes? One amazing structure, an infinite foam? Would the universe expand for ever, swimming endlessly outwards into the dark until its messages grew faint and were lost, or was there enough concealed matter to make it, at the last, turn back towards home? White distant swimmers, at the last, homing ... When he was a boy, he had loved that idea, that the universe was cyclical, expanding and contracting like a heart. The idea of perpetual repetition soothed him. At last, one day, the cards would fall out right. Davey could be the man he longed to be; the swimmer would home at the perfect angle.

How strange it was, how beautiful. One day he'd bring Delorice along to see. They would climb up into the sky hand in hand, and look together at the ends of time. Go on a trip across the wide star-fields, the hidden galaxies above the black waters –

– Which had started to smell, in recent days, as the city began to warm up into spring. Davey pressed a button, and rolled up the window. He reminded himself that nothing lasted. The floods had been bad, but they too would pass.

Moira rose to her feet, sighing, bleeding, and picked up her Bible, and found peace. Morning had come, a third day. Maybe her Master was in his morning. Maybe she was not unvisited.

God said, 'Let there be lights in the vault of heaven to separate day from night, and let them serve as signs for both festivals and years.' God put these lights in the vault of heaven to give light on earth, to govern day and night, and to separate light from darkness ... Evening came, and morning came. God saw that it was good.

She looked down for a second from the page of her Bible where the sunlight lay across her knee, the blue and yellow of her bruised knee, and Fool sat against it, his head on her flesh, she could feel the quick faint beat of his heart, the bridge of bone as light as egg-shell, and the sun painted a patch of his fur, lit part of it to such unbearable richness, such red fierce warmth, such a glow of red love, that her tears sprang towards it, the one good thing, of which Moira could never have enough.

May woke up from a dream of Alfred. He lay beside her: they were together; they were old, but they were curled like spoons, his dear hands joined beneath her bosoms, and he was whispering, 'I love you, May. I'll always love you, you know that May.' She woke on a crest of unbelieving joy that only slowly ebbed away.

She knew he was there; they had been together. Somewhere, not far, he must still be with her. (She wished so fiercely that he could see the children; when she'd left them yesterday, they'd hugged her to death, and Franklin had so much a look of Alfred, his Roman nose, and his grandpa's spirit; he was shy, like Alfred, but stubborn as a mule; and Winston had told her a fairy-tale, a rather muddled version of *The Snow Queen*.)

On the bedside table she kept her Tennyson, her other Alfred, who had not died. She picked it up and read, short-sightedly, drifting through the house to her little kitchen. She tripped on the carpet, and nearly fell. She heard him, impatient: 'What are you playing at? For heaven's sake, woman, look where you're going!'

She read 'Mariana' as the kettle boiled. May had always enjoyed her mornings.

'All day within the dreamy house,/ The doors upon their hinges creaked;/ The blue fly sung in the pane; the mouse/ Behind the mouldering wainscot shrieked,/ Or from the crevice peered about, .../ Old voices called her from without./ She only said, "My life is dreary, He cometh not," she said;/ She said, "I am aweary, aweary, I would that I were dead!"'

May liked the idea of the bluebottle singing. She'd always thought they were lovely things, with their hard, bright, blue-green, petrol-y sheen.

But all that 'weary, dreary' business …

If you were loved enough, it lasted.

I miss him, but I don't want to be dead.

'She's not at her best in the morning,' Lorna muttered to Henry, in the secretive, hissing tone she habitually used when talking of their daughter, who had sharp ears and a habit of silently appearing, barefoot, and getting annoyed.

Angela certainly wasn't at her best. Angela didn't need to be. Her mother and father got Gerda up, took her to school, then made breakfast for Angela, and brought it in, with the mail, on a tray. They were proud of their daughter, the famous author. Naturally she had to work late at night; naturally she couldn't get up in the morning. Since the two boys died, there had only been Angela.

After the sorrow of George's death, they had moved away to a flat on the coast, a new beginning, away from disaster. When Angela gave birth to their first grandchild, the baby became the apple of their eye, and they came up to the city whenever they could. But the father of the baby didn't want to know, and Angela started sounding down all the time, so they started to phone her every day. In the end there was only one decision they could make, though part of them wanted to be young again, get up without worries, walk on the beach …

Now they lived with her, and she paid for everything.

A world away from their life before, when treats were few, and they had to be careful. Now they could take mini-cabs if they went out; they didn't need to cook, they got takeaways; they never bought clothes from charity shops.

Angela had money for everything, since she had won the Iceland Prize. But sometimes they wondered if they'd done the right thing. Angela had meant them to be glorified housekeepers, running the household while she cared for Gerda and wrote her novels as before. Quite soon, though, it had somehow come about that Lorna and Henry took charge of Gerda.

Sometimes Gerda would peek in on her mother in the morning to say goodbye before she left, but Angela was usually half asleep. 'Mummy's tired,' Angela would whisper, eyes still closed. 'Kiss me, darling, then off you go. Mummy was working late last night.' Sometimes this was true, sometimes not.

An hour or so later, Lorna would bring her her mail. There were armfuls of it, since she had won the Iceland. Angela would scan it, and make two piles, one for her secretary to deal with, one for her to linger over: fan letters, free books, invitations. Not everyone admired her novels, but most of the dissenters were mentally ill, making critical remarks about her style or carping obsessively about small errors; after reading a few sentences, she would discard them. Then she'd leave her bedroom, so her mother could clean and take the breakfast tray away, and go up to her office at the top of the house, which had a whole wall of books by Angela, all six of them, in fifty-seven languages. Sometimes, when Angela was very bored, she would read a few pages of her books aloud in languages she didn't know. She sounded good in Finnish; more obscure in Basque. She wished she had a new book to read from.

In theory, Angela was spending her days writing her new novel, a follow-up to her Iceland winner, eagerly awaited by her publishers. Actually Angela was stuck, and spent most of her time reading old letters, and making, then forgetting, cups of herbal tea, which slowly cooled around her study, until her mother took them away. Sometimes she would pick up proofs publishers had sent, asking her for a quote for the jacket, but the writers were never as good as she was, so she tended to fling them down unfinished.

Still she believed she was busy, or ought to be busy, and when Gerda came home (picked up by Lorna or Henry) she knew she mustn't disturb her mummy till the latter stopped work, between six and seven. Then Angela might read Gerda a book, or briefly look at what her daughter called homework, though it didn't seem to be quite as advanced as what Angela herself was doing at that age. She might even put her daughter to bed, but Lorna or Henry usually did that. Gerda was so attached to them, and Angela was naturally tired by bedtime.

Gerda was a credit to Angela, though. Angela sometimes ignored Gerda's bedtime so she could take her to literary parties, beautifully dressed, with shining hair. Gerda would walk about, staring at people, and didn't interrupt her mother's grown-up conversations, though occasionally she would run up to Angela and hang, touchingly, upon her hand. Everyone asked about the striking child, and Angela modestly said, 'She's my daughter.' The last time this happened hadn't quite worked out – a literary editor with kids at the same school had asked, *en passant*, the name of Gerda's teacher, and Angela's mind had gone blank. He looked at her a trifle oddly.

Thanks to the live-in grandparents, it hadn't been onerous, having a child. Interviewers always raised the motherhood question, and Angela always had an up-beat answer.

'Don't you find having a child has slowed you up?' Nadia Samuels had asked, only last week. She herself was nearly forty, and anxious about not having one. The rumours in the book trade were that Angela was blocked. Some wanted her punished for winning the Iceland. 'People might ask you, well – five years have gone past; where is your follow-up novel?'

'I'm writing it,' Angela smiled, annoyingly. 'I think it will be worth the wait.'

'Are you putting motherhood before your career?'

'Some people make a great fuss about motherhood. I tend to take it in my stride. Of course I'm fortunate, Gerda's very bright. Precocious is the word the teachers use. And yet she's easy. She has a sweet nature.'

'But children need a lot of looking after, surely?' Nadia pursued, frowning.

'I suppose some do, but we're more like friends.'

Nadia frowned. The woman was a liar. Her sister had children. They did need looking after. 'Is the child's father around at all?'

'Oh, yes,' smiled Angela. 'He's very much involved ...' (with his Danian wife and family, she concluded, mentally).

Nadia stared at Angela, thwarted, and decided her profile would take no prisoners. 'The Silence of the Lamb' might be a good title.

'So life is perfect?' she inquired, cuttingly.

'Let's just say I've been very lucky.'

This morning, though, everything went wrong.

Angela woke earlier than usual, with a terrible wailing in her ear. Sirens, she thought, fuddled, anxious. It must be the floods. They're ejaculating. (She hadn't had sex for nearly six months.) No, that's wrong, they're evacuating us. The war, of course. I must save Gerda. She sat bolt up in bed, and switched her light on.

But she didn't have her contact lenses in, and couldn't make sense of what she saw.

A red drenched head, streaming with tears, features swollen beyond recognition, bulbs of cream snot pushing out of the nostrils, lay on her belly like a beaten dog, but all around there was screaming, yelling, and two desperate paws were scrabbling at the duvet, trying to touch her flesh underneath the covers, and then she realized that it was her daughter – Gerda, surely, but tortured, changed; and as she watched, the stubborn dog-like body was wrenched away, there was straining, heaving, and she saw, dimly, as she started to protest, started to reach out towards her child, that the grey-haired, purple-faced figure of her mother was pulling Gerda away by the feet, pulling her as if she were a heavy doll, and as Lorna fell backwards, clutching her grandchild, Gerda shot away towards the foot of the bed, still clinging on to her mother, still screaming, so the duvet and then the sheet went with her, and Angela felt the early morning chill hit her warm naked body like a shock of cold water, and the light was horrible, a flood of cold shame, for now Angela lay on the bed alone, Gerda was struggling in Lorna's arms, and the old woman's hand was across her mouth, her fingers had bandaged the child's wild mouth, soft pleats of full lip pinched between old knuckles, and a furious voice hardly recognizable as Lorna's was saying, 'Wicked girl! What have you done to your mother, your poor mother who needs her sleep, I'm sorry, Angela, I couldn't stop her,' – and then the two of them were backing out through the door, though Gerda's feet were still kicking, kicking, and she couldn't talk, she was crying too hard, but her grieved blue eyes, drowned and swollen with tears, were fixed in terrible pleading on her mother, and Angela, left alone in her room, where each morning Lorna brought her breakfast like a child, looked down the grey planes of her naked body. She was no longer a baby; she was growing old. She lay there rigid, trying not to think. Her mouth tasted bitter; her teeth were bad. Angela was terrified of the dentist. Only when the front door slammed, and Gerda stopped screaming, did Angela's panic begin to subside.

After about half an hour, there was a knock, and her

father brought in tea and juice. She had curled up foetus-like under her duvet. 'Sorry about all the screaming,' he said. 'We couldn't seem to do a thing with her this morning. There's better news though. The flood's going down. The TV says the rains are over.'

Davey flexed his hands on the steering-wheel. A night at the telescope always left him deeply tired; strained eyes, pain-clamped shoulders. He would have liked to drop in on Delorice and soothe all his aches in the warmth of her bed, but Delorice was staying with Viola, her sister, in the drowned no-man's land of the Towers.

He made a decision, and swung his car left. He would go for a swim in his local pool.

Outside the door, on the big bales of straw that had been packed together to make pontoons, a little girl was making a scene. She had dark red hair and a heart-shaped face, and was pushing, pushing, with all her might, at a protesting woman who might be her grandma. 'By myself! You're not coming in with me! I don't like you! By myself!'

The old woman looked at Davey, apologetically, as he tried to get past their tussling bodies. 'Little madam,' she said, and tried to smile, though her cheeks were inflamed and her eyes exhausted. The girl took advantage of her looking away. Shouting, 'I'm not a madam, I hate you,' she gave her one last almighty shove, and before Davey realized what was going to happen the frail figure of the woman was swaying, toppling, her face a single black O of fear as she clutched at his coat, feebly, in passing and then fell backwards into the water, sending gouts of black mud all over Davey. Her head went right under; one leg waved, shocking, a weak white twig with the shoe kicking off, then her feet went down and her head came up, black, slimy, clotted, without a face.

The little girl bent over the water, frightened. 'Grandma,' she said. 'Are you all right, Grandma?'

Davey was a good-natured man, and although he longed to sneak away for his swim he extended his hands to the gasping, sobbing statue of mud that weltered below him, up to her waist in dirty water. 'There are germs,' she was spluttering. 'They say there are. Because of the floods. I've swallowed some. There are horrible germs – you wicked girl. BAD Gerda.' She came lurching and churning back up on to the straw, gripping his hands with painful force, and stood there, shuddering, not letting him go, her back turned fiercely on the child.

'Shall I help you inside?' said Davey, politely, ignoring the mud on his arms and hands, the stains all over his new tan boots. Maybe he shouldn't have kids after all. 'Come along, dear,' he said to the girl, who now looked very pale and docile. Inside the pool, he asked for Zoe, who ran the swimming classes there. He had known Zoe for three or four years; Viola was her partner in business; in fact, Davey thought they might be more than friends, but Delorice dismissed it: 'Not my sister.'

When Zoe emerged from the staff-room, which had a big anti-war poster on the door, Gerda ran up to her smiling sweetly and put her arms around her, as if nothing had happened. Davey started to put Zoe in the picture, but

Gerda kept interrupting him, patting at Zoe to get her attention. 'It was a accident,' she insisted.

'She pushed me in,' said Lorna. Mud dripped from her hair. Now minus her makeup, she looked like a mushroom. Black yeti footprints covered the floor.

'Milly,' called Zoe, and a young white woman came hurrying across, clucking her sympathy, brandishing a mop. 'We've had a bit of an accident. Come and use the staff shower,' said Zoe to Lorna, and then to Davey, urgently: 'Have you seen Viola? She's still not managing to get in in the mornings.' To Gerda she said, 'Don't worry, darling, I've got some clothes I can lend your mother –'

And suddenly Gerda was angry again, all four foot of her aflame, indignant; 'She's not my mummy,' she said, loudly. 'You said she was my mummy last week, too. I wanted my mummy to come today, but she couldn't come, because, because, she couldn't come because –'

And here Lorna interjected, protective, 'Because your mum was tired from working –'

But suddenly all the fight left Gerda. She sat on the floor, and her red head drooped, and tears ran slowly down her cheeks. 'Because she never comes,' she said. 'Because she never, never does.'

'It's all right, deary, never mind,' said Milly, who could never bear to see children cry, crouching down on the floor beside her and taking the little girl in her arms. (She and Samuel, once devoted One Way followers, were thinking of having a child of their own – a boy, they hoped, and they would call him Saul – and now she saw children everywhere, and it didn't quite square with the end of the world. Jesus

loved children, didn't he? They were losing their belief in
Father Bruno. God was love: that was the point.)

The little girl's blouse was soaked with tears. She cried
steadily, fluently, without words, like a tap welling up when
the washer was gone. Milly held the child's hot wet face to
her own, and stroked her hair, and bore her sorrow.

Yet twenty minutes later Gerda was in the water, the clear
blue water with its minnows of sunlight, warm as happiness,
swimming, swimming, and Davey, on the other side of the
pool, cleaved powerfully, blindly through his programme,
and Lorna stood on the side and watched them, wishing that
she had learned to swim, wishing that she were young again,
understanding and forgiving Gerda, and all the knots of
passion and pain were dissolved in the moment, and floated
away.

But Zoe, on the pool-side, was not so happy. Too many
things to fret about.

She was worried about the war: not just the innate
loathsomeness of it, the way the rich were attacking the
poor, the lies that Mr Bliss was telling – but also the effect
on her social life (too many evenings at boring meetings, too
few evenings spent with Viola) and on her e-mail in-box,
which was swamped in gloom: half a dozen rants per day,
with giant attachments, too many to open, so she started to
dread them, and once or twice, guiltily, deleted them unread.
Zoe marched, she protested, she always had, but she didn't
enjoy it, or entirely believe in it. It was anger that motivated
her, not hope. War was such a stupid waste of human time
and effort. War kept her and Viola apart.

Now Zoe was having to teach two different classes because Viola was late again. Why can't she get a baby-sitter for that child and stay over with me? she thought, as so often. She quite liked Dwayne, but he complicated everything. If he weren't there, anything might happen. Perhaps they would have a child together. She would make Viola pregnant, yes. Put a heavy child in that beautiful belly. She desired Viola fiercely, totally, missed and wanted her every night. Zoe had been pregnant when she was sixteen. She had run away from home, and had an abortion. She knew life owed her another baby. Why shouldn't Viola give her one? They would be a family. For ever.

But her mind began to move in familiar grooves as she got her baby class to float under water, their necks relaxed, their hair streaming out. Six little bodies suspended in a line, plump, prosperous, well-fed bodies; well-dressed mothers looked on from the side; private swimming classes weren't cheap. Briefly, Zoe remembered the past, when she was a water baby herself, when her mother watched, and shrieked encouragement.

It had put her off swimming for years and years. Maybe Gerda was lucky that her mother didn't come. Zoe always suggested mothers keep praise for later. For half an hour, therefore, all the babies were hers. At first the underwater stuff seemed difficult, and the timid ones panicked and pushed their chins up, but in the end they had to trust the water; they would never swim well if they didn't let go. 'Well done,' she called. 'Now let's try again.'

They up-ended like ducks, adorable. 'Very good, Farouk. Lovely, Sejal. Now let's stand by the side and do breaststroke arms. No, standing, Daniel. And you're not a windmill. Please copy Ben, he's doing it just right. All of you listen: copy Ben.'

Zoe left the babies for a moment and walked further up the pool to see how the Junior Dolphins were doing. There were some gifted little swimmers there. She would have merged the two classes, it would have been safer, but some of the older ones were really good. Gerda, for example, swam like a fish; she was already preparing for her life-saver's badge.

'Staffing problems, these wretched floods,' she apologized to Lorna as she padded past her. 'I think you're great,' said Lorna, vaguely. 'People of my age never learned to swim. Gerda's been teaching the others to dive.'

'What?' said Zoe, anxious. 'They can't dive here,' and she ran past Lorna to the middle of the pool, but there she found Gerda standing on the side, hair stuck to her scalp in a gleaming dark pelt, saying 'One, two, three, *jump*! Go on, Dinesh. Copy me!'

They plunged in the safe way, splashing, feet first. Relieved, Zoe smiled at them. 'Well done, kids. Thank you, Gerda. I did need another teacher.'

'I always teach when the teacher's not there,' said Gerda, pulling herself up from the water, beaming, beaming, wanting to give pleasure. 'At school I read them fairy-tales.'

'Because you're sensible,' said Zoe.

Now they were all clustering round her, but Gerda was pulling at her hand, and her wide blue eyes weren't happy any more. 'I'm not sensible,' she said. 'Everyone says I'm sensible. I don't want to be sensible. I want to be a baby.'

Zoe laughed and took it lightly. 'You're a water baby,' she said. There was something needy about that child, but she couldn't deal with it today. 'Now back into the water, Dolphins! Three lengths of freestyle. I'm watching you! Ready, steady, go!'

There was hope, this morning, even in the Towers, where everyone lived who could do no better; the old, the mad, the poor, newcomers, and people like Faith, who cleaned the city. And rats, and mice, and bright mats of microbes. They liked the floods, and it was warming up, though to human beings, April still felt chilly. It didn't matter; in the sun, people hoped. Hope was all they needed to go on living.

Delorice and Viola were drinking coffee and staring down out of Viola's fifteenth-floor window, their ears cocked for the sound of engines. The two young women, one office-sharp in skyscraper pin-stripes and high waxed hair, the other cupped by a pale soft tracksuit clinging like peach-down to waist and breasts, sat waiting, princesses in chaos, at the breakfast bar of the ugly room. The radio was on.

'Did you hear him?' asked Viola, derisive. 'He goes, "We're going to do whatever it takes to get our people to the Gala." So who is this "our people" they're goin' on about? Where are these fancy river-buses? I can't even go to work on time, you get me, never mind some fancy Gala.'

'I couldn't care if I'm late to work,' said Delorice. 'I've started to think my job is rubbish. But I have got a meeting after lunch. And I do have to get to the Gala tonight.'

A look from Viola, half-glad, half-envious. She switched off the radio, trying not to get vexed. Delorice was always doing better than her –

What if she did? She was family. Family mattered, to the Edwardses.

There were only eighteen months between the two sisters. Viola, the elder, had always been the boss. They had gone to the same comprehensive school; shared lipstick, tights, shoe-sizes, been mistaken for each other any number of times, though Delorice was taller, and lighter-skinned – which Viola sometimes thought, in cynical moments, might be why she'd ended up doing better.

Viola's high-concept exercise machines shone out against damp, peeling walls. She noticed the stains more when she had company. How often had Viola asked the council to fix it? But nothing ever got done around here. Viola had the sense it was somehow her fault, the hopeless transport, the stains on the wall. Was her little sister judging her?

Viola remembered the end of the world.

'Delorice,' said Viola. 'It's not that I believe it. Not that I'm worried, or anything. But I saw all that stuff at the weekend in the papers, about this programme Davey's making. Saying that the world's going to end tomorrow. I mean, it is bullshit, isn't it?'

'Davey is not a bullshitter,' said Delorice. 'But most of those programmes aren't his idea. He doesn't seem bothered himself, Viola.'

'It frightens the kids though, dunnit?' said Viola. 'Dwayne was really scared, when he read that.'

'Don't stress, Viola,' Delorice said, with one of her high-cheek-boned, half-moon smiles. 'You know kids. They enjoy being worried.' (But under the smile, she worried too: could she really trust Davey, however much she loved him? The stupid white powder, like frost, like snow.)

'I think it's, like, irresponsible,' Viola said, suddenly vehement. Viola was the responsible one. She had taken in Elroy's boy Dwayne, now eleven, when his mother died in the same year as Winston ... It was down to Viola to hold the family together through all that horror and mess and grief. Everyone had to be looked after. Whereas Delorice couldn't even care for her own daughter.

'Do you mind if I read?' Delorice asked. She had something in her bag to read for Headstone, a vast new manuscript called *Living in Time* by someone whose name was completely unfamiliar, H. I. Segall. At first she had thought it wasn't a good sign that Headstone were giving her stuff from the slush pile, then she saw it came with a passionate recommendation from Mohammed Habib, their new editor, and was to be discussed at today's meeting, as a possible non-fiction lead for next spring. The note asked her to read a specimen chapter. She had started on one called 'The Unending Moment'.

'Don't ask,' said Viola. 'You was always reading.'

It was true, and Viola had never minded, but a new self-consciousness had come upon them. At school, where it wasn't cool to be a boffin, Delorice had read novels under the desk. Now she read for a moment, then stopped. 'It's unbelievable,' she said, looking out of the window at the blank bright water. The water-bus was two hours late. 'I don't know how you put up with it.'

'I told you, didn't I?' said Viola. 'It's been like this for effing weeks. The effing council have stopped answering the phones. Nothing here works except my exercise machines.'

She had taken up sport in a serious way after Winston died, going to college to do sports science. While Delorice had totally fallen apart. Then suddenly she was at college too, doing English, hooking up with Farhad Ahmad, getting herself a First, for Christ's sake, a *first class degree* and a posh job in publishing.

And Delorice wasn't shy any more. None of that staring at her knees, and whispering. 'I liked it, you know,' she had said to Viola, 'going to the opera with the Lucases. In one way it wasn't me at all, I mean gondolas and dinner-jackets and "sir" and "madam" and all that shit, but in another way, it just felt great. I was there, with Davey, and his mum and dad liked me, and I loved the music, and the food, and everything. I was telling myself, I could get used to this.'

Viola was watchful around this new little sister, with her new way of talking and new white friends. She sat there now, with her perfectly waxed parting and her high-powered suit, reading an impressively thick pile of paper. What was the word? She looked … classy. Viola found it all a bit hard to take.

'How's Leah?' she asked, not quite innocently. 'Did you go last weekend? Is her cough better?'

'Went over to Mum's for lunch,' said Delorice, without looking up from the page she was reading. 'I didn't notice Leah having no cough. Having a cough,' she corrected herself. When she was with Viola, the old phrases slipped out. She went back to her book; it was surprisingly good.

No, you wouldn't notice, thought Viola. Like you haven't noticed me and Zoe. No one in the family wanted to know.

Part of Viola longed to tell Delorice. But she imagined with horror what her sister might do: burst out laughing, refuse to believe her. Worst of all, pull a disgusted face like the one she had made, vexed, disbelieving, when their mother told them, wracked with sobs, that the police were saying Winston hadn't been normal.

Delorice was looking at her watch again. 'Sorry, Vi, it's just a habit.'

'You thought I was just bunking off from the pool till you came here and saw for yourself what it's like.'

'I knew there was something I meant to tell you. Last time Davey and me went swimming, Zoe was really missing you. She said you're the brains of the outfit,' said Delorice. Viola rewarded her with a smile. She was good at business, she always had been. Zoe would have worked for nothing for ever; only the actual swimming mattered to her. But Viola made sure that they made good money.

It paid for Dwayne's expensive day-care, though he hadn't been able to get there for weeks. For now, she was sending him five floors up to a young white girl who did child-minding, Kilda – which struck Viola as a sick kind of name, but it would do for the moment, till the floods went down. She was desperate to move before Dwayne hit his teens.

'It's been horrible here,' she told her sister. 'We couldn't get milk, or papers, or nothing. We, you know, bartered, some days, for food. That wasn't in the papers, was it? The government did fuck all for us. And then they're surprised when there's a little bit of trouble. It's like, "Violent Riots", and "Towers Mob Rule". In any case, let's hope it's over. I'd started to think it would rain for ever.'

The sun poured in through the bird-spattered glass, they were glad to be together, the news was good.

'You could have left for a bit, I suppose,' said Delorice. 'Some people did, didn't they?'

Delorice made everything sound like her fault. 'Why should I, like, leave my stuff behind?' Viola asked, reaching for a cigarette, half-breaking the box in her sudden longing.

'You're smoking again,' Delorice remarked.

'Want one?' The question had a touch of aggression.

'Bet Zoe doesn't like it,' Delorice said. 'It can't be good for your swimming, girl.'

'Zoe doesn't know,' said Viola, looking out over the shining water meadow that had replaced the usual sheets of concrete. The view from the Towers had got better since the floods. Were the waters going down? She squinted, minutely. Yes, on the facing tower, a band of dark wall showed where the flood had already receded. Maybe a metre in a couple of days. But the feeling of relief was mingled with anger; how would they ever clear up the mess? 'You don't understand. 'Ear me now. Your life is soft, girl. The people who left, all their stuff's got tiefed, and like nutters and weirdos have gone in and lived there. Singing and chanting and sticking up weird posters. I don't think the toilets are working or nothing. They're probably doing their business on the floor. It's just the way things are around here. It's just the way things have always been. At home we were poor but it wasn't like this. I smoke because it helps me get by.' She drew in deeply, fiercely, looked hard at Delorice, blew smoke across her.

'Well you could have moved in with me, for a bit,' said Delorice. But she knew her flat was too small for two. Something stopped her at the last moment from saying, 'You could have moved in with Zoe'.

Then Viola, still annoyed with her sister, said the thing she didn't usually say, sounding tight and nervous, not looking at Delorice. 'I could have moved in with Zoe, of course. She's practically begging me to live with her.'

Delorice said nothing, then, awkwardly, 'Right.'

Viola, with the nicotine powering through her, suddenly knew she had to say more. There were pictures of Zoe all over the house, and one or two snaps of them both together, laughing in the water, their arms round each other. 'You don't like Zoe, do you?' she asked. Both knew the question meant more than that.

'Stop being so feisty,' Delorice said. 'Cha! I'm not going to quarrel with you, Viola. I trekked over here to see you, right? And now I'm so late for work it's ridiculous. Zoe's going to sack you if you're always this late.'

One look at Viola said she'd got it wrong. Her sister stood up and blocked out the window. She was toned and muscled; she looked frighteningly fit. Delorice knew Viola could lay a man out; she had done it last year, after a man in the lift had touched her booty and whispered 'Black bitch'. 'Her not going to sack me, we're partners, get it. You don't get me, do you, Delorice? Don't you forget I'm your big sister –'

'I was only, like, having a laugh', said Delorice.

'I mean, *we're partners*. I mean, she loves me. You not the only one who got a lover. Smug little Delorice with her rich baby white boy.'

Delorice let the insult pass. She felt winded, thrown, but she clutched at straws. '*You* don't love *her*, though. You can't. You're normal. You've had more men than I have, girl.'

'It's not about normal. It's not about men. She's, like, just, you know, the person I love.' Viola sat down, her anger going, but she looked at the floor, at the window-frame. Her voice was different when she spoke again. 'Swear on the Bible not to tell Mum.'

A long silence, then the sound of a motor, a diesel engine, coming slowly closer. 'Are you telling me something?' Delorice asked, then, answering herself, 'You're telling me something.' She broke off, suddenly. 'I have to get my stuff,' as she saw the boat, an aged-looking thing with yellow paint and 'City Wonderama' on the side, creep slowly into view underneath their window. The same boat had brought her here yesterday. There were others, apparently, but nowhere near enough. They smelled of fumes; they were slow; they were packed. The yellow boat was already overloaded, heavy, sluggish, riding low in the water.

Both of them ran around finding things. They left, silent, abstracted with hurry, not looking each other in the eyes. Delorice was abstracted, her thoughts in turmoil. Maybe it was true about Winston, too. Maybe she had known about him, all along, but refused to accept it because of the shame. Maybe their mother had known, deep down. It was Mum who had accepted it, in the end, bringing down the fury of the family.

Viola slammed her door, then padlocked it. 'I got this yesterday,' she muttered, manoeuvring the metal hasp into the slot. 'Take a look at the posters on the way down. I'm not letting those bastards get in here with their creepy religious shit ... Zoe asked me to put up some anti-war posters. I goes, "Do you think we need any more of dem tings?"'

The lift was shut because of the floods; they hardly noticed, it was usually broken. They clattered down a stairwell wall-papered with posters. There were smells of seaweed, urine, mould. The notices were thickly bordered with black, printed in crude letters the colour of blood, with a picture of the Towers half-submerged in water, rising out of a crimson flood. 'THESE ARE THE LAST DAYS,' the posters shouted. 'Sisters and Brothers, come and join us. We are here to save, we are here among you. Open your hearts, and come home.'

'They're not coming in my effing home,' said Viola. 'They've wormed their way into all the empty flats though. This place is, like, crawling with them. There are Muslims as well, with their funny writing. The same posters, just different writing. They thump around the stairs. They preach. They sing. It's all doom and gloom and Last Days shit. They'll look right tits when the water goes down.'

'Viola,' said Delorice, a moment later, touching her shoulder as they reached water-level, one floor below the one they had expected, because the floods were draining away, because sun and wind were working their magic; pushed aside the wide drenched sheet of plywood that blocked the shattered landing window, climbed out on to the slimy window-ledge from which the boat would have to pick up, and were dwarfed by the dazzle, the cutting wind-chill, deafened by the engines slogging closer, their throats roughened by the smell of fuel – suddenly the world was all around them, raw, bright-edged, uncontrollable; two seagulls screamed and wheeled above them, their yellow beaks with a hungry look, and all that mattered was survival. 'Viola!' Delorice found herself shouting to make herself heard above the din: out here in the emptiness, what did they count for, the little hurts, the embarrassment? Suddenly she was fifteen again. 'Wait a second. Give us a hug. You're my sister, innit. We lost our brother. We lost Winston, we can't lose each other. Maybe – I dunno – you *should* tell Mum. You'll always be my sister, Viola –' They were hugging, kissing, both of them in tears, swaying together on the narrow window-ledge the boat was struggling to come alongside. 'Nothing is ever going to change that, right?'

'Right,' said Viola. 'Right. Safe.'

Some mornings, the water-buses looked like floating hospitals. Grey-faced people, packed together, slumped by pathetic small hills of possessions (there were regulations about how much they could bring, though the boatmen never seemed to know what they were). But the City Wonderama looked different, this morning. The passengers were smiling, and making jokes; hope had restored their sense of adventure; they could almost enjoy this, since it wasn't for ever. It would go down in history, the time of the flood, the time when the Tower-dwellers all stood together. They were coalescing, the myths of comfort.

The engine died, and the boatman pulled the women, one by one, across into the boat. Without the engine, the deck lunged, then plummeted, and each time a little sigh of fear and excitement rose from the packed bodies on the chilly deck as the swell left each sister in turn clinging on, a small living thing above empty air. Briefly, death caught at their chests again, and then as the strong arm of the boatman landed them, there was a communal ripple of relieved laughter.

'Safe,' said Delorice, touching fists. 'Safe.'

Ten

May sat in the little front room she had lived in for nearly fifty years with Alfred, clutching the arms of the maroon armchair; it was like her own body, once his, now hers. Here she could still feel the comfort of his fingers.

But today the familiar touch didn't help her. Her hands looked frail and thin in the sunlight; she hadn't much bothered with eating of late; the floods made it hard to get to the shops. In any case, she'd been getting thinner for years, since Alfred went, and with him, the pleasure of food.

May was staring at the newspaper. The same one Alfred had always taken, which she had gone on with, after his death, though she was more of an intellectual, more of a reader than her dear husband, a reader of real books, not papers. (She was getting on well with her *Greek Myths*, though the family stories were spectacularly bloody – the

White family were quite tame by comparison. She liked the sounds of the old Greek names, which she said to herself as she waited for the kettle: *Oedipus, Charon, Persephone*: it comforted her, like a skipping rhyme.) But even the unread papers were useful, for soaking up the water that leaked into her kitchen or stuffing wet shoes so they kept their shape. While May was alive, their old life would go on, his slippers in the cupboard, the daily paper. That way she would carry him onwards. Alfred, love, I won't let go.

Yet she sighed at the thought; men were so heavy. Alfred had taken things so hard.

And now there was this strange bit of news about Dirk, who she had imagined safe in prison –

She was shocked, winded. Her heart was racing. She read it again, unbelieving. 'His lieutenant, Dirk White, 28 …' 'His lieutenant, Dirk White, 28 …' Had they made his age up? She couldn't remember. Surely he couldn't have grown that old. The paper was dated four days ago.

There was a group picture, rather blurred, of people holding up a banner. 'Open your hearts, and come home,' she spelled, and then said it aloud, and the words upset her, because in her heart she knew *here* was his home, but could she ever have the boy back again, after what had happened, what he had done? The truth was, May was afraid of him.

But I mustn't be frightened of my own son.

Her head was spinning; she made a cup of tea. She'd started taking sugar since Alfred had died. She was losing weight, and she needed the comfort.

But the picture was still there when she came back.

She screwed up her eyes at the grey and white faces.

Perhaps that was Dirk, almost dead centre, next to the man who was dressed like a priest. (But he'd never been religious. That was more Shirley. Dirk hadn't really got the brains for it.) That was surely him, though. His thin bony face, the lantern jaw that had come in adolescence.

She couldn't help thinking it was silly of them to put him at the front, where everyone could see him. When she photographed the family, she'd done just the opposite, since Shirley had always been very pretty, and Darren, her elder boy, was a looker. Dirk was the smallest, but they stood him at the back. In the shots she kept, you just glimpsed the top of his head, his bright blond hair, which was his one good point. It wasn't Dirk's fault, but he lowered the standard, not that she'd ever say that to him ... There'd been such a big gap. She and Alfred were foolish, but then, they'd always liked – being together, and Alfred preferred them not being careful. People talked cruelly of 'the runt of the litter'. She was older, more tired, with less time for him, though of course May White loved all her children. Easier, though, with Shirley, who was lovely, and Darren, who was witty, and bright.

Nobody had ever called Dirk bright.

She had tried her best with him, hadn't she? She had even gone to see him in prison, for the first few years, every month or two. She couldn't do more, because she was grieving, she had lost her Alfred, it was like a black hole down which everything was sucked, even poetry, even Tennyson, the other love of her life, Alfred Tennyson, her other Alfred. She had lost her rudder. Hope was gone.

And then there was the horror of the murder. Half of her

still didn't believe he could have done it, flesh of her flesh, her own son.

He had killed a man. Who was black, homosexual, but a decent young man, by all accounts. Ignorant people said Dirk was queer too, but obviously he wasn't, he didn't even like them. She ought to know; she was his mother.

Everything had changed for the White family, then. Who had once had their pride. Been a decent family. Alfred, as park keeper, was famous, locally. And Shirley was a beauty, and Darren was rich. May held her head high in the local shops.

Now she stayed at home, as much as possible, because she imagined them whispering: 'There goes that woman whose boy is a murderer. Makes you wonder; it has to come from somewhere' (though a lot of them, in their heart of hearts, wouldn't mind there being one less black man).

She supposed they blamed her, since Alfred was dead. Yet Alfred had tried to make amends. Whatever he'd done wrong – and God knows he wasn't perfect – he had turned his own son in to the police, which went against nature; she herself couldn't do it. The strain of it all had finished Alfred. May couldn't help blaming Dirk for that.

The curious thing was, the lad had always refused to accept that his father had shopped him to the police. 'Dad wouldn't do that,' he had shouted at her, when the subject came up, on her first prison visit. 'Dad always loved me. You didn't.' (And Alfred had loved him, Dirk got that right.)

All the same, it was Alfred who'd insisted on justice. All of a sudden, colour didn't matter. All of a sudden there was only duty. 'Blood's thicker than water,' May had pleaded, but Alfred, as usual, overruled her. The man was dying, but he went to the police. In any case, Dirk blamed it all on her.

May's visits to the prison soon grew less frequent. What was the point? Dirk barely talked to her (not that he'd talked a lot at home). Bit by bit, she had stopped going. At first she had written, but he never replied. She had taught him to read, a lifetime ago, but it took for ever, and you never saw him reading. Perhaps her letters were a dead loss.

Sometimes she found herself forgetting she'd had him. As if there had only been Shirley and Darren. A mist of guilt drifted over Dirk's name. He must be, well, odd. Ill in the head. It could happen, even in a decent family. Perhaps there had been something on Alfred's side.

That was how May explained it to herself. And if he was ill, they should keep him locked up. There were murderers, poor things, who died in prison. Or she, of course, might die before Dirk did.

Sometimes May found herself wishing for death. What was the point of it, without her Alfred, with her children gone, with Dirk a convict? Nothing in her life had prepared her for that. When a Christmas had passed without either of them writing, she knew it was over, she buried it, and lay there at night clutching her pillow, trying to stifle his face, his voice.

But now Dirk was back. He was out of prison.

The blurred pale face swam out of the darkness.

(Compared to the news about her son, the full page headed 'Planetary Pile-up Looms' made little impression upon May.

She scanned it, briefly; they were going to line up, apparently, and there was an artist's impression of how it would look, little grey planets strung out like beads across a garish purple sky, but once she saw it was some TV show, May lost interest. It was bound to be rubbish.)

The two men sat across the wide black desk in Isaac Court's steely, minimalist office. One of them had just attacked the other, and they didn't quite know where to go from there. Isaac's fingers were just getting a hold on a bony, bobbing Adam's apple when his secretary knocked and he had to stop. Both of them were panting, lightly.

'Everything all right, Mr Court?' she said. She had heard raised voices; her boss was puffed up like a mating toad, face dark with blood, his short thick neck craning forwards oddly.

'Could you fuck off and leave us alone, Alice?'

She turned on her heel, thinking: boyfriend trouble. She put up with her boss, although he was a pig, because he was so successful; he had galleries all over the continent, but she had her eye on the New Work branch.

Isaac was too embarrassed to attack Dirk again. Because she'd interrupted him, the impetus was gone. But it felt like a lost opportunity.

'It was a fucking fake,' Isaac said again. 'You bloody made a fool of me. I can't believe you didn't know yourself.'

'Well you're the expert,' said Dirk, sulkily. 'You didn't exactly spot it, did you?'

It was just after lunch; Isaac had bad indigestion. *Foie*

gras with an elderly, obese female collector who had sat and yacked and picked yellow teeth and stared at him like a round glittering crab, waving cracked pincers encrusted with gold, while he laughed, flattered, pretended interest – and then at the last moment she didn't buy the Auerbach whose sale he had been setting up for months. (In any case, it was too good for her.)

Now this crim had turned up out of the blue at the gallery, sweating and furtive, reminding him of failure, of the stolen Bonnard that turned out to be a copy. He was small and twisted with thinning blond hair. Isaac stared at him hard for a moment of distaste and wondered briefly if he was gay. He had to be insane to come back here.

Isaac fixed Dirk with his little sharp eyes. 'So have you brought my money back, cunt?'

'That's not a nice word,' said Dirk, indignant. He didn't like swearing since he'd become religious. 'You should have fucking known about the wotsit, Boner. I mean, you're the expert. I'm just the one who nicked it. Your sister said you knew about art.'

'My sister is a stupid cow,' said Isaac, under his breath, to himself. A few years ago, Susannah had gone and got herself mixed up with nutters who believed in the end of the world; a few years ago he had got dozens of the cult thrown out of the house their parents had once lived in. Now they had the nerve to come flogging him rubbish.

'That's not very kind,' Dirk told him, smugly. Isaac glared at him again. Dirk made an effort to be agreeable. 'You have a point, though, she did seem a bit cow-like.' (The woman had stood there, fat, open-mouthed, when he and

Bruno made her a visit, gawping as if she was seeing ghosts. Bruno had known her years ago when the Sisters and Brothers were just getting started. She answered him like somebody not very bright, but then, Bruno had that effect on people – Dirk grinned to think of how scared she had looked. To make them go away, she'd given them Isaac's address.)

'You talk about my sister, I'll kill you. I can't believe I'm listening to you! Why are you here? Have you got a death wish?'

'Got something to show you,' said Dirk, surprised.

Isaac had never been able to resist the chance of getting something for nothing. His parents gave him nothing for nothing, so he always felt life owed him one. 'What are you trying to get rid of this time?' he asked, abruptly, leaning forward and pinching the flesh above his trousers. His roll-neck felt tight under his chin.

'Well it's another picture,' Dirk grunted.

'Probably another fucking copy,' said Isaac.

'I like this one better,' said Dirk, 'as it happens.'

'Oh yes?' said Isaac, sneering furiously. 'You like it better, do you? Why?'

'Well it's bigger for a start.' Dirk threw caution to the winds. 'The last one was very small, for the money … I think he's better at painting, too. You can actually see what he's trying to paint. I mean, it's a woman. With some of her kit off.'

'Don't speak,' said Isaac, covering his ears. 'Shut up and let me see it.'

But the thing that was finally revealed to Isaac, wrapped

in swathes of grey plastic, in the back of a van that was standing almost hub-deep in water, made the dealer exclaim and fall silent for a moment. He recognized its dimmed, familiar beauty.

Hopper painted the city like no one else. The woman with her unreal, carnival face stared out at the sunlight and the high red buildings. How did Hopper paint all times, all places? She could almost be looking out over the floods – Hopper had somehow foreseen it all. The beauty of the painting reached out to Isaac from its dirty setting, yearned towards him, but Isaac flinched and looked away. Yet part of his mind still thought like the painter he had wanted to be, a lifetime ago, before his stupid parents had abandoned their children, gone on holiday and never come back, leaving him lonely, resentful, suspicious, and Susannah at the mercy of Tom, Dick and Harry ... Was Hopper's woman lonely? She was raw, exposed, an unshelled animal, irradiated. Isaac could never bear so much sunlight. And yet, the woman luxuriated in it. She was happy, half-naked, as he could never be. He guided her gently back on to the plastic.

'*Morning Sun*,' he muttered. 'Yes, yes.'

His hands were shaking, and his voice wasn't right.

The newspapers had been full of the theft. Worth millions, of course. The police would be searching. 'But you're mad to think I can get rid of it. It can never be hung, never be shown. There's only one man in the world who will take it. I'm not sure even he would touch it.'

But I would like it, he thought to himself. How I should like to keep it myself.

The two men tracked across the shining slime of the art-dealers' quarter, back towards the gallery. Isaac wiped his feet on the pallet of rags that was stretched across the foyer to protect the carpets. 'You can't get the bloody stuff off your shoes,' he complained, sniffing distastefully. Before he could stop her, Alice brought coffee, and hovered, nosily, in the door of his office till Isaac told her to go away. Its bitter strength filled Isaac's gut with acid.

'You should turn it in,' he said loftily to Dirk. 'Leave it on the steps of the City Gallery. This painting is a Hopper, which won't mean much to you, but I can assure you it belongs to the world.'

'No, mate,' Dirk said, shaking his head with vigour. 'Belonged to some rich bitch of a woman. She can buy herself another one any old day … Iss the real thing, this time, wouldn't you say?'

His air of being a fellow connoisseur afflicted Isaac with a violent desire to laugh, or punch him, or kick him in the bollocks. He made up his mind in a split second. 'Right, fuck off out of here. Take the thing with you. Be grateful if I don't call the police.'

Dirk looked indignant, and sat there for a moment, mouth working, evidently thinking up a riposte. The moment extended painfully. 'You can fuck off, an' all,' he said at last, and looked delighted. 'Wanker,' he added, for good value. 'I was just going, in any case.' At the door he stopped, reversed, turned round and did something horrible which Isaac realised was supposed to be some kind of smile. It got into position, stuck, then grew. It was obviously meant to ingratiate. 'No hard feelings though, mate, eh? Can you give us the other picture back as well?'

Isaac sat there burping and massaging his gut, rolling a pencil across his desk-top, remembering the horrors of the One Way cult. His sister was a sucker for anything like that. He wasn't like Susannah, simple, helpless, a victim of frauds, hucksters, charlatans, people who battened on loneliness. He, Isaac, was stronger than her. (Yet he knew all too well why she was like that. Isaac had learned to protect himself, with money and rudeness and *savoir faire*, from the world which might possibly see him still as an overweight teenager in big round glasses, abandoned by his father and step-mother. He and his sister were left here to cope while the love-birds fucked off around the world. The kind of kids nobody liked or wanted – that was the message he and Susy got. But he had discovered the world of sex, while she had abortions and fell in with nutters.)

His thoughts turned to the coming evening. He was going to the Gala at Government Palace. He was sorry he had recently broken up with Caz, who looked buff and brutal, but did it with anyone. He would have felt good, with Caz on his arm, they would have been photographed arriving – though Caz never left with the same person.

Isaac had liked Caz, he had liked him a lot, though he couldn't trust him alone for five minutes and had never had bareback sex with him once in the couple of years they had been together. In the nineties Isaac had tested positive, and death became horribly real to him – would he end up a grinning, shivering monkey, gloated over by his guilty step-mother? He had been mortally afraid. But time split for him. At the last minute, a second, negative, result came through. Isaac woke up in another world, where he was not doomed, where he had to go on living; the sun was out, he was starving hungry. In this new world, he took all he could, lived all he could, lost out to no one.

Isaac liked parties: noise, colour, enough alcohol to laugh and not think, a reason for people to be with him, a reason for people to pretend to like him. The hope that he wouldn't go home on his own.

But if he did, it was bearable, here. That was why Isaac stayed in the city. Never the only one alone.

May sat and drifted as the sunlight strengthened. How she loved sun; butter, daffodils. The yellow cardie Alfred gave her one birthday, which didn't suit her but made her happy. *Oedipus, Charon, Persephone.* Slowly her thoughts about Dirk began to soften. He was out of prison, so he'd served his time. He'd 'repaid his debt to society', as they liked to put it, though he'd never been in debt, indeed Dirk was careful with his money. The 'repaying' bit must be aimed at robbers.

Whereas her Dirk had never been dishonest. A mother knew things, and May knew that. The thing he had done was more mad than bad. Getting rid of wickedness, he probably thought, being so set against homosexuals. (May was broad-minded about all of them – coloured people, homosexuals – she spoke as she found, and most of them were nice: but Alfred and Dirk were both funny about it.)

The sun made a golden pool on her lap; it reminded her of the cat, at home, her childhood home, how it sat and warmed her. Everyone had to have something to warm them. Since Alfred died, May wasn't needed. Darren didn't need her, Shirley didn't need her (only for chats and the odd bit of child-minding, now the boys were at nursery school).

Dirk, she thought. My youngest child. Somehow, Dirk had got in with loonies. He was – not a bad boy, but limited …

There was no one else to look after him. If Dirk needed her, May was ready. (And it might help her, as well, perhaps. Take away that tiny wireworm of guilt.)

In an odd way, Dirk wasn't unlike Alfred. The same big nose, the same blue eyes, though of course poor Dirk wasn't a patch on his father. Perhaps he would come and stay for a bit. She wouldn't mind, if it wasn't for ever. Just to help him get back on his feet again.

First, however, she had to find him. The newspaper said One Way was 'strongest' in the Towers.

May gave her appearance anxious thought. She should look respectable, but not too smart, for she knew how poor people were in the Towers. She had a little metal mirror from her mother, and she looked at her face in it, half-despairing; her eyes were still blue, but they were nested in wrinkles. Second-best coat, which dated from the sixties, with a little lamb collar, slightly tatty by now, and big patch pockets, blue rubber boots and a pretty blue paisley scarf, two dollars from a charity shop. No handbag, so there was nothing to snatch. Instead she put her money in her coat pocket, which made her feel curiously light and girlish, and a tortoiseshell comb, and her mother's mirror, thus relieving the ache in her arthritic shoulder, which had a little notch where her shoulder-bag cut.

Good job the weather was glorious. She had to wait for an hour on the floating decking the government had strung around the streets. Derelict water-buses brought in from the riverside serviced the Towers a few times a day. May had her favourite Tennyson stuffed in her other pocket. Taking off her coat, she bundled it into a makeshift cushion so she could sit reading, but the water she glimpsed between the wooden slats looked black and greasy and full of dregs, and she was too afraid of her leather-bound book slipping through the crack and being lost for ever, her other Alfred, her beloved friend, so she put her coat back on again and stood rather stiffly till the boat appeared, trying to read and keep her balance as the decking yawed and creaked in the wash.

Once she was on board, she felt bouncy again. The boat moved into more open spaces as it crossed a richer part of the city; the floods reflected the blue of the sky. May gazed with pleasure at the shining water, knowing it wouldn't be there much longer, enjoying the silly sight of orange beacons sticking out of the surface like short-sticked lollipops, the little hillocks of new green leaves growing out of the sea that had swallowed the tree-trunks, the everyday houses which had lost their gardens, paths, front doors, turned into Venezia.

But her mood changed when she reached the Towers. As

the land dipped downwards, the water grew deeper. Thanks to the long wait, it was already afternoon. May wasn't eager to stay too long. There was a hint of deep cold, striking upwards, but it smelled, as well, of rot, of toilets. This must be a frightening place at night. Because the water rose several floors up, there was nowhere central for her to get off, just a series of towers leading off into the distance, two dozen monoliths of stained concrete that reared up darkly between May and the sun, tall and narrow and without imagination, no arches or carvings or softening curlicues, the windows glinting like blind glass eyes behind which more hostile eyes might be watching.

I must be mad to come here, May thought. I'll never find him. I'll never get home.

As they drew closer, though, she felt less fearful. Several of the windows were flung wide, and music poured out to greet the daylight. May listened for hymns, but this was dancing music. Young people, people she didn't know ... but probably not murderers, if they were dancing.

'Come on, lady,' said the boatman, impatient. 'You're going to have to tell me which one.'

'I don't really know,' May said. 'Sorry. I'm looking for a – trying to find a – well you could call it a religious group. The One Way Brotherhood. Does it ring a bell? Where would they be?'

He looked at her with a little sneer. 'Oh, they've all gone mad for it, round this way. Why can't you lot find a proper church?'

May ignored the spite. She agreed with him. 'It's my son,' she said. 'I want to find him.'

'Here's as good as anywhere,' he said.

He put May off, without a word, on the balcony of the nearest tower, with one other woman, coloured, youngish. May stood there for a second, shivering, as the boat rocked away towards the other towers, getting smaller, less real, in the shining distance. She felt suddenly old, helpless, useless, with her loose, childish money slipping about between her icy sausage fingers. The water below her looked very deep. Things moved beneath the surface like sea-monsters, things slowly pushing up to the light. Perhaps they were only rotting car-tyres, but they looked black and slimy and warm and alive.

What had she ever understood? What did she know about the world? Had she been a good wife or a decent mother? Suddenly May felt she knew nothing at all.

The young coloured woman was disappearing through the shattered window that led into the tower, stepping gingerly across the sharp triangles of glass, carrying her shopping-bag with anxious care. 'Please,' said May, 'Coo-ee, miss. I'm looking for some, you know, religious people. The One Way Brotherhood, they're called. Christians.'

The woman looked blank, then nodded. 'Oh yeah, but they're Muslims, innit? They're everywhere here. You're in the right place.'

The staircase, which felt cold and clammy as a morgue, despite the lozenges of sunlight on the wall, was plastered with dramatic posters, lettered in red to look like blood: 'LAST DAYS' they said, and 'ONE WAY OUT': towering black storm clouds sprayed arrows of rain: beneath the clouds, crowds dressed in white were gathered piously

around a book, and the rain above them was mysteriously
diverted. Childish, thought May. Do they really believe it?
(In any case, they would soon look out of date. The rains
had stopped, the floods would vanish.) She felt nervous,
thinking of this new strange son who had put his faith in the
end of the world.

Her feet tip-tapped self-consciously upwards, loud and
alone on the blank stone stairs. On the third floor above
water-level, she saw two posters on a door. She hesitated. It
went against her nature, knocking on the door of total
strangers. She carried on upwards, then turned, uncertain.
Why had she come, if she hadn't any courage?

Alfred had courage. She begged him to help her. Screwing
up her money inside her pocket, May pressed the bell with
her other hand.

There was a long silence, then a slithering shuffle, then
she heard someone just inside the door. They were probably
looking through that peep-hole. That was good, if so; they
too were afraid. A bolt was withdrawn and the door swung
open. An elderly Asian man stood there, stooped. His hair
was a deep, boot-polish black. He looked up quickly at her
face, then down again.

May stood her ground, clearing her throat, and pointed
at the poster on the door. 'Is this yours?' she inquired. 'I
mean, is it your faith?'

'Why you ask?' he said: eyes up, eyes down. The roots in
his parting were startlingly white.

'My son,' May said. 'I need my son.' To her surprise, her
voice choked up. 'He's a good boy,' she said, pointlessly.
Once he was a boy; once he was good; once he had bought

his father sweets, with his own money, without being told, when Alfred was sick, in hospital.

'The God love the mother who love the son,' the man said, with a sudden flashing smile. Then his body seized up again, cramped, suspicious.

'I'm looking for my son. His name's Dirk White. One of the leaders,' May said, smiling, with her best, kindest, most motherly smile. Surely motherhood was international. 'Do you have a son? I'm sure you do.'

'Two children,' he said, flamboyant again. 'Daueid, like David, Mariam, like Mary. From the Koran, but same in Bible.'

Soon May was inside the over-heated flat, sitting drinking coffee by the old-fashioned gas-fire whose tight toothed grids of flame and ash reminded her of the (Islamic, were they?) patterns on the cover of a book on the table.

He told her his name was Jehangir, 'meaning he who holds universe in his hand … Jehangir build the Taj Mahal, madam.'

'That's famous,' May said, thrilled. She had a little brass box with a picture of it. She'd thought it was built a long time ago, but then, she'd never been good at dates. Lovely to meet a famous architect. The coffee was terrible, with powdered cream, but it was very kind of Jehangir to offer it, and shortly after he produced some biscuits, ginger-nuts, which were favourites of hers, setting them on a plate on a low carved table.

He was talking to her with an impassioned desire to

explain the world, to explain this life, which made May
think of the poets she loved: Walt Whitman, Matthew
Arnold. Alfred had not been a bit like that, so she'd kept her
poetic side to herself. She expanded, now, in the heat of the
fire.

'The mother,' he was saying, 'she always love the child.
Everything he do, she just love it. The father love it but he
say "No", he correct him, but the mother, she is pure love.'
(Listening to him, May believed she was; and if she wasn't,
she resolved to be. It was love that had brought her here, to
the Towers.) 'The prophet say, the mother has heaven
beneath her feet. Not the woman; no. There is man, there is
woman, wrong thing can begin. But the woman who is
under what do you say, under husband's name, everything
right. The woman who becomes a mother, who gives life
from her body and loves the child, this woman has heaven
underneath her feet.'

Suddenly May felt, life is wonderful. (The caffeine and
the sugar zinged through her blood; she had got starving
hungry, waiting for the boat.) The truth was here, it was
everything that mattered. This foreigner liked her, they
could be friends, despite all this rubbish the government
talked about foreign powers and sabotage. She smoothed her
hair. He made her feel womanly. A woman and a mother.
She was in heaven.

She tried to pay attention to the details, but after a bit he
was talking too quickly. Every good Muslim must respect the
Jesus. Jesus was a prophet in the Koran, who would come
again on the Doomsday. His name in the Koran was Isa, or
Esa-alaihis-Salaam, some hissing words she couldn't quite

make out; his mother was Mariam, the Queen of Women. ('That's Mary,' she told him. 'Which is close to "May".' She sat with her coffee, excited, queenly.) God had daughters, and their sons were all prophets. There were perhaps one hundred and forty thousand prophets ('perhaps a more, perhaps a less'). But there was only One Way, One Truth, One Path. 'God love the humans. Every one. But he is also a Judger, Mary.' She asked if anyone could join the Path, and he told her, eagerly, yes. 'The Christians, Muslims, even these Jews, which we call Yahudis.' He didn't sound keen on those but, he continued, 'They are all people of the Book, Mary.'

'May,' she corrected him, slightly coquettishly. He had fine features, a noble hooked nose not so different from Alfred's, though finer, thinner. She reminded herself she was doing this for Dirk, so there was no harm in sitting talking. 'What was your name again, Jehan…?'

'Jehangir, Mary, Jehangir. In the Koran, Jehangir is the son of Aqbar, which means the Mighty One. They call him Shah-han-soar, which is, the king above other king –'

'King of Kings,' she helped him out. She wished he would offer her another biscuit. In his culture, it might be rude to reach out and take one, from the small gilt plate on the pretty table, for May understood about different cultures, unlike her husband, who had been a little narrow. It was lovely, a man looking after her. Alfred hardly ever made her cups of coffee.

'Yes, Mary. Kings of King, Kings of King. Aqbar takes a Hindu woman, makes her Muslim, marries her …'

This was encouraging, to May. 'I once knew a nice

Hindu,' she confided. 'I like your religion, with everyone included. I didn't realize it was like that. My friend was the man who ran the post office. Mr Varsani. Very honest. Though Alfred didn't think so. My husband got a thing about his change ... But I like the idea we could all be together.'

But her new friend fired up at once. 'Hindu don't have Book!' he said, indignant. 'This is rubbish religion, if they don't have Book.'

'Mr Varsani was very sincere,' said May, thrown off course; she had thought he would be pleased. 'Indian, like you,' reproachfully. 'I don't suppose you knew him?'

'I am Pakistani, Mary!'

May had never really understood the difference. 'Don't you think all religions are good? Hindus do,' she suddenly remembered. 'My daughter told me that's what Hindus believe.'

But this was a definite wrong turning. 'Let me explain you Hindus,' he said, leaping up, flashing his eyebrows, smiling, mocking, looking rather elderly once he was in motion, with a little pot belly that quivered as he gestured. 'If I say to you, "Now we worship the cow", you say to me, "Rubbish, rubbish, dear". This is the Hindu: he worship the cow. God never forgive you to worship the cow.'

May decided to back off Hindus. It was One Way, after all; Hindus couldn't get in.

Now Jehangir returned to the theme of marriage. He didn't like cows, but he did like trees, and waxed lyrical now as he sat close to May and explained how the God made the trees pregnant, smiling at her with tender meaning. His breath smelled sweetish and peppery; he was very intense; his lips were red; after a while his voice was hypnotic. He was looking deep into her eyes.

May tried to hotch away very slightly, and a spring in the chair poked sharply at her buttocks. She blushed, hotly, remembering her mission. She reached for her coat (which she'd slipped off, as they chatted, embarrassed by its worn fur collar, wishing she had worn her best blue one) and pulled, from the pocket where her money was, her newspaper cutting with the photograph of Dirk.

'Please,' she said. 'This is my youngest boy. You must know him. Where can I find him?'

'White fella,' he said, sounding disappointed, as if her son should have been Pakistani.

'Do you know him? You don't know him.' Her heart sank. She had been buoyed up with hope, and the pleasure of the chat. Now it all seemed empty. Jehangir didn't know him. She started to gather her things together.

'There are hundred, hundreds hundred, thousands hundred, One Way people now,' he told her, whirling his hands about. 'I know only the Muslim people, Mary. Muslim people very good people.' There was a long pause while she buttoned her coat; her fingers felt like someone else's; the coat seemed unwilling to be buttoned, as if her body wanted to get out. He watched her, his eyes intent and hot. Suddenly they were gazing at each other; she was out of her depth, too old, too frail, but her eyes gazed, and her body sweated, and she failed to force the button through the buttonhole.

'If I marry you, you can become Muslim. I can have four

wives, the Koran say.' He smiled a complicated, ghastly smile, a mixture of lust and gallantry and despair because he knew she was going.

May was touched and upset by his need of her, but as pity began, her excitement vanished. Men were needy: she knew about that, but she made it to her feet, she extended her hand. In any case, he didn't really mean it.

'I'm going,' she said. 'You've been very kind. Thank you for telling me about your religion.' She stood there smiling with her hand stretched out.

But she had forgotten some courtesy, some essential stage in the dance of compliments, and now the good will was cooling, dying. She had got it wrong as she often did. Her friend was staring at the floor again, eyes darting up briefly to hers, then away. His parting, from above, looked very straight, and very white. Without meaning to, she had rejected him. Now he had some moral high ground to reclaim.

'My religion very strict,' he said, sullenly. 'All bad thing banneded, very banneded. I am always good Muslim, Mary.'

'May. I hope I haven't made you go against your religion.'

He bowed, stiffly, ignoring her hand.

Eleven

The sun kept shining all that day. It was only April; clocks had not gone forward; but this was the third day in succession the light had managed to survive the morning. People who were living provisionally, waiting for the world to heal itself, came out and dared to stand on the pavement. The centre, where flooding had only been minor, had for some time been grey and ghostly, since the outlying population had lost faith in public transport. Probably not much was different today, except for the sun and the government statement. But that was all they needed: hope.

Today was the Gala. Miraculously. Four days ago, people had been sneering at the thought of the city celebrating its history. Now they stretched and sniffed the air. The damp squares and the flowerless gardens soon became thronged with noisy people, smiling at strangers, almost skittish, not worrying how they were going to get home, enjoying air, movement, colour, the queer kiss of daylight on their skin. Blades of grass, sodden with water, shook off the drops, sprang up again. Birds sang deafeningly of spring. Beggars came out from their soaked smelly shelters: 'Lovely day, miss, sir' they said, and dared to smile into people's faces as they stretched out their caps and boxes towards them, feeling, for once, they were part of the others, all of them sharing the same good news. People were generous, because they were happy.

The clean-up campaign was really getting going. Soldiers had been working for seventy-two hours and the worst of the mud had been jetted off the buildings, scrubbed off the kerbs, washed into the drains. The big hotels sported notices, 'Open For Business As Usual'. Some had imported flowers for their window-boxes; looked at closely, they were spread thin, but passers-by exclaimed with delight to see red tulips and peonies waving, frail as butterflies, silk-skinned and fragile, warm small flames to burn away darkness. The commissionaires, who had slumped into depression, unable to show their caps and gold braid, burst like kings on to the drying sidewalk, blinking at the daylight they had almost forgotten, their drink-pinked cheeks like old rose-petals, shining and wrinkling in the sun, proud of their pitches, at ease, benign, doffing their caps to pretty women and customers, puffing their chests like turkey-cocks, booming their wares with baritone abandon, rib-cages straining at golden frogging: 'Taxi, madam? *Righty-ho*', tossing tips in the air before pocketing them, white in the light on their long spin down. '*Lovely* day, madam. *Lovely* day.'

They were starting to believe they had turned the corner. The way things had been going, the hotel trade was finished – no one would ever take holidays in a city sliding under the sea. Now suddenly they were going to have a good night. The most distant city airport, on higher ground than the others, had been re-opened, by government decree. The rumour was, plane-loads of celebrities were coming, attracted to the city by giant bribes. The heart of the Gala was a smart fancy-dress party, invitation only, at Government Palace, with fireworks in Victory Square at midnight. (There would be another, smaller display of fireworks just after sunset for the Towers; the government had to do something for these people, but the Gala brochures were slightly vague; the Towers were not on the Central Map.) Highlights of the evening would be shown on giant screens that were being erected all over the country. After months of staying in, the crowds streamed out: '*Lovely* day, madam, *lovely* day.'

Street sellers were out with trays, even a stall or two had been set up, selling flags and badges saying 'CITY GALA', and people bought them, and stuck them on their jackets.

One little boy had six on his coat, run across his front like medals. His young mother led him proudly along by the hand, enjoying the way people smiled at him. Joe walked with his head up, swinging his arms, solid, sturdy, the hope of the city, his ginger hair fire-red in the sun. He began to sing, loudly, 'Happy Birthday'; his mum had said it was the city's birthday. Torn between joy and embarrassment, she walked without looking at him, grinning at strangers, miming 'Isn't he a show-off?', but knowing show was what they needed.

'I came because it's such a lovely day,' said Angela, lying, as Gerda ran towards her from the gates of the school and into her arms, splashing her horribly, shouting 'Mum! Mum! What are you doing here?'

'Don't look so surprised,' Angela said, *sotto voce*. 'Anyone would think I never come to meet you.' People, she thought, were looking at her; they recognized her, doubtless; she felt ashamed.

'Well, you don't ever come to meet me,' Gerda said, factually, then with the acute sensitivity of the child who has to worry if Mummy is happy, 'It doesn't matter, Mummy, don't be sad.'

She clutched her mother's hand very tightly. 'This is my mummy,' she announced, proudly, to anyone they met, as they walked to the car. 'I was good at swimming,' she told her. 'I taught the others to jump in.'

Her mother liked it when she did well. Gerda tried to think of good things to tell her. Mum was looking pretty, in her fluffy pink coat, with nice lipstick and shiny yellow hair, so different from Grandma, all pleated and old, with funny damp skin and always worrying. She loved her grandma, but she was embarrassing.

Gerda spotted Miss Habib with a box of playdough. 'Oh Mummy, please, that's my teacher, she knows you're a writer, she's dying to meet you –' (Miss Habib had never said any such thing, but Gerda so wanted to show off her mother.)

'Do we have to?' asked Angela, but then she looked down and saw an expression of such disappointment that she said, 'Of course. It's just, you know, I want to take you into town.'

'Miss, Miss, this is my mother.'

Rhuksana was putting the playdough in her boot; her head was inside, so she couldn't at first tell whose mother she was meant to meet. Though she longed to get home to hear the news about Loya, she came up smiling, ready to please, but when she saw it was Gerda's mother, whom she'd never met, who never even came to parents' evening, the famous author, the Iceland winner – sleek and shiny, smelling of money, her lipstick mark clear as a wound on Gerda's cheek – she couldn't help stiffening nervously, and her smile wavered, till she hauled it back up again.

'Rhuksana Habib. Delighted to meet you.'

'Lovely to meet *you*,' Angela deferred, though she'd noticed that moment of instinctive dislike. She was a novelist; she noticed. 'I hear such wonderful things about you.'

'Thank you.' There was an uncertain pause. Seeing Gerda's upturned, eager face, Rhuksana made an effort.

'She's a delightful child. Of course, very bright.'

Angela nodded, modestly. Of course Gerda was bright; it was hereditary. 'Is she a good girl, most of the time?' she asked, remembering the scene that morning. 'I know they can all be terrors, sometimes.'

Gerda looked up at her, indignant. 'She's a pleasure to teach,' said Rhuksana, coolly.

'Bit wilful, sometimes,' Angela smiled, trying to indicate she knew her daughter. 'Bit of a bossy-boots, like me.'

Trying to disarm her, to win her over, but Gerda said, 'I'm not bossy.'

Rhuksana's smile faded. 'Not at all, Mrs Lamb. She's very sensible, in school.'

'I'm not sensible,' Gerda remarked, very definitely, with a stubborn face. 'Grown-ups have to be sensible. I'm not a grown-up. My mummy is a writer,' she added, proudly. 'She's a famous writer. Have you read her books?'

'I wish I had,' Rhuksana lied. 'But I know she's famous. Everyone does. My husband's in publishing, actually,' she added.

'Oh really?' asked Angela, and then, for Gerda, the conversation became infinitely tedious, the kind of conversation that grown-ups had, all names and places she knew nothing about.

'… but very commercial,' her mother was saying. 'Their books do sell, that's the main thing. I'm sure he'll be very happy there.'

'He doesn't like it there, in fact,' Rhuksana said. She wasn't going to be patronized. Mohammed got patronized every single day. 'He thinks they're, well, a bit patronizing.'

There was a silence. Angela blushed. Had she been patronizing? Surely not. But Asian people were hypersensitive.

'In any case, he's trying to change their image. He's found at least one remarkable book —' Rhuksana continued, and then broke off. She would never convince this woman of anything.

'What's "patronizing"?' Gerda asked, and then, not waiting for an answer, tugged sharply at Angela's hand.

'Why can't we go?' she said. She thought, with a small growing nugget of unhappiness, perhaps my teacher doesn't like my mother.

The two women began to edge away from each other, making small, ineffectual gestures of appeasement.

'Such a beautiful day,' Rhuksana tried.

'Gorgeous,' Angela agreed, heartily. 'Did you hear the news?' she added, shading her eyes against the light. 'The government says the worst is definitely over. Oh, and they think the flood defences were sabotaged.' She suddenly remembered this wasn't tactful; sabotage was usually blamed on the Muslims.

Rhuksana smiled stiffly. 'What nonsense,' she said. 'This government will try any lies.' Suddenly she had had enough, after a day of keeping her temper with the children. 'It's they who are wrecking our cities, in Loya. Have you heard about the Loyan National Library? Looters have stolen what your bombs didn't burn. And Mr Bliss's troops stood by and did nothing. My husband —' and here her voice became unsteady, but she forced the smile back on to her face. 'My husband wept, when he heard the news, for the first time since we were married.'

The woman was clearly a bit of an extremist. 'I'm not pro this war, you know,' said Angela, quite truthfully, though she wasn't really following it. 'In any case,' she said, not looking at Rhuksana. 'Thank you for all you do for the children.'

Miss Habib had got very red in the face. Gerda pushed her mother. 'Come *on*, Mummy.'

'It's my job,' said Rhuksana. 'I love it.' Slamming the car door and driving away, she thought to herself, But I don't love the parents. She wished she hadn't mentioned Mohammed.

At a quarter to four, Harold was lying on the floor of the second-floor sitting room, listening to Wes Montgomery playing 'Mr Walker'. He knew he should be getting ready for the Gala. Lottie was stomping about upstairs, issuing instructions at intervals, to do with his shirt, his hair, his tie. Harold listened to the music's velvet depth, its wondrous blend of bounce and melancholy, jazz guitar like the padded feet of a panther prowling through a warm spring night, and wondered whether his book was true: was the moment really all that mattered? Listening now, time became the music, a place of endlessly repeated bliss where nothing counted, not success nor failure, only the perfectly rounded chord which held all the particles of life in its hand, for he'd loved this track since he was seventeen years old, before he met Lottie, when he was alone –

'*Harold*! Have you started to run that bath?'

– When he was young, when he was someone.

Lottie's voice disappeared; he shut her out. He skipped back to Thelonius Monk. My man Thelonius. All my men … Women were obsessive about cleanliness. He didn't really want to go, tonight.

But he knew, underneath it, that he was depressed. The book, which had taken up two decades of his life, had gone into silence and emptiness. No one had even acknowledged receipt. It was too late now. No one ever would. It was worse because for weeks he had been buoyed up with hope.

Perhaps the book was mad, in any case. He had become

fascinated by simultaneity: at any one point in time, the thousand flowerings of event – the murders and weddings, mud-slides and military coups, the earthquakes, torture sessions, shy first kisses, the football matches, poems, invasions, dances, all of them gathered on the same string of time, all of them clustered together like a garland ... Going on for ever, now, now, all across this planet, stretching out into space like a great rope of flowers, and who knew if it was entirely nonsense, this business of Davey's about planets aligning – and even at this instant, as he lay on the floor, with the glory of the saxophone caressing him, great events were breaking, somewhere else, people were burning, people were laughing, soldiers were marching across the desert, little children were learning to swim, lives were being changed for ever – and then there were the ants, the bower-birds, the lizards, the intricate cross-hatchings of a thousand other species –

'*Harold, I'll kill you if you don't come at once!*'

The phone rang, disrupting the long camber of his jazz. He picked it up, trying to sound terse and cool, for it was bound to be somebody selling insurance, the industry was desperate because of the floods –

'Yes,' he said, guardedly. 'Yes, it is.'

And then, 'Really? ... Do you think so? ... Thank you. No, I haven't got an agent ... Should I have? Next spring? Really? "Inspirational", you say ... So is that, really, um, "where it's at"? No, I didn't actually realize that ... Oh yes, I'd love to meet you.'

He gets to his feet in a single fluid movement, switches off the music, stands, deep breathing, blood flooding his body, cheeks aching with joy. He jives round the room; he can't keep still. He is the man, the man, the man. Now it is his turn to do some shouting. He's pretty sure he can out-shout Lottie.

He bounds upstairs, but she's locked her door, which can only mean that she's shaving her legs.

'LOTTIE!' he yells through the bathroom door.

'Bloody hell, Harold, why are you shouting?'

'BECAUSE I'VE HEARD FROM A PUBLISHER!'

A pause. 'Oh darling, I'm sorry, never mind. A lot of people get rejections, you know.'

'No, Lottie, listen, open the door.'

She mutters, just audibly, but comes and opens, with a tiny trace of red on her shapely calf, and a little frown of tenderness; she really does love him. She doesn't like him to be upset. Besides, it's a bore, with the Gala coming. 'Harold,' she says, taking his hand, 'we'll go through this together, darling. Obviously they're stupid, and you are clever, cleverer than most people, cleverer than me –'

'I'm certainly clever, I'm a BLOODY GENIUS. Listen, Lottie, they've accepted it! They mean to pay me money! Rather a lot! They want it to be their spring lead, next year, which apparently is something really good!'

'Harold!' says Lottie, taking it in. 'Harold.' And Lottie is starting to smile. Her lovely soft mouth curls up and up; her tongue and her big white teeth are gleaming. *'Harold.* But that's, that's wonderful … Come into my bath. Come here. Let me kiss you. Harold. Oh Harold. You are a success!'

'We're going to have a treat,' Angela said, once Gerda was safely strapped into the back. Gerda didn't answer.

'Did you like my teacher?' she asked.

'No – I mean yes. Of course I did.'

'Will you pick me up tomorrow?'

'Maybe'.

'Will you bring me to school? Please, Mummy.'

'Maybe. But stop interrupting me. Tonight I'm taking you to a very big party.'

'That isn't a treat,' said Gerda, frowning. 'You always take me to parties. It's boring.'

'This one won't be.'

'Promise.'

'I absolutely promise it won't be boring! It's the City Gala, the best party for years! The Rapsters will be there, and Lil Missy M, and Gail Hadrada, and the president –'

'No. Promise you'll bring me to school.'

'Why are you going on about that?'

'It's *my* school. I want you to.'

'OK, I promise,' said Angela, annoyed. The child seemed completely unappreciative. It didn't matter what you did for them.

'And can we bring Winston home for tea?' This was daring. Gerda never had children to tea, but other children did, and Gerda wanted to.

'Who's Winston?' Angela asked, crossly.

'I *told* you,' Gerda said, reproachfully. 'The boy who brings me snail-shells at break. He's Franklin's brother. They're twins.'

'It's a bit awkward,' said Angela, nervously. It didn't sound so unreasonable. 'I mean, we have a routine, at teatime. You have a routine, with your grandparents. I generally write, and so on.'

'Stupid old routine,' shouted Gerda. She had never shouted at her mother. 'All the other children have people to tea. Why can't I?'

Angela couldn't answer. A tiny headache was beginning to grow.

'It's because you're old,' Gerda yelled, furious, saying the worst thing she could think of. 'It's because you're too old to have children. I hate you!'

Angela found tears running down her cheeks. Her first reaction was to give in. Besides, she did want Gerda to come to the Gala. 'I'm not old, I'm in my forties,' she whispered. 'You can have your stupid twins, if you want them.'

'I only want Winston. I don't love Franklin …' Gerda peered forward; her mother was actually crying. This gave Gerda a pain in her belly. 'I'm sorry, Mummy, you're not really old. You're not very wrinkly. You look nice in your makeup.'

Angela vowed not to speak to her again, and put the radio on loud, but the radio was talking about the Gala.

'This is the party you don't want to go to that they're going on about,' she said crossly over her shoulder. 'They're supposed to have spent millions of dollars on it. There are going to be tigers in cages, it says. And an ice-rink. And dancers dressed up as swans. And that person on the television that Grandma says you like so much, what is his name, Davey Duck –'

Gerda had suddenly burst out laughing. 'Davey Duck! Davey Duck! Mummy you're a Idiot!'

Angela's headache got sharply worse. Angela didn't like being laughed at. 'What is the matter with you, Gerda?' she said coldly. 'Really, stop acting like a child. I don't know why I bothered to pick you up.'

'His nickname's Davey *Luck*!' Gerda shouted. 'He's a Nastronomer! He's totally famous!'

'I didn't happen to have heard of him. But I know you like him. I take an interest. Why is it so funny if I make a mistake?'

Gerda thought, in the back of the car. 'It's like, if they called you Angela Ham,' she said, and started to giggle again. 'Angela Ham! Angela Ham! I think I'm going to wet myself.' It took several minutes for her to stop laughing. 'I think I might marry Winston,' she said, apropos of nothing, but her mother wasn't listening.

'They just mentioned me on the radio,' Angela said, turning round in her seat and almost hitting a man on a bike. 'If you weren't laughing so much, you'd have heard it.' But her voice had softened, her mood had improved. 'They said, "famous writers like Angela Lamb and Farhad Ahmad are among those on the guest-list." Admittedly Ahmad's a bit of a fraud, but still it's quite pleasant to be mentioned.'

'Mummy,' said Gerda, quietly. 'Mummy, can I ask you something?'

'Uh-huh.' Angela was trying to park.

'I don't really want to go to the party. I want to stay at home and do a painting and watch TV and have a bath with you, and *you* be with me all the time, and *you* read me my bedtime story –'

'It's totally unreasonable, of course,' said Angela, not letting her finish. 'Most children would give their eye-teeth for this. Why can't you just be normal, Gerda?'

'What are I-teeth?' asked Gerda, briefly distracted. They must be some kind of special bones, like the magic bones that they had in Australia, the ones that Miss had told them about, the ones that had your spirit in. 'I wouldn't give you my I-teeth, Mummy. In any case, you didn't listen.'

'I did listen. You're not coming.'

'I'll come if Davey Luck is really coming. And if you take me to school tomorrow. And if Winston can come to tea.'

'Deal,' said Angela, relieved. 'Now please get out of the car, darling.'

'Promise?' Gerda showed no sign of moving. She was staring her mother in the eye.

'Promise.' If I manage to wake up, Angela thought.

'Promise that Davey Luck is coming? Hope to die?'

'Hope to die.'

She thought, they have no idea how much we love them. Simultaneously she remembered there wasn't any school tomorrow; it was a public holiday. She didn't mention the fact to Gerda.

Gerda was looking up at the clouds, riveted by something her mother couldn't see. Then she turned her face back to Angela, curious. 'But do you *really* hope to die? I don't ever want to die.'

The boy with his chestful of paper medals stopped singing 'Happy Birthday' in the middle of a note, pulled his hand from his mother's (who was smiling at a stranger, her eyes intimating 'Isn't he great?'), with a sudden jerk, fun, easy, and ran across the road without a care, glimpsing a park on the other side, the tops of trees under a blue and rose sky; football, of course, after a gap of two months, the happy game from a lost green life – 'Come on, Mummy,' hope called, peremptory, over his shoulder, not missing a beat, and as time split, he skipped off the pavement – dodging and weaving between the traffic, which screamed to a halt, hooted, braked – his mother tried to run after him but the stream of cars as the sun went down was suddenly thicker, blinder, more pressing; crowds were driving in to watch the celebrities; they surged on, pitiless; she couldn't see him, only the red-lit metal flanks of the cars, their lights flicking on as the pink sun set, so that everything became a confusion of signals – in the end, with a hopeless, nameless, terror, and because not to go was impossible, she threw herself out into the flashing river, suddenly skinless, a bag of wounds, was carried across by luck, and fear, telling herself, 'They will not kill you, they will not kill you, you have to save him, then you can die'; all that she held in her mind was love, love and the horror of losing it, but that silver thread pulled her through the maze; she saw him, suddenly, curled in a ball of blue coat and old shoes on the traffic island, shocked, stunned, a boy of stone, and as the cold draught from a speeding lorry pulled her up short just before it hit her, she plunged through a gap, she had him, her boy; love crushed his medals, she snatched, she held. 'You could have been killed, you could have been killed.' He clutched her, sobbing. He had not been killed.

The cars press on towards the Gala. Some stars are going early, to check sound and lights.

'Did you see that?' squeaks Lil Missy M, peering through the window of her limousine. 'Crazy little kid ran right across the road.'

'Kids are freakin' crazy,' says her bodyguard, swallowing a pill, then taking another. 'Don't worry, baby. Everything's cool.'

In the rest of the city, life is nearly normal, in the afternoon, in the early evening, normal for a city recovering from chaos, a city eager to be normal again. The swimming-pool where Zoe and Viola work stays open till ten, six days a week. It is warm and bright: people feel happy. Milly feels good, washing and polishing. She's talked to Samuel about Father Bruno. They will stay with the Brothers, because they are needed, stay and remind them that Jesus is love. Milly likes to clean, because it makes life better. She likes the children who come to the pool. She likes Zoe, who's a good person; she's seen her at the market, making a speech against the war; the mike didn't work, and hardly anybody listened, but Zoe kept on talking, to the muddy water. Milly cleans Zoe's office especially well, and sticks back the curling corners of her anti-war posters. Like Milly, Zoe always comes in early.

Viola manages to come in around lunch-time; Zoe sulks for a bit, and then forgives her; it's just that she can't get enough of Viola.

The swimming-pool has its familiar rhythms, rhythms they like to think of as natural, forgetting order is rare and exquisite, forgetting life is rich and brief.

There are the tiny private classes before school which

bring in more money than the rest of the day, then therapy sessions for the local hospital – Zoe does the therapy groups for free, because the hospital has no money – while large school groups use the rest of the pool: then at lunch-time, the club swimmers arrive, hard and lean and slathered with cream, robot beings with goggles and swim-hats and sharp black insect-clips on their noses; they power mechanically down the lanes, smooth as salmon or bucketing like speedboats as they break into glistening butterfly stroke. Then comes the sleepy afternoon, when more teachers bring classes of school-kids; Zoe and Viola can doze in their office, if they are abreast of the paperwork; they kiss or gossip, or make each other laugh, usually about the quirks of the parents. (Milly is cleaning the toilets again, singing 'Swing Low, Sweet Chariot'.)

It is sweet, sweet, this life together. This afternoon, because they've missed each other, because they quarrelled, slightly, at lunch-time, they lock their door and make tender love; small animal purrs and gasps of contentment are heard by people in the corridor: 'Did she bring her cat in to work?' wonders the eighteen-year-old receptionist. At four, life starts to rev up again; more private classes, more kids, more clubs, more bossy parents, cheques, enrolments. Life goes on, banal, beautiful; the swimming-pool breathes in and out; the life it supports takes its rhythms for granted; everyday, peaceful, miraculous life in a city reclaimed from the edge of disaster.

At four o'clock, May has got nowhere, back out on her own

in the deathly cold stairwell. She feels she has come to the end of time. A place she never expected to go, when she had her children and lived with Alfred. She'd thought they would always be safe together. Alfred, she thinks, where are you, love? I need you now. You have to help me.

But Jehangir's words still ring in her ears; there are thousands, or hundreds of thousands, of this cult; how to find Dirk among so many?

Should she try the higher floors? But it is too alarming, pressing on upwards, going ever further from her line of escape. On her way downstairs, she hears something shuffling below her, and slows her step, and the other feet slow, and she is afraid, but she thinks of Alfred, and, as Alfred would have done, she walks on.

What she finds, hunched against a cold damp wall, is a thin yellow girl with marks on her arm who offers to take her to the nearest two towers, saying 'I'm the local taxi. Don't laugh!' The amount she mentions is pitiable. Her boat is tiny and ramshackle; there is a silt of dirty water in the bottom; the girl looks too skinny and weak to row, but she manages it, pulling with animal ferocity, the muscles in her arms long pallid cords.

May knows she is stepping off the edge of the world, lost with this child, riding low in the water, while the sun sinks down in the April sky, swooping red and large between the lines of buildings as the boat traces long unsteady arcs.

Each tower, from a distance, looks blank and menacing, but once she is inside, they are just cold, and poor, and full of posters, but her son is not there, though more than one of the pale, frowning people whose doors she knocks on claim to know him. In the end a short, tough-looking, busty Irish woman smoking a fag takes pity on her. 'My daughter Kilda's got in with 'em,' she said. 'They're all mad as knives though, if you ask me. My daughter's got it into her head she sees the future … You're not going to have much luck today. There were special boats took 'em all off this morning, all wearing their robes and carrying their placards, Prods, Pakis, the whole blooming lot of them. They've all gone off to the Gala together. Come back tomorrow, love. You might find him. If he's not too busy with the world ending.'

Out on the balcony above the black water the pink sunlight poured down on May. She felt terribly alone, despite her Tennyson – the last reader, at the end of the world. She had gone to the bottom of the tower and waited, after the yellow girl abandoned her. The wind licked sharply at the dazzling pink pages: a gang of young boys skimmed stones across the swell at the crimson disk of the setting sun; every so often, May had to duck, but she was afraid to tell them off. After what seemed like hours of waiting she heard the tired chug of a City Wonderama bus.

The boatman was black, and very thin, cadaverous, almost, hollow-voiced, barking with some kind of irritable infection. Round dark glasses concealed his eyes. His jacket was rusty, soiled with age. ''Ear me now, missis, get in,' he coughed, but the gap between the balcony and the boat looked too wide and frightening for May to attempt, the sides rushing apart and briefly together, and she said, 'Can't you help me?' but he didn't hear, so she shouted, 'Oi! Give us a hand!'

Cold as death, his hand gripped her like iron and pulled her across into swaying limbo. Close up, white bristles prickled out from his chin. The boat behind him was frighteningly empty; this skull-like man was her only hope.

He was waiting for something, fixed, blind-eyed, his engine stalled as the boat swung dizzily. 'Oh – my fare,' she realized, and reached in the pocket of her coat for money. He took it from her, without a word, and the boat set off jerkily into the beyond.

'Me don't nar – ma – lly answer to "Oi",' he said, over his shoulder, in his mournful voice, after they had travelled for a few minutes.

'Sorry,' said May, meekly. 'What's your name?'

'Wrong,' he hacked, fighting for breath.

'I didn't say anything.' May was affronted. He didn't have to be quarrelsome.

'Cha!' he sucked his teeth at her in irritation. 'R-O-N, woman. Me nyame is *Ron*.'

'Hello, Ron. My name is May.' Perhaps another man was going to chat her up, though he didn't strike her as the talkative sort. She patted her coat pocket, feeling for her mirror; she would tidy her hair, while she had a minute, while the boatman had his back to her, while there was still a little light from the sun.

At six p.m., the end would begin.

Twelve

Shirley said, 'You go, honestly. I'm not quite happy about Winston.'

The sun was going down, having shone all day, waking up the sparrows on the patio. The bird-table had grown tall again, as the level of the water sank earthwards. Shirley had donned her Wellingtons and put out some crumbs from the breakfast table; birds skipped about, gilded, gladdened. She dipped through *Study Skills: Achieving Concentration*, turning her head when the blackbirds sang or the breeze blew in from the window. A day at home; a beautiful day. Time had passed slowly, gold drops dropping.

Elroy had had a good day at the hospital, a sheet of sunlight glossing his desk. They had both felt blessed; the world had got lighter.

Now suddenly the boy was ill. Elroy stood in the kitchen,

undecided. He had come home early to dress for the Gala. 'If you're worried about him, I should stay home.'

'I'm not sure, really … his forehead is hot. It could just be this stupid thing at school.'

'We should have put our foot down,' said Elroy, meaning 'You should have put your foot down, Shirley'. Elroy's sphere was earning the money; home and the boys were down to Shirley. Elroy was trying to be patient, but he wanted to go to the Gala with Shirley.

'You could get a baby-sitter,' he said. 'What about this Kilda girl?' But Shirley had waited so long for these children that she rarely let them out of her sight when they were poorly. She could have left the twins with his sisters if their whole relationship wasn't so vexed. They were a close family, full of passionate loyalty, but ravaged by the past, and the deeper past, by the shadows of the shadows of unspeakable crimes. Why had his own father deserted his family? He, Elroy, would never do that. And yet his son, Dwayne, lived alone with Viola, and she made it hard for the two of them to meet.

'Don't want to go on my own,' Elroy said, and was suddenly a boy, his handsome head drooping. 'Felt good today, with the floods going down, and hearing the Gala was going ahead, and seems like we won't have to evacuate the hospital … Forget it, I ain't going, either. I'll get some food in. We'll all stay home.'

But she knew Elroy. He liked to have fun, he liked to dress up and see and be seen. She didn't want to stop him, or cramp his style. 'Go,' she said. 'Go, really. Come back and tell me all the news. Everything, mind. I want to hear what

Lil Missy M was wearing. And you're to get autographs for the boys. It'll be fun, Elroy. It'll be great.'

'You really think Winston will be all right?' When the boys were poorly Elroy veered between complacency and terror. Part of Shirley's job was to even things out.

But today she herself was at a loss. It could all be to do with the problems at school. A teacher had decided to split the boys up. For the first time, they were in different classes. Perhaps it was her fault for not resisting.

Then just by coincidence a mother from school, Angela Lamb, rather plummy voice, had rung out of the blue and asked if Winston could come and play with her daughter Gerda. The name was definitely familiar – yes, that strange young girl at the zoo, out with her doting grandparents. Pretty little thing, red hair, precocious. Not both the boys, as usual, just Winston. 'He's my daughter's special friend,' the woman explained. 'I suppose so,' Shirley had answered, surprised. They fixed for tomorrow, the Gala holiday. When she told the boys, Winston was wildly excited and Franklin had cried and thrown his drink on the floor.

Shirley sighed, and tried to sound reasonable. 'Yes. Like you say, it could be this school thing. In any case, the funny thing is, Franklin cried all day because he couldn't be with Winston, wouldn't eat his lunch and so on, then after they got together this evening they fought worse then they ever did in their lives. Then Winston was sick and fell asleep, and I slipped him into bed, but Franklin seems fine ...'

'If you're sure, I'll go.'

She hadn't said she was sure. Why did Winston have a temperature?

'You're a good mother. I love you, Shirley,' Elroy said, putting his arms round her soft thick waist, feeling her silky blonde curls against his cheek.

'Kiss me,' he says, and kisses her, passionately. 'Nothing could ever pull us apart. It's you and me for ever, Shirley. You and me. It's all going to go right.'

(But she has a slightly absent air, she is in a different world, of maternal worry.)

Viola, Zoe notices, with dread, has the absent air she knows so well, sitting by the side of the swimming-pool not quite watching as the Junior Dolphins swim. Viola, she sees, has started to worry. And Zoe is worried; there is something in the air.

'Zoe,' says Viola, as Zoe knows she will. 'I'm starting to worry about Dwayne.'

'Why?'

'I hardly saw him this morning. Delorice was there, he went off upstairs to be minded by this Kilda girl. She had to go out this evening.'

'So? She must have made arrangements for the kids.' Zoe can feel herself losing her temper, and starts breathing deeply, breathing like a swimmer; relax in the water; let it come easy.

'She's got a mother. A fat woman called Faith. I'm not crazy about her.'

'Right. You had better ring her, then.' Zoe knows quite

well Viola doesn't want to ring her. She knows Viola wants
to go home.

'I just don't like her. She shouts at her daughter.'

'Well, you shout at Dwayne sometimes.'

'I want to go home,' says Viola. Her beautiful dark eyes
are fixed on the slippery glaze of the grey tiles beside the
swimming-pool.

'You didn't get in till lunch-time, Viola.'

'I want to go home.' Viola never really argues, just says
what she wants, with increasing conviction.

'It's, like – I feel – you're letting me down.' There; it is
out; Zoe has said it. Fortunately they have a few minutes
between sessions, while the old classes shower and the new
ones get changed. 'We're in this together. It's *our* business.'
Zoe catches her hand; holds it, hard, her white fingers trying
to enlace with Viola's dark ones, but Viola's are still slippery
from the pool.

'Something's spooking me,' Viola says. 'I can't explain it.
I'm, like, edgy.'

'What about?' asks Zoe, still breathing deeply, but Viola
can't answer.

'It's, like, instinct.'

'*Please* go and phone up.'

Yet she wants to tell Viola, I'm frightened too. It's the way
Bliss has been talking on television, the evangelist's air of a
man who believes, whose mission to convince himself has
been too successful. A man like that could do anything.

And if we're frightened, we should be together. But Viola
doesn't want us to be together. Viola only cares about
Dwayne.

The first girl comes out, shivering, skinny, in a yellow bikini she's far too young for. The parents have no sense, thinks Zoe, remembering how little sense her own mother had, how the nagging nearly put her off swimming for life, and then her mind returns to Viola, her pointless worrying. No fucking sense.

Life starts to crack open; nothing makes sense. Zoe knows she is starting to lose her temper; if she loses her temper she will shout and scream and Viola will never love her again; if she loses her temper the world might end.

She sees there is no point arguing, no point persuading, nothing to say; but just as Zoe decides to give up, a voice comes struggling up from her chest, from the place of deep breaths, the helpless place where her feelings are too raw to be silent: 'Why do you always put Dwayne before me?'

Viola looks at her, silenced, stricken. More of the children are emerging from the changing rooms, pushing, giggling, expectant. 'I love Dwayne,' she says, simply.

Zoe wants to sob, to howl, to hit her. 'You'd better go,' she says, and turns away.

She teaches the next lesson in a fugue state, closing her mind to the pain in her body, grinning and encouraging on automatic pilot, wishing them away, wishing it over, her eyes darting constantly up to the clock-face. At half-past five she has a twenty-minute break. At half-past five she can slip away and weep.

But she unlocks the door of their office to find Viola sitting there waiting for her, dressed to go home, with her pull-down peach hat, her velvet tracksuit and tight leather jacket – but her face is naked with love and sorrow. 'Sorry,

Zoe,' she says. 'I feel awful. I know it's like doing a runner on you. I've just got this weird, like, bad feeling – like I ought to go and get Dwayne back. It's only a feeling. I should ignore it.'

But she sits poised to leave, not removing her jacket.

'Nothing's going to happen,' says Zoe, as she bends to kiss her, to take her in her arms. 'You should go and get Dwayne, of course you should. But nothing's going to happen, is it?'

They stand together for a few minutes, tender, stroking cheeks, wrists, hands, little solacing movements of discovering and leaving the curves, the folds, the skin's small secrets. There are ten minutes left of Zoe's break. There are five minutes left of giving comfort. They hang in the moment; everything is slow; it goes on for ever; it is happiness; they are grateful for this; they look; they kiss. Then the telephone rings, and Zoe pulls herself away. 'Go,' she says, 'I'll answer it, it's probably just the anti-war brigade,' but before she answers it, she says one last thing, letting the telephone ring and ring; 'One day we'll have a child of our own. I'm so happy with you. I'll love you for ever.'

The phone-call comes at six p.m.

Davey Lucas, meanwhile, is trying to get through to the mobile of Kylie Spheare, of Extreme Events. It is constantly engaged; her voice in the message sounds hyper-relaxed, breathy, off-hand, so just for a moment he thinks it won't matter, they aren't expecting him, everything's cool, though in real life he knows she must be demented; things at the palace will be moving to their climax.

Davey is realizing, with shock and relief, that he isn't going to make the Gala, that he will dare to let them down. At first it seemed unthinkable; Davey is performing for Bliss, and the government, and every famous name in the city, for more money than he earns in a year ... What had Kylie said? 'You're the man for us. Frankly, you're the only one who can do it.'

But great events are in the air. Events that dwarf the City Gala.

Zoe picks up the phone, and the night leaks in.

Viola is letting herself out of the office door when she hears Zoe's sharp intake of breath as she listens to a voice in the electronic distance. 'Now? Right now? Are you kidding?' And then lower, more worried: 'But how has that happened? ... I don't understand ... Right. At once ... Never mind.'

She puts the phone down and stares, for a second. Her voice, when it comes, is flat and strange. 'Sorry, you'll have to stay and help. We've got to evacuate the swimming-pool. Something weird. There's been some breakdown between our system and the flood-water. The water-table seems to have risen again. I didn't get all the technical details – but from what they're saying, it's dangerous. They're shutting down all the city pools ... There's talk about some virus, too. And people are saying it's water-born.'

'But the floods are over,' says Viola. She has taken her hat off, though, and her jacket, as if she already knew this was coming. 'That's why they've gone ahead with the Gala.'

They run together towards the pool. 'I knew,' gasps Viola. 'I had this bad feeling.'

At Government Palace, the guests are arriving.

Elroy went off to shower, singing to himself. He liked to work out; he was slim, toned. Being married didn't mean that you let yourself go. He padded down the landing, naked, passing the lit door of the bedroom where Winston was already asleep, and glimpsed Shirley sitting on Franklin's bed, the bedside light warm on her fair, soft curls, whitening the page of the book she was reading. She paused for a moment, reached gently across and felt the forehead of the sleeping boy. 'He's a little bit hot,' she whispered to Franklin. 'But don't worry, I know he'll be fine.'

Elroy loved her voice, creamy, kind, that sleepy lilt that would calm the boys down. He sprayed some cologne, put on his dinner jacket, went back and stood in the boys' doorway. Shirley was just tucking Franklin in, bending to kiss him and put off the light. 'Shirley,' he whispered, 'give me a hand with my tie.' He could never manage to fix his bow tie. 'You look wonderful,' she said, and he did look good, the black and white making his skin-tone glow. 'Love you,' he said. 'I won't be too late.'

'Don't believe you,' Shirley said, but she smiled her love. Suddenly they were together again; after a week of living like virtual strangers. 'Love you, Elroy.'

'Love you more.'

Trying to decide which woman to call, he inspected himself briefly in the long hall mirror.

May's face in her mother's small metal mirror, floating against the darkening sky, shocked her: tiny. And wrinkled. A grandmother. The light wasn't good, but she saw what she saw. Ron had shown no more interest in her. She thought, with a pang of regret, of Jehangir, who must have been desperate, or short-sighted. She knew she would never be loved any more. She shouldn't expect it, those days were over. The boat wove its course between the dark shores. She felt frail, and small, and very alone. Her head sank softly on to her chest. She wished she could rest on Alfred's shoulder. She'd thought he would be there for ever … Frightened, her little hands groped for each other. The next moment, she fell asleep, and sat dozing and twitching as the boat chugged onwards, butting on into the gathering night.

As she fell into the void, Alfred came to find her. He had always been waiting, beyond the black water. He stepped, with a creak and a gasp, into her boat. 'I'm here, May, darling. I've kept a look out. Surprised to see you're still wearing that coat.'

She couldn't see him clearly, in the boat's low electric. He sat close to her, with his back to the light. He had always liked her to look her best, but then, she hadn't known she was going to see him. May didn't like to offend people, and the boatman might be from these parts, so she whispered, 'I purposely didn't dress up, Alfred, because they're, you know, quite poor around here.'

'Let's have a look at your face,' he said. 'You've got so thin, love. Haven't you been eating? Shirley should be making you keep your strength up.'

'She's got her own life,' she said, protective. 'I'm cold, Alfred. Put your arm around me.'

'I can't,' he said, 'it's not allowed. Not till you go the whole hog, so to speak.'

She didn't understand. She never liked regulations, though he had always been strong on them. 'Why not?' she asked. 'You're my own – dear husband.' Her voice caught in the middle, turned into a sob. It was torture, having him near, but not touching her. Watching the silhouette of his head, the way his neck joined the narrow shoulders, the bony, noble bulk of his nose.

'It would make you colder, May. Cold as death. I never wanted you to be cold. I'm trying to sit near. It's the best I can do.'

Then she realized a miasma, a slow fog of ice, was stealing across the small gap between them. 'But *I* can touch *you*,' she said, boldly. 'Can I?' (She thought she could; she felt so full of life. Sometimes she'd had to take the initiative. When they first married, she had to help him; he'd been too eager, and then despaired, and though she was a virgin, she'd made things right, just by loving him, encouraging him.)

'May, I don't know. Be careful, love. You've still got things to do, back there, for the kids, I mean, for the family. Things I didn't manage to set straight.'

There were so many questions she wanted to ask him. 'What's it like, Alfred? Are your people there? I've thought about you, you know, so often –' (and yet she winced in case it wasn't enough; not all day and every day, as she had at first. And perhaps they knew, on the other side. Perhaps it made their loneliness worse. And her sorrow and pity made her reach out to touch him; without fear or forethought, she stroked his rough cheek.)

'Don't worry about me,' he said, gruffly. 'That's lovely, May. You don't know how lovely. You always were – a lovely wife.'

She kept on stroking him: cold as ice. 'Won't you tell me, Alfred? Is it – too bad to tell?'

'It's not too bad,' he said. 'Bearable, duck. I'm here because I don't choose to forget. If I took a drink of the river, see, it would all wash away, the kids, and you, our whole life together, every bit of it ... the things I done right, and the things I done wrong –' ('*Did*,' she corrected, as she always had) '– our little garden. The park, in summer. The lake, under the willow tree. Sometimes I start to feel so thirsty ... but I'll wait for you. I don't want to forget.'

'There were wonderful times. Ooh, I miss it, Alfred. You think, don't you – it will go on for ever.'

'I think it does, May, but I don't know where. It's like I've slipped into black-and-white, from colour. There is a way through, but I can't find it.'

'I'll help you, love, when the time comes.' Firmly, tenderly, May kissed his cheek. 'We can do anything, together.' Yet she was afraid of having to stay here.

'How's Shirley?' he said. 'She's a good girl. I didn't quite manage to say my piece. I reckon she knew I was sorry, though. I hope she's happy, up there in the sun … You don't see a lot of young people, here. The ones you do see – they get very down. Though I've heard it said we're not here for ever.'

'She's got babies,' May said. 'Two coloured babies. Don't upset yourself, they have a look of you, Alfred. Lovely boys. Brainy. Healthy … Did you know that, love? Do you know about us?' she asked, then, urgently, seizing his hand, tugging it towards her, telling herself she could make him warm. 'Can you see us, from here, or is it too far?' It mattered to her more than anything, to know if they were able to see or hear, Alfred, her father, her poor dear mother.

But his answer came back hoarse and strained. 'I don't rightly know what I know any more. I seem to be sleeping more than I should. I'm letting you down, May, leaving my post – the cold does something to your brain. Maybe I'm not the man I was.'

'Don't fret, Alfred,' she said, quickly.

'Not getting any younger, you see,' he announced. 'But I'll wait for you, May. No worries on that score. I wouldn't like to think of you here on your own. And then we might take a little trip together. There are other places. The world's your oyster.' But his voice was thinner, reedier, and his hand in hers felt less substantial, and the noise of the engine was growing louder.

Suddenly someone else was in the boat, and Alfred was moaning, moving away. 'Not you,' he was muttering, 'not you in here.'

He was frightened: Alfred, who was frightened of

nothing. A tall dark young man had climbed into the boat. There was a faint smell of salt, and iron. For a moment the light caught his eyes, light golden. May saw those eyes were her grandson's eyes. Sadness came into the boat with the youth, a little mist of regret, and longing. He sat across from Alfred, and stared at him.

'Don't forget me,' he said. 'You won't forget me.'

May knew who he was without being told. She wanted so much to put things right. 'We haven't forgotten you. You're Winston, aren't you? Your brother gave one of his boys your name. He's my grandson. And *his* grandson.'

'I'm cold,' said Winston, shivering. Perhaps he couldn't see her but he spoke to her. 'I wanted to live, the same as you.' Very low and urgent, his teeth chattering. 'I had my chance, but he took it away.'

Now Alfred seized his head in his hands, and started to make a low terrible noise, a noise that May could not bear to hear. 'Oh-oh-oh-oargh,' it sounded like. 'I try to give him my jacket,' he groaned. 'I offer it him, but he'll never take it.'

'Leave him alone, he's upset,' she told Winston, but the skinny youth didn't seem to hear her. He went on talking in the same low voice, bent over Alfred, smelling of blood, and she suddenly glimpsed his great scarf of wet red. 'Jesus, man, just take a look,' and then lights were flashing, and the boatman was shouting –

'Jesus, man, jus' tek a look!' Suddenly May was fully awake, and Ron was waving and shouting at her. It was dark overhead, but great flowers of scarlet were bursting, blooming, everywhere. Then electric blue star-bursts, silver-pink tree-ferns of flickering glitter, lianas of purple, unfurled in sequence across the night. There were explosions, too, like muffled guns, or else people were shooting under cover of the fireworks; perhaps the war had come to the city.

Alfred had gone. She hoped he could see it, but he would worry about the cost. May stared in wonder, all the same.

It went on for ever, more bangs, more colours, and soon she said, 'It's burning money.' She would say his words, if he could not.

''Dis fule fule government,' Ron said. 'Dem 'ave to 'ave some kin' of a show for the Towers.'

And then May started to see, or imagine, orange faces staring out from the balconies as the boat rocked past the last of the towers. There were mirthless cheers as the display climaxed.

May thought suddenly, painfully, of Dirk. Dirk would like the fireworks; he always had done. They'd made less of an effort, because he was the youngest. For the first two, Alfred did proper displays, nailing Catherine wheels to the washing-line posts and bedding rockets in sand-filled bottles. Dirk just got sparklers and a few Vesuviuses which didn't always manage to explode. Darren and Shirley had all the luck.

May ached to make it up to Dirk, before he had to go into the cold for ever.

Thirteen

The Gala! The city must have its Gala.

'EAT, DRINK, FOR TOMORROW YOU DIE' said some of the posters of the One Way protesters. There were hundreds of them; they had cloned themselves, quietly, effectively, down in the dark, through the long winter of wet and fear. They were human; they hoped; they bid for salvation. Now they would be saved, while the others would perish, the rich, the lucky, the lovely, the sinful. They had come here today on a tide of excitement, for round the Towers and in the poor north-east — in the south-east reaches down by the river – in the broken-down estates near the Western Gardens, the refugee centres and 'Canvas Town', in all the districts where One Way was strongest, there weren't enough lucky people to hate. They wanted to see them, they were hungry for the enemy; to sniff their perfume, to snack on their flesh, to feast their eyes on the gloss, the wealth –

Here's Lottie, on cue, arriving with Harold, in a pale velvet coat like frosted cream, her cheeks plumped out with designer hormones, her curls a crisp cap of sculpted gold, smiling, smiling for the cameras as she glides up the steps on Harold's arm; smiling for the unexpected joy of today, smiling with happiness for Harold; smiling for the sex that they had in the bath; smiling as if she had never been hurt, never lost her youth or Hopper's sunlit morning; and that shining smile on a face that can't see them (but Lottie truly can't see the protesters, she's blinded by the flashes of mega-watt lights) drives them to a frenzy of righteous hatred. They scream 'One Way! One Way!' and she flinches: is she driving up a one-way street again? Ah well, it has never stopped her before. Lottie will go wherever she wants to. And Harold is looking particularly handsome; usually melancholy and distinguished, tonight he looks rubicund and rich; onlookers guess that he's a lawyer or banker, when he is just flushed with happiness; Harold's had his phone-call from the publisher; Harold bounds up the steps a success.

Bruno is glad to examine the guilty before they are flung into the fiery pit, though Samuel and Milly, who have recently been quieter, hanging back from Bruno, unsure about Dirk, are trying to restrain the Brothers and Sisters: '"Judgement is mine," saith the Lord,' cries Samuel. 'The Lord will judge in his own good time.'

All the protesters have come tonight. The anti-war lot are out in force, with whistles and hooters and drums and megaphones, furious, howling with their longing for justice, trying to deafen Mr Bliss into peacefulness. 'BLISS OUT!' say dozens of rainbow banners of the blissed-out anti-drug-law protesters. A long-haired boy waves 'GALA IS LA-LA'. 'WHY DO YOU NEED TWO SKINS?' scream the placards of the anti-fur protesters. 'DISS THE BLISS!' shout the teen-friendly slogans of the anti-government campaign. 'BLISS A DEAD LOSS' shouts a hand-lettered poster. 'PISS OFF BLISS' says a turquoise banner. (President Bliss has made further allegations, that afternoon, about sabotage, which he claims 'has endangered the safety of our nation, and is a clear and present danger': the airforce, already flying nightly missions, is promising 'swift, resolute action'; tonight, it is confidently expected, an escalation of the war will be announced, though luckily, it's happening a long way off; nothing to depress the mood of the Gala.)

The politicians who stream to the party in official cars and gleaming suits are feeling liberated from the floods; they sink their rears into the soft leather, they snicker and wisecrack on their phones, they give salty quotes to the newspapers, they wave and give thumbs-up signs to each other. Not many believe in Mr Bliss's war. Now the worst of the flooding is officially over, Bliss's own party can turn on him. Life is going to be fun again.

There are other, quieter protests, held by still figures standing at the back of the crowd packed in round Government Palace. 'WAR REFUGEES' one banner says, and dozens of Loyans stand stiffly beside it, carrying big photos of their ruined homeland, carrying placards with the names of the dead. 'NO HOME, NO MONEY, NO HOPE' a thin-faced woman has written in crooked black letters on a piece of card. It hurts her to see so many happy people, it hurts her to know they don't see her. She thinks that the people invited to the Gala must all have nice homes, and hope, and money, she believes they are smiling, not just for the cameras, which go off round the foyer of Government Palace like a lightning storm against the indigo sky, but at themselves, in invisible mirrors that whisper to them what their lives amount to; theirs are enormous, hers is nothing.

Only the *crème de la crème* have been chosen, the people the city defines itself by, the rich, the celebrities, the people who count, the styles and the faces that are known and copied, stars, actors, leaders, beauties, all the names baptized in the tabloids, famous chefs and fashionistas, ballet-dancers and fancy hairdressers, horoscope-writers and football-players, game-show hosts and TV presenters, all the showmen who make people happy, plus a salting of 'real people' like Elroy, people who have climbed to the top of something worthy, firemen, ambulancemen, doctors, police, who are glad and embarrassed to see the celebrities, staring at them hungrily, sharply assessing, wanting to laugh, to sneer, to wave, sharing space-time with them at last, the dream-figures, the screen-figures ... And yet, they are proud the celebs are here. All the guests have a glow, as they mount the stairs, their shoe-soles massaged by the rouge-red carpet, and caressive little thoughts flit around like bluebirds – 'everyone who's anyone is here, my dear' – and *they* are here, thank God they have made it; the bluebirds of happiness perch on their shoulders; against long odds, home safe, home free; anyone who's anyone, my dear, is here.

'Have you got a permit to do that, sir?' A uniformed man asked Ian McGregor, who has set up an easel near the parapet of the gallery overlooking the stairs, commanding a perfect view of new arrivals.

'Absolutely.'

He looked hard at Ian: decent dinner-jacket. But reddened cheeks, as if he lives outside, and something not right about the mouth. 'Could I see your invitation, sir?'

Ian produced it, left-handed, yawning, without pausing in the sketch he was doing. 'Friend of Mr Bliss's, in fact,' he drawled, his eyes never lifting from the line which unscrolled with complete assurance from the point of his pencil.

His lack of concern convinced the flunkey. 'Right, sir. Sorry, just doing my job,' the man apologized, and turned away. 'Perhaps I can bring you a drink, sir?'

'Well, I'm working – just a glass of water.'

'Thought we'd all had enough water, sir.'

Ian chuckled, obediently, and went on drawing.

As soon as the man was gone, Ian's head swivelled. He resumed watching, with amused interest, something odd going on at a nearby window. A dark-haired, wild-eyed, female figure was hauling itself up outside the glass; first the head, staring through and then disappearing, rising and falling like a cuckoo in a clock; then slender shoulders and golden arms, ringed like a pigeon in thick silver bangles; then finally a curvaceous torso, but it was immediately apparent to Ian that the girl was stuck; she couldn't open the window.

There weren't many people in the gallery. Soon the meeting and greeting would be over and the mass of the crowd would push up the stairs. With a quick glance around, Ian strolled across, saw the eyes out in the night open wide with fear, a convulsive attempt to get away, but he pushed up the window, swiftly but gently, saw there were two of them, tall, pretty, young girls staring and shivering with terror as they tried to cling on to the window-sill. Raising his eyebrows, he pulled them inside.

They fell in, gracelessly, giggling with fear. They were half-naked, in party-clothes. He helped them up; their hands were very cold.

'Are you going to chuck us out?' Lola asked, recovering her confidence (which never took long, for she had drunk it in with her mother's breast-milk). Hearing Lola's bold voice, Gracie stopped shivering.

'Why should I do that?' Ian asked, coolly. 'I'm sure you both have invitations.'

'Are you a proper guest?' Gracie asked him, peering.

'What a rude question,' he said to her. Just at that moment the flunkey arrived in his immaculate jacket, bearing the water on a silver tray with a snow-white napkin. 'Could you bring my two friends champagne?' Ian asked him. 'Come and see my pictures, girls,' he said.

Lola had fallen in love on the spot, but Gracie wasn't quite on Ian's wave-length. He seemed to be taking them too much for granted.

'We haven't really got invitations,' she said.

'Shocking,' he said, waving his finger at her.

'We're anti-capitalist protesters.' It sounded rather silly, said like that.

'Prove it,' he said, and to Lola, showing her the sketch on top of his sheaf of paper, 'What do you think of that?'

It was a picture of a troupe of monkeys, capering across a stage, grinning.

Gracie was tugging at Ian's arm. 'Look,' she said, rather sulkily, and pulled her teensy silk jacket apart to reveal a tinier, tighter top, and conical breasts, lettered in red: 'GLOBAL CAPITAL IS BUST'. 'Do you think it's witty?' she asked, anxious.

'You look very nice. And ... You, um, make your point,' he said gravely. 'But better do it up. People might look.'

'My pants say 'BLISS IS A ARSE', said Lola.

'*AN* arse,' he said. 'You don't have to show me.' But he smiled at her as if he liked her.

'Aren't you going to draw the people here?' she asked him, looking at his sketches of monkeys.

'Oh, I did that this evening, from life,' said Ian. 'I'm doing a sequence, actually. I'm calling it "Party Animals". What are you girls? Mountain goats?'

'My mother's here somewhere,' said Lola, anxious.

'So's mine,' said Gracie, clutching her. 'We'll both get in terrible trouble if they see us. But everyone who's anyone is here.'

Ian gazed at her quizzically. 'So they tell me. But I'm sure there must be other people somewhere.'

He turned back to his easel and started work, frowning down into the crowded foyer.

'I think you girls should go and look around. Lil Missy M is here.'

People were beginning to come upstairs. In the soft bright light from the high chandeliers, under the opalescent glaze of good makeup, everyone looked like film stars; the women had shining, perfect skin, set off by thick milky swags of pearls or dewy filigree wreaths of diamonds, borrowed stones, spectacularly bright; no one was grey, or dusty; the colours of the clothes were luminous, brilliant, the colours of flowers against a summer sky, honeysuckle, morning glory, bougainvillaea, the best dyes on the best fabrics, wool, cashmere, satin, silk, the clear, confident colours of money. Their hair was set like sculpted glass; their nails smooth as bevelled gem-stones. Lola and Gracie watched, impressed, before they remembered they were here to protest.

Everyone was slightly larger than life, laughing more loudly, smiling more radiantly, turning their heads every second or so, so they didn't miss a celebrity. Whispers ran across the shining heads like winds in a field of summer corn. Whole golden rows trembled and quivered. Lola and Gracie darted out like butterflies, following the rumours, skimming the breeze (and older women tracked the two girls with their eyes, envying the silvery youthful something which makeup artists could never copy).

'There's Angela Lamb,' somebody hissed, and the name repeated like a water-mark, 'Angela Lamb', 'Angela Lamb'. 'And that must be her little girl.'

But something wasn't going quite right. 'Gerda,' called a

woman's voice, polite, at first, then louder, 'Gerda', then almost screaming, 'Gerda, will you come back here!'

Some puppyish thing was charging through the flowers, an unseen whirlwind, a little sprinter, half-knocking people over as it ran.

'It's the painter man, Mummy,' Gerda was shouting. 'Look, look, it's the painter man!'

Angela blundered after her, apologizing as she went, suddenly afraid of losing her daughter; there were too many people; too few children, something she had never noticed before when she'd taken Gerda to grown-up parties, but this was a new Gerda, today, a six-year-old tyrant, an adolescent.

Gerda dived for Ian's knees. He looked up, startled, from the pen-and-ink sketch he was doing of a group of vicious penguins. She smiled up at him, confident, but for an instant he didn't know her, used as he was to seeing her windswept and scruffy at the zoo, tugging along her grandparents; he looked down at her shining red hair, her little dress of scarlet satin, her wide blue eyes, staring up at him, and suddenly had it: 'Hello, Gerda ... I'm glad to see you. Have you brought your grandparents?'

'This is my mummy, Angela.'

A blonde woman shot through the crowd, flushed, ruffled, in brilliant pink, her matching boa sliding off one shoulder. 'Gerda, don't run away like that!'

'Mum, it's the painter man from the zoo.'

'I'm sorry,' panted Angela to Ian, registering a handsome man, smiling rather artificially as she tried to conspire with him against her daughter: 'she seems to think she knows you.'

'Oh, I know Gerda,' he said, coolly, and looked Angela up and down, not entirely agreeably, then went back to sketching, with fluid movements, men in dinner-jackets, human penguins, waddling self-importantly across a ball-room.

Gerda watched, intent, as the drawing took shape.

'Do you mind us watching?' Angela asked, in a vain attempt to make him look at her. 'I'm Angela Lamb, the writer, by the way.' His gaze at the paper didn't even flicker, and his expression seemed to say, 'Never heard of her.' She drew her boa around her, nervous; the soft feathers didn't comfort her.

'Please yourself,' he said, but he winked at Gerda.

Angela stared rather hard at Ian, and decided he looked like an ex-alcoholic, with his flushed complexion and mobile mouth, though some people might have thought him attractive. 'How do you know my daughter?' she asked, haughtily, patting her hair, which had been cut and streaked very expensively that day, before she picked up Gilda. It was maddening that he didn't notice her. The pink was skin-tight, and flattered her figure. She ran her fingers across her hip-bone and crossed one ankle over the other, which she'd read somewhere in a magazine made your legs look longer and slimmer. It seemed a lifetime since she'd had a man.

'Menguins,' Gerda suddenly said, then exploding with pleasure, 'They're *menguins*, aren't they?' Ian pointed his pen at her in tribute; the two of them fell about with laughter.

Angela stood there, upstaged by her daughter. The pink feathers were perhaps too youthful. Suddenly she felt very exposed.

Perhaps she would never have a man again.

In two more minutes, though, Gerda was bored. 'I want to find Davey Luck now,' she said.

'They can't concentrate, can they?' asked Angela, one final try at getting Ian to like her, but he had embarked on another picture, a disquieting sketch of a large pink flamingo, its legs entwined without elegance, lost in the middle of a sheet of black water.

Gerda had darted off into the crowd. Peering, preening, Angela followed her.

Everyone was there.

The stars: Lil Missy M, Baby Nana, Woof Daddy Woof, Franky Malone, Desiree D, the Lites, the Three Bones, Cleft (minus their lead singer, stuck in the traffic coming in from the Towers, where she's had a huge row with her boyfriend for letting her lucky stage-shoes get wrecked by the water); the great tenor, Vincenzo Da Vinci, whose luggage has been lost in the half-drowned airport, in a borrowed suit whose waist-band's too tight, unable to resist the lobster creams, which he's throwing down his throat in twos and threes; the young lions of the art scene – Shona Goff, who arrived so drunk she had to be helped up the steps by her dealer, one breast falling out on to her thousand-dollar shoulder-bag, which is a witty *trompe l'œil* of a hamburger; Terry Gribbin, Haroun Al Jezir, and their posse, and Walter the Wank, who is wearing a cod-piece from which there protrudes a shiny pink phallus, perhaps his own, but everyone hopes not; big-name journalists – Darren White (May White's son, Dirk White's brother, over from Hesperica for the Gala, fresh from his third divorce, the 'famous brother' who has always upstaged Dirk, making him feel smaller, stupider, meaner); he has written a daring attack on Bliss exposing his 'sabotage' claims as a fraud, to be published tomorrow in the *Daily Mire*; Darren can't wait, but this evening he's talking with great animation to Bliss's press secretary, Anwar Topping, and anyone would think that they were best mates (Darren's hedging his bets, for if Bliss should survive, he may swallow his medicine and court Darren again, for how many 'radical' journalists are there who went to the same college as him? Darren White has his eye on an honour); Paula Timms, Gracie's journalist mother, who has always thought Darren a total chancer because he earns more money than her, is boring two dancers in skin-tight red latex who unwisely sat down within range for a rest, as she explains how the floods have been unfair to women; Petronella Bella, the gossip columnist, furiously clicking names into her palm-top while throwing tiny yellow pills into her mouth; Amina Patel in an exquisite sky-blue sari, wishing she had never come to this city, wondering how soon she can slip away and help her teenage son with his homework; a yapping kennel of tabloid hacks, tanking up fast on Gala champagne, eager for titbits, sniffing the air, talking to each other till they find someone better, staring shamelessly over their shoulders; the PR people, pushing forward their clients, smiling and oiling at the journalists; a scattering of prostitutes, still young and immaculate, still hoping to alchemize into wives or actresses, still half-believing they are escorts, starlets; and, occasionally cocking an eyebrow at the prostitutes, here are the generals, admirals and air vice-marshals, enjoying the chance to wear all their medals but playing their other cards close to their chests (they are a little abstracted, they have something on their minds, you catch them in pairs, shaking their heads, in corners); and the city's cash-cows, the arms manufacturers, sweating, in mohair suits, and smoking; but why are they so happy? Smiling, high-fiving.

And here are some old stars: Lily de la Lilo, in a metre of cracked makeup and crooked dark glasses, on the arm of Freddy Flatter in his corset and wig, with an emerald silk suit and built-up shoes, both of them baring bleached tusks for the lenses; they try to edge close to some younger stars, in the hope that a little silver youth-dust will blow off, in the hope of being photographed with movers and shakers. Here are some new stars – some very new stars, for Bliss's people, desperate to attract the youth vote, have cast their nets wide: look, Kilda is there!

Yes, 'Madam Kilda the Clairvoyant'! In the first week of her first real job! Introduced to the *Daily Atom* by Davey, amazed, last month, when he was at his mother's, to have his whole past revealed to him by Kilda, who read it from his hand, in a matter-of-fact way, though she did get very weird about his future, where she saw him with a girl in the top of a tree ... Kilda is there, very shy, but radiant, waiting to do a gig in a semi-transparent 'boutique tent' in the Upper

Gallery, its gauze-grey chrysalis enamelled with stars; a very camp young man is sitting taking bookings, and the list is already surprisingly long for a gathering of people scornful of horoscopes; many of them are politicians' wives, and indeed, Berta Bliss herself has signed up, no longer able to predict her husband, who has grown increasingly strange and distant.

(On her way in, Kilda was shocked to see the howling crowd of One Way protesters, stretching clawed hands towards the cars. It felt as if they hated her. They didn't, of course – they couldn't recognize her, behind the smoked glass of the limo, could they? And yet there had been a bad, gut-wrenching moment when the protesters pressed right up against the car and she found herself staring at a thin grey face, twisted with anger: surely Dirk White, and he looked straight at her. But Dirk and she always got on well; he must have thought she was someone else, someone lucky and wealthy who deserved to be hated. What did it mean to be hated so much? Was hatred really in the One Book? She herself only hates her mother. But she loves her mother, deeply, as well.)

As Kilda waits for her gig, she is protected from lechers by the *Atom*'s tiny entertainment editor, Arnie Pippin, who's looking, when she isn't, down her white calm cleavage, and then around the room, with enormous complacency, telling Kilda that 'absolutely everyone is here'. Even *he* has made it: little Arnie Pippin. Arnie Pippin, with the best view of all.

('Would you really say I've, you know, made it, Lottie?' Harold asks Lottie, tongue loosened by champagne. 'If Headstone really want to publish it, and if they like it as

much as they say – will you, you know, be proud of me?'
'Harold! I have always been proud of you.')

'But nobody is here,' Ian mutters to himself, looking round
the room and then down at his paper, where he's sketching a
mob of starving hyenas, jaws splayed wide for wine and
food. So many of the city's people weren't there.

The builders' labourers, the rat-catchers (though the rats
are there, just beneath the floor, in the U-bends of the staff
lavatories, and round by the bins, in a frenzy of activity,
sniffing and whiffling at the wonderful plenty, the prawn
heads, the chicken skins, the lambs' feet, the creamy shell of
cooling fat skimmed off the gravy); the door-to-door
vendors of dish-cloths and oven gloves; the sanitary
engineers, the plumbers; the bus conductors with their
ticket-machines; the lice inspectors with their nit-combs; the
primary school-teachers (no one wants to be told things);
the hospital auxiliaries, the midwives.

The babies: the future hasn't come to the party.

The past isn't here: the old, the dying.

The bin-men with their grinding lorries, unable to service
their normal districts, the rubbish-bags bobbing away on the
water, splitting and rotting into the future.

The illegal immigrants aren't here, with their stuttering
vehicles and singsong accents, their second-hand clothes,
their makeshift lives.

The mini-cab drivers, with their long sad stories of study
and exile, their cigs and their prayer-beads, their hopes for a
future unutterably different in a decent country with jobs

and money, their humbling knowledge that none of their passengers ever remembers their names or faces, their cab-drivers' destiny of driving the ignorant to places beyond the ends of the earth – the mini-cab drivers were left at the door.

The cleaners, getting up every morning at four, to be at work at six, with their roughened hands; no one invited them to bring their knee-pads, no one wants to see their broken shoes; no one wants the cleaners to arrive till tomorrow, when the dregs of the party are vomited out.

The young offenders, hiding drugs in their anuses and crying at night because they miss their mothers, packed in four to a cell since the flood-waters entered the lower floors of the city prison – the young offenders haven't been invited, though those wretched kids would like nothing more than a glimpse of Lil Missy M's big mouth and booty; her picture is stuck to the walls of their cells, but no one has heard of them, nobody likes them, nobody wants them, none of them is here (but the drugs are at the Gala, in a thousand different stashes, in pockets, in cummerbunds, in bras, in purses, being sniffed and injected in the elegant toilets).

The has-beens aren't here; the entertainers who would have been here a decade ago: the former beauties, the stand-up comedians now wobbling badly in the provinces, the It girls who lost whatever It was, the actors who never made it in Hesperica, the PR moguls who drank it away, the writers who didn't win the Iceland Prize, the politicians who were voted out and ended up selling crooked time-shares –

Oh, and by the way, Mr Bliss isn't here. The president! He

hasn't arrived yet; he is too important. He has orders to give
to the military; decisions to make about what to tell the
country. Bliss has equal billing at tonight's Gala with Trinny
the Tranny, the most famous female impersonator in the
world! Yet Mrs Bliss waits for him anxiously: what Madam
Kilda told her was most alarming, though some of the
details are blurred with champagne – but Mr Bliss still isn't
here.

Actually, most of the world isn't here.

May isn't there. May has never been asked to balls or galas,
nor expected to be.

   She was thrilled, though, when Shirley and Elroy were
invited. As May carries on her interminable voyage back
from the Towers to the land of the living, she imagines her
daughter, in the warm, in the light, dressed to the nines, with
Elroy, and smiles: Shirley should have the good things of life.
That's how it is, for the young generation. Life must be
better, warmer, brighter. The knowledge fortifies May
against the night.

   But Dirk – she thinks, with a sinking heart.

Dirk White could never get in to the Gala, though if he had,
it might have satisfied something, a long ago need for fun
and lightness, the years of hopeless birthday parties –
('When you've got more friends, we'll have more of a do.')

Dirk is outside on the street with his placard. Dirk is having a not-bad time, prophesying against the godless, shouting and screaming and blowing a whistle. But something, a small sharp painful something, is nipping at him, underneath all the noise, and the nips get ever sharper, more spiteful. It was Kilda he'd seen, he knows it was, driving up in a dirty great white limousine and poncing up the steps with an ugly little midget, all tarted up, not looking at him. Kilda, who'd once acted like she liked him. Kilda, who'd made out that she was his friend. A great fury picks Dirk up and lifts him; they always disappoint him; they always let him down; there is nothing worth having in life except anger.

He will tell Bruno. Kilda will be finished. Crushed, humbled. *Vengeance is mine.*

(And why should she get in, a mere girl, a mere woman – a bit of a loony, who thinks she sees the future – while Dirk is left outside on his own?)

And Davey isn't at the Gala either; 'Mr Star-Lite' isn't there. Famous Davey, beautiful Davey, billed to introduce the stars; Davey Lucas, nicknamed 'Luck', just as his lucky mother once was. On every invitation his name is engraved, as large as the names of the stars, in gold. (When she saw the stiff card with its bevelled edges, Lottie shrieked 'HAROLD! Davey's really made it!' and Harold smiled, he has a soft spot for Davey, but for a few hours he was a little low.)

Something's up with Davey. He is ultra-reliable; that was one of the reasons for inviting him, because Davey claims to be a Straight Edger; Davey, in theory, doesn't drink, or take drugs; such a great role model for all his young fans; yet Davey has cancelled. Davey isn't here. Hundreds of young women will be disappointed.

Kylie Spheare is listening to her messages. 'Fucking Straight Edgers,' she snarls, furious. 'Fuck fuck fuck fuck fuck fuck f-u-u-u-ck! I mean, fuck. Fucking, *fucking* astrologer ...' But she has other things to think about; the amplifiers have been giving problems; Vincenzo Da Vinci has been sick; there is total confusion among Bliss's advisers as to whether or not he is going to make it. She runs her eye briefly down the guest-list. 'Find Freddy Flatter, he'll jump at it. He's an old ham, he can do it standing on his head –'

'Hope not,' someone says, 'his wig'll fall off.'

'Somebody should tell that little cunt Lucas he's not as hot shit as he thinks,' Kylie spits.

Shirley isn't here, though May believes she is. Shirley has fallen asleep, accidentally, the thermometer still clutched in her hand, wearing a sick-stained dressing-gown, on the floor of Winston and Franklin's bedroom. Her last thought is, 'It's much too high,' before sleep comes to dissolve her worry.

The Gala speeds along its programmed groove. The crowd feels good; the crowd feels great. The rains are over; the flood's going down; the city is back under control again. Spring has sprung, and they long to be happy. Hundreds of faces flush with alcohol; drink trickles through into their brains, their spines, at first a stimulus, later a quietus; thousands of blood-vessels circulate the alcohol that livers are too overloaded to deal with; dozens of brains start a pleasant short-circuit; laughs get louder, gestures wilder; on the fourth or fifth drink, speech slurs, eyes blur, but the drinkers are still feeling pretty terrific. Dozens of endangered species are eaten, flown in for the occasion from all round the world, plucked or skinned, pulped or tenderized, smoked or grilled, glazed or in paté, marinated, macerated, boned, *done,* their animal nature vaporized. Several hundred cards with contact details are whisked by slick digits from pocket to pocket; unmeant promises to call are lavished; married couples meet up and quarrel, because one of them has had too much fun; sexual assignations are requested, and granted; a couple has sex in a cupboard on a landing at the back of the tent where Madam Kilda is performing; a lot of white powder has drifted like fine silver snow on to the plains of polished parquet, but more has slip-slithered through mucous membranes; pupils are dilating, heart rhythms jitterbugging, coke-heads are pelting like anorexic greyhounds round silver race-tracks of lucid psychosis, higher, faster, now spinning off skywards ... A fight has begun between the entourages of Woof Daddy Woof and the Three Bones; security's summoned to the dressing-rooms, and Lil Missy M has a hissy fit, saying she won't perform without her boyfriend, the road manager for Woof Daddy Woof; the police appear to reinforce security, thus missing messier things elsewhere – two journalists break each other's noses in a brawl over a woman uninterested in either; three security guards rape a prostitute who had climbed on to the roof to look at the view (lucky for her she is a prostitute, because if she were not, they would have to push her off; as it is they know she won't dare complain).

Elroy has come to the Gala alone, finding every one of his girlfriends was out. He feels virtuous that he didn't bring a woman. He stands by a window where the crowd is thinner to telephone Shirley and tell her he loves her; but he looks a little pensive when he flips off the phone. Biting his lip, he stares out into the darkness, where part of him registers a woman is screaming, an unearthly sound blowing down from the roof-top which must be part of the entertainment ... Shirley said Winston was fine, but was she just being noble? And she sounded sleepy; he'd woken her up. Elroy wishes he hadn't phoned. For a second he wonders if he should go home, but it's not even twelve, the night is young, and the Bengal tigers will soon be performing. Shirley wouldn't want him to miss the tigers. Elroy can't hear the screams any more. He beckons a waiter: more champagne.

Rhuksana and Mohammed aren't at the party. Mohammed wasn't at work today. Helena Harp had rung; he had missed a big meeting; he would not talk to her; he did not care.

Now Rhuksana is taking a phone-call from Loya. She stands there shaking with the phone in her hand, looking through the doorway into their bedroom. She cannot breathe, she cannot think. Her ears are ringing; the world has turned red. Perhaps this is what dying is. Mohammed is praying, as he has been for days, since the news came through about the burning of the library. His dear dark head is prone on the floor. Such pain as this she cannot bear to give him, for it is his mother on the phone, sobbing, ringing to tell them his sister's been shot through the head in a ricochet from a soldier's bullet, walking through the streets in search of bread, his beloved sister, the pearl of his heart, and everything precious dissolves in blood.

The One Way protesters outside Government Palace have sloshed the front steps with scarlet paint while the guards were distracted, peering in through the doors at Lola and Gracie, half-naked and gorgeous, skanking to the music of Baby Nana, surrounded by an ice-storm of flashing paparazzi (Lottie and Harold look across with a smile and say doesn't that girl remind them of Lola? – though thank God she'd never wear *quite* so little); Gerda is sitting on Angela's lap, watching the beautiful big girls dancing while her mother spoon-feeds her wild-raspberry ice-cream; they are both, for once, completely happy. The kitchen staff are still working full tilt, their arms and hands flying like demented knitters as they try to keep pace with the mouths of the guests, their appetites doubled by drugs and alcohol; the party-goers want to keep on climbing, they want to be bigger, higher, *more*, they need the pleasure rush to come faster ...

But quite soon, most of the dancers will tire. Most of them

start to feel gravity tugging, a twinge of fatigue, a sour
dottle of glut, their eyelids beginning to granulate in the
yellowing stare of the chandeliers; their cheek-muscles drag,
their jaw-bones sag ...

The night can't be over, at only half-past midnight. Where is
the president, Mr Bliss?

You must understand, he's been awfully busy.

There's a fuss going on, by the main doors. People in dark
coats; the night has swirled in, surrounded by police, lights,
cameras. Ah. At last, Mr Bliss is here! ('Keep Berta away
from him,' the word goes out. Berta Bliss, his wife, has spent
more than half an hour in the tent of Kilda the Clairvoyant;
and emerged very tired and emotional, clutching an empty
bottle of fizz.)

He's a little late for people's full attention. People are
slumped together on the dance-floor; sitting in corners,
wound around each other; crouched in toilets, reviving
themselves. Freddy Flatter is both drunk and nervous; he had
let himself relax, at the end of his gig, and the quiff of his
toupee has slumped on to his forehead; he tries to hold it up
with his limp left hand as he introduces Bliss with his be-
jewelled right; he hopes that this looks more coquettish than

desperate, but as he leaves the stage, with a debonaire snicker, he trips on the mike wire, and the thing falls off, lying on the floor like a lost bit of wild-life.

Mr Bliss doesn't notice the thinness of his audience. He's used, after all, to performing to parliament. And he is surrounded by his own people, his gleaming place-men, smiling and nodding. They are salt of the earth; they understand him. He begins quite blandly; he celebrates 'our history' (meaning twenty-five years of the tourist industry); he says how successful the city is, how people flock here from all over the world (he's referring to tourists, not refugees); and then he moves on to the momentous present. History, he says, is in the making. Mr Bliss's lieutenants clap and whistle when he talks of 'deep conviction', of 'decisive moments', of 'necessary resolve'. 'No precipitate action' (they exchange veiled glances), but 'we shall prevail' because 'our cause is just'.

He comes to a climax, and looks down, modestly. He's done his best, as he always does. Now he waits for the guaranteed tide of applause. He doesn't hear it, but he still looks up with the engaging grin that says he is pleased, the reward he habitually gives his audience, telling them he likes them all, *personally*. It is true, alas. Bliss loves and needs them. 'Look, guys, I'm happy to answer questions.' He knows the answers to the ones that are coming.

But he isn't prepared for the red-headed child who suddenly rushes down the room towards him, evading his bodyguards, escaping her mother, so he has to smile sweetly and answer her question, though kids are always unpredictable: 'I'm Gerda,' she says, as clear as a bell, into the microphone a reporter has given her. 'Mr Bliss, why have you got your clothes on?'

He laughs, as amiably as he can, a politician enjoying children. His red shirt had been carefully chosen. 'Wouldn't I look funny if I came to a party without any clothes on? You've got a very pretty dress, Gerda.'

He grins at the cameras, ready to move on. But then, to his horror, the wretched child, who must have been put up to it by one of his enemies, informs the room, 'My friend Ian is a famous painter. He says you're the Emperor with No Clothes.'

Her red hair glints as the room sniffs blood.

At four a.m., when all the humans have gone, the last waft of pink boa and flicker of snakeskin, and the last of the kitchen-staff, trying to close the bins, which bulge open, gleaming, in the stormy moonlight – at four a.m., before the cleaners arrive, before the sun comes up, though the sky has begun to have a pinkish tinge, an uneasy, flesh-coloured, nauseous underbelly – there is a sudden wave of smell on the air: an acrid, musky, urinous smell, a smell like a swipe from the rough paw of a bear.

And then they arrive, sprinting through the water, seen only by terrified, fleeing rodents, twenty, thirty, a hundred foxes, a tide of muscle and bone and bite, shoulder to shoulder, brush to brush, a brazen army of invading red dogs, snapping and sniffing and straddling the dustbins with their strenuous paws and strong narrow bodies, rooting up the lids, the moonlight catching the coarse silver hairs on their strong hind-quarters and the smudge of dark fur down their whipcord spines. Their nostrils flare at the scent of meat, fat and roast skin and split marrow-bone, all the glorious detritus of the human banquet; and out in the open, as the moon starts to fade and the sun heaves up behind dreary cloud, the foxes drip spittle and truffle and gorge, and, sated, spat and gavotte with each other, nip each other's necks, bare teeth in greeting. Time for the foxes to have their Gala.

Then they melt sinuously away. Most of the foxes are leaving the city.

Fourteen

Professor Sharp has tried all the official channels, but Mr Bliss doesn't want the population alarmed. He has serious issues for them to think about: national security: patriotic duty; protecting freedom; pre-empting the enemy. A meteoroid would upstage him totally. The government refuses to issue any warnings. If there's to be alarm, Mr Bliss means to cause it. And the media are surfeited with cosmic disasters; the weekend newspapers have all run 'exclusives' about tomorrow's *End of the World Spectacular*: radio and TV news already have Davey Lucas booked for the morning. When Professor Sharp, not half so well known (though infinitely better qualified) with a boring voice and a skin problem, rings up and says there is an cometoid coming, they say they will ring him back, and laugh.

Now Sharp and his colleagues think laterally.

When the first news about the cometoid reached him from

the Observatory – Professor Sharp himself, ringing urgently – Davey was cockahoop to be called by the man who so recently dismissed him as a charlatan, in the thick of the outcry at the weekend. He didn't really listen to the content of the call. Obviously Sharp wanted to get himself on TV. Davey cut in and said he was too busy to talk, he would try to get back to the professor tomorrow.

He was, in fact, busy; he was choosing shirts; the blue was his favourite, but poor for TV; he had been warned that Bliss would be wearing red, to project a positive, optimistic image, and most colours seemed to clash with it. He was starting to think he would fall back on white: white, white, white delight: he had taken just a little of his white powder, just enough to keep dancing above the gulf that very occasionally opened beneath him, way beneath him, he was rising, rising ... The performer's adrenalin is already in him, a net of wired nerves winding slowly higher, he has left the foothills, he will soon be flying –

Then Sharp's voice came again from far below. It was faint, pointless. Sharp understood nothing, or else he, Davey, understood nothing.

Besides, the drugs are dancing today. Davey has also taken one more valium than he usually uses before his show. (Delorice didn't like it, but she was at the office. He wished she were here to hear his speech. He wished the Observatory would stop ringing.)

Davey took another valium, and lay on the bed, and tried to think what his life was about. Nothing at all came; just blankness. He thought, my parents. Lola. Delorice. But they had no faces, they were just a list. They seemed to come, though, with a weight of pain, as if they were slipping away into the dark, as if something very heavy might fall on them, soundlessly, slowly, from very far away. Usually the valium made him numb. He took another tablet, irritably; thought, with sudden clarity, about his step-grandmother, Sylvia, Harold's mother, the sense of white nothingness after her heart attack, the nagging question, where could she have gone? Where do we go, he thought, mind slurring, why are we going, going, gone ... The drugs were failing to keep their promise, to hold him tight in their sealed white moment; terror and loss were leaking in.

He woke at six p.m.; the phone was ringing, but he rushed to the bathroom, and vomited. His whole being was pulled out of his throat, surge after surge of wracking retching. After he was finished, he washed his face, brushed his teeth, felt suddenly sober. His head was clear. The fog was gone.

Davey goes and listens to his messages to see if he has dreamed it all, but the professor's messages all say the same thing, and he understands that the drugs were the dream, the drugs and the shirts and the money and the palace, his weekly programmes, his teenage fans, the scripts he reads that someone else has written, the nonsense about the alignments of the planets on which he has wasted so much spacetime, the second-rate telescopes he advertises, the makeup girls who fake-tan his skin.

There is a noise at the back of the house, and he turns to look out of the basement window, hoping Delorice has changed her mind and come home, though she's due to meet him at the Gala. He has to talk to her, to tell her everything. He loves her completely; he needs her to love him, but first she has to know the whole truth about him. He thinks he can trust her to go on loving him.

Something else is standing on the wall in the light. The fox, his fox, alert, intent, red as the earth, its breath steaming. Davey looks out, and the fox looks in.

A moment later, Davey picks up his mobile and calls Kylie Spheare to apologize.

Davey rings round the taxi firms so he can work on the journey to the Observatory; he doesn't want Professor Sharp to think him a fool, though he's uneasily aware that he *has* been a fool: the floods of letters, phone-calls, e-mails challenging last weekend's saturation publicity for his *Planets Line-Up!* programme has taught him he is a bit of a fool, though the TV station was sanguine – ('It's a *response*, Davey, it's great, it shows the whole world is going to watch us'). He calls Delorice, again and again, but her phone battery's flat, though she doesn't know it, the thing lies dead in the bottom of her handbag, she is walking round the Gala looking for him, and the tender electric artery between them is broken.

The cab carries Davey on the motorway through the flooded land on the way to the Observatory. The orange sky over the city gradually gives way to silvered darkness. Looking up, as he does, every now and then, from the rough calculations on his palm-top, he glimpses the constellations and shivers. They look white, distant, as they always do. Tonight's starlight set off towards him thousands and thousands of years ago. But the planets, thinks Davey, looking at the moon, which is bright, today, on this cold clear night, the planets are a thousand times nearer. Usually the planets lie well-spaced; they are plot-able, predictable, as novels. The asteroids and cometoids are wilder, more eccentric, shooting far out in space, far beyond our own galaxy, then plunging back steeply in to the centre, nearer than the planets, crossing and re-crossing them. Each time the orbits are a little different, and each changed orbit changes other orbits, though most of the time, in a short human lifetime, they all whiz safely round the asteroid belt.

But every so often, the pattern fractures. Maybe the galaxy is bored with balance. Maybe it gets tired of a life-form's persistence. Perhaps it wants to make room for something different, something less myopic than the city-dwellers ...

Not so very rarely in a human lifetime, many times in a hundred years, a near-earth object careens towards us. The tiny ones flare into golden dust, but sometimes a large one keeps right on going.

Then senior professors call TV astronomers.

Then stories enter a phase of chaos.

Fifteen

Moira is awake an hour before usual. She claws her light on, the bedside light which is the one luxury she has kept (for her books are work, the works of the Lamb – she longs to lose them, but not yet, not yet) and reads her daily pages of the Bible. Her dog cocks an ear, moans, turns over and runs in his sleep as she intones: 'Let the waters teem with countless living creatures … sea-monsters, and every kind of bird'.

Moira feels unaccustomed happiness. This morning, at last, she has her mission. Moira is needed; she has been called. There is thunder below, as there often is, as if someone were battering up at her floorboards, but this time she has an official message. Yesterday a servant had come to her door, a fat scratching woman with a piece of paper: 'It's the, you know, radio. They want you to ring them.'

She had wondered, at first, if it was a trap, but if it was, she had to endure it. The man she got through to sounded hectically keen; they'd managed to trace her through the Institute. 'We want a nice little item about the Gala. If you happened to have any thoughts about that, you're a cultural critic, I believe, you might want to put the case against, a lot of people feel it wasn't, let's say, appropriate –'

'It's sinful,' Moira had told him, firmly.

'Oh good,' he said, 'I hoped it would be simple, I'm sure you've done this kind of thing before, nothing too heavy, there's a three-minute slot, and we're hoping to find at least one more speaker –'

(He didn't add, as he might have done, 'But we can't find anyone, they're all at the Gala, all the halfway decent speakers have their voicemail on.')

A car would arrive for her at seven. So Moira had become important again. Life pushed anew through her poor shrivelled fingers, her dry veiny legs, her stiffened bones. 'Let the waters teem with countless living creatures …' She contained multitudes; sea-birds fluttered under the pale freckled skin of her breast; her hollow belly held sea-monsters; she is distended, she is pregnant.

'Flood sickness.' All over the city, people woke up, stretched out, half asleep, to the radio or their TV remotes, and heard the phrase; it didn't mean much. It was just something new, in the bones of their heads, a new little swimmer, dim and featureless, struggling, quietly, to make some headway against their conviction the floods were over.

Party-goers woke who had hardly slept, tossing and turning through the short chilly hours when the highs drain away and the headaches begin; when the brilliant conversations they thought they were having start to snag, and convulse, and torment the speakers; everything false, stupid, dead; they remember they loved the things they betrayed, the wife, the children, the faith, the party; shame abrades them like sandpaper. There is no escape. They twitch with horror. They remember the laughter, the howling faces, the cards scattered and already forgotten, dropped in a taxi like dirty snow, the principles they did not stand up for because so many people were laughing, the shallow promises they'll never keep: 'Stay in touch': 'You must come to dinner': 'I'll send you a postcard': 'Let's have lunch'. The bed is rigid, comfortless, wrinkled. They are very cold, and very hot. Nothing can calm their restless limbs. They are longing to sink down deep, deep into the dark place where it can all be forgotten, but light has imprinted itself like a migraine; they see it again, hear it again; the Gala will go on happening for ever, a fluorescent stage where they gibber like monkeys, bare-arsed, helpless, and everyone sneers.

Hands reach out and click the switch on. 'Flood sickness …', they hear. 'Flood sickness.'

May woke at six, looked at her watch, and tried to go back to sleep again. She had planned to have a lie-in, this morning, after the awfulness of last night, to fortify herself for her return, but instead she lies wakeful, tossing and turning.

May believed in goodness, and trying to be kind. She hoped she had passed that on to her kids, though she wasn't what anyone would call religious. Yet all her kids had turned into believers. Shirley was always in church with the kids, Darren had his Marxism, which was like religion, because he held on to it no matter what, even though he was so wealthy, and never seemed to share it; and now Dirk, who she thought could never be religious, because things like that were beyond his ken, had turned into a pillar of this One Way lot. Who weren't properly Christians, nor Muslims, nor Jews. They just wanted to be better than anyone else, more this, more that, more pure, less worldly – yes, that was the word, 'fundamentalist'. A world that had no light and shade.

Did it come from Alfred? Perhaps it did. Alfred believed in things like Justice, with a capital 'J', and Standards, with a capital 'S'. May had more sense, because she was a woman ...

As May lay there, sleepless, trying to understand, Dirk became more than ever like Alfred, a solitary figure who needed comfort. Something stirred, something new she had never felt for Dirk, something tender started to grow inside her, something warmer than duty, stronger than guilt.

She was over seventy, yes, but she wasn't useless. She fell asleep with hope in her heart.

But she woke again still tired from her journey, knowing she had to go back again, to the chilly world of stairwells and water and crying children and needle-marked arms, of coloured people and blood-red writing. She flicked on the radio; her arm was aching. 'Flood sickness,' she heard. 'Flood sickness.'

She turned over on to her good shoulder and drifted off, briefly, over the water, in a safe warm ship, with Alfred as pilot ...

The radio suddenly screamed in her ear. It wasn't a dream; it was an old woman, screaming. 'These are the LAST DAYS! It has all been written! There is One Way, One Path, One Truth ... There is rushing water and the deep roar of thunder ... the Lamb is standing on Mount Zion already, and with him are a hundred and forty-four thousand people with his name and the name of the Father on their foreheads ... They alone from the whole world will be ransomed! No lie will be found on my lips; I am faultless ... but those who have worshipped the beast and its image, they shall drink the wine of God's wrath ... they shall be tormented in sulphurous flames ...'

'Thank you very much,' the presenter was saying, having vainly tried to interrupt the woman every other scream or so, 'Thank you very much, Dr Moira Penny. I'm afraid we have to leave it there. Our next item is about the kind of boots people are wearing to beat the floods ...'

Religion, May thought. It could turn your brain. She imagined a giant lamb on a mountain, surrounded by thousands of normal-sized people. You couldn't take it seriously, could you? Though she'd have to be careful not to laugh at Dirk. It wasn't a good idea to laugh at men.

She got up, sighing, pulled her dressing-gown on, resigning herself. Let the day begin.

Moira is hustled away to the front door of the radio station
by youthful minions who try not to look at her, though she
notes the glances of wild amusement they shoot sideways
under their brows at each other. She doesn't care; she rises
above them; she flays, with her eyes, the pasty young faces;
God has prepared the lake of fire and sulphur. She clings to
the door frame, suddenly tired. Recently she has not been
eating.

'Aren't you going home?' the girl asks her, rudely.

But the boy touches her arm. 'She isn't well. We'll get you
a taxi, Mrs ...' He consults his notes. 'Mrs Lamb.'

And then the madwoman is screaming again. 'Angela
Lamb? Angela Lamb? How dare you call me Angela Lamb?'

He hurriedly looks at his notes again. 'Sorry, sorry. Dr
Penny.' 'Moira Penny' had been pencilled in after the Lamb
woman cancelled at the last moment. Extraordinary reason,
for such a well-known writer, who you would expect to be
well-organized; she said she had to look after her daughter.

Angela Lamb's got parent trouble. Her parents have always
got up early in the morning; something to do with the jobs
they once did, when they always had to be up by six. They
have read the paper; they have heard the news, while most of
the city is still sleeping.

Angela has always had trouble with her parents, since she
was a child, long ago, and Henry drank, and fought with
Lorna, though he hasn't drunk for thirty years. She has
always been dragging them, shyly, unwillingly, into the
present, into the future. They hadn't really wanted to come

back to the city; they had managed to buy their flat by the sea, in the sleepy old town with beach-huts and donkeys, but they gave up their safe quiet life, and came. And now perhaps they must lose it again.

'You leave, if you want to,' Angela said, furious. 'You go and fight your way on to the buses. It's not going to happen. It never does. I used to get so scared in the eighties, I used to believe every scare meant war. This is just the ridiculous Mr Bliss. And this other thing you're talking about, this TV astrologer, whoever he is, probably the one that Gerda is in love with' (unlike her parents, she hasn't heard the news, she's done nothing of late but look after Gerda, who hasn't let her mother out of her sight since that terrible morning of begging and weeping; but the Gala – so decadent, so theatrical! – has given her lots of ideas for a novel, and now that she's absolutely raring to go, her parents are asking her to leave the city!) 'We aren't going to take any notice of *him*. I mean, really. An asteroid! It's a cliché from a Hesperican movie.'

Her daughter's scorn was always unpleasant, but this time Lorna decided to withstand it. 'What if it happens?' she said. 'What if it actually happens, Ange? Gerda's just a child. She hasn't had her life. This man was just saying we should move inland.'

'STOP TRYING TO MAKE ME FEEL GUILTY,' screams Angela, agonized, turning away. 'I have important work to do. She's my daughter. I can look after her.' (This statement is manifestly untrue; other people have looked after Gerda for years.)

Lorna goes very red in the face. She will not let Angela

make her cry. She loves her granddaughter. She's going to say it. 'Don't you love her, Angela? – Don't you love Gerda more than your work?'

As she asks the question, Gerda walks through the door. She looks rather fancy, for an ordinary day, in the red satin dress that she wore to the Gala, which has dark sorbet stains across the front, but she has decided to wear it again. After all, it was the dress she wore to see all the famous people, and finally, to meet an emperor, though her grandma wouldn't believe it when she told her.

Gerda hears the question Grandma asked her mother. Her mouth drops open with pity and horror. How can people say such things, and not die? Her mother has her hands over her face, and is crying big splashy interesting tears that burst through the gaps between her fingers. 'Naughty Grandma,' Gerda says. 'Of course Mum loves me. You made her cry.'

'I do love you,' sobs Angela. 'And I love Granny. I love her too.'

The three women sit there, hugging and weeping.

'Isn't it time to go and pick up Winston?'

On good behaviour, trying to be Mummy, Angela wipes her eyes and agrees.

The taxi-driver has his radio on. Moira knows she has to suffer it, it is all foretold, the tittering youngsters, the blaring voices, the hot rough car that shakes her exposed bones painfully against the seat. But then something catches her ear, and she finds that God has been good to her, yes, his mercy, yes, it is infinite, towards all those on the One True Path.

He is using a young astronomer, whose name is Davey, which means: David, beloved of God. He is talking of stars and portents. His tired young voice – for they are all tired, all God's true prophets are tired by their work, though they take it up gladly, the cross of endeavour, but mercy, mercy, show me mercy, show me a sign oh Lord, she weeps, for her ribs are painful, and her crumbling backbone – explains that the planets are lining up. Mercury, Mars, Venus, Jupiter, Saturn, Neptune, Uranus … For a minute she thinks he says it isn't important, that there is something else he wants to tell us, but she knows her ears can sometimes deceive her; besides, she is counting, feverishly. Seven. And even seventy times seven …

'To the angel of the church of Ephesus write: "These are the words of the One who holds the seven stars in his right hand … From the throne went out flashes of lightning and peals of thunder. Burning before the throne were seven flaming torches, the seven spirits of God, and in front of it stretched what seemed a sea of glass, like a sheet of ice."'

Her eyes stare out across the empty water, her fingertips wander across the car-window, its shining, blank, inhuman surface, wanting to touch something, to grasp, to feel.

Shirley opens her door, bleary-eyed, half-dressed, expecting to see their familiar postman, but instead she is faced by a smartly dressed woman, smiling a bright, rather tense, smile; but her eyes look red, as if from weeping.

'How do you do,' the woman says. 'I'm Angela Lamb. And this is Gerda.'

Peering round from behind her is a laughing little girl.

'Say hello, Gerda,' the woman instructs her. 'We are so looking forward to our time with Winston.'

The girl ignores her mother. 'Where's Winston?' she asks.

Shirley stands looking at them blankly. 'Sorry, I've overslept, Franklin's not well …'

'When I phoned last night you said Winston was better?' the woman inquires, with the hint of a frown.

'Yes, Winston's fine, he's up watching TV –'

'I'll go and find him.' Gerda darts inside.

'I'm just not sure –' Shirley rubs her eyes. 'Franklin wasn't well last night.' She hasn't even had a cup of tea this morning; she slept with the boys; she hasn't seen Elroy; she doesn't quite know what day it is.

Angela's first impressions are poor. This woman is hopelessly disorganized. But she makes an effort, and smiles once more. 'Shall I wait in the car while you, er, get ready?'

'I'm just not sure –' Shirley mumbles. 'I don't know whether it's infectious.'

'Oh, Gerda's terribly healthy,' says Angela. She still sees doubt in the woman's eyes. 'I'm going to take them to the Western Gardens. I've planned it all. I can't disappoint her.'

Afterwards, the visit is dream-like, to Shirley. Gerda ran around like a little whirlwind, fetching Winston's coat, getting his trousers on, making sure he has his Bendy Rabbit, which she evidently knows he won't move without. Winston's so excited he tears from the house without saying goodbye to anyone, and to Shirley's surprise, the woman drives off without any further attempt to make contact. It's almost like a kidnapping.

Shirley stands in the hall; she has no shoes on; her lids are heavy; Winston has gone.

She checks that Elroy's asleep in their bedroom. Then she slips back in to have a look at Franklin. He has his back to her. He is sleeping. Shirley lies down on the fluffy rug, just for a moment, beside his bed, pulls the duvet over her, just for five minutes, and then falls deeply asleep until ten. She is half-aware that Franklin has joined her.

Faith wakes up in a steaming temper. In fifteen years, she has been late once. Now thanks to her lump of a girl, it has happened again. Switching off the alarm, she's slept stubbornly on to the hour when normal people get up, people who don't clean, lazy buggers. Civilians, she thinks, for she is a soldier. But soldiers are never allowed to be late. She rolls out of bed in a single movement. No holidays for people like Faith. If she had a holiday, what would Lottie do? (And yet part of Faith would love to stop, just once, to lie in and dream or watch the world go by ... but today is the opposite of a holiday.)

Kilda had come in at half-past four, stinking of drink, and with money in her handbag, which Faith searched when her daughter collapsed on the floor, just in case the great lummox had been taking drugs. There were hundreds of dollars, in crisp new notes, and the girl was slurring about telling fortunes, and a luxury tent, and her own show. She was drunk as a lord and babbling rubbish. Faith shouted at her, and when Kilda ignored her, the two of them had a fight on the stairs.

Faith snatches up her mobile as she runs to clean her teeth. No one answers at the Segall-Lucas household. The machine is on, so she makes her excuses. Kilda is ill – and she *will* feel ill, Faith assures herself, grimly, banging the bathroom door, wrenching the taps on with special violence. Then she makes herself coffee and a doughnut with jam, and puts on the TV as loud as she can, hoping to give her daughter a headache.

Kilda's sleeping with people for money, Faith knows, though she has only the vaguest idea what that means, for Faith has only ever slept with one man in her life, and that was Kilda's father. She didn't much enjoy it; it was quick, and furtive, but it wasn't hard work, and Kilda is lazy … Besides, the girl has no other talents.

My daughter is a prostitute. Faith starts planning how to deal with it. The magazines sometimes have articles about them, the ones Mrs Segall passes on to her from the tottering piles by Lola's bedside. They look a lot better turned out than her daughter.

She will lock her in, for a start, Faith thinks. She will beat her, though when Faith tries to imagine it, she remembers Kilda's much bigger than her. A slap is different to a good beating.

Jam spurts from the doughnut, all over her shirt. Faith sponges it, disconsolate. 'Jesus Mary and Joseph,' she says.

Her best efforts, and it all goes wrong. Kilda had been such a lovely baby.

Mrs Segall's boy, Davey, is on the TV. Doing very well for

himself, that one. Usually she never watches his show. She wishes that Kilda had a boyfriend like that. But when she starts listening to what he's got to say, she finds Davey is talking about planets, and comets, and Faith remembers the stupid piece in last weekend's paper, the *Sunday Atom*, warning about all sorts of disasters. So is he an astrologer, a horoscope man? Does Kilda get her daft ideas from him?

Faith switches it off in disgust. 'Kilda!' she yells. 'Get your arse out of bed.'

Kilda doesn't get her arse out of bed. Since she was just a mite she liked lying in bed. From Kilda's room, only heavy silence.

Faith calls twice more, with ascending volume. Her throat starts to hurt. Her temper worsens. In a moment, she snaps. Though for many weeks Kilda's not let anyone in to her bedroom, Faith hammers on the door, and then bursts in.

She expects to see mess, slathers of clothes, dirty plates, and some evidence of prostitution: whips? High heels? Do they wear fur coats? Her imagination won't go any further.

But what she sees is a tidy room, tidier than she ever remembers, and Kilda peering from under her duvet, but the room has changed, has it grown extra windows? She stands on the threshold, taking it in.

There are two pictures. Faith knows those pictures. The great big yellow one lights up the room. The room feels airy, bigger than before, as if it opens on to other worlds. A woman sits staring through a sunlit window.

Kilda has got Mrs Segall's pictures.

It's theft she's into, then, not prostitution. A wave of

emotion lifts Faith: relief. And she's never seen Kilda's room so nice.

'Mu-um. Please. I'm no good in the morning.'

'Will I make you some coffee?' Faith inquires.

The two women have a long, noisy hug, with lots of small kisses like hungry birds. The bed sags badly beneath their weight. The pictures glow on the walls above them. They move apart a bit and look at them.

'I like the yellow one best,' says Faith. 'That woman feels like a friend of mine. I saw her more or less every day. I always thought, she knows about cleaning. She's got a bit of muscle, like me. As if just this one morning, she's on holiday. And she sits there thinking, "This is my moment" ... I never did like the little blue one.'

'I like the blue one,' Kilda says. 'Bedrooms make me feel, you know, happy. I like those people going to bed. I get, like, visions when I lie in bed. I think both pictures are beautiful ... You were horrible, Mum. I've got a headache. Get me some coffee. It was true what I told you.' She sees from Faith's face that she does believe her. She'll never say it, but her mother is sorry. 'A milky coffee. And some biscuits.'

'I'm just out of milk,' says Faith. 'I'll pop and get some. Viola, Dwayne's aunt, might let me have some.'

So Faith isn't there, and Kilda is dozing, still in her pale blue cotton night-gown, when half a dozen of the One Way Brotherhood, led by Dirk to the right front door, which Faith has left on the snib for the moment, burst in, rudely, and enter Kilda's bedroom.

'Dirk?' says Kilda, not understanding. Dirk is her friend. He gave her the pictures. 'What have you come here for?' Dirk can't answer.

They lay hands on Kilda, and take her away.

'So is your father actually a doctor?' Angela asked Winston, as she drove along.

'Shut up, Mummy,' Gerda instructed. Her mother was asking too many questions, and trying too hard to be a hostess. 'He wants to talk to me, not you.'

'Look, don't be rude to me in front of other people!' Angela said, exasperated.

'So can I be rude to you at home?'

For the rest of the journey, Angela was silent. In the back, the two children giggled and farted. Gerda was more sensible when she was alone.

Still Angela decided she rather liked it, all that laughter, all that silliness. They were listing the things they would do in the Gardens; there were no floods, in the world of wishes. It helped her to suppress the worm-like worry her mother and father's words had started. *Of course* she was a responsible mother.

Still the day did have a peculiar feeling. There was almost no one else on the road.

As she drove over the Bridge of Flowers, where the river marked the boundary of the city, the sky got lighter, the air freshened, and Angela thought, I'm a lucky woman. I can finish my book, I know I can.

The car skidded, the steering-wheel spun, and she had to turn all her attention, briefly, to staying alive, and saving the children.

Almost no one was parked on the street around Flowers

Green, which was normally a rectangle of glass and metal, but Angela drove on through the dirty water towards the car park, on higher ground. That must be where all the cars had gone. But no one at all was in the car park.

They walked to the gates. Winston went very slowly, because he kept making essential detours, to pick up a frog, or a Wellington boot, though Angela drew the line at poo. (Was Gerda like this, a year ago? Angela didn't think she was. But then, how often had she taken her out?)

The man on the gate seemed cheered to see them. 'I thought the whole world was staying in bed,' he said. 'Nice to see the children.'

For a while, the two of them played near the gates, where there were some sheltered islands of land, and flowers blooming in great stone horse-troughs, irises, ranunculi, small mauve pansies. Gerda had brought along the tiny optical kaleidoscope her grandfather had given her, and was trying to make Winston look through it.

At first he trained it on a large snail. 'Snail,' he remarked. 'It goes curly whirly.'

'Now it's lots of snails,' said Gerda, moving it for him. 'See? If you turn it, it's more and more snails. Millions of snails. It would go on for ever.'

Winston pulled it away and used it as a gun. 'Duh-duh-duh-duh! I can shoot your mummy!'

'Don't,' said Gerda. 'She's a nice mummy.'

They didn't know she was listening. Angela's cheeks flushed with pleasure: *a nice mummy*. She heard it again, she would always hear it, however many times Gerda criticized her.

Now Gerda had got the little instrument and turned it on the ranunculi.

'They're like roses,' she said. 'Lots and lots of petals. Mum, look at this. It turns into millions of roses.'

Angela tried, but at first she couldn't see it. Then she found the flower. It was red, so red, on a frame of green grass. Despite the rains, its form was perfect. She pulled back a little, and it multiplied. The beauty repeated again and again, became a green lawn with dozens of blossoms, each one perfect, in a perfect garden, an Alice in Wonderland rose garden; it all depended on how you framed it. 'It's amazing, darling. It's wonderful. The longer you look, the better it gets.'

'Winston is bored,' Gerda interrupted. 'Winston wants to see the glass-houses.'

But the boats for the visitors weren't running. This was a shock, since most of the Gardens were still under water. A few staff were buzzing around in motor-boats, abstracted, carrying plants in pots and boxes.

'Mummy, we *have* to go in the boats,' said Gerda, pulling at Angela's hand. 'Winston wants to go in a boat.'

'I'm going,' said Winston, and splashed across the path, sending up great arcs of water, and threw himself head-first into a boat, his small bum in the air, his kicking feet following. He disappeared completely, then popped up, grinning.

'Come back, please,' called Angela. 'You can't go in a boat without grown-ups.'

'You're a grown-up,' said Gerda strictly. 'You could drive a motorboat.'

Angela couldn't, to Gerda's scorn. ('Any of the other mothers could do it.') But as a novelist, she could lie. Who was to say what was truth, what was fiction?

A very young gardener stood staring out at nothing with a look she read as frozen sadness; no time to speculate about the cause. The children, behind her, were getting restive. This was a definite motherhood test.

Making sure that neither of the children could hear her, she touched his arm, and looked into his eyes. 'This boy,' she said, 'has been seriously ill. His twin brother is still in danger. It is his first outing for many months. He wants so very badly to sail in a boat and see the rest of your delightful gardens' (out of the corner of her eye, she could see Winston pulling the heads off the ranunculi; Gerda was weaving them into her hair).

'I'll take you,' the young man suddenly decided. He was pallid; she realized he looked afraid – that was the expression she had read as sadness. 'They can run around like ants,' (gesturing towards his colleagues, scurrying insect-like in the distance) 'but it's not going to make a dime's worth of difference.'

But his frown relaxed as the four of them sailed in the puttering boat under a thin skin of cloud; the grey, blue and cream was reflected in the water; there was an operatic, multi-layered chorus of bird-song; small birds were everywhere, singing, waiting, their existence more vivid in the silence of the humans; the birds had become the voice of the Gardens. Even Winston and Gerda grew quieter, more reflective, dwarfed by the great shining sheet of pearl-grey, so still it was like ice, like peace. They drifted together; for a while they were tranquil. It was half-past ten; it was nearly eleven.

Winston scooped water-beetles up with his hand, and began to play kicking feet with Gerda, until she got cross and kicked him hard. Then she remembered that he was her friend.

'Winston and me want to see the big glass-house,' Gerda said to her mother, pulling at her dress. (Her mother had silly high-heeled shoes on. How could she play catch in shoes like that?)

The young boatman changed course towards the Palm House. From far off it looked as magnificent as ever, a series of domes and arcs of bright glass, but close up you saw that its crystal cliffs rose straight out of the plain of grey water.

'Course, you can't go inside,' he said, over his shoulder. 'The heating's broke down. It's a bit of a mess. We managed to move quite a lot of the stuff, but some of the palms is bloody enormous, you'd have to demolish the whole bloody house.'

The boat bobbed along by the big fogged panes. Giant green palm fronds pressed up against them; some of them looked brown; some must be dead. Some of the tropical plants looked huge and powerful, leaves like great bears' feet walking on the glass, vast hairy limbs like swimming mammoths, scaly grey trunks like dinosaurs. Winston spotted a section where the glass had been removed, perhaps when they were trying to get the plants out, leaving a perfect, iron-framed, way in. The inside of the Palm House looked tremendously exciting.

Briefly, fiercely, for the first time today, he wished that

Franklin were here with him. Together they could do anything. But Gerda, though a girl, was very good at swimming. Without another thought, Winston jumped in, and dog-paddled the metre or two to the opening.

Angela screamed, 'What are you doing?'

Clutching Bendy Rabbit, Gerda followed him.

Elroy has always been good in the mornings. Elroy has sometimes been bad at night, but Elroy is excellent in the mornings.

Most days Elroy gets up first, pads through the flat, puts the kettle on for a cup of tea for Shirley, quietly enjoys the peace of his home, the little cave with its breathing humans, its cleanliness, its warmth, its goodness. This morning, though, he's had four hours' sleep, and wakes up very late, with his heart beating wildly. Shirley is not in the bed beside him. Now he lies there anxious, trying to remember why he's woken with a weight of fear on his chest.

He'd been called by Shirley at the end of the Gala to say Franklin's temperature has gone through the roof. 'Liquid paracetamol,' he told her. He didn't want to know about Franklin's temperature, when he was at the Gala, enjoying himself, when he couldn't do anything except worry. And it wasn't fair: only hours before, when he'd rung up to check how his family were, she had reassured him, more or less: Winston was cooler, both boys were sleeping …

Then Elroy's worry becomes specific.

Elroy remembers what happened next. An epidemiologist he knew slightly from another hospital came across and

chatted. There was a solidarity between successful black
men in the Health Service. They had a smoke together,
decided that they liked each other, arranged to meet for a
game of squash. As the man turned to leave, he paused for a
moment, and said, in a low, conspiratorial tone, 'We've been
told to keep it quiet by the government, but there's
something big in the pipe-line … We've got eight cases of
flood sickness. The thing they had in Makaria.'

What's the matter with me? Elroy asked himself. Am I
deaf, or insane?

It hadn't occurred to him that the boys –

But now he is running down the corridor, clumsy, heart
pumping, mouth dry with fear. He looks in through the
door of the twins' room; Shirley is lying on the floor, covered
by a duvet; but the boys must be up; their beds are empty. A
wash of relief. They must be watching television.

Then he spots the bulge of a boy's body and tight-curled
head under Shirley's duvet. Sleeping, Shirley looks utterly at
peace, creamy, flushed, beautiful. But the first brief glance at
the boy's exposed cheek shows the strange red buboes he
had so dreaded, the sharp stigmata of flood sickness.

Sixteen

By lunch-time on the day after the Gala, Davey, who did not sleep last night, is utterly exhausted. Davey's warnings have not been heard; he has been treated as a showman by the 'experts', which means those astronomers who aren't up to speed on what is happening at the moment; he has been ridiculed as a TV lightweight, an accusation that cuts him to the bone; he has been comprehensively mocked and doubted. It was only a couple of days ago that the papers were full of the planetary line-up – and now before his programme has even gone out, Davey's telling them the problem is a runaway comet. Most of the people who interviewed him insisted on talking about the planets, because that's what it said in their briefing notes; when Davey told them it was a red herring, they asked him why he'd made a programme about it; there was no answer, except the money. 'The point is,' Davey says, hearing his voice grate and break, not his usual pleasant, humorous voice, the one they like and pay him for, 'the point is, if this object hits, it may be two thousand kilometres away, but there will be massive tsunamis – tidal waves, to most of us – ironically, just as our programme predicts. But this time it's real. It's serious. Thousands of people will die on the coasts. Lives can be saved if people move inland.'

Not a single interviewer seems to believe it. And half of Davey can't believe it either. It is not a certainty, just possible, according to the measurements Sharp's team is taking – with every second, becoming more likely, as the course of the comet narrows towards them – depending on the balance of delicate forces, the movements of other astral bodies whose movements may vary minutely, vitally. No one is willing to credit that there is a fifty, fifty-five per cent chance of this happening.

In a way, Davey agrees with the dissenters. There is never a fifty per cent chance of anything. Merely two worlds: one where it happens, where everything returns to nothing, and one where all of life goes on. Time splits, and splits, and splits again: what matters is being in the lucky fraction. Now he must find his sister, his mother, now he must make his way to Delorice – Davey will not be leaving the city, although Professor Sharp has gone already.

Davey has never been a praying man, but Davey finds that he is praying. For all the people he knows and loves, for all the people of the city. Davey, after all, is not really a scientist. He puts himself in the hands of the gods.

All those who slept little, or not at all, have a day of dread, after the Gala. Lottie, Ian, Elroy, Lola, Gracie, Isaac, Freddy ...

And although it's a public holiday, quite a few people are feeling gloomy. The sun, which has shone for three whole days, has vanished behind a thin veil of cloud. People start to realize the flood-waters have hardly receded, despite yesterday's official claims; they just looked better with the sunlight on them. Perhaps they went down a metre, if that.

Now some people say they are rising again. The swimming-pools are closed, and the tap-water tastes funny, as if it has been doused with chemicals.

Yesterday they knew they had turned the corner. Today, outside the centre, the smell is still there, and the dirty, irregular water-buses, and the little bodies, of drowned rats and mice, and the bin-bags, festering, decomposing.

The hissing whisper is 'flood sickness'. No one is worried about astral bodies.

On the long strings of space-time, events are gathering.

Mr Bliss is upset. The papers have shown themselves, as usual, utterly base and trivial apropos of his glittering Gala performance. 'Look, guys, I'm happy to answer questions,' he'd told his audience, frankly, freely, awaiting the questions he'd pre-arranged. Mr Bliss takes risks! He meets the people! But instead of the photo-opportunities he'd planned, all the papers have photos of the horrid little girl, even the centre-centre *Daily Bread,* and some have photos of a dancing teenager, with 'BLISS IS A ARSE' on her tiny pants.

'You are the Emperor with No Clothes!'

There had been howls, gales, roars of laughter. He had shrugged, likeably, grinned, grinned, held the expression till his cheek muscles ached, said, 'Thank you, guys! I think that's enough questions!' though Anwar was gesturing strictly from the rostrum; he fled down the long bright room feeling sick, knowing everyone was whispering and pointing at him: 'There goes the Emperor with No Clothes'.

Life was real, life was earnest, but no one would listen. The indignation burned a hole in his chest.

Today he had caught Anwar Topping laughing at a particularly hurtful cartoon. His wife had also been unpleasant to him; instead of praising his handling of the flood situation, she'd poured out a tide of nonsense she'd got from some clairvoyant (every week, she found a new one) predicting plague and tidal waves. Meanwhile, the *Daily Mire* had rubbished his very good dossier on sabotage, which some of his people had spent hours compiling. (Darren White, of course, was always a loose cannon: he'd been footsying with Anwar about an honour, while secretly writing this sabotage piece.) And now there were more cases of flood sickness, and accusations of a cover-up … Granted, the first cases were weeks ago, but the government's job was to prevent a panic. And then on top of it, this TV astronomer was screaming about the end of the world!

As the day went on, his mood worsened. A chap did his best, but people were ungrateful.

At eleven a.m., Berta called him. 'It's all very well, what you say about the floods, but there's still loads of stinking black sludge in our garage. Come straight home and clean it out.'

He was somebody, wasn't he? He was the Leader! Now he would make his wife realize that.

The children have disappeared into the Palm House. Angela stands in the boat, screaming. She can see them, quite clearly, through the gap in the glass, black shapes crawling down the branch of a tree, ending up clinging to the white spiral staircase that leads up into the upper gallery.

'Gerda!' she yells. 'Come back at once!'

'We're OK, Mummy,' Gerda calls.

At least, in chaos, they have something to cling on to. The white curved iron is like a helix. They are scurrying upwards. They are out of sight.

'Do something,' Angela shouts at the young gardener, who is sitting open-mouthed, looking after them.

'You'll have to go, missis,' he grunts. 'They're your kids. And besides, I can't swim.'

Angela kicks off her shoes and jumps in. It's a very long time since she has been swimming. The dirty water closes over her head. It feels like death; she knows she is dying.

That afternoon, all over the city, in the newly cleaned centre and on Two Zoo Hill, in the drowned parks and the beleaguered libraries, around the grey Towers with their tide of debris, rocket-sticks, defunct Roman candles, helicopters begin to hover. The residents hardly notice; they are used to the drone of helicopters, chasing burglars, monitoring demonstrations, keeping an eye on the city's pleasures, making sure nothing gets out of hand. It's a public holiday, and people have hangovers, so most of the city stays in their houses, watching TV, catching up with the papers. But when a few people put their boots on and step outside for a breath of air, they find the city has been covered with leaflets, bright yellow, slim, ubiquitous leaflets. On the front is a picture of Mr Bliss, but his face is half-obscured by a gas mask, and he is holding out another one to a child, who is looking up at him adoringly. 'PROTECT AND SURVIVE', the yellow chits shout. Unbelieving, reluctant, gingerly holding the flimsy pamphlet with Bliss's masked face, the people of the city begin to read.

The city has launched a pre-emptive strike on the hostile power which caused the floods. It's been done to make the city safer; we could not do nothing in the face of aggression. As always, Bliss thought of our children's future (as he OK'd the draft, he thought briefly, sourly of the red-headed child with her unfair question. He wasn't committed to that child's future).

But in the short term, there might be reprisals. The enemy were ruthless, and would stop at nothing. The people of the city should be vigilant. If an incident occurred, they should stay at home, and switch their TVs and radios on. The government would keep them fully informed, and

explain the safest course of action. At the last minute, Mr
Bliss had decided to cut the last passage, which asked people
not to stockpile food, and told them not to try to leave the
city. Of course, the awkward squad would do precisely that.

The leaflet ended opaquely; 'Home is the safest place,' it
said. But it didn't explain how they were to get home, if the
boatmen themselves had all gone home, and all the people
who should save or help them, the police, the firemen, the
doctors, the nurses; or how they should deal with the heavy
knot of terror that clenches as they read this pamphlet.

Gerda, however, is perfectly happy. The helicopters haven't
reached the west. The Gardens is one of her favourite places.
The top of the Palm House feels almost normal, with its
narrow iron walkway running round under the roof so the
children look down on the crowns of the palm trees, like
huge green stars or octopuses, though there's only water
below and between them, where usually she can peek
through the gaps and see people's heads bobbing like
toadstools. There's an 'up' spiral staircase and a 'down'
spiral staircase, but today, she thinks, there won't be any
rules.

She chases Winston round the walkway. Gerda's fast for a
girl, and Winston gives up. Being chased in this empty place
is too frightening. When he looks at Gerda close-up, she
looks funny: her dress has gone brown, and there's weed on
her neck. Then he sees, in her hand, his Bendy Rabbit. Bendy
Rabbit looks changed, all skinny and black. It scares him to
see Bendy Rabbit look different. It scares him that he forgot

his rabbit. It scares him that he's forgotten Franklin. How can Franklin be managing without him? Does he still exist without Winston there? Is his life going on at the same time? A frightening void opens up before Winston, where everything keeps happening, squillions of things, not knowing about him, not caring about him, and he can't control it, or keep anyone safe.

'You changed Bendy Rabbit,' he says to Gerda.

'I saved it,' she says. 'You forgot to bring it.'

'It isn't a it, it's a he,' he shouts. He punches her, and snatches the rabbit.

Isaac decides to get out. There are too many straws in the wind, today; Isaac isn't ready to die just yet. The pamphlet lies stupidly yellow on his desk. He picks up the directory of luxury services, and starts looking for helicopters. It isn't easy; firm after firm has had its fuel requisitioned by the government. When he finally finds an outfit with fuel, all three machines have been booked today, but Isaac stays on the line, wheedling, cajoling, doubling his offer, trebling ... In the end he offers the price of his house; what good is a house in a wrecked city? And, after some weaselling, they agree.

Then other decisions have to be made. The helicopter seats four to six. Isaac no longer has a lover. Caz, whom he loved so very recently, left in a way that gave him pain; Isaac, who bears Caz no ill feeling, nevertheless decides not to save him. The gift of life! It is too rare, too precious! How can he spare some for a man who spurned him?

Besides, there aren't really five spare seats. Isaac must take some pictures along, and some little comforts that make life worth living if you don't have a lover, a father, a mother. He needs his two-thousand-dollar bottles of wine, the ones he has been saving for happiness; he must have his jazz and opera CDs; his small bronzes, including the one-off Paolozzi, cast just for him; his smokey, Goya-esque Paula Regos with their children larger and freer than their parents; his Michael Andrews; his Cornell box, a world under glass, blown sand, torn paper; his tiny Freud, with the feet to die for, the exquisite red-silver-cream-blue flesh; his haunted Auerbach drawing of a head; he is shocked to find how heavy they are, and to see that some of his favourites are dusty – how have they got dusty, if he loves them so?

Perhaps there is room for one other passenger, as long as they will come without cargo. Isaac thinks about his sister Susy, whom he loves, though they quarrelled years ago, when he drove the One Way-ers out of the house ... Susy. A little pain in his chest. He dials her number; it rings once, twice. Then he imagines what will happen; if she comes with him, she'll never come alone; ever since she was little she's adopted things, birds, puppies, human wreckage; he imagines them, scrabbling at the helicopter, helpless, dirty, hysterical ... Four rings, then he puts it down. He sits there thinking, his packages all round him, his best leather overcoat tightly buttoned, the water and heating already turned off, the flood- and bomb-proof storeroom sealed. After a while he dials another number.

Angela has struggled, sopping wet, furious, into the hulk of the drowned glass-house. She feels ancient, and stupid, and very tired. She left her new shoes in the boat with the gardener (she wore them in case Winston's mother was smart; but Winston's mother had not been smart). What if the young man abandons them?

She is too old for the thing she is doing, inching along the branch of a tree, scratching her feet every step of the way, the leaves whipping and scratching at her cheeks, but she hears the children up in the echoing roof, and there's no other way to reach the white staircase.

'Gerda!' she calls. 'Win-ston!' No answer. She listens a moment. They are quarrelling. 'Gerda,' she shouts. 'Come down this instant!' She peers awkwardly up through the tangle of branches, but as she does so, something falls straight past her, something wet and black, which splashes her cheek, and suddenly both the children are screaming.

Swinging over the void, she reaches the white handrail, grips it, pulls herself across, clings, for a second to catch her breath, then finds herself slapping up the steep narrow staircase, wet feet slithering perilously. She tries to shout, but her ribs are hurting. She reaches the top gasping like a grampus. Gerda, she thinks, you'll suffer for this.

But just as she gets there, she sees them below her, they have both run down the opposite staircase, and crouch side by side on its bottom rung.

They seem to be fighting. Gerda's clutching Winston.

Aching, shivering, Angela follows them, crossing the walkway, descending the staircase, holding on tight because the view makes her dizzy, the enormous trees, tiny heads of the children, the dirty water stretching out all round them.

Now there's no way that they can escape her. She slips, nearly falls, tells herself *take care*.

Twenty metres below her – fifteen – four –

There's a splash like the sound of a world exploding. One of the children has fallen in the water.

She can't lose Gerda – her life – her daughter –

But straining round the ironwork, she sees it's Winston.

Gerda is shouting: 'Don't! Come back!'

Ian, Gerda's 'painter man', picks up his phone, and finds it is Isaac. The two of them are old – not friends, but acquaintances. Isaac would say 'friend', Ian 'acquaintance'. Ian is one of Isaac's few straight friends. Isaac's always considered him phenomenally talented, though Ian would never listen to advice. Isaac represented him for years and set up some absolutely key commissions, but Ian frequently didn't play ball – Ian only wanted to work for himself, and at first that sometimes included portraits, which Isaac sold for a lot of money, but then something odd started happening, the portraits slipped towards caricature, so some clients laughed, and some were offended; then they slipped a little further, a little broader, and the point of the caricature became clear: Ian saw people as animals, jackals, hyenas, wild-cats, snakes. Isaac admired them, but couldn't sell them, though later, after the two of them had parted, the great museums started buying them, and Ian became one of the world's most successful artists, though almost nothing was known about him. On one of the rare occasions they had met, after their business partnership had broken down,

Isaac congratulated Ian on his marketing tactics. 'Absolutely brilliant! The Beckett touch! You have created such mystique!' But Ian just laughed, and turned away, and started sketching something on the back of a napkin.

Isaac no longer knows Ian's number by heart, but he flicks through his palm-top and swiftly finds it. Only ten minutes till he has to leave. They're picking up from the pad in the north-west of the city. Shall he phone, or not? The power of life and death ...

A silverfish flicks across Isaac's desk.

He squashes the silverfish, but rings Ian's number.

The question he puts is a little self-conscious, aware of his beneficence, almost shy.

But the answer is succinct. Ian isn't coming. 'I can't do it. Got to go to the zoo. OK then, mate. I hope you make it.'

Seventeen

May finds her son as the second wave of helicopters starts to rumble over the city. The Towers are decked with feeble yellow bunting where occasional leaflets have stuck to windows, caught on mouldings, blown like leaves on to balconies. The flood waters have a freight of dirty yellow paper. The Tower-dwellers carry its stain in their hearts, a grim leakage of fear down the edge of the day. They veer between terror and forgetfulness. They cannot accept it, because they don't have an enemy; nobody, surely, could hate them so much as to want to bomb them, poison them, gas them, any of the fates the leaflets threaten ... Any of the things that Bliss may have done, in other words, to the other country, their new, faceless, invisible enemy. But now, slowly, under the surface, in the depths of their hearts where there is no argument, where knowledge never reaches, beyond

logic, they start to hate, because they start to fear. The
yellow leaflets are the first poison.

May, however, has lived through the war. May doesn't take a
lot of notice. It's just that smarmy Mr Bliss, trying to get his
face on everything. She feels sorry for the child in the
photograph, though. She dimly remembers the mask she
wore as a teenager for gas-mask drills. It was hot, and heavy,
and suffocating, like a dream from which you could not
wake up, and she briefly wonders, as she searches the
Towers, as she goes up yet another flight of empty, inhuman
stairs, panting, resting, aware of a nagging pain in her foot,
as she knocks on yet another peep-holed door, no longer
afraid of what she will find because she has already seen it
all – the enormously fat man propped up against a packing-
case, dressed in a parka and underpants, his legs stretching
out like two alien life-forms behind the skeleton who cared
for him, his starved yellow daughter with her withered skin;
the old black woman who came to the door clutching the
shoulder of her crawling son, dragging himself intently
along, but he could see, his eyes yearning upwards, while his
mother's are milky, lightless, blind; the crack dens, where
young people twitched and dozed and a skinny dog wolfed
the forgotten hamburgers spilled like excrement across the
floor – she briefly wonders, as she knocks on a door, this
tenth, or twentieth, or thirtieth door since she started
searching, today, yesterday – if her life since the death of her
dear Alfred has been just such a dream, heavy, comfortless,
a dream where everything is seen through pain – so she

might still wake and turn and find him, not dark and cold as
he was last night, but somewhere where they could be in
colour, his dear red face and funny mouth, the pale blue eyes
that always softened to see her; and the door opens, this
thirtieth door, this door no more hopeful than any other,
and suddenly she sees him, at the back of a crowd, that face
and body she'd forgotten to love, that form so familiar she
could close her eyes and still see him there, against that
bleak window, Alfred's narrow shoulders, his wiry arms ...

But the angry crest of fair hair is Dirk's.

'I'm his mother,' she says to the young white woman who
opens the door, pointing at Dirk, and the woman frowns,
uncertain for a moment, then suddenly beckons her in.

'Dirk?' May says, a little bit shy, for everyone's turned to
look at her. Perhaps fifty people are packed in this room.
The fluorescent light is bright, after the dim cold landing.
Dirk looks at her with his mouth open, and she wants to tell
him to shut it again, for it isn't an expression that makes him
look intelligent.

There is a weird-looking man like a priest, at the front, in
a kind of long white dress, with a scarf, and his eyes are
strange, dark-ringed, scary, as if he hasn't slept for months,
but the iris is paler even than Dirk's. Eyes as white as glass
or ice, fixing on her like a bird of prey's. Now he's talking to
Dirk, who he calls 'Brother Dirk', and motioning him to
deal with her. May starts to feel she is intruding on
something. There is an atmosphere, tense, electric, not just
to do with her bursting in.

Dirk looks older, thinner, than she remembers. He too
has a garment like a priest's surplice, but shorter than the

other man's. It is a physical shock when he comes near. She remembers this; once he was hers. She finds herself thinking, but he's half my Alfred. She catches her breath; she wants to cry. Something is coming to a close at last, something is happening that had to happen.

Angela clutches at her daughter, but Gerda shakes off her mother's arm. She is crouching on the bottom step, looking down. Her cheeks are bright red; she's just starting to cry.

'Winston jumped in, I told him not to –'

Angela sees the boy, swimming about, a plucky, not very fluent dog-paddle: the hanging branches and leaves look threatening, arms of things that want to trap him.

Anger comes to suppress her fear. 'What on earth does that boy think he's doing?'

'He dropped Bendy Rabbit. But he can't dive. *Winston!* Come back, Mum will get your rabbit – you will, won't you, Mum, say that you will –'

'But Gerda, we'll never find it in here. We'll have to buy him another one –'

'Stupid Mummy! You don't understand!'

'What are you doing?' Dirk says, grumpy. Suddenly it's all very ordinary, for how often has May heard him sounding like this. 'I don't know why you've bothered to come. Matter of fact, I'm very busy.'

She was going to embrace him – all kids loved hugs, but Dirk, as a boy, had been hard to hug – but, hearing his sulky voice, stepped back.

'I read in the papers you were out of prison,' she says, very quietly, mouthing the last bit with meaningful gestures of her eyebrows, for no one need know he had been to prison.

'Fat lot you care,' he said, and suddenly looked young, he looked like the skinny blond boy she remembered, imagining the other two were loved more than him.

'I didn't think you liked it when I visited,' she said, simply, but she did feel guilty, she was in the wrong, she couldn't explain why she had just given up on him. (She had got so tired, it was her age, perhaps, but she knew that Alfred would never have allowed it, if he'd been alive they would have gone to see him, no matter what the boy had done.) 'Your poor nails, Dirk,' she said suddenly, reaching out and taking his hand, for the quick of the nail was raw and bleeding and the skin on the knuckles was flaky and pale. He snatched it away, with a harsh little breath, then looked at the floor for a second, hunched, then with a violent, unreadable convulsion of emotion, tried to put it back again. She took it, she held it. It felt like wood; wounded, awkward. A limb re-attached after a terrible accident.

'I'm sorry,' she said. 'I didn't know what to do. I didn't know anything. I never did.' It was there again, that sinking feeling. Her whole life as a mother, her whole life as a wife, she had never known anything, she'd just reacted, just done the next thing as the next day came, and mostly it was wrong. Her whole hurrying life. It was only afterwards you understood things.

(But maybe it had been like that for Dirk. Was it possible?

She stared at him. Perhaps it was even like that with … *a murder*. Perhaps a great bird snatched you up in its claws, perhaps you were muffled in the dark smelly feathers, perhaps the thing happened in blind, deaf panic, and then the cruel feet dropped you again. And then, in the light, you saw you had done it, and everyone was standing staring at you. For a second May felt as if she had murdered. Perhaps she and Dirk had done it together.)

'Brother *Dirk*!' a frightening voice shouted now. May blinked, and returned to the crowded room. Everyone was silent. The light was too bright. Everyone stood there staring at them. May felt very shy. She held Dirk's hand tighter. The voice was the voice of the priest at the front.

'We are in process of judgement on Sister Kilda. We require your attention, Brother Dirk.'

'It's just my mother,' Dirk mumbled, looking down (she had tried to teach him not to mumble; had constantly told him to stand up straight, and she nudged him, with her elbow, as she had done so often, but he twitched away as if she had kicked him, and his head went forward, as it often did, into what May used to think of as Dirk's head-butt position).

'The court will continue,' the priest announced. 'Brother Dirk, you have promised to forsake all others. Is this woman to stay, or go?'

Dirk looked confused. 'It's not a woman, Father Bruno,' he muttered. 'It's, you know, my mother. She's only just got here. I can't chuck her out, like, *straight away*.'

For a moment Father Bruno's face became completely blank, a queer shivering contortion that left it like a mirror, and what May saw in the glass was so frightening that she looked away, for she saw her own death, but it was only a moment, then the image was gone, and the man waved the two of them forward together.

'Gerda, I never learned to dive.' Angela is trying not to cry herself. She ought to be able to sort this out, if she were better, if she were stronger. Winston is not responding to her shouts.

'Zoe taught me, in the diving pool. Because she said I was the best at swimming.'

'You're not going!' Angela shrieks. She manages to scrabble a hold on Gerda's dress.

Gerda watches Winston splashing about. He keeps pushing his little face down into the water, and comes up choking and coughing out slime.

How long, thinks Angela, can he keep this up? The water on her body feels cold as death.

Outside the glass, there is a deafening droning; it must have been growing louder for ages, but Angela, preoccupied, has hardly heard it. But now she does, and thinks 'motorboat', and she starts to shake, with joy, with relief, for the Gardens staff must have come to save them.

But in another moment she sees she is wrong, it is helicopters, swooping low above them. A yellow drizzle seems to be falling, in the old world, the world they have left.

May gets to the front of the packed gathering and sees a

strange woman sitting on an armchair she somehow manages to make like a throne. Facing the crowd as Father Bruno was.

Then May thinks again. Big, but not a woman. She is beautiful. She is just a child. She sits there, tall, grave, heavy, wearing a pale blue dress like a night-gown (and then May realizes, it *is* a night-gown) and bare feet, and dishevelled red hair, but her face is beautiful, the kind of high forehead that in May's youth would have been called 'noble', her eyes are large, grey, steady, her skin gleams with health and youth; she looks as if she's fed on milk and apples; she could be a queen, in her long loose dress, a country queen, or Persephone; she has a look of the young Shirley.

But there's something wrong, May sees at once, for her mouth is swollen, drooping, sulky, almost as if someone has hit her, and her body (with her big legs wound round each other, her heavy arms folded across her chest) says, 'Do not touch me: do not hurt me.'

'Who's that?' May hisses to her son, but he shakes his head, impatient, shushing her. In any case, May soon finds out, because Father Bruno turns and addresses the girl.

'And so, Sister Kilda, these are the charges.'

'I still don't get it,' Kilda says.

'SILENCE!' Bruno yells, in a wire-taut scream that cuts the air and leaves them all still. Only Kilda stays human, stirring, shuffling, but her face quivers, for a second, with fear, and her mouth stays immobile, slightly open.

'You have left the true path, the One Way. You have prophesied in your own selfish voice, without consulting the One True Book. You were tempted away by money, and frivolity. You were seen at the Gala, consorting with sinners. You tempted others, you led them away, offering them visions of worldly things. This is your crime, your sin of sins. You have defied your Father's instructions. You have tempted Adam as Eve once did. Sister Kilda, you have abused our trust, you have tried to undermine the One True Faith. Because we are just, infinitely just, you shall have a chance to acknowledge your guilt, to renounce your sin, to come back to us. Acknowledge the Book, and you will be forgiven. God is an angry God, his wrath is infinite, he takes you up and he casts you down, but if you humble yourself, he can also have mercy. Repent, Sister Kilda. Accept the Book.' He paused, leaning forward towards her like a vulture, his arms extended, casting sharp shadows, strong, wiry arms that could kill or bless.

Gerda is calling across the water. 'Please, Winston, you're making me scared. We got to go back now and find Franklin.'

But Winston doesn't take any notice. He is tiring now. His body is drifting.

Kilda rises to her feet, ungracefully. Standing in the light, she looks more beautiful but no older than she did before. To May, a mother, she is just a child; she looks at her and again sees Shirley, before she was comfortable in her skin, trying to live in her new adult body.

Kilda doesn't talk at all like the priest. 'Thing is,' she says

'I haven't done nothing. I hear the voices, I see what I see. It wasn't my fault that, like, the papers got on to me. First of all, you all, like, go mad about my visions, you're all, like, "Kilda, this is amazing, oh Kilda tell your visions to me."' (There is a flash of mockery as she says this, a flash of the teenager, suddenly, and May feels afraid; she sees Bruno is dangerous; but as quickly as it came, it fades away, and Kilda is just sad and slightly sulky.) 'Then suddenly it's all, like, "They're not the right visions". But I do see it, now, I see a big wall of water. I do see, like, the end of the world, the thing you're always going on about. What you don't get is, there's lots of different endings. It isn't, like, One Way, not at all. There are worlds that are all bright, like worlds of light, and a world of darkness, but it all, like, splits, it goes on and on, so there's lots of worlds, and the pieces get shuffled ... It's doing it now. Every day, every moment. And now you're all, like, trying to keep me locked up. Like I'm the devil. But I'm not. I'm like you. And my mum will be worried if I'm not home soon.'

Then she turns to Dirk, who is staring at the floor, his head and shoulder twisted slant-wise, crab-like, a creature protecting itself from hurt. 'And you,' she complains, 'what's up with you? I thought you were, like, a mate of mine. I never did anything against you, Dirk.' (It may be the first time she's said his name; actually said his personal name, which his mother chose, and he never liked, but which somehow slipped under his skin, and became him.)

Kilda's speech, which sounds touching, and truthful, to May, makes that curious blank shiver come over Bruno's face. 'She condemns herself,' he hisses, sudden as a snake, his small head darting from side to side, and all around May, the faces work and shudder. 'SHE CONDEMNS HERSELF! She is without faith! She has rejected the peoples of the Book! She has rejected the faiths of the Book! This woman is damned for rejecting the Book!'

The hubbub which broke out is stilled again, as his furious mouth issues the condemnation. But Kilda, who at first slumped to her seat as if exhausted by the strain of speaking, is standing again, talking again. 'It's not my fault,' she cries passionately. 'It's not my fault. I can't even read. I can't read the Book. I CAN'T fucking read it, I can't, I can't. It takes me too long. The letters go crooked. And it's not just me. Loads of you can't.'

And then they are all howling, mad with anger. May realizes that they will kill her.

Then she looks at Dirk. He has covered his eyes. His fingers, clamped into yellow claws, are kneading, pawing his cheeks and forehead as if he wants to re-make himself. His poor pocked skin looks wet and greasy.

But it can't be true. Dirk can't be in tears.

Gerda can't bear to watch any more. Angela thinks she has a hold on the child, a miser's grip on her soaked red satin, but suddenly, everything flicks upside down; with a fluid movement like a fish escaping Gerda twists away, stays for one instant poised on the narrow white iron of the step, staring at her mother, is comforted as she looks in her pupils and sees, in their circle, for one split second her own small image, safe in its robe of scarlet satin, queen of the world, but then she dives.

They are fleeing, fleeing; they are falling over; they are dragging trunks and boxes of paper; they are telephoning taxis, airports, heliports, rushing the banks, rifling their storerooms. The rich are trying to leave the city. The rich believe they can always leave, that money will always get them away; but most of the phones aren't answering, most of the taxis have already gone, and the helicopters hang there, sky-born, swinging dark bellies over the city, droning, droning, deafening.

Frightening the people who do not leave. The poor believe they can never leave. There is no escape; life simply happens, the wheels roll forward, crushing them or sparing them. The helicopters hang there above them.

Gerda and Winston are swimming, swimming.

The rich have choices. What will they save? Jewellery, art, their Slim Jim Shoos, those silvery slender kid-glove stilettos that will surely dance to dry land again, the gliding wheels of their Rollon watches, their Verso shirts, their Parade purses ...

Suddenly Lottie changes her mind. She tosses the whole lot on to the floor, runs up to their bedroom, and raids a cupboard. When she toils down the stairs again, her arms are full of photograph albums; pieces of light, pieces of life, Lola and Davey when they were babies, Harold laughing on a sun-blanked beach, Lottie, so young, in a room full of roses. She stands for an endless moment and stares: the past, unshadowed by this future, and yet it was always waiting for her, and then thought fails, because time runs out, Harold is shouting, pleading, desperate, if they don't leave now they will lose their chance, and she slams the case shut and totters downstairs, toes crammed, at the last, into her Slim Jim Shoos.

Moira Penny is getting ready. She is not in the Towers, with the Sisters and Brothers (though had she but known that today was the day they were going to try Kilda, she would never have missed it). But love; Moira Penny was looking for love; it has never come from her colleagues, or students, and now she has missed it, too, with the Brothers. Father Bruno hurts her with his many favourites, the young, like Kilda, with her empty faith, her Bog Irish ignorance, her brazen beauty, the way she rubs her big breasts in your face.

He has not praised Moira for her radio triumph: the way she brought the One Word to the people. He forgets to consult her about the Book, although he must know she is a doctor, an expert. She has always known about books, always; has spent her life reading, studying, lifting the pages one after another, abstracting the truths, weighing, measuring, telling the less lettered what the books contain, wicker-works of text, immurements of meaning. She has not cheated. She has suffered it all. The aching eyes; the wasted muscles; the long evenings in yellowing libraries; the lunatic strait-jacket of language, crushing her arms against her ribs.

But they don't value her. They don't love her. She savours the bitter taste of the truth, the thing they have tried to conceal from her with faint, false fibs of brotherhood: Moira Penny will never be loved. The terrible engines and propellers of judgement that droned above her all afternoon have made her certain it is over for her. She has glimpsed a pale arm, waving goodbye.

Moira has given up almost everything, her teaching position, her salary, her warm office, the respectable house where her dog could play outside in the garden, where Fool and she were almost happy: but till now she could never give up her books; her books and her paper were the things she most needed. At last she sees there is no more need.

She collects them together. From all the thousands she once possessed, using up air and space and life, a mere hundred or so remain, and she makes great towers of them near her window, her attic window, her view of the world, extending over the empty roof-tops, the flooded playgrounds, the useless spires, the tree-tops ringing what was once a park, where she glimpses the movement of an empty boat, and beyond the motorways, more roof-tops, empty, empty, emptiness ... But perhaps, and she cranes, she peers through the window, she has opened it to let the cold air in, perhaps in the last dim glimmer of the distance she sees something other, outside the city, something surviving, a blueness, a greenness. Perhaps there is grace, though Fool is desperate, she hears him barking in the kitchen below where she has wedged the door shut with yellow pamphlets, she has to teach him, for he won't be quiet … Eyes on the hills, Moira Penny waits.

Elroy and Shirley will wait for ever. At half-past three, in intensive care, where they are living a life quite insulated from the world where the city dreads and waits, after everything possible has been done, their beloved Franklin slips down into a coma.

And now something happens that no one's expecting except Professor Sharp and his colleagues, but they have all gone away inland.

With an unearthly roar, with a schlooping sound as if giant dinosaurs are sucking the drains, with a rushing of wind and a shiver of motion that suddenly grips the whole city, the water-levels plummet, the floods sink down, the dirty water pours back into the sea, moiling and boiling blackly downwards, shooting boats and buses along like matchwood, baring dark grass and sodden brickwork, dragging along sheds and lawn-mowers and cars on their backs like drowned beetles – and inside the buildings, and on high ground, everyone stops what they're doing and listens: something very big is breathing above them; after months of wishing, praying, cursing, it retreats in minutes, the flood is gone.

Gerda and Winston are suddenly pulled down, kicking and struggling, deep, deeper, down between the silver-slimed trunks and stems, down through the boggy roots and suckers, down past the water-fleas and half-grown frogs and blushing sticklebacks and spinning toadlets, and whorls of rotting, forgotten objects, shoes and handbags and hoses and nozzles, thrashing like snakes in the force of the water – and Winston spots it, his Bendy Rabbit, stuck in the angle of a black drowned branch, and grabs it to him as he hurtles past – but Gerda knows they cannot fight it, their only hope is to ride the tide-race, and as it sweeps them down deep underground, into a labyrinth of drainage channels, she kicks her strong feet, and holds on to Winston, and breathing the air bubbles in her red hair (but it suddenly loses its red and goes dark, the colour shuts down, it's a black and white world) the two children shoot along the grey chill tunnel which leads on for ever, and only gets colder.

There is a long pause, in the sucked-out city.

Eighteen

And then it comes, the white line of water, moving in from very far away, and at first, to Moira, it seems to come slowly, but she crawls out, shivering, on to her balcony, into the light where she can see at last, and she stands, staring, transfixed by joy

but duty, duty, the drumstick of duty, taps her shoulder, peremptory, and she blunders back through to rescue her books, strains her arms as she tries to embrace them, sharp-spined, heavy, why always so heavy

The Brothers and Sisters are all looking inwards, watching

the infinitely interesting thing, the prospect of seeing justice done; this is the beginning of Judgement Day. Bruno Janes has Sister Kilda by the hair, and then by the neck underneath her hair, and is shaking her, slightly, as a dog would a rat, and she is too terrified to resist; limp, eyes glazed, head lolling forwards, a useless bud on a broken stalk. She is finished, thinks May, he will finish her off, and she tries to force herself to her feet, but the old fear crouches like smog on her chest, crushing her lungs, thickening her tongue, freezing her body on its chair – No, she can't bear it. No, not possible. 'Dirk,' she whispers. 'Dirk. This is mad.'

She says it quietly, timidly, but the room is quieter than she can be, and in that cold, electric silence, Bruno's head swivels like the head of a weasel, he lets go of Kilda, who slumps to the floor, and those terrifying eyes stare into them, at May, who is old, who is only a widow, who has shrunk, with age, to a paper doll, who feels her mouth shrivel, pucker, dither, whose heartbeats lurch and then cascade, May White, who is weak, who has never been brave, and Dirk, poor thing, her youngest son.

'Brother Dirk.' Bruno breathes. He pauses, smiles. 'Brother Dirk. You will come and execute the sentence.'

The room gives up a low sigh, a faint roar, as if they had all been holding their breath, but suddenly May becomes unsure; perhaps the roar is outside the window; 'No,' she hears herself say, quite distinctly, 'No,' and she catches her son by the sleeve, but only Bruno seems to have heard her; the Brothers and Sisters are on their feet, they run to the window, tripping over each other, shoving, falling, and

Bruno is shouting 'Order, ORDER', but no one looks at him, no one is listening any more

Mohammed is praying in Parliament Close, ten metres away from Government Manse, as near as the policeman will let him go; it seems he's the only policeman on duty; they eye each other, warily, but the policeman's trained not to be frightened of foreigners; he tries an official grin at Mohammed, who thinks the policeman is sneering at him. Neither man's heard the news this morning: both of them wonder why the close is empty.

Mohammed has marched from the station, sweating, a man with a mission he doesn't want, a man who is no longer himself, whose subtle heart has been squeezed and twisted, whose head is irradiated by grief. Mohammed, today, is superhuman; he is emptied out; he has become a message. He moves in its wake, a walking cipher:

I will have such revenges that
  What they are yet I know not but

He prays to be spared from doing this thing: he prays to Allah for help, for grace: he prays that the woman with the peace placard will go away, somewhere else, somewhere safe, for she has done nothing, she is just a woman; his eyes flick across her, constantly, tormented by her youth, her sad eyes; she's not so much older than his beautiful sister; Jamila, Jamila; the world goes red, but he makes himself focus on

the young woman; she sits on the ground with her mobile
phone, dialling then muttering to herself, unhappy; perhaps
she has parents she needs to contact, perhaps she is worrying
about her baby (how much Rhuksana had wanted a baby)

Moira smiles to see the wave coming, she laughs;
   in another life, there is a dog, barking;
   she hears her Fool in part of her brain, the oldest,
simplest part of her brain, but her feeling self is lost in the
future, finding the relief of an end, at last, the washing away
of her words, her wounds

how very much she had wanted a baby. Mohammed's glad
now not to have children, no child to suffer from what he
will do. How many children have lost their fathers? Let Mr
Bliss's children lose their father, let Bliss's children know
pain and shame. But once again Mohammed starts praying:
Spare me, Allah, from this great sin ... Spare me, Allah,
from hating children

Shirley is weeping in Elroy's arms, deafened, blinded by
helpless loss: 'It makes no difference that there were two, he
was just himself, he was Franklin, Franklin' –

Mohammed's prayers have gone wrong again, for the anger

is burning and twisting inside him, the new mad anger, the tungsten heat

– must every pain be endured again? The lost child, the shattered family – Winston, Franklin, the names of love, darkening into names for torment

It must be time for Bliss to arrive. 'Excuse me, miss,' says Mohammed, most politely, he knows city people find Muslims frightening, even peace protesters might find him frightening, 'have you got the right time? My watch is slow,' but Zoe (whose phone is losing its signal, who is crouched there tensely beside her placard, trying to reach her beloved Viola to tell her she loves her no matter what, to thank Viola for making her happy) shakes her head, glowers, *leave me alone*, she's noticed him staring at her before, now the stupid bastard is making a pass, and, desperate to talk to her darling girl, furious with his dull male face, on impulse she gives Mohammed the finger, although she is here protesting for peace, although she can see he's a foreigner and Zoe believes in being kind to foreigners

Lottie and Harold are in their helicopter, jammed in with Lola and five other people who paid so much they could not be left behind, but the helicopter is overloaded, it is struggling on across the nearby fields, there is a smell of hot diesel, of straining metal; then it lurches, yaws, in a sudden wind, in the strengthening torrent of air from the wave that is racing nearer, blank, enormous, its summit blocking out the sky. In the first sheet of spray, the thing slips, tries to climb, finds a blind silver wall, a final valley

Zoe jabs one finger up, hatefully

'Shirley, I love you,' Elroy sobs. 'I know,' she says, 'but it's not enough –' they sit there, struggling to contain the pain, which is wilder, larger, than their wracked bodies
      Together, separately, they long for death

Lottie thinks, I loved brightness, luck, light
      but then it is dazzling, and all around her

Ian's in the zoo, waiting for the wave, his easel set up on the top of the hill. Though he knows that the image will never be seen, never collected, sold, kept, he determines to draw the wave as it comes, to catch the beauty with his hand, his eye, for in the end only the moment matters, the glass bead swung on its rope of sunlight

the angry child jabs with one hate-fuelled finger: die, you bastard, she prays, just die

at the last moment, Ian sees the wave coming and thinks of

the birds in their aviary, he has no ark, he can do so little, but
he leaves his easel, he leaves his art, he runs like a madman
down the hill, he snatches a gardener's discarded loppers
and hacks, smashes at the birds' wire cage, and at first they
are stunned, they cower together, but as the first tide pours
over the ground they flutter up, crying, dizzy, crazed, they
find the raw hole he has cut to the light, and spin past his
shoulders, a column of smoke

all over the city, the birds flare upwards, a shawl of starlings,
a cape of crows, a staggering, hurtling volley of pigeons,
herons up-ended into broken mayflies, thin legs splayed by
the weight of the wind, but the highest flyers, the boldest
wing-tips, power up the air, their mountain slope, needing
nothing at all in that single second but steely hope, *survive,
survive*

as others smash into flurries of feathers
      drenched, dulled, death drags them down

as Zoe stabs at the air with her finger, a low black car purrs
past the policeman and up to the president's glossy door;
Mohammed assumes it is Mr Bliss, not knowing the
darkened windows conceal a nervous delegate from his own
country, part of a desperate last-ditch attempt to negotiate
(or buy) a peace: *Goodbye, Rhuksana, goodbye my love*:
and one final time he prays to be spared, clutching the

masbaha beads in his pocket: '*Oh God, you are peace, from you comes peace*,' but the other voice says

> *I shall do such things, I know not what*
> > *I shall do such things*
> > > *They shall be the terrors of the earth*

But Allah instructs him, 'Incline towards peace'

Moira stands proud on her balcony, stretching her painful bones to the sky, shouting, 'Come, Come, O Lord, I am ready', but the kind water takes the sound away, she is spared the noise of her own screaming, she is safe to do it, dwarfed, deafened; the roaring water is below her feet, the moil that comes before the crest of the wave, and she takes the first book, the first torment, the first of the bricks in her life's dark walls, and she flings it, opening, its pages like wings, and a second, and a third, out on the bright water, the free muscled shine of the water's skin, the finally accepting, limitless body which has time and room to take them all, to dissolve her prison, to take her home, and she flings them, laughing, one after another, book after book, bird after bird, they can no longer peck her or make her suffer, no longer make her care for them, they are free at last, they are on their own, and so she can be free, now they are gone, it is over, over, the lover has come death crashes in through Shirley's window and takes her and Elroy in its arms

on Daffodil Hill, the highest part of the city, people are running, scrambling upwards, the unfit straining as they puff up the slopes, young parents sprinting ahead of them, children straddling their skinny shoulders, turning briefly to look at the great wall of dark with the crest of silver pouring onwards – impossible, unstoppable

the final, unthinkable, astounding thing

and the sun lights up the detailed beauty of each distinct figure, each bright life, running, falling; sculpted by light; the only thing that can never be copied

Look, there's Davey, hand in hand with Delorice – he pulls her up into a cedar tree: 'I can't,' she says, 'I can't, Davey,' but 'Yes,' he says, 'you can, we can do it,' and they climb, from a distance like a couple of children, starting in the cradle of the lowest branches, then up, up, she is giggling with terror, 'Trust me, Delorice,' and at last she trusts him, the essential Davey who could always be trusted, clutches his shirt, and he hauls her upwards to the highest branches, till the wood is too slender, and wavering, dizzy, they can climb no more – at the top of the tree, they cling to each other

but the crowd on the hill pushes on upwards, struggling, now, pushing, screaming, red and contorted, insects

scrambling on top of each other, a mill of ants in its final
terror, but till the wave comes they will fight to survive

and then the wave comes; then the wave comes

Allah the beneficent, the merciful, has asked too much of his
servant Mohammed: to ignore a lifetime of slights is
inhuman: he groans as the small white finger prods the air,
she has no reason to insult him; smash the rude girl and the
monkey-grin policeman and Mr Bliss, who murdered
Jamila, crush the scorn and the ignorance, the lies and greed
of colonialism; they will find at last that Islam is strong, it
will end in flames, it will end in fire

Moira is happy, but something is scratching, something is
tearing, a pain, a sound, something she tries not to hear, but
hears, as she throws out the last of Angela's books, the
books which have given her so much trouble, the texts which
made Moira a drudge, a slave, and as they fly, she no longer
hates them, they do not need her, they can go alone: Moira
Penny is finally free; then she hears the sound for what it is;
it is Fool, barking, her dog, her Fool, the warm animal body
trapped inside, and Moira at last is free to feel pity, and she
crawls back inside, she runs down the stair, she unlocks the
door to her animal's prison, and it hurtles out, huge, warm,
slobbering, loving, it thunders with her up to the roof; and,

hugging its neck, so warm, so silky, so infinitely soothing to her thin cracked fingers, she climbs with Fool through the attic window; the water is only an arm's length below; barking, laughing, they jump together, they swim together away into the distance, his curled ears floating out like wings, her long grey hair like silver weed, she kicks her shoes off, she kicks her clothes off, she lets it all fall away to nothingness, nothing, any more, but their tired bodies

and the wave sweeps towards them from Daffodil Hill; when they have to let go, they let go together

but Mohammed is spared, as he asked to be

in Parliament Close, there's a roar of cold wind as Allah unveils a different future, Zoe turns to see where it's coming from and pauses, transfixed, by the cliff of the wave, and her very last thought is still Viola: a second later it crashes across them: they do not end in fire, but water

'Are we high enough?' whispers Delorice. Delorice and Davey hold each other, riding the tree like willowy gymnasts as it bends with the movements of their beautiful bodies. 'Yes,' Davey answers, and thinks of the stars: how faint, how far: invisible, but shining above them, the heavenly bodies he's loved since boyhood, spread thicker than Delorice's electric hair, thicker than leaves, thicker than grass, is it time to say goodbye to the stars

and at first, because the wave's far away, the top of their tree seems to float worlds above it, they shiver with hope, *survive, survive*, they breathe the bright pollen on the sunlit air, but as the water roars towards them they suddenly see how puny they are, the cold wind rushes before the wave and their cedar bends and snaps like a match-stick two ants flying two specks of stardust

the Brothers and Sisters plunge from the Towers; One Way, One Path has become survival; Father Bruno is trying to keep them inside, they must preserve order, it is Judgement Day, and he is the Judge, and they must obey, they must follow the Book, they must keep the Faith, but no one is listening but Dirk and May, who are stuck at the back of the rush for the windows, and May is struggling to wake Kilda, who fainted when Bruno shook her and dropped her

as time concertinas, this is May's daughter, Kilda is the child she failed to save from the paralysing rage of her father: 'Wake up,' says May; 'come with me, my dear,' and her pounding heart lifts her over the fear that has always held her in a cage of knuckles and suddenly turning on Father Bruno, who is bellowing about Sin and Greed, she remarks, quite loudly, in her 'mother' voice, 'And you, young man, had better pipe down, I think you've said enough for one day' – then to Dirk, who is watching, biting his fist, wishing his mother would think of him, she says, 'Good boy, Dirk, we can lift her together,' and they link arms, clumsily, to try and lift her, Dirk has the strength and May has the courage

her fingers beat a small tender tattoo on the biceps her son has worked into whipcord
    touching him, she approves of him
    at last his mother approves of him

but Kilda opens her big grey eyes and sees the immense water coming, the amazing thing she had always known since the first bad dreams began to wake her

the water surges above the window, the last People of the Book must drown

and the last day splits down a thousand tears, each minute, each second, each broken moment, into light and dark, presence and absence, the dead and the living, the lost, the found white flash of a wing where an arm is swimming

dissolving, now, to a ghost image
    blurring, doubling in the haze of the future –

one last white curve would complete love's circle
    the future bending to find the past
    life from the end to the beginning

three thousand generations of humans
    stiff and damp from their spell underground
    pushing up alive from the flood-washed catacombs
    pulling themselves to their feet like apes

After

Gerda and Winston burst up, soaked. They are panting like dogs. The light is blinding; they gape and squinny; water shakes off their hair in a fountain. They are in a round house full of water-lilies, pink, cream, purple, with golden stamens, in a round calm pool, in a round calm house. It is all in colour: it's glorious. The leaves are bronzed green, like giant plates, the largest over a metre across, with a delicate upturned rim like pie-crust. Winston capsizes one by sitting on it. It's warm in here, as warm as life. One of the visitors strolling round the pool spots Gerda's shining, heart-shaped face and drenched red hair among the lily-cups, and says to his wife 'See that? I swear that child just came out of the lily.'

Winston is peering through the windows, which are silvered with moisture, wreathed in creeper. Suddenly he sees his brother: 'Franklin!' Winston is off like a rocket, but

Gerda, being older, runs a bit faster, and by the big creaking cast-iron doors with their Victorian name-plate, 'Kew Gardens, London', she catches him, and kisses him on the lips.

'Errrhh!' he shouts, and wipes it off, but when he is reunited with Franklin, he whispers something in his ear, and laughs, and just for a moment Franklin looks jealous. But they stand there, rocking, holding each other, punching and patting, wordless with pleasure.

Out in the sun, it's a holiday.

Everyone has come for the summer solstice. The yellow-green grass is spread lightly with bodies; people picnic in little groups. Bees drowse over the buddleias. There is a heat-haze of butterflies; Gerda pauses to watch her red one; its velvety eyes are blurred, sleepy. People drift slowly between the families. Ian has his arm round Angela, who looks entirely different today, more human and more animal; she has lost her shoes, her clothes are rumpled, but Ian tells her, 'You're beautiful.' Ian has plans for Angela, later, if he can stay awake in the heat.

The children dart about like gnats, picking titbits from the grown-ups' picnics, all of them bossed about by Gerda, though Dwayne is nearly twice her age. Gerda has got them all doing handstands: 'Copy me, I'm the one who can do it!' The boys jerk gracelessly about like frogs, then Leah, looking at Gerda disdainfully, dips into an effortless series of cartwheels, and instantly has Gerda in thrall.

This is the place of perpetual summer. Harold is

watching a V of birds, pointing its arrow in the golden instant; just as he catches it, his lashes fall. Bruno is here; there is room for Bruno. Sent to the island in the middle of the lake, opposite the earth of a pair of foxes, the cubs not ready to be adult, yet, their noses snub, their look a little bashful – he lies in the grass, where no one can get to him, no one can hurt him, no one can judge him, soaking up light, soaking up sun.

Kilda is here. It has all come to pass. She is recognized. She is somebody. Her mother is beside her, smaller than her. Faith's legs are bare. She stares at the sun. No more cleaning, no more struggles. She is the woman in the Hopper picture.

Alfred stumps back from the distant café, bringing May and her mother a cup of tea. 'What do you think of Kew, Alfred?' 'Not bad at all, duck. Well, a bit showy.' The two women sit there, quietly. May is stroking her mother's hair; it is infinitely familiar, but different. May reads, and dozes, half-wakes for a second, gazes into the blue beyond.

Lola and Gracie doze and sunbathe, happy nymphets in bra and pants, rocked to sleep by their favourite Tupac; no one but Davey and Delorice can hear them, because of the magic of the solstice, although they are playing it fabulously loud: *I ain't mad atcha, I ain't mad atcha ...*

Every bone and muscle springy and weightless, Davey and Delorice dance in their moment.

No one is mad here, no one is angry. Moira floats with her dog down the river, the sun on its coat as red as love, and Milly and Samuel watch and pray. The greatest of these was always love ... 'Love one another' is the whole of the law.

Winston (tall Winston) and little Dirk White are playing

football with Mohammed, who hasn't told them he once
played for Loya; neither Dirk nor Winston is much good at
the game, but they're having fun, they could play all day –
'Nances,' says Alfred, but very quietly, pausing to watch, and
when the ball comes over, missed yet again by Dirk's left
foot, Alfred can't resist, he traps it, neatly, and dribbles in
masterfully from the wing, running, surely, like he did as a
boy, but 'Pass, Dad, pass,' yells Dirk, excited, and Alfred
remembers not to show his son up, passes, and Dirk pokes it
into the net. Mohammed, in goal, pretends to look
astonished. May puts her book down and gives Dirk a clap.
'Alfred! Come and sit down with me.' The heat is terrific:
soon they will rest, lie down easily among the others.

Some of the children are already dreaming. Lottie sleeps
near the long rose-beds, blonde head lolling in Harold's lap.
She has been happy; that was her gift; she has loved it all,
every moment of it, each touch of the hot sun on her body
– loved it more than words could say; life in the light was a
glory, a wonder; but nobody can bear the day for ever. All
over the garden, they are softening, yielding.

Safe in the grass, the bodies lie, stunned by the arc of the
sun through the sky.

Dreaming themselves, they are as they wish. All that they
ever hoped to be.

Here they come now, arm in arm, flowing like water into
their future. They pass without seeing us, homing, home,

here in the city whose name is time, glimpsed long ago, across the river, the ideal city which was always waiting

– the lit meadows, the warm roof-tops, caught in these steady shafts of sunlight. City suspended over the darkness. Above the waters that have covered the earth, stained waters, bloody waters, water heaving with wreck and horror, pulling down papers, pictures, peoples; a patch of red satin, a starving crow, the last flash of a fox's brush. City which holds all times and places.

See, here they come, where all are welcome.

Here we come, to lie down at last.

Maggie Gee

The White Family

Shortlisted for the Orange Prize for Fiction 2002
Nominated for the Impac Dublin Literary Award 2004

'Maggie Gee's novel takes flight.' *New York Times*

'Finely judged and compulsively readable.' *The Guardian*

'A transcendent work.' *Daily Telegraph*

Alfred White, a London park-keeper, rules his home with ferocity and tenderness. May, his clever wife, loves him but conspires against him. When Alfred collapses on duty, his beautiful daughter Shirley, who lives with Elroy, a black social worker, is brought face to face with her younger brother Dirk, who hates and fears all black people. The scene is set for violence. This ground-breaking novel takes on the taboo subject of race as it looks at love, hatred, sex, comedy and death in an ordinary British family.

'A triumph of hope over despair, reconciliation over bitterness.' *The Independent*

'One of the year's finest novels. It deserves the widest possible readership.' *Literary Review*

'Outstanding . . . tender, sexy and alarming.' Jim Crace

SAQI
www.saqibooks.com

Maggie Gee

Light Years

Lottie Lucas is the luckiest person she knows. She has looks, money, three houses and a teenage son she adores . . . So why is her husband Harold walking out on her?

Lottie and Harold track each other across a bizarre mid-1980s Britain and a hot summer in Paris. As the year turns full circle – the time it takes light to travel six million million miles – the power of love is affirmed.

Light Years is also about zoos and the zodiac; the seasons and the stars; and how humans see the natural world. It is a novel about the possibilities of happiness, a surprising and beautiful contemporary love story.

SAQI
www.saqibooks.com